THE OTHER PLACE

THE OTHER PLACE

Ibrahim Abdel Meguid

Translated by
Farouk Abdel Wahab

THE AMERICAN UNIVERSITY IN CAIRO PRESS
CAIRO NEW YORK

The American University in Cairo Press
113 Sharia Kasr el Aini
Cairo, Egypt

First published in Arabic in 1991 as *al-Balda al-ukhra*

Dar el Kutub No. 7811/97
ISBN 977 424 456 7

Printed in Egypt

TO FATMA

TRANSLATOR'S ACKNOWLEDGMENTS

I would like to thank the following friends and colleagues for help with various aspects of the translation: Anne Broadbridge, Sooyong Kim, and John Meloy (University of Chicago); John Eisele (College of William and Mary); Peter Heath (Washington University of St. Louis); Gregg Reynolds (Chicago Tribune); and Neil Hewison (The American University in Cairo Press).

I owe special thanks to my teacher, Professor Fatma Moussa-Mahmoud, for suggesting the present title, based on the following lines from *Hamlet*, Act IV, Scene iii:

CLAUDIUS: Where is Polonius?
HAMLET: In heaven. Send thither to see. If your messenger find him not there, seek him i' th' other place yourself.

THE OTHER PLACE

1

The door of the plane opened and I saw the silence. A rare sensation: to feel the cool air-conditioning at your back as your chest and face meet the sun before you've even left the door of the plane. The person behind me pushed me gently and I took the first step. The moment I descended the few steps and my feet touched the ground, I felt that I, the earth, and the air, had become one thing: hot and empty. I had to walk the short distance to the airport terminal. It was a small airport with only one other, small, ochre plane a little way off. On its side I saw the American flag and under it the words 'US Air Force.'

✧

At the door of the terminal I saw some dark-skinned soldiers. One of them shouted, "Men in one line, women in another." Behind a glass wall at the side of the terminal I saw a broad belt making a circle on the floor and figured that my baggage would arrive on it.

"Move on, boy," one of the soldiers shouted at me. The people ahead of me had entered the terminal and I had dozed off as I stood in line.

✧

"Have you forgotten me?"

"Not at all. I've been waiting for you," I replied, confused, almost apologetically.

"Don't leave the airport without me," he said.

✧

The baggage began to arrive on the belt. I found myself leaving him and going toward it. What was it that made me dislike this young man?

I took my small red suitcase and placed it in front of one of the customs officers, none of whom appeared to be over twenty. I opened the suitcase quickly and the officer examined it quickly. But as soon as I closed it he ordered me to open it again.

"What's this? Books?"

"*Your Own Physician*, an Egyptian magazine."

"It's prohibited."

I stared at him. I had nothing to say.

"Tell me, why is it that you Egyptians love to read?" he asked as I remained silent. Should I tell him that Faruq, who had sent me the job contract, had asked me to bring this special issue on pregnancy and birth? Should I tell him that I didn't know the law of the land?

"Go," he said nonchalantly, and closed the suitcase quickly, leaving the magazine inside. I left, incredulous. I saw Faruq looking at me through the glass partition of the terminal, with a smile on his face.

✧

"I told you, you keep forgetting me."

I was quite embarrassed. Here was Abed, catching me for the second time. I sat next to Faruq in the car as Abed talked to me through the open window, almost poking his long face in, with its narrow eyes and thick eyebrows joined in the middle. I overcame my embarrassment and introduced him to Faruq, who said as he started the car, "Hello. We've met before."

Abed asked, "Is he really your relative? He's very shy."

"This is the first time he's ever left Egypt. He'll come to work tomorrow," said Faruq, without even bothering to look at Abed, who now really had put his head through the open window, and was breathing so close to my face that I didn't know where to look. Abed left and I asked Faruq as he drove the car, "Why didn't you invite him to ride with us?"

"He's got a car."

"But he's just arrived with me from Cairo."

"Don't worry about anybody else."

It seemed that I wouldn't understand anything. So I shut up, and felt the stifling heat.

✧

The Datsun sped along the long, narrow road flanked on both sides by sand dunes. Faruq was driving at an incredible speed. True, the road was empty, but I had never ridden in a car that was almost flying. I shrank back in my seat. Faruq turned the radio on and I heard Muhammad Abduh singing "Don't send my letters back." When a few wooden sheds appeared at the side of the road, Faruq said, "This is your company."

I saw two children playing in front of the sheds. A car sped by on my side of the road, scaring the daylights out of me.

Faruq smiled and said, "Everyone here drives at breakneck speed and they pass on the wrong side."

I kept looking at a white dog, far away among the scattered dunes. It was huge and looked more like a stray donkey. Faruq must have seen it too.

"Here they kill dogs," he said. "They consider them unclean. That one knows it, so it stays away from populated areas."

He laughed. I thought back to the plane and to the coincidence that seated me next to Abed; how we began talking and I found out that he worked for the same company that I was on my way to work for. He had been spending his annual vacation in Cairo. He offered to put me up the first night, but I told him I had a relative waiting for me in town. Housing was expensive, he said. The company had its own house, but it was occupied by Asians and it was rare that a bed became available. Then he asked me about my previous job and how I got the contract, and my plans for the future, and whether I was engaged or married, and all sorts of other things too. I was irritated but thought that perhaps he really wanted to help.

"I noticed that you were a little late in the airport terminal," said Faruq.

"*Your Own Physician*—they said it was prohibited."

He laughed and said, "It's no use now anyway."

I smiled and said, "So, you're a father!"

He accelerated, and replied, "I'm a bachelor. I divorced my wife."

✧

The small town appeared and disappeared in a flash. Faruq had taken a road that bypassed it to the right. At the end of the road I saw a group of low houses—while the town, from the glimpse I caught of it, had some tallish buildings.

The car lurched over bumpy alleys. I saw a lot of cars parked in front of houses with narrow steel doors.

"Each street here is an auto showroom," Faruq said.

"You've been married less than a year," I said.

"Don't worry about it. She wanted to buy land in her village and I wanted to buy land in my village."

I didn't understand. The few times that I had met Faruq he hadn't seemed to be reckless or to have a short fuse. Actually he was one of my mother's cousins, who had appeared suddenly in our lives five years before, the year I graduated from college. He said he had been appointed as an engineer in the Alexandria Department of Streets, and so he thought of paying us a visit. My mother asked him about lots of relatives from her village—names that I was hearing for the first time. Faruq told her they were all dead. Then he stopped visiting us for a year, then appeared again, chiding me for not visiting him and for not bringing my mother to see her uncle—his father—who had grown old but still remembered her. The uncle even remembered me, from the time he used to come to Alexandria in the fifties to buy cattle fodder from the Oil and Soap Company, when he would spend the night at our place. My mother confirmed everything he said, so I was reluctant to admit that I remembered nothing of it at all. I felt it was rather awkward that a relative should suddenly appear in one's youth and that a strong relationship should arise between the two of you. I also remembered that I didn't know anything about my mother's village. I wasn't born there and I had never visited it. Then, once again, Faruq disappeared. I don't know how my mother found out he'd gone to Saudi Arabia, and I don't know why he sent me more than one letter offering his help to get me a job contract. I had never complained to him or hinted that I needed anything like that.

But I had to travel. Who would turn down such an easy opportunity? It was something that people envied me for, as my mother said. My teaching job was a dead end, and waiting to be seconded to Saudi Arabia by the Ministry of Education would mean waiting until the oil ran dry, as Faruq said in his letters.

"You could both have postponed buying the land," I said, suddenly.

Faruq snapped back, "And why doesn't a wife obey her husband?"

I fell silent, and he did too for a few seconds. Then he said, "I gave her three thousand Egyptian pounds. I spent a similar sum on the marriage. I'll recoup that and marry a better wife. Here's the house. I live with a doctor and a teacher."

He parked the car in front of a small, one-story, cement-brick house.

✧

The cold shower was truly wonderful. I had hoped they'd let me be by myself, but they insisted that I sit with them and watch a rather intense game of backgammon.

The house did not feel comfortable on the whole; there were two rooms on either side, separated by a big, unroofed courtyard with a bathroom and a kitchen on the far side. Faruq said it was a typical Arabian house but to me it was just blocks of cement, and narrow rooms with windows that looked inward to the courtyard rather than to the street. The windows were small, like the peepholes in prison cells.

From under the cold water I could hear the sounds of the

dice and backgammon pieces as they hit the board, and the cheering and the laughter. I thought of going quickly to my room, which Faruq had furnished with a small plastic armoire, a single metal bed, and a fan. But they saw me as I was getting close to the room and all shouted, "No sleeping before midnight. It's a law of nature."

I walked toward them. My legs and my chest were dripping with sweat just from walking the short distance between the bathroom and the middle of the courtyard where they were sitting. It was already evening but there was no change in the weather. Was it really September? In Alexandria, September cools people and houses with waves of lovely breeze. Here the air was so heavy you could hold chunks of it in your hand.

"Do you have any riyals?" asked Wagih, the doctor. I was baffled by the question, but the explanation was furnished by Said, the teacher. "We gamble."

I sat on a chair they had provided for me in the courtyard. We heard knocks on the steel door and Faruq got up quickly. I saw Abed's face peering in at us, so I got up too. Faruq had opened the door just a crack and stood in such a way that Abed could not enter.

"A bed has become available at the company house. If you'd like to move there, I can assign it to you," Abed said.

I wished I could move Faruq from the door and invite Abed in, but Faruq held on to the door, almost blocking it entirely with his body, and said, "We'll see about it tomorrow."

"I had a very hard time finding your house. I learned about the bed as soon as I arrived at the company. You must have seen the company on your way. Nabil—he makes coffee there—told me that one of the Pakistanis had died while I was on vacation, so I thought I'd let you know. It's a rare opportunity. Don't let it pass you by."

He sounded very sincere to me. I was embarrassed by Faruq's attitude and the way he blocked the door, but once again Faruq beat me to it and said, "Thanks."

Abed left and as soon as he turned his back, Faruq closed the door and came back. I remained standing for a few moments then followed him.

"I'll lend Ismail fifty riyals," Faruq said before I sat down. I didn't comment. Wagih said to me, "Don't worry—whatever you lose you get back. It's our rule."

I said nothing. Said added, "We play each game for ten riyals and write down what's won and lost in this notebook."

I remained silent, and Wagih said, "At the end of each month, the winner returns to the loser whatever he's lost and we begin again."

We were all silent for a few moments, then Wagih spoke again.

"You must be wondering what the point is, if everyone's guaranteed his money back. To tell you the truth, we don't know."

2

"It's all right to be late the first day," Faruq said as we drank our morning tea.

"I was thinking of staying with you until I see you off at the airport," I said.

I was exhausted. I'd had a nightmare the previous night, in which I saw myself backing off slowly, fearfully, from four black men with bulging, rolling eyes, each as large as an egg. They were closing in on me, with long whips raised high. I didn't know where to go. They were surrounding me, driving me as I backed off into a small dark alley. Behind and close beside me were high walls of huge black basalt stones like those in the walls of old fortresses. They kept whipping me, slowly, as their eyes turned, also slowly. And, as if in slow motion, I began to scream. Nobody from the other rooms came to wake me up; perhaps they didn't hear my screams, perhaps my screams never left my lips. I awoke, panting, and looked around—and realized that I was in a small, narrow room in a faraway country.

I couldn't get back to sleep for a long time, during which I thought about the long stretch of time in my life when I had neither dreams nor nightmares. I read once that after twenty, daydreams become rare and after thirty, dreams stop almost altogether. After twenty, one begins to realize one's dreams and after thirty, one should have realized many of them. I am thirty, but I haven't realized anything and I don't have dreams. My fellow teachers in Egypt often spoke about their dreams and how hard it was to figure out what they meant. Most of them, like me, had not accomplished anything of value. But they had dreams and they spoke about them.

I asked myself, "Really, why don't I dream like them?" I arrived at the conclusion that I was a contented person, an extremely contented person, who saw nothing in life beyond taking care of my mother and my brother and sisters after my father's death. I've often thought that perhaps I had become a person with no desire to live. What brought me to that? Was it my old habit of reading, which I had given up? Was it some kind of dust in the atmosphere, which thwarted longings in the soul before they even arose? Perhaps it was my profound hatred of my extreme contentment that made me agree to travel. If I gained nothing else, at least I would shake off the stagnation of my soul, if only once. I couldn't go back exactly as I had come. If I didn't achieve anything, I would at least receive a small wound. If I didn't succeed, I would have reasons for my failure. And already my soul had been shaken, had been beset with nightmares even though I had committed no sin—and I hadn't had a heavy meal that evening, either.

"My plane takes off at one," said Faruq. "It's eight now. If you go now, this will count as your first day of work."

The night before, he had surprised me by announcing that he was flying to Cairo the following day. He said he had postponed his departure in order to be in Saudi when I arrived. I was genuinely grateful and asked him if this was the time for his annual vacation. He smiled and said he was leaving to get married. I didn't speak with him again the rest of the evening.

✧

"You're late," Abed said as soon as I entered his office. I didn't answer him. I sat down on a big leather chair and looked around the small room, feeling the cold air pouring in from the air conditioner. That, I felt, was unnecessary. It wasn't even ten o'clock. The noise of the air conditioner bothered me. The walls of the room were gray. The air conditioner was gray. The carpet was gray, as was the desk behind which Abed sat. The whole room was cheerless. The piano-like ringing of the bell sounded a few times, persistent and impatient. Abed jumped up from behind the desk, stood for a moment with eyes closed, then put out his cigarette in the ashtray. He then calmly went to open a door that I hadn't noticed, leading to an inner room. He entered, closing the door behind him. I heard a powerful voice, "Who's that in your room?"

"The new Egyptian colleague."

"Bring him in."

Almost instantly I saw Abed in front of me, saying in a whisper, "The director," and motioning me to follow him.

The director's office was large and the smell of jasmine filled the air. I felt the thick carpet under my feet; rich, dark green carpeting the same color as the six low chairs with broad armrests covered with smooth velvet. The walls had white, silvery wallpaper. The oval wooden desk was shiny white with four telephones on it: a rectangular red one, a round black one, a cylindrical yellow one on a square black base, and a white one, the size of a pack of cigarettes. The director sat behind the desk, invisible except for his face, which, when he raised it toward us, I saw was light brown with sharp eyes, a small nose, and thin lips. The *ghutra* that covered his head was shiny white and the *uqal* around it was shiny black. The director began to look at a piece of paper on his desk, and I continued to look around. I saw a glass cabinet with ebony corners, containing a few small, elegant folders of different sizes and colors. The air conditioner was working noiselessly. It was so quiet and fresh-smelling that I almost dozed off as I stood. I forgot all about Abed, who was still standing next to me, and I thought to myself, "Does that powerful voice I heard a short while ago really belong to this fragile man?"

"Hello," said the director, reclining a little. I responded politely, smiling. "Hello."

"Do you type?"

"No."

He looked displeased.

"Do you drive?"

"No," I said, in a voice that I wished had never left my lips. He looked at me for a while, then addressed Abed.

"Tell Arshad to teach him how to drive and get him a license."

Then he asked me in English, "Do you read and write English well?"

"Yes, sir," I answered right away in a conspicuously loud voice. I remembered soldiers receiving orders from their officers in American movies, and almost laughed. I saw him smiling, though he did not want to show it. Perhaps he was surprised by my loud answer.

✧

There was nothing much to the job. I was to sit in the office next to Abed's. The whole building of the company consisted of a row of three wooden rooms and a bathroom and, perpendicular to that row, another one with three deserted rooms and a kitchen. In the middle was a big, dusty forecourt in which were parked the director's cars, Abed's car, and visitors' cars. The whole area was surrounded by a high white brick wall with a wide gate. There was not a single tree.

As soon as we entered my office, Abed went to open a metal safe attached to the wall. I stood, puzzled, for a few moments. I couldn't help seeing the bundles of shiny blue banknotes inside the safe. Abed didn't put anything into the safe or take anything out of it. He just opened it and then closed it a few moments later.

He motioned me to sit down, so I sat behind a large metal desk with rusty corners and he sat behind the other desk, near the safe. There was not much else in the room apart from those two desks—two old leather chairs, and an open metal cabinet containing dusty, unorganized sheets of paper.

Abed told me I would be in charge of the administrative matters, that the job consisted of simple routines, that there were fewer than eighty workers. He sighed and said he had been dreaming of the day when someone like me would work with him. He was the director's secretary and financial officer, and was also in charge of personnel. Now he would be relieved of personnel and the problems of absenteeism, reporting for work, sickness, travel, vacations, contracts, and terminations. I was going to take care of all that and also translate the reports that came from the technical department where the American technicians worked. The Americans worked at remote job sites and had fancy houses but were part of the company. Here there were only ordinary workers, in cleaning, construction, and maintenance jobs related to the air defense of the Northern Region. They too were all foreigners, mainly Asians. This was the Services Sector. The

Americans handled the Technical Sector, which was more sophisticated and from which we sometimes received reports that we would translate for Amm Abdallah. Abdallah was his name and *Amm* was used as a respectful form of address, like *Ustaz* in Egypt.

"Do you know that Amm Abdallah kept me in the dark about your job contract?" said Abed suddenly.

"Really? No, I didn't know that."

He smiled and said, "Sometimes he behaves strangely, this Amm Abdallah, but he's a good man."

"He does appear to be," I said, not concerned with the veracity of what I said.

A young man of medium height, wearing an off-white *gallabiya*, came into the room. Looking at his face, I realized he was Egyptian. He was carrying a silver tray with a can of 7UP and smiling.

"This is Nabil, he looks after the kitchen. He lives with me in a room behind the offices. It was him who told me that a bed had become available where the Asians live, as I told you."

I was smiling and shaking hands with Nabil, who said as he smiled, "Welcome to your own country."

I felt at ease seeing Nabil's face. It was truly striking: a broad nose, thick lips, and very small eyes. The asymmetry did not bother me. I sensed a goodness and spontaneity behind the appearance. He asked me, "Are you brother Ismail, sir?"

"Yes."

"Abed told me about you yesterday. The truth is, I've been waiting for you. I wanted to ask you: an empty room like this one and an empty town like this one and a safe like this one, full. What does one do with it? Tell me, please."

He was laughing as he spoke, and I had no answer except a smile.

✧

I sat in my office a long time, alone and in silence. I thought about the furniture I would buy for the office. All I needed was a glass cabinet instead of that old rusty one, and a few new folders. Abed had told me we could buy whatever I needed today. Suddenly I started thinking about my mother. She must be missing me by now. She had been the one most enthusiastic about my travel, even though I knew she didn't like me to be away from her. I wished I had written a letter and sent it with Faruq. I couldn't leave work on my first day on the job to catch up with him at the airport. I would write her in the evening and send the letter by mail.

I know that everyone loves his own mother, on the whole, and I am like everyone else when it comes to that; but ever since my father died, my love for her and for my brother and sisters has doubled. It's a love fraught with anxiety, a quasi-paternal love. So, I am different from the rest of humanity. But my mother, like all mothers, undoubtedly knows that thousands of Egyptians come to this country; and, like all mothers, she can think only of her own son, as the only expatriate in this world. From now on, I must write, and I must lie and say that I am fine and tell every nightmare as if it were a beautiful dream. This is what all expatriates do, out of love for others. This indeed is the age of beautiful lies and I am a man of this age.

I felt the light from the forecourt being blocked, and looked at the door, and saw him—a young man of dark complexion and sullen face, blocking the door, with a monkey, yes, a monkey on his shoulder.

The young man was wearing a spotless white, loose-fitting *gallabiya*. The *ghutra* on his head was also white and clean, the *uqal* around it black and clean. But it was the monkey that drew my attention. I didn't stand up as the young man came in, without asking for permission, and sat behind the other desk close to the safe.

I kept looking at the monkey. It was small, brown, not generally very hairy, but with long hair around its colored eyes, and thick, fluffy hair around its neck. Its bluish testicles, visible above the young man's shoulder, shone like marbles. With its tail raised up over its owner's head, it was a truly beautiful monkey.

"Where is Abed?" said the man.

"In his office."

"He's not there."

"Maybe he went on an errand. He'll be back soon I expect."

I was still looking at the monkey, which had now placed its hands on the young man's head.

"I know," he said, curtly. I placed my head on my left palm, leaned my elbow on the desk and fell silent.

"Are you the new Egyptian?" he asked.

"Yes."

"What's your name?"

"Ismail."

I smiled, hoping to get over my irritation. He sighed and repeated my name to himself, sounding surprised, then heaved another deep sigh in a vexation I did not understand. Nabil appeared at the door, laughing.

"Ha, Mansur."

He came in quickly to shake his hand, but Mansur did not offer his hand. I noticed a faint smile on his face. Nabil reached his hand out to the monkey's head and Mansur recoiled a little. Nabil laughed and addressed me.

"This is Mansur, ha ha, with little Mansur on his shoulder. Ha ha ha ha."

He began to laugh convulsively and Mansur got up, anger on his face, and left the room without a word. The monkey looked around, upset. I was surprised when Mansur directed a sharp, angry look at me.

✧

In the Toyota pickup truck, Abed asked me, "Have you thought about moving to live with the Asians?"

I was thinking about Mansur and his monkey. Why was Mansur hostile to me without knowing anything about me, and why did Nabil treat him with such familiarity? Nabil spoke to me about him after he left. He said he was good at heart and harmless, that I shouldn't fear him.

"Are you comfortable living in town?" said Abed.

"Yes."

We fell silent. I kept my eyes on the asphalt road, which was now very shiny, quite different from how it had been in the morning. The sun was in the middle of the sky. The light reflected in waves on the road showed how uneven it was.

The moment I saw the white dog running out there among the dunes, the same dog that looked like a donkey, a yellow dust storm started to blow so hard that Abed had to slow down the car. We were engulfed by dust so we closed the windows and Abed turned on the headlights and I saw the dust flying in front of us in two columns of light, swaying in the air.

"This is the *ajj*, a dusty wind that blows without warning, sometimes every day, maybe more than once on the same day. Then sometimes it doesn't blow for long days on end."

It seemed the storm wasn't about to ease. We were almost suffocating. Abed turned on the windshield wipers, which began to remove the dust as if it were rain water. We could hear the sound of the dust hitting the outside of the car and I began to be frightened.

"We've got to stop," I said.

Abed was reducing speed considerably and making for the shoulder of the road to stop, but the storm started to abate little by little. Eventually the horizon was once again white, the asphalt black, and the sky above us blue. I saw the town approaching, stretching on both sides of the road with its low, white buildings. As we entered the town Abed said to me, "This is the main street in town. It's a small town with only a few neighborhoods: Sulaymaniya, Faysaliya, Aziziya, and Omdurman. The whole town is the size of Tahrir Square in Cairo. You must have seen it. Suffocating, isn't it? They've even built a pedestrian bridge in it. Can you imagine that?"

I was drawn to the crowds and the cars crawling along the two lanes of the street, with stores open on both sides. This main street was where the market was, where I was to buy the things I needed for my room and my office. I looked up and down the fabrics hanging high in front of the stores. I looked at the hardware, the electric appliances stacked everywhere, and the shining mirrors, and the perfumes, and the watches, and the books, and the loose-fitting, garish dresses: shiny black, shiny red, and green, and yellow, and blue, all shiny, with large floral patterns in the midst of the colors, with very little white. Empty cardboard boxes were strewn everywhere on the sidewalks, and wastepaper littered the street. Groups of young Koreans were laughing and running around; there were men in *gallabiyas* and men in pants, and Indians with black beards and huge turbans walking slowly along, old men with fair complexions and red beards dyed with henna, walking, tired. I found out later they were Afghans. Young Pakistanis, their eyes gleaming, walked fast in their loose-fitting pants and shirts. I saw Americans and Egyptians wearing jeans. As for women, I only saw their faces as you would see an apparition that disappeared as you closed a window. The sun was high in the sky over the white, open space with cars crawling on both sides. There was the smell of grilled meat. In my mind's eye I saw dancing girls from *A Thousand and One Nights* handing out cups of strong drink to the passersby, as one of Shahrayar's processions went by, flanked by pretty boys and singing girls, followed by banners and cymbals, as the sounds of horns mixed with those of blaring tape players.

"'Tabuk makes you forget your mother and your father' is a saying that the Egyptians here use all the time," said Abed.

Silence descended.

"What's that? Listen."

He slowed down the car, which was not going fast to begin with. I pricked up my ears. He opened his eyes as wide as he could and stretched his head forward, almost through the glass. We heard the words "middle school."

Everything came to an absolute standstill; you could see the silence.

"A new scandal," Abed said, gesturing to me with his finger not to speak. I didn't speak and the voice kept coming closer. A police pickup truck appeared from a side street. A policeman stood on the truck holding a microphone and next to him stood a girl or a woman—something so totally covered in black from head to toe could not be anything else. The policeman spoke into the microphone in an amplified and discordant voice. His beard was long and the *ghutra* on his head was pale green with some old black thread, and around it the *uqal* was faded; his yellow uniform had brass buttons that shone in the light.

"Wadha bint Sulayman ibn Sabil," he was saying, "a student at Aziziya Middle School, went out every day after school with the Yemeni, Yami ibn Abdallah al-Yami."

Crowds of people gathered on the sidewalks and at the entrances of the stores and the light grew more intense. I saw the girl, fragile and small. The black *abaya* shimmered and delineated a place for itself in the white, wide open space and attracted the eyes of all.

"She went with him every day to the deserted Tayma road."

I didn't know how Abed managed to get his car alongside the police car. Now the voice was like big chunks of rock falling on my head.

"Al-Yami did not dishonor her, but because of her heinous deed she has been expelled from school."

"The whore," Abed shouted, clenching his teeth. Nothing at all like that came to my mind. My eyes were fixed on the small, featureless body under the loose-fitting, black *abaya*. All I wanted was to see her face. That became my only need, growing as sorrow welled up in my chest. Her veil was black and heavy but the sunlight was so brilliant that it could have revealed her face to me if it had wanted to. I was certain that she had died as she stood there and my only painful hope was to see her move. If only she would move! She was not even swaying with the movement of the car. And that huge ape of a policeman never ceased to stand and bend as he bellowed into the microphone, "Al-Yami has been sent to jail for three months, after which he will leave the Kingdom for good."

I looked at the sun in the dome of the sky. It was far away but the light filled everything around as if it were bathing it in pure white milk. My eyes were still glued to the blackness of the *abaya* and the motionless body. O God, Most Merciful God, the little body quivered a few times. There was no wind, not even a breeze. The only thing causing the *abaya* to move was the quiver of the body and the tremor of the soul.

I no longer heard the policeman or Abed who was now madly twittering away, cursing the girl and the Yemeni boy. I kept following the police car as it moved away and the *abaya* as it moved and the body as it quivered. She was alive. People and cars once again moved in the street, and the *Thousand and One Nights* dancing girls sprang up, serving the drinks as Shahrayar's procession kept moving with the singing girls and pretty boys, with the banners and the cymbals bringing up the rear. Once again the Koreans ran, laughing, the svelte Indians walked slowly, the Pakistanis smiled and caught reflections of the sun's rays in their eyes. The old Afghans' mouths gaped in bewilderment. The Egyptians loitered in front of the store windows. The Americans, their left hands on their hips and dark glasses covering their eyes, drank soda pop. The goods and the blaring, discordant sounds of the tape players totally surrounded me. Once again, I smelled the grilled meat, and could see no women at all in the street.

3

I began to like the house and to like going home. At three o'clock, the world would open up before me. I hadn't learned to drive yet. Every morning when he came to sign in, Arshad would ask me, "When are you coming to the garage, Mr. Ismail?"

And I would answer, "As soon as possible."

But I hadn't gone. I don't know why.

Abed gave me a ride every day. I usually arrived home around half past three to find that Said had prepared lunch. Said was the first to come home.

Sometimes I helped him but often he would have prepared everything already. We usually ate lunch alone together. Wagih came home at five and would often go back to the hospital later. Our lunch was usually big chunks of boiled meat, and rice, and whatever vegetable was available, and a salad. For fruit we would have grapes or pears or watermelon. Everything came in fresh from Jordan, according to Said.

Wagih often protested about the huge amount of meat that we ate and drew attention to the harmfulness of eating rich food in such a hot climate, and the necessity of eating sautéed vegetables. But Said would laugh and pay no attention. He did not change the way he cooked, nor did Wagih stop wolfing down great amounts of the food.

I became convinced that Wagih was right after noticing how sleep overcame me soon after lunch, the stupor I felt in my chest and my head, the strange movement I felt in my intestines, and the insistent pressure to break wind. But I didn't try to get Said to change the way he cooked.

I had come to love the house and every day, from the moment the hands of the clock met at twelve o'clock, I longed to go home. Why did I buy that wall clock for the office the day I went to the market? Why did I go along with Abed's idea? I placed it before me as if to torture myself, raising my eyes to look at it from time to time. When the hands met at twelve o'clock, I began to follow the movement of the minute hand, minute by minute, seeing it or hearing it move. By twelve o'clock I had usually finished most of the work; the remaining hours, three of them, felt like an eternity. So I would think about home.

I could not leave work, or the office, for more than a few minutes. Nabil could not spend a long time with me, and Abed would either be in the office or outside the place altogether. Abed usually spent most of his time looking after Amm Abdallah's private business, which had nothing to do with the company. He would tell me to sit in his office until he came back, and usually he didn't come back for a long time, during which I had to do secretarial work, usually nothing more than answering the telephone.

"Hello."

"Who are you?"

"Ismail."

"Is your boss there?"

"No. Can I do anything for you?"

"Tell him that Shaykh Salih called."

I put the telephone down and it rings again.

"Who are you?"

"Ismail."

"Where is Abdallah?"

"He went out."

"I know. Where did he go?"

"I don't really know."

"How come you don't know? Are you a jackass?" And he hangs up on me.

Then the telephone rings.

"Hello."

"Abed, is the money ready?"

"This is Ismail."

"Ismail?"

"A new employee."

He hangs up.

The telephone would ring and I couldn't complain. I just had to take down the names so that when either Abed or Amm Abdallah came back I could give them to him.

Now that two weeks had passed, that no longer bothered me. I got used to it and the people calling got used to my being there and to my name. They became less irascible; some even joked with me and asked me about Egypt and what was happening there, even though I didn't know them, or at least had never met them. But I couldn't forget about looking at the clock at twelve, even if I was in Abed's office; I just looked at the identical clock that he had bought for his office.

After twelve, the world here appeared vast and empty, with the sun lighting it as if intent on setting it on fire. The appearance of a person or a car became a rare occurrence, except for the old Yemeni man who wore European clothes and who always surprised me by sitting on the ground in the forecourt next to the wall, placing a *siwak* in his mouth and moving it around. I never saw him enter the forecourt. I only saw him after twelve o'clock, sitting, moving the *siwak* around in his mouth, disturbed neither by the sun above nor by the dust on which he sat. I would look at him and he would look back and smile. I'd see Nabil bringing him a cup of tea, which he would take in silence. Nabil would also return in silence. If a car belonging to Abed or Amm Abdallah or any visitor came into the forecourt and blew the dust around, he never moved. Only when I looked at him would he look back at me, smiling, his eyes gleaming with sharp intelligence. He was a truck driver, about fifty-five years old. I once told Abed, "This Yemeni's name isn't in the signing-in or the signing-out book. I have no work file on him."

"He and Amm Abdallah have an agreement that he gets his salary without being officially appointed," he said.

"But being appointed doesn't impose any obligations on Yemenis. They're treated like Saudis and they can leave work anytime they choose."

"True. He knows that. But he says who can guarantee that things will remain the same? Amm Abdallah likes him and accepts his conditions."

I said to myself, "So, this man will never come into my office."

I really do not know why I thought about that nor why I wanted this man to come into my office. I once invited him in with a gesture of my hand. All he did was smile and turn the *siwak* around in his mouth. Then suddenly I thought to myself, "How come I only see him sitting in his place after twelve o'clock?" I became almost obsessed with this thought and I watched the forecourt two days in a row to see him as he arrived, but somehow something always distracted me at the crucial moment, and when I looked again there he was, sitting, looking and smiling at me, his eyes gleaming with sharp intelligence, as if he knew exactly what I wanted and didn't want me to get it.

I had come to love the house. Every day after twelve o'clock I couldn't sit still. What was it that made me so restless? I could, if only I closed my eyes, give time room to pass. The remaining three hours passed slowly only because I waited for them to pass.

The house was really nice. After the siesta we would place the backgammon board in the middle of the courtyard together with the notebook and the money box. I rarely lost; every day I would win thirty riyals. Whenever I caught myself taking the game too seriously, I'd say to myself, "Come on Ismail, there's neither winning nor losing. Everyone gets their money back." But I would soon forget and show that I was taking the game very seriously. Said and Wagih laughed at my transformation.

The courtyard in the house was lovely in the evening. It was late September and the breeze seemed to be a little cooler. The television set was always placed in front of us even when we were playing backgammon. It was me that moved the television from Said's room to the courtyard. I always saw to that.

I had come to love television and I followed its programs intently. In Egypt, I never caught myself even once developing the slightest interest in watching television. Here, however, an incomprehensible relationship developed between television and me. Here I almost imagined that its programs were real events taking place in real life around us. I became addicted to watching episodes of *The Six Million Dollar Man* that were shown more than once a week. I had never paid any attention to this program in Egypt, but here I watched three long episodes. Then they announced that the program would not be shown anymore because of several incidents in Riyadh and Dammam, in which some children had jumped from tall buildings in imitation of Steve Austin. They announced that episodes of a new series called *The Incredible Hulk* would be shown, starting the following week. I awaited these episodes with great anticipation. Everything shallow and trivial on television here had come to captivate me. They showed the film *The Knight of Bani Hamdan* twice, and both times I watched it as if I had never seen it before. Both times I loved Farid Shawqi and hated his rival, Mahmud Mursi, even though I realized that the whole film was rather naive.

In the courtyard, under the high sky, with a cool, soft breeze blowing, the voices of the singers sounded enchanting. In the courtyard, under the high sky, the voice of the muezzin, calling the faithful to prayer at sunset and then at the time of the night prayer, carried me to heights of sorrow. The voice of the muezzin sounded like the cry of a bird being slaughtered on top of a tremendously high mountain.

After the muezzin, I listened to the heart-rending voice of the announcer reciting one of the Prophet's hadiths. O God, what is the secret of this deep modulation of the voice and that unutterably sad tone that carried me to the valleys of tranquillity and serenity? It opened the gates of comfort in my soul, almost bringing tears to the eyes of this sinner who didn't know what sins he had committed.

I had come to love the house. I now turned down any invitation to go out, even an invitation to an Arabian dinner—and there were many such invitations. Said and Wagih sometimes accepted these invitations to the houses of their friends, or friends of friends, from the town. They would come back talking of *kabsa*, the famous Arabian dish of young lambs, grilled whole and served on huge platters, on beds of rice cooked with pine nuts, almonds, and walnuts. People ate with their fingers. A smart person would control his appetite because diarrhea was often the fate of those who attacked the meal with too much gusto. Said used to say, "It's not important to eat, just to watch." But once I came home, I preferred not to go out again.

Television transmission would end. I would go to my room and leaf through the newspapers and magazines that Wagih and Said bought and left in the kitchen after reading them. All the papers spoke about Sadat and cursed him. One of the magazines had the headline, "If only a bullet would find its way to the traitor's head!" and above the headline a photo of Sadat in German military uniform, and the famous pipe in his mouth. I didn't linger long on politics. I looked for women in the advertisements, pictures of naked women. I couldn't find a single one, despite the scores of ads touting Swiss and Japanese watches, French perfumes, Italian furniture, British castles, and Singapore Airlines. I had not been thinking about women before coming here, but now it seemed that I must have come here for them. But why did I really come here? To make money? For the sake of my brother and sisters? For the lie that my father had placed like a noose around my neck? Whatever, I had to dive into the sea of women one of these days—a sea into which I had not even cast a stone before. Because of the accursed embracing of that lie and the continual self torture that afflicted me, from where I didn't know, I had lost many a heart, and big hearts at that. What a miserable wretch! But I had come to love the house when we moved our mattresses to the courtyard to sleep. Wagih said that the practice would prove most harmful later on, but he couldn't stay inside even so. Said would say there could be nothing more beautiful than a man and a woman sleeping there under the sky, and the birds, and the stars, and we would laugh. He had an engagement ring on his right ring finger but I didn't try to find out anything from him. He didn't speak about it, but once, as we watched the dome of the star-studded sky, he recited:

O Umayma, let me tend this wearisome anguish
and suffer this slow-star night.
It has tarried so long I said it would never end.
One who shepherds the stars is not likely to
return.

We laughed and Wagih said, "But your friend's name is Widad and not Umayma." Said winked at me and said, "What an ignoramus!" I wondered how Said, the physical education teacher, came to know poetry.

I wanted to say that I, too, knew a lot, even though my memory was now covered with dust, and that I had spent my early youth with *The Book of Songs* and other classical literary compendia, that I had read this and that—but I didn't say any of it. To myself, I said, "You had a lot of time. No regrets."

I wondered why Said never said anything about his fiancée, about whom I knew nothing except her name. I also knew nothing about Wagih except that he was married, which was obvious from the wedding ring around his left ring finger. Then one day Said said to him, "A man whose heart is big enough for two women does not suffer the pangs of love, Doctor." I fell silent out of embarrassment and was surprised that Wagih was not fazed. He laughed and said, "God knows more than we do; therefore he permitted a man to marry four women. I am now looking for the third one."

He looked at me and said, "Do I look like a man with two wives?" I smiled, embarrassed, but he laughed and said he had left them both in Mansura in Egypt. He didn't want to bring one of them along for fear of upsetting the other one. He wanted to be gentle with the little dears, he said. Then he left us and went to his room, for one reason or another, and Said whispered to me that his two wives were splendid beauties, that one of them had a very handsome son, and the other had a very beautiful daughter, and that if Wagih spoke about a third wife, he would definitely go ahead and get one. I didn't feel it proper to discuss the private affairs of either of them if they had not broached the matter themselves. I had gotten used to that and I preferred to know about them only what they wanted me to know. I didn't feel any annoyance; I'd come here only for a short period of time. I should be like a smooth mirror to which incidents and facts did not stick. I shouldn't spoil my peace of mind at home nor try to seize the opportunity of one of them not being there to learn anything about him from the other. I had a long enough time ahead with the two of them. Many secrets would reveal themselves to me.

✧

"How come you're playing so absent-mindedly today?" Said said as we played backgammon in the courtyard. Wagih was on call at the hospital that night.

"Faruq. I haven't had any letters from him."

He laughed and said, "Are you expecting a letter from a man who traveled to get married? Play." He threw the dice hard. We heard a few soft knocks on the door.

"I wonder who that is. Maybe Wagih's left work and come back to play backgammon," Said said as he got up to open the door. Then I heard him exclaim, "Hello, Dr. Rafat. Come on in, we have a new customer."

A tall man came out to the courtyard and shook my hand warmly. I reciprocated and Said offered him a chair and said to me:

"Dr. Rafat, a great urologist. It was his idea that we play for money then return the losses at the end of the month. You must play with us, Doctor. It's been a long time since we've seen you."

Rafat smiled calmly and said, "Actually, I haven't come for the evening. I just came to say good-bye. Where's Wagih?"

Said asked in surprise, "To say good-bye? Why, what's the matter, Doctor?"

"I'm going back to Egypt, for good."

"Really?"

"Why not? I'm leaving in the morning. Didn't Wagih tell you?"

"He told me nothing at all. He's on call at the hospital today."

Rafat shrugged and smiled, and said to me, "The hard decision to make here is when to go back. It's boring here. It doesn't seem to be boring but you soon discover that time's rushed by and taken five years of your life. Some people have spent ten years here. How many five- or ten-year stretches are there in your life? Nobody thinks about that. Youth and the money make us forget. Lots of people have tried to talk me out of going back. But I've made up my mind. Five years is more than enough for any country other than your own. If you really think of it, you realize it's really just a big prison. You can visit people and move around, but the people are the same, mornings are the same, evenings the same, there's nothing new."

He didn't realize that he was going on too long. "I cannot live more than five years in a country where you travel from one city to another by airplane. Besides, what do you need except a reasonable amount of money to start your life in Egypt? I've already done that. I have a practice in Tanta and I'm going to the United States to buy some equipment, then I'm going back to practice and live like any citizen who relies on his wits and his strength to live. Do you think I'm wrong?"

I smiled and replied, "On the contrary. I think you're absolutely right."

Said had left us to make some tea for Rafat, and now came back and offered him a cup.

"Tea without sugar, Doctor."

"Thanks."

He took the cup of tea, saying to me, "I'm diabetic, you know. It's happening to a lot of people these days."

Said said, "I don't think Wagih will be late. He's on call in the evening only. He's not staying there overnight."

"It's rather strange that he didn't tell you. He knows I'm leaving tomorrow and doesn't even think of paying me a visit."

"He might do that on his way back. Perhaps he's arranged it already. We'll miss you very much, Doctor. It is Ismail's misfortune that he didn't get to know you. You haven't visited us."

"I am happy to make your acquaintance, brother Ismail," said Dr. Rafat. "Would you like me to take a letter back to Egypt?"

"Just say hello from me, Doctor."

"Imagine, Ustaz Ismail, it's me that needs to stay here the most. Said and Wagih know that. My son's polio eats up most of what I make. My son is back in Egypt and I've decided I can't stay away from him any longer."

I felt very awkward and said, "Perhaps your being with him is the best therapy, Doctor."

"You really think so?"

"Absolutely."

We both fell silent. I noticed there were tears welling up in his eyes. Then, just as he was about to get up, we heard the key turn in the door.

"Here's Wagih!" cried Said.

And indeed Wagih came in saying, "Good evening, Egyptians."

He shook our hands and said to Rafat, "I've just come from your place. Needless to say, I didn't find you. Please forgive me. What happened tonight is horrible."

"What?" Rafat asked, and after he sat down Wagih replied, "Tabuk won't sleep tonight. Three southern Egyptians killed their employer. A month ago. They cut him up in small pieces and put him in a concrete mixer, so the corpse disappeared into the building. The crime was only discovered today. They were arrested and they confessed. One of them was brought to the hospital, almost dead from being tortured."

4

"What a beautiful day!" I said to myself, as I stood in front of my office looking at the high, blue sky bathed in the brilliant sunlight. The silence had not yet been bruised by the heat. It was about eight in the morning. The workers had come and gone after signing in. I had done nothing since then except drink some coffee and sit around. I remember how they came in at seven in a hurry.

"*Sabah al-khayr.*"

"Good Morning."

"*Al-salaamu alaykum.*"

These three greetings I heard every morning. In the afternoon when they came back to sign out they only said, "*Al-salaamu alaykum.*" They spoke as quickly as rabbits eat. I smiled at their faces because they were always smiling. But they were always in a hurry; there was no chance of getting to know any of them. Occasionally some of them would come to the office during the day, but only for a short time—for a meeting with Amm Abdallah, to get a referral to a doctor, or to request permission to leave early to take care of some business at the bank, or for something to do with bringing the wife and children over.

It was Philip Sousay Biliya, the old Sri Lankan electrician, who stopped sometimes to chat with me. Once he produced a pocket-sized copy of the Quran from his jacket pocket, and opened it and pointed to the verse, "Verily we have created man into toil and struggle" and asked me what it meant. I was amazed that he had a copy of the Quran at all, and particularly this bilingual edition in English and Arabic. I answered him, "It means into difficulty and hardship."

"You mean everybody has a hard life?" he asked.

"It means that there is no rest in this life. Real rest comes in the afterlife."

He said in surprise, "But people here are quite comfortable."

"Who do you mean?"

"The Saudis, Mr. Ismail."

I smiled and asked him, "Are you a Muslim, Philip?"

"I am a Buddhist but I am going to convert to Islam. I don't want to go back to Sri Lanka."

It surprised me that a man over fifty should think that way, but I smiled and shook his hand as he was leaving. No day passed now without Philip asking me about the meaning of an expression in the Quran. When I asked him when he was going to convert, he said, "When I've understood the whole Quran, Mr. Ismail. I am quite serious about it."

Besides Philip there was Munzir, the Jordanian who always came in and left in a great hurry. He would mouth a quick greeting, sign in and leave without waiting for me to return his greeting. More than once I thought of asking him why he was in such a hurry but I always forgot. In the end I said to myself, "The Lord works in mysterious ways."

Of all the other workers, only Aaron Bounkerd, the Thai with hazel eyes and a Mongolian moustache caught my attention. He caused me some perplexity every time he came to sign in or out. He signed in in English and looked for a long time at me, smiling broadly, then took his time leaving. He did this every time he came into the office. Sometimes he asked how I was and I would say "Fine," but he never said anything else and then left. He seemed like someone who had known me a long time ago and who wanted to remind me of himself.

I saw Abed suddenly standing in the door of his office. He looked at me and said, "Beautiful day, isn't it?"

I smiled and said, "I was just saying that to myself a few moments ago."

"Amm Abdallah has a meeting at the Emirate today. I'm not going to leave the office, so you can go to Arshad to learn how to drive. You must learn to drive so you won't need anyone to give you a ride home."

At the same moment I saw Nabil coming from the kitchen carrying a tray with two cups of coffee. Nabil usually did this twice in the morning, then he wouldn't serve anything unless we ordered it. Suddenly he shouted, "God save us! Gomaa is here." He was speaking to Abed. I looked at the gate he had pointed to and saw a huge, young Egyptian crossing the fore-court, smiling.

"Good morning, Egyptians," he said as he drew near to us. Abed took him by the hand and went into my office. I followed. The young man shook my hand hard, while Nabil stood, holding the coffee and looking at the young man in surprise. Then Nabil said to me, "Get ready to pay fifty riyals from your first salary."

We had been paid the day before. Before I could say anything the guest said, "Not for me, I swear. It's for the dead man."

I must have looked extremely perplexed as I sat down. I saw

Abed go to the safe, open it, and take out fifty riyals. Gomaa remained standing as Nabil put down the coffee for me and said to Abed, "I'll put your coffee in your office." He turned to leave and Gomaa said, laughing, "Aren't you going to pay anything, Nabil?"

Nabil laughed and said, "Next death."

He left as Gomaa laughed, and Abed smiled as he gave him the fifty riyals. I took a fifty-riyal note out of my pocket and gave it to him. Abed said, "Gomaa works for Bazei's company, the biggest contracting firm in town, almost the biggest in the whole country. Bazei has ships at sea and a fleet of trucks that could go to war against Israel, if he wanted to. No day passes without one of his workers dying. Bazei and his directors always refuse to pay the dead man's benefits and they refuse to pay for the repatriation of the body. They even refuse to pay the price of the box! They always say, 'Bury him in the Kingdom, it's sacred ground.' Everyone knows that each nationality has a representative who collects money for the dead at Bazei's company."

No sooner had it sunk in than Nabil came into the office saying to Gomaa, "Maybe if they sent somebody else, even once, nobody would die after that."

Gomaa's face turned red but he didn't stop smiling. He looked extremely foolish.

✧

I drank my coffee alone. Gomaa left and Abed went back to his office, while Nabil got busy washing the Cadillac parked in the forecourt. It was a beautiful white car that stood like a giant goose swimming in a sea of light. Amm Abdallah had several cars and would often ride in more than one on the same day. Each car had a cellular phone. I couldn't get Gomaa's face to leave the room. After he left, Nabil said he knew him, and saw his coming here as an evil omen. He said that originally he lived in the cemetery area of Cairo, and his father was a gravedigger. Then he laughed and said, "Like father, like son," but I didn't laugh. I was thinking about what he had said.

I got up to go to Arshad. I felt I shouldn't spoil his splendid day. I crossed the forecourt bathed in the light of the day. Nabil stopped working on the Cadillac and caught up with me at the gate.

"Where are you going?"

"To Arshad. To learn to drive."

"Take me with you."

We walked. Nabil must have known that Amm Abdallah was busy at the Emirate today, otherwise he wouldn't have dared to leave.

"I want to learn to drive, like you," Nabil said as we walked in silence.

I didn't respond.

I looked at the nearby garage, next to the compound where the Asians lived. This was my first time there. The ground between it and the company offices was not paved, but nor was it rough ground. It was limestone covered with a thin layer of sand. Nabil kept talking.

"The problem is I don't have time during the day because Amm Abdallah might come back any time and need coffee."

"Why don't you learn in the evening?"

"Arshad is afraid to use the cars after hours, and Abed won't let me use his car."

I was perplexed and thought, "Why did he come today, when he knows he may not get a chance to continue?" As if reading my mind, he said, "I wanted to watch you today as you learn. I'll learn from watching you, in other words, without actually driving myself."

I smiled, almost laughing, and he said, "Yes, I swear."

I burst out laughing and felt the air echoing my laughter even though there were no mountains around us. He said suddenly, "Why don't you believe me? Why are you mocking me?"

It was as if the wide open space around us had suddenly opened even wider. I felt as if there was nobody else in the whole wide world except Nabil and me. I also had a very strange sensation, a sensation that I will never forget: I wanted to kill him. If I had had a knife in my hand, I would have stabbed him and stood watching the blood glistening as it flowed onto the ground under the light.

"Would you believe that I have come to love you very much, Ustaz Ismail?" he said. I was surprised, particularly since he was suddenly so formal.

"I think you are a kind man, Ustaz Ismail," he continued. "Abed is a snake, a cobra. He sleeps in the same room with me and I know him. Can you imagine that sometimes I get up in the middle of the night in panic, for fear that he might kill me. Why is that happening, Ustaz Ismail? Am I going insane here?"

I stopped walking. An overpowering mixture of emotions caused me to stop.

I didn't know whether I wanted to comfort him, curse him, or order him to go back. I said as I held his arm, "Don't make me dislike people, Nabil."

With a very hurt look, almost crying, he said, "I didn't mean it like that. I just wanted to remind you not to go too far making friends with people. You are here only to make money, like everybody else."

I let go of his arm and walked in silence. I noticed that we drew apart from each other, then drew closer. We didn't walk for long, since it was quite a short distance. A few steps before we reached the door of the garage, I asked him, "Did you really come along to learn how to drive? If you want, I can persuade Arshad to teach you in the evening."

He said, "If I steal what's in the safe, would they kill me?"

✧

I asked Arshad, "You work alone in the garage?"

"Wahhajuddin works with me," he replied. "He's out test driving a car. The garage is small, as you can see."

We had just finished the first lesson, which involved getting to know the dashboard and how the stick shift moved, all while the car was parked. Nabil had left me as soon as we arrived at the door of the garage. He said Amm Abdallah was a wily man who might return any moment. He did not wait for my answer to his disturbing question.

Arshad turned his attention away from me for a short while and began to fill two cups with tea from a thermos flask that he had taken from a small wooden cupboard. I began to look around the garage and the workshop.

A few cars appeared to be in need of repair. Old tools filled the corners. The floor was black and dirty. Arshad's face had great presence, always wearing an expression of disbelief and resentment that became more intense whenever he came to the office and had an argument with Abed about food purchases for the compound. Arshad was also in charge of the living accommodation for the Asians.

Arshad had sharply intelligent hazel eyes and a complexion fairer than that of most Pakistanis. Like most of them, however, he had a meticulously trimmed moustache and smooth black hair. Arshad's features would change whenever he argued with Abed about provisions. At the beginning Arshad would be nice, carefully choosing his English words to make sure that Abed, who didn't speak English well, would understand. He would even throw in a smattering of Arabic. But his features would begin to change as his face turned red in surprise and aversion. Arshad always appeared earnest, while Abed talked to him as nonchalantly as one would toss a piece of paper into the wastepaper basket. Abed would say, "Much *kammun*!" and shrug his shoulders, whereupon Arshad would say, "Yes, much *kammun*, Mr. Abed. Cumin is necessary." They would then have a long argument about the amount of spices that Arshad requested. And even though spices were extremely inexpensive in Saudi Arabia, Abed loved to give Arshad a hard time about them. Arshad, now losing all patience, would say, "Mr. Abed, please remember how many times I told you that *kammun* and *shatta* and pepper and all *baharat* are necessary for our food!" I half laughed at the odd mixture of Arabic and English, all in an Urdu accent.

Actually I was surprised at Abed's attitude, since he must have realized how important spices were for Asian food. I told Arshad once, as they were in the thick of their argument, that Abed was only joking, and I was surprised when Abed said to me, earnestly, "I am not joking with him. They do consume huge amounts, at great cost to the company." After that I never got involved in their arguments.

"Drink the tea, Mr. Ismail," Arshad said.

I picked up the cup and had a sip. "Arshad," I said, "You know that Pakistanis are different from the Thais and the Sri

Lankans. But morning or afternoon when they speak to me I can hardly tell the difference; their voices sound almost the same when they say anything, in Arabic or in English. You're now speaking to me in English but your voice is no different from anyone else's. When I hear you speak, I am reminded of everybody. Strange, isn't it?"

Arshad smiled and kept looking at me with a bright gleam in his eyes. He was suddenly cheerful. I had no idea why. I had spoken without thinking; I didn't know when or even if I'd had these thoughts before.

"Your voice also will become similar to ours, Mr. Ismail."

We both fell silent and drank tea. I happened to notice a book on a chair nearby. He got up, picked up the book and put it in the wooden cupboard, then came back saying, "I'm sorry, Mr. Ismail. I brought this book here by accident. I have no time here for reading."

I looked at his face for a while. He closed his eyes. Why did he fear me so much? I drank the rest of the tea in one gulp and got up to shake his hand. We agreed to meet the following day.

✧

As I went into my office back from Arshad's garage, I saw a car drive fast into the forecourt, churning up all the dust. I heard the door of the car as it opened and slammed shut. Abed leapt into my office.

"Quick. The Sri Lankan's file."

"Which Sri Lankan?"

"Philip. Do we have any other?"

We did have other Sri Lankans but I chose not to reply. I stood amazed as he gave me no opportunity to bring the file.

He rushed to the filing cabinet, opened it and snatched Philip's file, then ran out of the room, dropping a few other files on the floor as he went. I began to rearrange the files and started pacing the room. I wished I could scream something at somebody, anybody. I saw Nabil coming in, carrying a tray with a cup of coffee.

"Would you like some coffee? I took it to him but he didn't want any."

How could he have made coffee so fast and taken it to him already? It must have been Amm Abdallah's car that blew up all the dust. I almost burst out laughing.

"He refused to take the coffee and yelled at me to get out. Are you going to kick me out too?"

"Put the coffee on my desk and sit down. Did you find out what happened?"

"A catastrophe! Philip stole a radio from the market and was arrested."

"How did you find out?"

"I heard Amm Abdallah tell Abed as I went in."

He started shaking with laughter, which he tried to hide. As Amm Abdallah left his office we heard him tell Abed, "You sit right here, and tell that one"—I am sure he meant me—"not to leave his place."

I heard the door of the car open and slam shut again. I heard it start then saw Amm Abdallah back up quickly, not forgetting to look sharply at me, then drive off fast, filling the air once more with more dust.

✧

I looked at the clock. It was twelve o'clock. I looked at the forecourt and saw the old Yemeni man turning the *siwak* in his mouth with his hand. He had come in with the dust blown by the car. I would have been able to see him coming in if it hadn't been for Amm Abdallah's dust. He smiled and his eyes gleamed, shrugging his shoulder when he saw me looking at him. I smiled and sat at my desk wondering at people. Really, what had made Philip steal? A man like him, over fifty, dignified, chief foreman of all the electric workers, one who wanted to spend as much time as he could in Saudi Arabia, ready to convert to Islam? What was he going to tell his wife Rosalina and his ten children—five here and five left behind in Sri Lanka? His tenth son was born here and he named him Fernando. He told me Fernando was not black like him but rather chocolate-colored like Rosalina. He was two years old now. He would get up in the morning with Philip and hang onto his leg, not wanting him to leave without him. Philip would lift him up and put him on top of the armoire. Fernando would laugh and Philip would leave and when he came back at the end of the day he'd find Fernando still on top of the armoire, crying. Rosalina, who was petite, never thought of standing on a chair to get the child off the armoire. Fernando, Philip told me, was a miracle. Who would have thought that Rosalina would get pregnant at forty-five? "But it is the blessed land, Mr. Ismail. I and my wife are like the prophet Zakariya in the Quran, Mr. Ismail." Now Philip had ruined everything by stealing a radio. He would not convert to Islam nor would he stay in Saudi Arabia.

I was feeling depressed so I got up to leave the room and hang out with Nabil in the kitchen but instead I saw Mansur come in, asking, "Where are you going?"

I stopped, surprised at his return after a long absence. He was heading for the other desk next to the safe. He sat down, the monkey still on his shoulder. He was asking me a question as if he had been with me only a few minutes ago, though in fact he had disappeared for more than twenty days. He didn't even bother to say hello.

The telephone rang. I picked it up and said, "Hello."

"Put down the receiver."

It was unmistakably Amm Abdallah's voice. He also must have recognized my voice, otherwise he wouldn't have said that. He wanted Abed. Was it my fault that the two telephones shared the line? Once again I sat at my desk very irritated.

"Hello Ismail!"

Mansur was reminding me that he was there. I decided that if he wanted to be rude to me, I'd be even ruder to him.

"May I sit down?"

"You already have."

We were both silent for a while, then he said, "I drove to Amman. It's a very beautiful city."

I didn't say anything. Nabil appeared at the door carrying a plate that had a few peanuts and pistachios on it.

"Put it on the floor," said Mansur.

Nabil put the plate on the floor, and the monkey's eyes gleamed. Mansur shrugged his shoulders lightly. The monkey jumped off to the desk then to the floor and began to pick up the peanuts and pistachios so fast it was funny. Nabil laughed and said, "It's a circus! Master Mansur's circus!"

Mansur blushed and I saw him trying to hide a faint smile. Suddenly I found myself laughing heartily. When I stopped laughing Nabil said, "Mansur visited us last night. He brought us some pistachios from Amman."

I didn't react. Mansur told Nabil, "Amman's pistachios are fresh, not like what we get around here. But remember it's not all for you. Don't forget the monkey bag." Then, addressing me, he asked, "Does it bother you that the monkey is eating here?"

"Certainly it does."

"If you want me to leave I will."

I didn't answer. Nabil, who must have sensed the tension, left.

Mansur asked me, "Are you from Masr, brother Ismail?"

"What exactly do you mean?"

"I mean, are you from Cairo? They call Cairo 'Masr,' don't they?"

"I'm from Alexandria."

"It's a beautiful city, with a beach and a sea."

"It has the most beautiful beaches in the world."

"I saw Cairo but not Alexandria. Can you swim, brother Ismail?"

"I'm a champion swimmer. I've won lots of medals."

I was lying. I had never swum ten meters.

"You swim in the midst of women in the sea?"

"In the midst of women wearing bikinis. And now they're swimming topless. You see their breasts swimming in front of you. What do you think of that?"

I saw him looking at me, then he lowered his eyes to look at the desk. He began tapping the desk with his fingers in a quick, rhythmic motion. I noticed that he had dirty fingernails even though in general he looked clean. I saw his face suddenly frown and cloud over. He stood up and walked around the desk. It was as if the monkey sensed what was happening; it stopped eating the few remaining peanut and pistachios. Mansur extended his arm; it climbed on it then sat on his shoulder. Mansur dashed out without a word.

✧

Munzir was the first one to arrive for signing out. Amm Abdallah had called Abed to join him at the Emirate so I asked Munzir to give me a ride. I knew that he was always in a hurry, so I told him, "Signing out won't take that long. Don't worry."

"Take your time," he said.

He sat on the big leather chair and fell asleep. Yes. He stretched out his legs, covered his face with his hat, and slept. I heard him snoring after a few moments. "Is Munzir's job so exhausting?" I asked myself, and then saw Aaron Bounkerd standing in front of me with that enigmatic smile. I noticed, for the first time, that his teeth were haphazardly placed in his mouth.

He said as his Mongol eyes stared at me, "I need a three-month advance on my salary as a loan, Mr. Ismail."

I almost laughed at his accent in English, saying "tree" instead of "three" and "mon" instead of "month."

I said, "That's Abed's job."

He said in despair, "Oh, Mr. Ismail. This Abed is very difficult!"

He patted me on the arm, saying that he had to get the loan to send to his wife so she could buy a house in Bangkok, a small house.

Then he said, "What good is my working in Saudi Arabia if I can't buy a home in the capital, Mr. Ismail?"

I looked at his short, stout body, his yellow complexion, his bald head, and the protruding bones of his face. He went on talking.

"Don't you wish to buy a house in Cairo?"

"I live in Alexandria, Aaron."

"I also don't live in Bangkok."

"Alexandria is more beautiful than Cairo."

"This is true, Mr. Ismail. It's a very beautiful city."

I thought he was just being nice to me but he added, "I saw it, Mr. Ismail, in the cinema, in a beautiful American movie called *Ice Cold in Alex*."

I patted him on the shoulder and said, "I'll help you, Aaron. I'll talk to Abed about it."

He said sadly, "Thank you, Mr. Ismail. You are a very kind man."

Then he stood on tiptoe to whisper in my ear. "Do you like wine?" he said in English.

At first I didn't understand. When it dawned on me, I was surprised at the question. I didn't know what to do or say. Once again he whispered, "Don't be afraid, Mr. Ismail. I make my own. Aaron's wine is wonderful."

His eyes were gleaming strangely as if in total ecstasy.

"I don't like it," I said.

The words almost didn't leave my lips. I was so taken aback that I didn't notice him leaving.

✧

On the way home a sandstorm hit us hard with heavy yellow squalls. Munzir turned on his headlights but they did nothing to dispel the yellow darkness engulfing us, almost suffocating us.

"I can do nothing about the dust in this land," shouted Munzir. "I, Munzir, who nothing can stop. I do everything: they want electricity? I do electric work; carpentry? I am a carpenter; a blacksmith? I am a blacksmith; supervising? I am a supervisor; death? I die. I, Munzir, unable to stand up to this yellow dust?"

"It's best if we stop."

"We'd suffocate. It might take a long time. Everybody's

stopped off the road. Everybody is afraid. The road is open and clear in the middle. I say we go at the same speed."

I heard the sand hitting the car. I felt as if someone was flying and carrying me with him in a closed box. The problem was, I knew I was in a car. What should I do? Should I beg him to stop?

"Munzir! Stop the car," I yelled.

"Are you shouting at me? Are you yelling at Munzir? Do you want us to die? Don't you know that there is a curse on this town?"

He didn't slow down and started laughing hysterically and raving, "Munzir is better than Shazam! Munzir challenges Superman! Ha ha, don't be afraid, man."

"Don't be afraid, my good man, sir, Egyptian. Do you like Sadat? I hate him. I hate him very much. Ha ha ha."

The sound of the sand hitting the car was now more like torrents of stones. What should I do with this madman?

"Don't be afraid. I'll stop the car. As you can see I am slowing down. Don't be afraid, brother Ismail."

I felt the car slow down, then it went off the road and stopped. But by then the storm was beginning to let up and the houses in town were becoming visible.

"See? We came a long way and nothing happened. Munzir's theory is correct: everyone stops off the road. Munzir does not stop; he drives down the middle."

"I don't think I'll ride with you again, Munzir."

"You will ride with me a lot, Ustaz."

He started driving slowly even though the storm had stopped.

"I will let the cars that we left behind pass us. I won't bother anyone. Tell me, Ustaz, do you live alone?"

"I live with some friends."

"In an Arabian house?"

"Yes."

"That's the best thing you've done. I used to live in an Arabian house but when I got married I moved to an apartment. The worst thing here is to have neighbors."

I didn't understand what he meant, so he started telling me about his landlord who lived in an apartment across from his. The landlord was over seventy and had a twenty-year-old wife, his sixth. Coming and going, Munzir saw the young wife in front of the door of her apartment, her face uncovered. She was a very beautiful blonde who could be mistaken for one of those Turkish women whose ancestors had stayed behind in Saudi Arabia for decades. He was afraid of this young woman.

I asked him, "Are you Jordanian, Munzir?"

I hadn't thought about the question beforehand and I don't know why I asked. I knew he was Jordanian.

"Is that important, Ustaz?"

"Not at all. I just wanted to ask you about Jordan. Mansur says it's beautiful."

He laughed and said, "That Mansur is a cuckoo, Ustaz. His is a strange story—which I'll tell you later on. I think your house is nearby."

I had given him directions before I rode with him, and indeed we were there. As I opened the car door to get out he said, with a strangely defiant look on his face, "Ustaz, I am not Jordanian. I am Palestinian."

5

"Why don't you like to go to the market with me?" Said asked out of the blue, as he closed the backgammon case. We were sitting in the courtyard. It was early evening. "You've been playing absent-mindedly today," he added. "You lost a bundle."

I didn't want to tell him anything. What good would it do to tell him I was thinking about the silent treatment I had been getting at work for days now? I didn't know what wrong I had done Arshad. When he came to request something from Abed and if Abed happened to be in my room, he would ignore me totally, wouldn't even look at me. He would finish the conversation with Abed quickly then leave, agreeing with everything Abed told him, showing no protest and no anger. When I went to him to continue my driving lessons, he treated me in a very formal manner, closing the door on any other conversation. Munzir still came in and left in a hurry but coming and going he looked at me with a defiance that I failed to comprehend. He seemed to be waiting for the slightest excuse to challenge anything I said or did. Even Philip, for whom Amm Abdallah interceded with the authorities so he was not deported or punished, no longer asked me to explain verses from the Quran that he couldn't understand. He seemed to be unwilling to talk about anything. He knew that if he talked with me I'd ask him why he stole the radio and he didn't want to get into that. But was it really necessary to stop talking altogether?

It seemed to me that for the last few days I had been a person who nobody trusted. Just like that, and for no fault of my own. I seldom remembered my pledge to myself not to be part of anything, to be like a shiny smooth mirror off which raindrops slid. I felt so depressed that I didn't know what to do to get out of it. Even Mansur, who seemed to provide so many diversions that allowed me not to dwell on my own annoyance, disappeared again. There was nobody left at work except Abed, who spent what little time he stayed at the office busy with Amm Abdallah's private business. There was also Nabil, who had told me a few days earlier, "Forget what I said about the safe," then stopped speaking to me altogether. He would serve me coffee in silence then go. Only the old Yemeni man and I exchanged distant smiles.

"I need to go to the market with you," I told Said.

We both went to our rooms to change. It was Friday, the day I did most of the work at home. Said usually got up late then went to the mosque and stayed until prayer time. Wagih would be on call at the hospital the night before and would come home Friday morning to sleep.

Thus it fell to me, who neither prayed nor worked nights, to prepare lunch. Our Friday lunch was usually Egyptian: fried fish, fish in tomato sauce, fried eggplant, fried potatoes, fava beans, fried green peppers, pilaf, a big green salad, and lemonade or orange juice. I learned how to make all that from Said.

After the prayers, Wagih would get up to have lunch with us then he would go to the hospital, usually coming back after ten o'clock. Said and I would watch television or play backgammon. We both made sure to watch Shaykh Ali Tantawi's program. Shaykh Tantawi was a man over fifty with a pleasant, radiant face surrounded by a trimmed gray beard. He spoke as if he were sitting and talking with you alone, as if you were an old friend. He tackled the most profound issues in jurisprudence with such simplicity that every viewer understood what he was talking about. For that reason apparently every group claimed him as one of their own. They said he came originally from Egypt. Said said he was Syrian. Other groups said he was Moroccan, or Jordanian, or Palestinian.

I didn't want to go to the market only because of the silence I was encountering at work. There was another kind of silence here at the house that I'd come to like and to which I loved to come back and stay as long as I could. It seemed to me that our life was following a certain, fixed routine. We had nothing in common except for all being expatriates. We laughed a lot over stories that we told about others. None of us had ever broached any personal subject with his two roommates. I didn't share anything personal either, but not intentionally. Nor was it intentional in their case. It must have been that each of us was still attached to the other, faraway circles of homeland and family. The fact that one day we would go back must have had an effect, building barriers between ourselves and our immediate surroundings. And because each of us was confident of a triumphant return, it didn't seem that fear or worry on that account could find its way to us. What kind of life was it that appeared as neat as a set of grammatical rules? Everything around me was cold. My going to the market today was nothing more than a faint smile.

✧

We rode in Said's Datsun and drove around in some side streets and alleys until we made it to the main street. This was only the second time I had seen this street, even though I had been here for more than a month. The street was still as crowded as it was when I saw it for the first time, as if I had left it only a short while ago and was now returning to it. It was evening now and the street lights on both sides were on. I saw the moon high in the sky, a mere crescent.

"It's better to walk," Said said as he parked his car in a side alley after we reached the middle of the main street. We left the car and continued on foot.

The sidewalk of the main street was packed with passersby and goods. A strange human silence hung in the air, which was heavy with the high humidity that had set in suddenly the day before. It seemed that summer was breathing its last. It was the middle of October, approaching the end of the Islamic month of Dhu al-Qida. In a few weeks the Feast of the Sacrifice and the pilgrimage would be upon us. Television had already started to show a special program about the pilgrimage and its rites. Haberdashers and sewing notions stores were all over the place. I thought of buying something for my mother and brother and sisters, but I didn't know anyone going to Alexandria any time soon.

I was now seeing the market better than I had seen it the first time. I took my time walking around. Said did not rush me. It did not feel strange being there. Was the market itself really strange that first time or was it the sight of the police car and the poor girl paraded on top of it? Now I couldn't see anything that was radically different from the Manshiya market in Alexandria, except that no one was hawking the merchandise here as they did in Manshiya. Also, the people looked different.

"You can transfer your money to Egypt via Rajihi Bank. It's the most famous bank here," Said said when he saw me looking at the bank sign.

"Actually I need to send my mother a hundred Egyptian pounds."

"And I need to inquire about the price of gold pounds," Said said as he pulled me by the hand to enter the bank. "Wagih will ask me in the evening," he added. "He likes to buy gold. He says gold is better than dollars."

We went in through a narrow door. The small bank was packed with people, breathing and sweating. Said stood in front of a young Pakistani teller to ask him about the price of gold pounds.

"One hundred and ninety-four riyals," I heard the teller say. I stood in front of another teller separated from him by an iron grill. I asked him for a hundred pound check in Egyptian currency. He took five hundred riyals from me and wrote out for me the check that I would send to my mother by mail. I felt as I stood waiting for the check that a beam of light was piercing my cheek. Something was forcing me to look at a far-away corner in the crowded bank. I knew that when someone looked at you, you felt their gaze even if you couldn't see them. That feeling usually became sharper the greater the scrutiny of the gaze. I didn't realize what was happening until I turned around and saw him far away in the middle of the crowd, his eyes like two spots of light in an extremely dark room, fixed on me. It was none other than Mansur, without a monkey on his shoulder this time. I didn't know what to do: should I go to him or ignore him? Said tugged at me, saying, "Why are you standing there like a statue?"

I saw Mansur's face contorting with anger. His eyes grew wider and had a threatening gleam. He rushed at us like a sharp arrow. I don't know why I always expected him to be rude. He passed us quickly and went out, pushing his way through the crowd.

"Why are you standing like that? Don't you hear me?" Said said as he shook me. My neck and face were bathed in sweat. I took the check prepared by the Pakistani teller and let Said pull me by the arm as we left the bank.

✧

"What's the matter with you?"

I didn't answer. We walked, encountering dark Pakistanis and fair Afghans with red beards. You could tell the Afghans by their beards and perhaps also by the bewilderment in their eyes. They had the same clothes as the Pakistanis: the same long shirt and loose-fitting pants that Nabil once said, laughing, were made especially for floating in the floods that were reported in broadcasts every day.

We also encountered groups of Koreans who walked fast. Whenever we came across two women walking together, Said would say, "Egyptians." He explained to me how they walked in twos and how rare it was to see an Egyptian woman walking by herself; she would be either with her husband or with a woman friend. In front of one store I saw a number of Europeans, perhaps American, drinking 7UP. Among them was a girl in jeans, a blonde without her face or her hair covered. She was laughing out loud. I hadn't seen anyone like her on the street.

We stood in front of a huge grocery store. The attendant came over to us, ignoring the other customers. I noticed at the far end of the store a man reclining on cushions on the floor next to the wall, stretching out his legs and smoking a waterpipe. Said gave a list to the attendant, who shook his hand, smiling.

"We'll be back in an hour," Said said. The attendant's smile grew wider as he said, "With God's protection."

We left. Said said, "The man smoking the waterpipe is the owner of the store. The attendant is a Yemeni whose name is Muhammad. He loves the Egyptians and they love him. He's very sharp. All Yemenis are intelligent. We'll be back in an hour, and everything will be ready."

We kept walking. The street lights were dimmer and it was less crowded. The stores were few and far between. There were some old buildings and ruins. We arrived at a place that was pitch dark, and stood there, as the smell of pickles filled the air.

It was a small store with a single, feeble lamp and a very old man whose back was bent. Said and I stepped up to him. Said asked the man to fix us a bag of pickles for five riyals. I looked at the barrels that were stacked up to the ceiling and at the small open barrels, some of which had yellow and white onions floating in red water. Other barrels had pickled cucumbers piled up, the seeds floating. In others you could see pink and white pickled turnips and green peppers. There was nobody else except us. The faraway crescent moon did nothing to dispel the darkness. In my imagination the barrels were filled with dynamite that would explode instantly. I looked in the dark at a mosque that appeared clearly in front of me. It was a big mosque but it was closed. There were low white houses behind it.

"This is the main mosque of the town. All the *sharia* punishments are administered in front of it. Almost all—the beheadings take place in Mecca. They say this mosque was originally built by the Prophet himself when he conquered Tabuk. I think he only prayed here and the mosque was built later."

"So is this where they do the flogging and the stoning?" I asked.

"Most probably there's no stoning. I haven't seen any to date. Foreign adulteresses are usually deported. Nobody's found any native adulteresses yet. As for flogging, it's no more than caning. The Egyptians here call it 'dusting off the clothes.' It's mostly funny. If you'd come last Ramadan you'd have seen the flogging on the morning of the first day of the Feast. Maybe you'll see that next year. Most of the flogging is done here during the Lesser Feast: a person caught breaking the fast is usually jailed until the end of Ramadan then flogged on the day of the Feast. The real flogging is done at the Emirate: the emir himself administers it. He doesn't use a cane or a whip, but an *uqal* on the bare skin. Wagih can tell you about people sent from the emir's compound to the hospital, sliced."

I trembled as he spoke in the darkness, which I never liked to begin with. Said took the big plastic bag that the man had filled with pickles. Before starting back I asked him about the houses behind the mosque.

"This neighborhood is Omdurman," he said. "The people who live there are all black. Perhaps that's why they call it Omdurman, after the city in Sudan." He smiled and added, "Or perhaps the people became black because they lived in Omdurman. It's notorious for alcohol and other things. Most of the people who live there—men and women—sing and dance at weddings, like the artistes and chanteuses of Muhammad Ali Street in Cairo. They don't sit at cafés or in front of their doors here, though. Do you know, in my four years here I've never set foot in that neighborhood? It's very dangerous."

He turned to go back. I followed suit, leaving behind Omdurman and the closed mosque, fixing my gaze on the distant lights. Said said, "Every time I come here and see the mosque, I remember the conquest of Tabuk and a strange story that people tell. They say that when the Prophet passed by a certain tribe, that tribe refused to give him water to drink and blocked his army's way to their well. So the Prophet invoked a curse on them: that members of the tribe should become extinct except for twenty people and that that number should remain constant until the Day of Judgment: twenty men, women, and children only. Every time a baby was born, a member of the tribe would die. It's the curse people here talk about. Do you think it's true?"

Before I could answer he added, "Don't say anything. It's a horrible story that I'd rather forget."

We walked in silence. I remembered that Munzir said the town was cursed when we were in the middle of that dust storm. This was probably what Munzir meant. It really was horrible. I didn't think the Prophet would do something like that to anybody. I didn't think anyone had seen any members of the tribe. It was a horror story invented by a madman. However I felt real fear, which only began to dissipate when I heard the call to the night prayer coming loudly from a faraway mosque. I saw the stores closing, and the passersby going into alleys, and two old men with long gray beards walking on the sidewalk, each holding a small whip, with which they lightly beat anyone they came across, saying loudly, "Perform the prayers."

"These are members of the Society for Enjoining What Is Right. They close the market down and force people to pray," Said said as he pulled me into a dark side alley to hide for a little while. We found a number of other Egyptians who had beaten us to the alley and stood there watching us and laughing.

The prayers finished. Everybody came out from wherever they were. The stores reopened their doors and the people who had hidden behind them emerged. Little by little the street came to life. The lights grew brighter, and we kept going. Many of the faces I had seen earlier began to reappear. Said took me to a big open area behind the Riyadh Bank where we found a vegetable, fruit, and meat market. We bought mangoes and oranges, and went back to the main street to go to the grocery store before it closed down. Said asked me, "Have you forgotten what I told you a few days ago?"

"What was that?"

"The private lesson."

Said had talked to me about the possibility of making some extra money by giving private lessons. Holding two jobs was forbidden in Saudi Arabia, but giving private lessons was not officially a job. Private lessons were also forbidden, but only to teachers. For people like me, who had some other type of job, it was all right.

I hadn't paid much attention to the conversation and had forgotten about it. But apparently he had taken it seriously. He took me to an elegant school and office supply store where a smiling young man welcomed us. Said introduced the young man to me as Khalid.

The young man shook my hand heartily and took us to a far corner in the store where he opened a little refrigerator, took out two cans of Vimto, and went back to talk to a customer who had been there before we came in.

We finished the drink and Khalid finished his business with the customer. He came back to us smiling happily. His white *gallabiya* was clean and shining as were his *ghutra* and black *uqal*. He seemed totally overjoyed.

He took from the upper pocket of his *gallabiya* a piece of paper, which he gave to me saying, "This is our address, Ustaz Ismail."

I held the paper, not knowing exactly what to do or what was expected of me. Khalid said, "Don't worry about your fee, Ustaz. We'll pay you well. My sister is an intelligent student who needs only a few lessons in English."

So, Said had arranged everything and set me up to teach this man's sister. My God! Giving lessons to a girl? In Saudi Arabia? My blood must have rushed to my face, for when I looked again Khalid had left. Then he came back carrying a case holding two golden Sheaffer pens. He gave me the elegant case, saying, "This is a little token of our friendship, Ustaz. When will you come?"

"In a week."

I don't know why I said that. Anyway that's what happened. I saw disappointment on Khalid's face but he soon smiled and said, "God willing, Ustaz."

I took my leave and held out my hand to shake his. He took my hand between his two hands and shook it very warmly, then he shook Said's hand. As soon as we turned to leave he called out, "Ustaz!"

I stopped. He came closer and whispered, "Please come. Don't let me down."

I didn't know how to respond. I was thinking, "Why did I accept his gift so easily?" I said, "Don't worry. I'll come as I promised."

He shook my hand again very firmly, like someone making a pledge of loyalty forever.

✧

After supper we were watching television in the courtyard at home when Said asked me, "Are you going on the pilgrimage?"

"No," I said.

"Then you will spend the Feast alone," he said.

We were both silent for a while, then he said, "I'll be on my second pilgrimage. Wagih will be on his fourth. Isn't that so, Doctor?"

Wagih said, "True. But this time I'll be doing it on behalf of my mother."

I smiled and asked, "Is that possible?"

"Yes," Said replied. "Didn't you see *Pilgrimage Special* on television yesterday? What matters is for a person to go on pilgrimage for himself first." Then he laughed and added, "Actually he's going on behalf of his mother to save money. Instead of sending her a ticket and going to meet her and fuss over her, he'll just go on her behalf."

I was surprised when Wagih said in a matter-of-fact tone, "That's true. But it's also true that the pilgrimage has become very hard on people. I'm sparing my mother the hardship. You think I am wrong, Ismail?"

"No. So long as Islam permits it, it's all right," I said. I wasn't really convinced of what he said but didn't see the use of arguing when Wagih would never budge from his position. Addressing Said, he said, "Here's a man who's not going to make the pilgrimage, but he tells the truth and doesn't resort to insinuations or innuendoes."

Said laughed. Wagih started to write a letter in the flickering light of the television. I thought about Said, who had told me that day for the first time about his fiancée, Widad, who was a schoolteacher in town. Her mother lived with her as a chaperone and he could not visit her or see her except, by chance and briefly, in the market.

This was hard to believe, but why should he lie, I asked myself as we were coming back from the market. He was still speaking. He said he was going back to Egypt for good at the end of this school year: "All my work here was lost there," he said nonchalantly. He had purchased an elegant apartment in a huge building in Heliopolis, but it collapsed soon after construction was completed. He thanked God that he had not moved in before it collapsed and that his fiancée Widad understood his circumstances and used her own savings to buy another apartment. She convinced him that this should be their last year in Saudi Arabia. "Vanity of vanities, all is vanity and vexation of the spirit, my friend," he said as he laughed and drove the car. But I understood his agony. "All our engagement days here are wasted without the chance to meet and get to know each other," he had said more than once. Then it struck me that the young man we met in the market, Khalid, might have been a brother of Wadha bint Sulayman ibn Sabil. Said had told me earlier that he knew her brother, who had a school and office supply store on the main street. At the moment that the thought hit me that the girl who Said had arranged for me to give private lessons to tonight could be Wadha herself and just as I was about to ask him, the announcer began to read the last newscast of the day in a firm, authoritative voice. He said:

"In the name of God, Most Gracious, Most Merciful. *And there is life for you in retaliation, O men of understanding . . .*

"Today the Mufti of Mecca has approved the application of the *sharia* punishment, by sword, on Malik ibn Abdallah ibn Malik, who during the last glorious month of Ramadan, kidnapped a girl who was tending sheep in the outskirts of Mecca and took her to Taif. There, he and Satan set up a tent in the mountains and began forcibly to have intimate relations with her. The hiding place of this atheist was discovered this week. A police task force conducted a raid on his hideout but he was armed with a machine gun, that he used to kill a member of the raiding force. God Almighty enabled the force to capture him alive."

"Have you ever seen a beheading?" Wagih asked me matter-of-factly. I answered, "No."

And I felt my neck.

6

A great crush of large and small buses and different makes of cars: Peugeot, Mercedes, Chevrolet, Toyota, Datsun, Honda, and others that I didn't know. The road from the north, the southbound airport road, was jammed. Tabuk was the first big town in the northwestern part of Saudi Arabia. Pilgrims would spend a night or two here in the open air next to the cars. Making it to Tabuk was reassuring. From there on, it was an easy journey and in the holy land. The hospital in Tabuk served as a quarantine station where pilgrims arriving from the north, Syria and Turkey, would be examined.

On my way to work every morning I saw the crowds: men, women, and a few children sitting on the ground next to their vehicles eating their breakfast in silence, with cars and buses parked along both sides of the road. It was the groups of Turkish pilgrims that struck me most, on my way to and from work. They looked poor, barely clothed, with gray beards and red complexions. They were mostly elderly, their faces spoke of silence and waiting. They were always some distance from the cars. They had come on foot and would continue until they made it to Mecca. They slept outdoors; it helped that the cold had not set in yet. They had very few belongings, maybe just some coarse wool blankets.

I wasn't as much surprised by the number of cars and buses as I was by those who were making the journey on foot. It was as if we were still in those earlier times we had read about, when trains of pilgrims traveled on foot from Morocco and Muslim Spain, or in caravans on camel back escorted by Mamluk forces to protect them against Bedouin raids. All the Mamluk rulers took pains to secure the pilgrimage route against raids by the Bedouins until the time of Muhammad Ali, who, by occupying the Hijaz itself in 1810, provided a more permanent solution to the security problem.

For centuries, all the rulers of this region took pains to secure the pilgrimage route, until Israel came onto the scene. Israel encroached on the old pilgrimage route when it encircled Sinai from the south, just as it encroached on the northern coast, where Abraham walked; it seized al-Arish, which Abraham first settled, and it rushed from the center through the wilderness where the Israelites once disobeyed Moses, who spoke with the Lord. This time Israel did not wander nor did it get lost: it had learned the lie of the land. Israel has marched and trampled over all the holy routes in unprecedented security. It said, "The land is our land; we know it. The prophets are our prophets. No pharaoh can force lies or an exodus upon us. Our father Abraham was good; he lied to escape with his wife from the pharaoh. Our brother Moses was good; he convinced us to flee. Today we are back and the daughters of Abraham are swimming in the water in front of you. Who amongst you can stop them? The pharaoh has finally come to us to ask forgiveness. We will give him back what we have taken from you on condition that the daughters of Abraham stroll through your markets. Our men will not have to lie anymore.

Israel would leave the pilgrimage route in Sinai, but nobody used it anymore. People took ships and planes to make the pilgrimage, except the poor, tired Turks. The pilgrimage here was so quiet. Neither Layla Murad nor Muhammad al-Kahlawi was singing the praises of the Prophet Muhammad, there were no white banners flying from cars, no joyous, shrill, trilling ululations. I thought that people here didn't know much about the Wahhabi movement and the strict codes of behavior it established. The pilgrims who came by car and on foot were tired, busy trying to figure out and prepare for the rest of the journey and getting provisions. They went to the market and strolled the streets of the town. But you couldn't tell them apart from the townsfolk; they were strangers in a town full of strangers. No one entered into the state of ritual consecration to begin the actual rite of the pilgrimage here; you didn't see people wearing the special seamless sheets necessary for the rite. You could recognize pilgrims only outside town, where the northern road bypassed it to cut quickly to the south past the hospital and then into the desert sands.

These days, however, the pilgrimage was all that anyone ever talked about.

✧

Arshad came into my office and said the Pakistanis had organized themselves to go on the pilgrimage and wanted me to intercede with Amm Abdallah to give them a big truck for transportation. I smiled. Arshad was talking to me. I had completed my driving lessons and the day before had been given an old pick-up truck to use. Arshad had kept strictly to the driving lessons. Today he was talking about something else. I asked him, "You're going to travel by truck?"

"Yes. Our colleagues will ride in the back and Wahhaj and I will take turns driving."

"Isn't that hard? Why don't you rent a bus?"

"That's very costly, Mr. Ismail."

I knew that if you split the cost of a bus rental, it wouldn't cost that much. But the Pakistanis in the company held mostly janitorial or simple technician jobs and had to save every penny.

"Will you talk to Mr. Abdallah, Mr. Ismail?" Arshad asked again, visibly worried. I asked him to sit down and he did. I ordered a coffee for him and he drank it. I wanted him to talk a lot, and he did. He said he had graduated from art school; he was a painter who kept his small paintings in his room in the camp but didn't show them to anybody. He told me not to be surprised; his father had taught him to drive and to repair cars when he was a young boy. His father was a driver. He needed to travel, so Arshad had to get a passport showing his occupation as a mechanic so that he could easily get a job contract. "There's no room for artists here, Mr. Ismail," he said, smiling, then asked me, "Is it the same in Egypt?"

"It's the same," I said.

My surprise did not end there. I didn't believe the story, but I didn't wish to inquire further about it. Arshad said he was married, that he had a beautiful daughter named Zaynab whose picture he always drew in his room. He said he was from Peshawar.

"What's so special about Peshawar, Arshad? Isn't it like other towns?"

"No, Mr. Ismail. Peshawar is the poorest town. Almost all the janitorial workers here are from Peshawar. They don't take annual vacations, just keep working to get double time. They only go to Peshawar after four or five years, at the end of their contracts."

"Isn't that very difficult?"

"It's more difficult to go to Peshawar and come back here," he said.

He fell silent for a short while then suddenly said, "Pakistan is an unfortunate country."

I didn't understand what he meant. He said, "Zia-ul Haq is very evil, Mr. Ismail. Haven't you seen his eyes? Bhutto is better. Do you know Bhutto?"

"I know that he's in jail now."

"They will kill him, Mr. Ismail. It was Bhutto who made Zia-ul Haq, but Zia-ul Haq turned against Bhutto. Zia-ul Haq is like Sadat, Mr. Ismail."

I was disturbed by what Arshad was telling me. He went on talking, quite freely.

"You hate Sadat, don't you, Mr. Ismail?" he asked.

I didn't answer; I was at a loss for words. He was speaking like a very innocent child.

"It is a duty, Mr. Ismail," he said. "A duty to hate them all. I know a lot about Egypt, about last January's riots by the poor. We need to have such riots in Pakistan, but military men are stupid and they shoot people. They are all against us, Mr. Ismail, all these presidents. They are against us. We are truly very wretched."

We were both silent for a long time. Arshad, who was usually so silent, had opened up like a waterfall. How come he, who seemed so afraid of me, had opened his heart to me? He got up and asked me again, "Will you intercede for us with Mr. Abdallah?"

"Don't worry, Arshad. He will say yes."

"Thank you, Mr. Ismail. Aren't you going on pilgrimage?"

"Not this year."

"So, you will spend the Feast by yourself, Mr. Ismail."

He left.

✧

"Aren't you going on pilgrimage, Mr. Ismail?"

"No."

"So, you will spend the Feast by yourself."

I was surprised that Philip Sousay Biliya should say this. He spoke with me that day too. He found himself face to face with me and had to wait with me for some time. Abed had gone on one of Amm Abdallah's private errands, and I had moved to his office. Arshad had been there less than one hour ago and I was still thinking, "How come he opened up his heart and spoke with such candor to me so easily? Were things weighing so much on him that he wanted to get them out of his system?" Anyway, he talked to me and that gave me some kind of mysterious delight. Arshad did not fear me. I didn't frighten anyone. Philip asked me about Abed and I told him he was in the town. He looked at his watch irritably and said, "He asked me to come here at twelve."

I looked at the clock on the wall; it was indeed twelve o'clock. I found myself leaving him standing in the room, and hurried to have a look at the forecourt in the hope of seeing the Yemeni man as he entered, but I found him sitting in his usual spot, turning the *siwak* in his mouth. When he saw me he smiled. I smiled and returned to the office. I sat behind the desk and Philip sat on one of the chairs. We were both silent for a few moments, then I asked him, "Does Abed need you for something important?"

He answered impatiently, "He said it was important."

I looked closely at Philip's face with its protruding cheekbones, a strong face despite his age. He was wearing prescription glasses that I hadn't seen on him before. I said without much thought, "Did you know that Mr. Abdallah was going to save you from the police?"

I immediately felt sorry I had said it. Some time had passed since the theft. I shouldn't have reminded him of it but it seemed my curiosity about his motives was stronger than my ability to watch my words.

He said, "No."

He smiled and I smiled and grew bolder, so I asked him, "Do you know the laws of this land, Philip?"

"I know them, Mr. Ismail."

"So, how come you did it?"

"It's a very wonderful radio, Mr. Ismail, seven bands."

"But it almost cost you a lot of grief. You could have bought it."

"It sells for one thousand five hundred riyals. It's a magnificent radio. I wanted to listen to broadcasts from Colombo. Have you ever seen a radio with seven bands?"

"No."

"Well, there you are."

He said that in Arabic. I don't know what devil possessed me to say, "You are ready to convert to Islam, Mr. Philip. Theft is a sin in Islam."

"I know. But there's nothing in the Quran that says one shouldn't steal a seven-band radio."

I burst out laughing. He smiled broadly in such embarrassment, occasioned undoubtedly by my laughter, that his face turned red.

I said, "Now you have to hurry up and convert so that people forget what happened."

"I will do that soon, Mr. Ismail. But tell me, aren't you going on pilgrimage this year?"

I was surprised by Philip's question. Abed's car stopped in front of us in the forecourt but he did not get out. Instead he motioned to Philip, who went to the car and got in. Abed drove off without speaking to me. I had to stay in his office for some time.

✧

I expected, when Nabil entered the room and stood looking at me without saying anything for a moment, that he too was going to ask me whether I was going on pilgrimage or not. The repeated question had begun to irritate me. How should I explain? I had been working there for less than two months. I was surprised by the Feast of the Sacrifice forcing itself on my attention. When somebody came here they thought of nothing but work. One realized only too late that time was the same everywhere in the world. The Feast of the Sacrifice came at its appointed time, even if you were in China or Japan. But I really was surprised by the Feast of the Sacrifice and surprised by the whole business of the pilgrimage. Pilgrimage was associated in my mind with elderly men and women. I had seen no other types of pilgrim in Egypt. To my mind, pilgrimage was preceded by rituals that I saw repeated year after year where I lived in Alexandria: there were decorations, and slaughtering of sheep, little kids dipping their hands in the blood then imprinting them on the wall to ward off the evil eye, young men painting pictures of a camel ridden by an old man being led by a boy, a faraway mosque and palm trees on the road. There were groups of men coming to shake hands with the pilgrim before he left, cars bedecked with banners and flowers driving up and down the streets, Quranic recitations in small pavilions, and banquets for the poor. I never thought a young man like me could go on pilgrimage so early in his life. I was amazed at how, in this country, you could ride in a car only one day before the pilgrimage rites started, do the pilgrimage, then come back.

That was the puzzle for me, which nobody else would understand and which I hadn't mentioned to anybody yet. However Nabil did not mention the pilgrimage. He sat down and asked me to listen closely to what he was going to tell me.

"Okay."

He said, "It's not okay."

I smiled. I had become accustomed to his way with words. I said, "Be that as it may. Go ahead."

He said, "You know I am engaged."

"I see you're wearing an engagement ring."

"I have a great dilemma. Shall I go through with the engagement or break it?"

He didn't wait for an answer. I had no answer, of course. He continued to talk. "I make one thousand two hundred riyals. That's about two hundred and forty Egyptian pounds. I send my fiancée one hundred and my mother fifty and live on the rest, saving nothing. My fiancée has opened an account with Bank Misr. No, Citibank, a foreign bank. She told me a week ago and asked me to transfer the money directly to her account and not to send her checks or money orders because trying to cash them took too much time. Besides, it was always crowded at the bank and often they didn't have any dollars so they'd give her Egyptian currency at the official rate of exchange and she would lose a lot. They exchange a dollar for sixty-eight piasters even though on the black market it's worth eighty. As if that wasn't enough, sending checks was a very risky business; postal workers opened the letters and took the checks for themselves. Postal workers in Egypt are very poor, as you know. You must remember what they looked like."

I laughed and asked him, "They'd do that even if the check was made out to somebody else?"

"Postal workers in Egypt can do anything."

I laughed heartily as he went on.

"My mother sent me a letter yesterday," he said, "advising me to stop sending money to my fiancée because she's going out with a driver from Kitkat; no, not Kitkat, from the camel-market neighborhood in Imbaba."

I laughed and said, "It doesn't matter where he's from. I'm from Alexandria, if you haven't forgotten. I don't know Cairo that well."

He fell silent and said very calmly, "What I am telling you about isn't in Cairo, it's in Giza."

I started laughing again. He smiled and said, "What do you think?"

"About what?"

"Should I break the engagement or not?"

I thought a little. I decided to take it seriously even if he were speaking in jest. I said, "Stop sending money to your fiancée and wait. You'll find out if she loves you or not."

He was silent for a moment then said, "If she loves me, I will be very sorry that I stopped sending the money. If she loves somebody else, she will leave me. It is not proper that a man should wait until a woman leaves him."

I found the situation most perplexing. I said, "Well then, why don't you go back and find out for yourself?"

"You are complicating matters. I can't go. I'll do like the Pakistanis and spend my annual vacation working. I need every penny."

We fell silent. I thought how this man who needed every penny was sending back almost all his salary. He said as if talking to himself, "The problem is, I love the bitch. She reads magazines and newspapers."

I kept looking closely at him as he seemed lost in thought. Then he said, "Do you think I should ask Abed too?"

Giving up on the whole matter, I said, "No one can do you any good. I don't quite understand what you mean. The right thing to do is to save the money you are sending yourself so that when you go back to Egypt you'll be able to get an apartment to marry in. How do you expect to get married without an apartment?"

Once again he seemed lost in thought. He didn't seem to have followed what I was saying.

Then he got up, saying, "I should go on pilgrimage first, then think about it afterwards."

He took one step to the door than turned to me and said, "Is it true that Islam allows a person to go on pilgrimage on behalf of another? I heard something like that on TV."

I remembered what Wagih had said and told him, "Islam permits you to do that on condition that you go on pilgrimage for yourself first."

I could see surprise in his eyes and his face. He said, "Well, if my mother is sick, almost paralyzed, and if I'm not sure she'll live another year and I want to go on pilgrimage on her behalf, is God going to reject that pilgrimage because I haven't gone on pilgrimage for myself first? I don't think so."

As he left my heart shook for fear he'd ask me whether I was going on pilgrimage or not. He didn't ask. Nobody talked to me the rest of the day.

7

"Why are you going so fast?"

"Why go slow?"

I asked and Dr. Wagih answered.

He had invited me to go along and spend a night at the hospital. He said, "Tomorrow is Friday and you can stay up with me till the morning."

I had accepted straight away, saying to myself that this was another chance to break the rigid routine of our life. I had gone out with Said to the market, and tonight I would be in Wagih's company at the hospital.

Wagih was talking a lot about how stressful working was around that time. The hospital was overcrowded because of the pilgrimage season, its surprises and road accidents. The day before yesterday he had told us about the shock the pilgrims had when they found out they had to be tested for infectious diseases, especially cholera, the bugaboo of the pilgrimage season. The pilgrims had to uncover their rear ends in front of hospital orderlies of the same sex, who would scrape the anus with special medical spoons, and the samples would be quickly tested.

The day before yesterday a whole busload of pilgrims refused to bare their rear ends. With great reluctance the men finally complied but when it was the turn of the women, everyone, men and women, protested. Dialogue became impossible; everyone was screaming and no one could make sense of what was being said in the angry Syrian dialect. The passengers were all Syrian and were all going on pilgrimage by land for the first time. They left swearing never to go on pilgrimage again. Quarantine rules were well known, but still the tests always took the pilgrims by surprise. I asked Wagih, "Why don't they get it done in their own countries?"

"Even if it were done in their own countries, we wouldn't accept it. They have to be tested here."

"Isn't there another way to test for cholera besides this scraping business?"

"Of course there is: stool tests. But where do we get the time for all these pilgrims to bring samples of their stool? The only choice we have is to stand them in line and have them bend over and bare their rear ends, so the orderlies can scrape off the samples."

"It's really quite awkward," I said, laughing. It was perhaps because of these stories that I agreed to go with him that day.

✧

On the way Wagih told me that the hospital was a small one, a two-story building with four small clinics: surgery, internal medicine, obstetrics, and pediatrics. Each clinic had two rooms with four beds in each. He said they were building a huge new hospital but that it wouldn't be finished for another three years. He also told me that there was a big American hospital on the military base, called Whittaker, but that no Arabs worked there. According to Wagih, a foreign nurse there made several times the salary of an Egyptian doctor in any other hospital.

We arrived at the hospital. There was a continual hustle and bustle in the big hall that took up a large area of the ground floor. Men and women were coming and going quickly and silently. It was no longer hot; the summer had begun slowly to make room for winter. It was November. Dhu al-Qida was gone and only three days remained before the pilgrimage.

We went up to the second floor, and into a not very clean room. Wagih sat behind a small, old desk and I sat on a chair next to the desk. In the room there was another chair and a glass cabinet that contained some lusterless white medical instruments. The paint on the walls had flaked off in several places. Behind the plastic folding screen I saw the edge of the examination table covered by an off-white sheet.

As soon as we sat down, a nurse came into the room. Wagih introduced her to me as Aida. She smiled faintly, barely hiding the serious look on her face. She appeared edgy, I didn't know why. I was struck by her wide, dark eyes and the gleam of their whites in the dimly-lit room. I said to myself, "This is the first woman's face I've seen here." She said to Wagih that all the patients were doing fine. He asked, "And the pilgrims?"

"There were no new groups this evening. They say the day shift was very busy."

"That's our good fortune. Even though I wanted Ustaz Ismail to watch."

She looked at me, smiling, and said, "What could he see here that he hasn't seen in Egypt? Have you been to any hospitals in Egypt, Ustaz Ismail?"

I answered right away. "I stayed in a hospital once for a hernia operation."

I don't know why I answered so quickly. I saw her try to hide her laughter.

Wagih asked, "What's the matter, Nurse? Did he say something funny?"

"No. But he looks too young for a hernia."

She seemed very embarrassed, and blushed. I lowered my eyes in embarrassment myself and heard her say, "I am sorry. Very sorry."

She left quickly. Wagih looked at me, stretched out his lips, and said, "In Egypt nurses are a dime a dozen. Here a nurse's salary is sometimes higher than a beginning doctor's."

I said to myself, "There he goes again talking about the material worth of things." A middle-aged man came into the room and stood silently. Behind him stood a small policeman. Wagih got up quickly and came around the desk to shake the man's hand warmly.

"Hello, Doctor. Hello. Please have a seat."

He offered him the empty chair but the policeman said angrily, "Don't sit. Stay as you are."

Wagih stood in silence. I looked at the man who the policeman had prevented from sitting down. He had a scruffy beard and there was a look of dejection in his eyes. His clothes were dirty and unkempt. Wagih went back to the desk quickly, took out a closed envelope from a drawer and gave it to him. The man took it with a trembling hand and didn't say anything. He turned to leave and the policeman grabbed him by the arm and dragged him along. I saw them in the long corridor outside the room, the policeman hurrying and the man scrambling along, almost stumbling. The man appeared shorter at a distance than he had in the room. Wagih sat down sadly. He placed his head between his hands and lowered his head, staring at the desk. Another man, a black, wearing a *gallabiya*, a *ghutra*, and a tattered *uqal* appeared at the door and said, "Miss Aida sent me, Doctor."

Wagih said without looking up, "Make us some tea, Numan. We have a dear guest."

I told myself this must be the servant, sent by Aida to make up for the gaffe. I didn't forget about the first man, who had come in with the policeman, the Egyptian wearing the shabby suit who Wagih addressed as "Doctor." I asked Wagih, "What's the story behind the man who came with the policeman?"

Wagih sighed and said, "It's a strange story. He's an Egyptian doctor who's been here for five years. A year ago he made a horrible mistake. A young Saudi man came to him with a young woman who he said was his wife and asked him to perform an abortion on her. We don't know how Dr. Gharib, that's his name, Dr. Sayyid Ali al-Gharib, could make such a mistake. He should have taken precautions. Abortion is illegal to begin with, except as a medical necessity. Any doctor can go against his conscience and make up medical reasons for an abortion, but that doesn't happen. Dr. Sayyid al-Gharib did it—he wrote a report indicating that the abortion was medically necessary. Why did he do it? Nobody knows. I don't think the young Saudi tempted him with money; Dr. Sayyid had been here long enough to make a lot of money. The matter would have passed, except the young woman died during the procedure. Worse yet, the young man disappeared. It turned out that he wasn't her husband nor was he related to her in any way. Since that day, Dr. Sayyid al-Gharib has been placed under house arrest. His pay has been suspended until the court decides his case, which it hasn't done yet. They confiscated his money and placed him in a beautiful house. Can you imagine? The only house in town with a garden, and palms, and lemon trees. He's been there a full year now. Every month they allow him to go out once with a policeman to come to the hospital and take whatever we can come up with to help him. The Egyptian doctors and nurses collect some money for him every month. His family in Egypt has stopped sending anything to him since the incident. If we didn't help him, he'd starve to death." He fell silent for a few moments, then got up, saying, "I wish you hadn't seen that. Anyway, that's that. I'm going to make the rounds quickly. If Numan brings the tea, don't wait for me."

✧

It wasn't easy to forget someone like Dr. Sayyid Ali al-Gharib. He had looked long at me while Wagih was busy getting the envelope from the desk, as if he didn't want me to see him. After all I was an Egyptian like him and he didn't want me to witness his tragedy. He probably knew that his story was well known but he must have wished it to stop there. I wanted very much to see him again, I don't know why.

I felt very dejected. I realized that Numan had come and placed the tea glasses on the desk and that they had gotten cold, undrinkable.

Wagih returned, followed by two Saudis. As soon as he came in he said, "How come you're so depressed? Still thinking about Dr. Gharib? We've gotten used to it and so has he."

I said nothing. He turned to the two men, one of whom was middle-aged and the other an elderly man with a bent back. Wagih addressed the former, "What's the matter with the old man?"

I was struck by how dirty and tattered their clothes were. The younger one had no *ghutra* or *uqal*. The old man had on a very old *ghutra*, which he tied on his head without an *uqal*. He wore an old black jacket over the *gallabiya*.

The younger man said, "He's complaining about his stomach, Doctor."

Wagih motioned to the examining table behind the folding screen. The two men disappeared and were followed by Wagih, who I heard asking, "Does it hurt here?" I heard the elderly man making feeble moaning sounds then Wagih's voice once again, "Here, old man?" and this time the old man made noises that were more like tortured meows. Then Wagih emerged and sat at the desk. The younger man appeared. Wagih said, "I am going to prescribe some pills to strengthen and cure him."

"Please prescribe some injections. They get into the blood and nourish him."

Wagih looked at me as if asking me to be a witness to this weird meddling in his job. The old man reappeared, so bent he could hardly stand up. The younger man propped him up with his arm. Wagih said, "He cannot tolerate injections."

"Please prescribe them for him, Doctor," the younger man said. Wagih said nothing then opened one of the desk drawers and took out some wooden sticks, which he handed him and said, "No pills and no injections. Take these. Have him boil them and drink their water every morning."

The younger man snatched the sticks saying, "These are much better. May God be pleased with you, Egyptian."

He turned to the old man and both left slowly. I said, "I see that Arab medicine still commands a following here."

Wagih fell silent for a few moments then said, "These are hopeless cases."

I asked, "Is the use of herbs permitted here?"

He replied, "Those were just some old sticks I found in the street. They believe in my method and I save the state money."

Numan returned. Wagih asked him to make two fresh glasses of tea for us. I began looking at my watch; it was getting close to midnight. I wanted to leave. I had seen a side of Wagih that I didn't want to know. Besides, I didn't see anything extraordinary. I saw an Egyptian prisoner and two Saudis who were poorer than our own poor. This country is full of riddles. It wasn't easy to leave. Wagih was talking non-stop.

He said what puzzled him here was not merely how many car accidents there were, since that was the same in all Arab countries, where everyone drove with unbelievable recklessness. He was puzzled in particular by the endless accidents that happened in the village of Qaliba on the road to Medina. Every time he was on night duty, he expected to have at least one accident at Qaliba, and all night long he would keep an ear out for the sound of the ambulance arriving at the hospital. He hoped there wouldn't be accident at Qaliba that night. My being there with him would allay the worry he always had when he spent the night there alone. I asked him, "Don't they have a hospital in Qaliba?"

He replied, "It's a small village. Do you notice that its name is derived from the word for a car overturning? They have a small clinic that works only days and cannot handle accidents." He smiled. "No doubt you remember Dr. Rafat, who visited us a few weeks ago to say good-bye before his return."

"Of course I remember him."

"When he first came here, he was assigned to the clinic at Qaliba. They have no bakery and no place that sells bread. Rafat worked there for a year and every week he'd buy a week's supply of bread from here. Somehow he ran out of bread one time. It was during a very cold stretch of winter and the poor man was a diabetic who couldn't tolerate hunger. He had fifty thousand riyals. He kept looking at the money and twisting in pain. He was prepared to pay the whole fifty thousand riyals for a loaf of bread. Unfortunately, the ambulance had stopped going there for three days. He was about to eat himself; he caught himself actually biting his arm. When the ambulance arrived he was almost a goner. He rode the ambulance here and stopped in front of the Lebanese bakery and asked the owner to sell him a thousand riyals worth of bread. The man was shocked and thought he had gone mad; nobody had ever bought so much bread. But Rafat kept shouting, insisting that the man sell him bread for that sum. The baker sold him all the bread he had. Rafat put it in the ambulance, but he didn't go back to Qaliba that day. He had been transferred here. He distributed the bread among us and we had a good laugh."

I didn't laugh. I was still feeling down and I wanted to leave. When Aida came into the room I felt secretly relieved. Behind her was a Saudi man. She told Wagih, smiling, "He has an abscess."

It was past midnight, and Wagih said disapprovingly, "Is this the proper time?"

She said, still smiling, "He's here. Should we keep him till morning?"

Wagih asked the silent man, "Where does it hurt?"

The man extended his right hand. It was a strange abscess at the top of his index finger just below the nail. Wagih looked at me, still disapprovingly, and said to the man, "Put your hand on the desk."

The man placed it on the desk. I saw Aida's face turn pale and her eyes almost popping out in consternation. She wanted to speak but could not. Wagih was bringing his face closer to the man's hand as his hand fumbled for something in the desk drawer then brought it out. Wagih stood up suddenly and held the man's wrist with his left hand. Then, with his right hand, the one that had been fumbling in the desk drawer, he stabbed the man with a scalpel directly in the abscess. The man screamed. Blood and pus erupted from his hand. Wagih shouted, "Cotton, Nurse." Aida ran to the cabinet to bring the swab. I stood up as if a scorpion had stung me and moved back toward the wall. I thought the blood and pus would erupt in my face. I saw the man's face turn pale, and he almost collapsed. Aida threw the cotton on the desk and quickly placed a chair behind the man, who actually fainted and collapsed on the chair. Wagih dropped the scalpel and, with his right hand, began pressing the abscess with the cotton without letting go of the man's wrist. Aida was now looking at Wagih with utmost disapproval. He asked her for gauze and ointment for the wound, and began to bandage it. He let go of the man's hand and he fell from the chair to the floor. Wagih said as he came from behind the desk and left the room, "Remove him."

Numan came and carried the man out. I saw Aida following him with tears in her eyes. Wagih came back. I hadn't sat down yet. He had gone out to wash his hands and was now scrubbing them with disinfectant and drying them with cotton.

"Why are you standing?" he said.

I couldn't sit down. I was reminded of jungle movies and the white explorers who cleared patches through the forest with machetes. Aida came back and stood at the door and spoke to Wagih.

"How could you do that?" she said.

"Has anything happened?"

"He could have gone into shock."

"This is my job, nurse."

"You are heartless, Doctor."

"Nurse! Don't forget your place!"

Her eyes were still moist with tears and she looked very angry. She left. I sat down again, surprised to see Wagih cave in so easily to Aida. There was silence for a few moments then he said, "I cannot lance an abscess under anesthesia. They have great fear of operations. When he comes to he'll thank me. You'll see."

I wasn't about to stick around to see. I got lucky. We heard the ambulance outside and Aida came in a few moments later, saying, "A terrible accident. Six injured. Their car overturned in Qaliba."

She ran out and Wagih hurried after her. I got up quietly and went down to the ground floor where there was a commotion of orderlies around the ambulance. They brought the injured in as Wagih, Aida, and a number of young doctors and nurses that I hadn't seen before hurried after them. I stood alone in the forecourt of the hospital looking at the ambulance driver, who was still in his place. Then I approached him.

"I am a friend of Dr. Wagih," I said. "I've been with him here and I want to go home."

He smiled at me. I saw a gold tooth shining in his mouth.

"Get in," he said.

I got in and sat next to him. He started the ambulance. He was a young Saudi, wearing clean clothes. He spoke only when we were halfway through. He said, "The bend where these accidents take place in Qaliba is very easy for a driver to negotiate. Why then all the accidents? I swear it must be some kind of witchcraft."

I didn't comment and he didn't speak again. I only gave him directions to my house.

8

"Why am I here?"

A difficult question, Wadha. Even more difficult was seeing you face to face. As if I had known. Ever since I saw you under the sun, in the white light, and I yearned to see your body quiver, I knew that I was going to meet you. It must be like the witchcraft that's causing the cars to overturn in Qaliba, as the driver with the golden tooth said. The question is, am I destined for you? I didn't think either of us was destined for the other. Why then was fate placing you in my path? Was it because this was a small town? Had it been Cairo, nothing would have changed.

You were the second female whose face I saw and the second one that I spoke with. Only yesterday I saw the first female, Aida. Today I saw you. What made me go to give you the lesson? I had forgotten the first appointment and one more week had passed after that. If only I hadn't taken the Sheaffer pen set! I saw it and I remembered that I had forgotten. I hadn't really forgotten. Said reminded me more than once. You don't know him. Your brother does. Every time I'd tell him I remembered the appointment and he'd see me not go. I told myself he would understand that I didn't want to go and would leave me alone. He didn't, and I didn't come. I saw your brother's gift and I felt guilty and I came, afraid.

I knew that nobody else but me saw your body quiver. The sun and I. The sun that was bathing the universe in a light as pure as milk must have seen your body move. Now I was going to see your body right before me. Would it quiver, or was it my body that would this time?

Khalid welcomed me with childlike joy. He led me into a big room with soft red carpets and little green cushions around the edges. I saw a small desk in a far corner with two chairs. It was a small desk that looked out of place in a room that was otherwise purely Arabian in design. I told myself that Khalid must have prepared for the lesson in a hurry. He didn't ask me why I was late for the appointment that I myself had suggested. He appeared to have a truly noble character. He spent some time telling me about himself. He said he had graduated from the Business School in Jedda, that he wished he had gone to an Egyptian university in Cairo. He said his grandfather on his mother's side was an Egyptian who had come here in the thirties to go on pilgrimage and stayed, that he was still alive, that the whole family loved Egypt and the Egyptians. He said he refused to continue his studies in America. He went there for a year but left school and came back. He hadn't overcome the feeling that he was an Arab who could not savor the thought of moving suddenly from a tent to high concrete walls.

He laughed and said somewhat angrily, "How could I live in a country where I didn't hear my grandparents' stories?" He said the best time he had was in the tent set up in the yard behind the house, the tent where his two grandfathers lived. His grandfather on his father's side had fought with King Abdul Aziz in the twenties and, if he talked at all, still talked about nothing but Ibn Saud and his legendary feats. Khalid laughed when he said that his grandfather never tired of repeating the strange story that was told about Ibn Saud. According to the story, Ibn Saud was gravely wounded in the abdomen. A rumor spread among the troops that he was about to die and his forces were on the point of being defeated. Then he surprised everyone by consummating a marriage with a new wife. Khalid said that his grandfather would shout for joy as he described the troops' adoration of their inimitable commander, who neither blade nor bullet could touch. A man who got married when his abdomen was slit open. But Khalid's grandfather was now angry and hadn't spoken for a long time.

Khalid fell silent for a long while then said, "My sister is Wadha bint Sulayman ibn Sabil."

I said, "I know." I spoke simply.

He said, "They decided that she would not go to school but take the exams as an external student." We were both silent for quite some time until he said, "Ustaz Ismail, you are an Egyptian and we have Egyptian blood in our veins."

Wadha entered, preceded by a mysterious perfume. A small trembling hand shook mine. Why did it tremble? Khalid introduced us to each other. We needed no introduction, I thought. I somehow harbored the notion that just as I saw her in that bright white light she saw me, even if I didn't see the face, which was invisible behind her heavy veil. Khalid went out of the room leaving us together. I was extremely surprised; I was alone with a girl in a cool, big room in a big, silent house in the middle of an expansive desert in a huge country.

I wasn't prepared for the lesson anymore. I felt that Wadha had sensed that. My mind was not organized and I wanted to get done quickly. I wished to run away. I just listened to her tell me about the difficulty she was having with the English language. Suddenly I said, "Uncover your face."

I felt at that moment it was necessary to see how her eyes were receiving my words. If I couldn't see her face clearly, she probably could not see my face either. How then could we get to know each other and how could we remember? I was on the point of apologizing, had she not acquiesced right away.

A small mouth, glistening teeth, dreamy hazel eyes, long eyelashes, a surprising light brown complexion, the bangs of black hair over the forehead and under the green cover promising rich, abundant hair.

"What, besides grammar, bothers you about the language?"

"The story is long."

"But it is interesting."

"Read it with me."

"We will read it together and we will rearrange everything and we will laugh a lot about what Passepartout does as he goes around the world with his master, the gambler."

Suddenly I caught the fragrance of her breath. Her mysterious perfume became more pronounced and spread. The lesson had lasted more than two hours. Whenever I looked at her, she lowered her eyelashes and whenever she handed me the book our fingers touched and hers trembled. She probably hadn't been listening to me for the whole lesson. She pushed the book aside and asked me, "Is Egypt beautiful, Ustaz?"

"Very beautiful."

I looked at her and she looked long at me.

"Why are you here, then?"

✧

That was a tough one, Wadha. I couldn't find anything to say. I am here because it made certain people happy. Nonsense. I am here because all Egyptians are here. Nonsense. I am not the last one nor was your Egyptian grandfather the first one. Nonsense. I felt nothing but your mysterious perfume so why did you make me end the lesson that had lasted longer than it should and that I did not want to end? But I was so eager to meet you, I came again the following day. You came without a head cover, your thick black hair descended down your back like a deep sea or a night filled with mysteries. "Beautiful perfume," I said, and I wasn't just paying you a compliment. You gave me a bottle of perfume.

"For me?"

"For your fiancée in Egypt."

I couldn't say that I had no fiancée and no wife. How could you not figure that out yourself when my hands are in front of you the whole time? You are young and you are playing the game of student and teacher with me. But your question is not young and nothing could save me now from your thick hair that enticed me to swim. But would I be able to?

"Are you coming during the Feast?"

"No."

Idiot that I was, I only said that because I usually took Feast days off.

"Are you going on pilgrimage?"

"No."

"So, you will spend the Feast by yourself."

I couldn't take my word back. I became dejected. I forgot that I had seen in two days two beautiful faces, one with tearful eyes and one that lifted the veil.

9

My mother did not wake me up today to the sounds of the radio, the chanting, the clamor, the voices of the children in the street, and the songs celebrating the Feast. Today I did not have to play host to my married sister, her husband and her two sons, nor to my divorced sister and her two daughters. My querulous college sister would not insist that they make room for her to sit next to me. Neither would my college student brother display any sign of discomfort about being so big yet holding his hand out to take whatever money I gave him. Anyone else in my place now might be reduced to tears over being alone in such a vast house where he would also have his Feast meal alone. But I turned the volume on the radio to the maximum and smiled.

It had been years since that last time I had gone to the mosque early in the morning to perform the Feast prayer. Today I got up early, true, but I spent the time preparing the festive meal for the Feast: boiled meat, broth with cardamom and *fatta,* and there was nobody to sit with.

On that occasion, a fight had erupted all of a sudden; nobody knew how it started. My father had returned from the early Feast prayer and mother had almost finished making the hot Feast meal. We had no idea what the fight was about.

Loud voices were also coming from the apartments of the neighbors next to us, above us, and below us. Men's and women's voices, children's whimpering, and our fear created a cacophony. My father backed off. "I am sorry, Um Ismail," he said. "Happy Feast!" Everyone fell silent; then loud laughter burst out everywhere. The doors to merriment swung open. Why did all of that happen—the fight, the screaming, the conciliation, the laughter, and the merriment? To this day I do not know. Why did it stop happening? Was it because the children in all the apartments had grown up like me? Was it perhaps because all the fathers, like my father, had died? Or the mothers, like my mother, had fallen ill? My God, could my mother die while I was here? I ate voraciously, driving off the memories and miserable thoughts that were assailing me.

✧

I went out to the street. I had no need of a car. I was going to go on foot and see if the town was really empty. I couldn't spend the Feast alone in the house. During the Feast all the rich people usually went to Syria and Europe, and all the poor went to Egypt. The women and the children stayed glued to their television sets and VCRs. Muslim aliens went on pilgrimage. Non-Muslim aliens stayed home. Could this be real? I walked, crossing dusty roads between low houses to reach the main street. I saw nothing but a few goats climbing over the cars parked in front of the closed doors of houses that also had closed windows. I kept walking. Suddenly a door opened and out came a man, and a woman who was totally covered in black, and some children. They got into a big car. I heard the noises they made when they spoke but I couldn't understand a word they said. The car moved slowly then disappeared. I kept walking. I made it to the main street. There was no market today. The doors of all the stores were closed. I was reminded of the stores on Max Street in Alexandria at night. The street was strewn with wastepaper; empty cardboard boxes filled the sidewalks, and cans of soda pop were everywhere. It was a clear and splendid day. I read the store signs: watches, perfumes, school supplies, a grocery store, a jeweler, cassette tapes, electrical appliances, the Rajihi Bank where I saw Mansur get angry, in front of it Riyadh Bank, and behind it the vegetable market, also closed today.

The street was not as long as it had seemed before. I counted the lampposts on one side; they came to about a hundred. So there must be two hundred on the two sides; no need to count the other side. I was almost done with the street. I came across ruins, and undeveloped lots, and houses with collapsed walls, and houses that were being rebuilt. I saw cats as big as tigers or sheep gathering in the empty lots around things that I couldn't see, the remnants of food, perhaps. The sun was climbing higher in the sky and the open space stretched out. How beautiful the open space was when you discovered it while you were in the middle of a crowd and how wretched both you and it were when you had it all to yourself, your only company in a faraway land on the day of the Feast. Here they didn't kill cats. The Prophet blessed them, they said. But dogs didn't stand a chance. So what was this white dog, as big as a stray donkey, doing in the street? It wasn't even looking around. It looked as big as the one I had seen earlier in the desert. Maybe this was another dog or maybe it was the same one. Maybe someone had told it that today the town would be a desert. It stood there watching me making gestures to it with my hand, pointing at the cats so that it might attack them. It turned then moved away slowly.

I kept walking until I reached the mosque at the end of the street. It was open but empty. In front of it stood the pickle store. It was closed.

✧

Should I explore Omdurman? There were no open windows or doors. The low houses were built of white plaster. There were a few cars here and there on dusty narrow roads, and mounds of garbage around which there were neither dogs nor cats. There was a slightly fetid odor in the air. The sun seemed to be walking with me. Where have all the singers, musicians, and purveyors of good times gone? Today there were no weddings and no street decorations. A lewd laugh rang out, extending like a shiny knife reflecting the rays of the sun, followed by the broad and strong laugh of a man. Was that real or did I just imagine it? I didn't know, but then I heard and saw a man running across the street on which I was walking at a leisurely pace, then disappearing into a narrow alley. Another man, whose *ghutra* would have fallen off his head had he not used his hand to keep it in place, also passed quickly then disappeared. Nobody appeared after that, not even a cat or a dog. I didn't know whether to keep going or to go back. There was no fear of getting lost; you could see the whole town if you climbed on a chair. I decided to keep going.

A large square in a devastated city. All the houses around the square are on fire, smoke billowing out of the windows. A soldier among the corpses rises, looking around in fear, aiming his rifle at nothing or anything that might appear suddenly. The soldier walks in the midst of the smoke rising from the burning cars and tanks on top of which are more corpses with heads bent down. The soldier keeps circling, turning around, expecting an enemy every moment. He sees a woman with an agitated face in front of the door of a house with burning windows. The sun lights up her white face framed by a black shawl; the dazzling, attractive face gleams; the contours of her svelte figure are defined under a dress that is also black. The camera moves down to her black shoes and shimmering legs, follows the tap-tapping of her shoes as she runs across the big black tiles of the square and enters a narrow, dirty alley.

Washing is still hanging on broken clotheslines on the balconies of the houses in the alley. The soldier hesitates for a moment before running to chase the woman. He goes into the narrow alley and sees her disappear into one of the doors; he goes faster. I see her splendid legs and black shoes as she quickly climbs the metal stairs. When she makes it to the roof, I see the soldier in the stairwell looking up; seeing her feet, he goes up quickly. She scrambles across the roof sending the ducks and chickens running noisily everywhere. She enters a room; he is now on the roof. He sees a door close. He advances slowly, pushes the door. They are now standing face to face. She gasps in fear, backing away with her hand on her mouth. He looks at her with ravenous eyes, his face framed by a dusty beard. He advances, letting the rifle fall to the ground. As she backs away she hits the brass bed behind her, its white lace mosquito net hung from high posts. He comes closer. Their eyes meet in some kind of vague understanding. He reaches with his hand to her neck; tears well up in her eyes. He pushes the hair from the side of her neck; she rests her head on his hand. Calmly he reaches with his other hand and pushes aside the collar of her dress baring her full, rosy shoulder then part of her chest. Her lips tremble in muted appeal and she closes her eyes. A bird on the roof screeches. A plane passes over the city, a bomb falls. She falls into the arms of the poor tired soldier.

On the distant battle front cannons go off in rapid succession. I see the soldier afterwards in bed smoking a cigarette, his torso bare, a white sheet covering his lower half. She is lying with her head on his chest, her back bare over the sheet. She has a little mole on her right shoulder. Her fingers play with the hair on his chest.

I was still going down the streets of Omdurman, where the houses were still silent. The windows and doors were closed; not a soul stirred. What mysterious cause killed all the singers and musicians on the day of the Feast? Not a single face, black or white, appeared. Should I knock on the doors? Then I heard someone singing in a voice that sounded like moaning coming from a distant cave. As I went on the voice grew louder and deeper and the sadness of its notes grew more pronounced. It was a woman's voice. I could almost see her tears. She was accompanied by the weeping chords of a lute:

> *I appealed to the soothsayers of Yamama and*
> *Najd, both skilled, to cure my heart.*
> *They tried on me every medicine and potion*
> *known to them.*
> *Then they said, "We have no cure for you; only*
> *God can heal you now."*

Silence fell. I was now standing under the window. The singing started again, mixed with sobbing, then it was just the sobbing. I found myself moving away. I was oblivious to the houses around me, until I realized that I had come out onto the street that separated Omdurman and Aziziya from Sulaymaniya in the western part of town where I lived. I hurried back home, feeling that I had lost something I had had, but that earlier I had not fully grasped.

✧

I lay down on the bed and laughed so hard that my whole body shook. Ever since I arrived I had rarely sat on a chair in my room. I realized that now. It was difficult to sit on a chair if there was a bed in the room. I got up and turned the television on. What else was there to do? There was a shot of the pilgrims in Mina, a tremendous crowd in white. People and tents. I smiled at the thought that I might see someone I knew in the crowd. The call to the noon prayer must already have been made because the shot showed the pilgrims praying in the open air. There was a circus show for two and a half hours. The woman acrobat on the horse had long legs. All circus women have long legs. Then an hour of singing, to which I didn't pay any attention.

Next there was an exciting American film featuring Burt Lancaster, Sophia Loren, and Ava Gardner, about a train beset by the plague. I missed the name of the film, which had started before I realized it was on. I knew all the actors well except that I thought Ava Gardner was Elizabeth Taylor. Ava Gardner had grown older but her face retained some of its beautiful old wildness. I could recall the old, stagnant air in the alleys of our old neighborhood, Mitras, in Alexandria, and the smell of cheap cinema houses where we relentlessly chased after *The Barefoot Contessa* whenever it was shown. I could see Kamal al-Far shouting, "The Barefoot Contessa in Cinema Concordia," "The Barefoot Contessa in Cinema Cleopatra," "The Barefoot Contessa in Cinema Layla," and all over the neighborhoods of Alexandria. He was an avid fan of Ava Gardner and pushed us to go along as we laughed. Why did we do that, really? Tuberculosis took Kamal from us early on, and I never saw *The Barefoot Contessa* afterwards:

nor had I seen Ava Gardner's full lips again, nor her body that called you to take it in your arms, until today. Now it no longer called you to do anything. Twenty years had passed.

I kept tossing and turning. The film was over. I turned the television off. It was evening. I was going to eat lunch for supper. It wasn't easy to eat meat twice in the same day but it was the Feast.

Between the room and the kitchen, the short distance across the roofless courtyard, I felt cold. This was one of the early signs of a harsh winter coming. I returned with a big tray on which I had placed a bowl of broth, a plate of meat, and a plate of *fatta*, all hot. I carried the tray close to my face to let the steam warm up my face while I returned to the room. I was very hungry.

As I ate I realized it was too quiet. It was as if someone mute and blind was sitting with me. I turned on the television and got up to close the door of the room, which was keeping the big dark outside well-lit. I turned on the other room light. I wanted bright lights. I finished eating and turned the television volume up then slipped under the bedcover and stretched out. I began to watch an episode of *The Incredible Hulk*. A man who knows the secret of the Incredible Hulk turns himself into another, even more incredible hulk and uses his power for evil ends. Now the first Incredible Hulk, the original one, the poor scientist mistakenly hit by radiation while conducting experiments, has to defeat the evil man, the more incredible hulk. And what a battle between the two titans! It ends with the original, good, Incredible Hulk beating the dark, evil one.

The two lamps began to shake and I felt a taste of fine dust in my mouth. A sandstorm had started blowing and the dust was coming in through the space under the door and the shutters of the window. There was nothing I could do except wait. I couldn't open a window or door. But why were the lights shaking? I saw the bottle of eau de Cologne placed on top of the television. Here they drank eau de Cologne and stood at night under lampposts, drunk. I wasn't ready to go out again. The food weighed heavily on me and sleep tugged at my feet.

✧

The first night and day were over. They were bound to end, and I knew it. The second day, at midmorning, I went out for a walk. I wanted to see the town come back to life little by little. I found an open grocery store near the house, but nobody was there buying anything and nobody was there to sell anything. The owner of the store lived in a house behind the store and most likely would come out of the house in a short while. I put off buying cigarettes until my return. I walked to the Lebanese bakery just where the Aziziya neighborhood began, and looked at the owner's red face. I put off buying bread until I returned. I kept walking. I had an almost certain feeling that I wasn't going to see more of the town than I already had, but I kept walking. I decided I'd play a game with myself: yesterday I had walked through Aziziya and Omdurman, today I would go left from the main street in the direction of the Emirate. There was no difference between one quarter and another except in name. The houses all looked alike; they were low, white or yellow, with steel gates. Apartment buildings did not rise above three floors. But nothing said I couldn't walk where I hadn't walked before.

Then I realized this road was taking me to Wadha's house near the Emirate. I couldn't have done that deliberately, could I? I decided to walk without a plan, to make up something and think about it so I could pay no attention to the road. If my feet took me to Wadha's, I'd knock on the door and ask after Khalid to wish him a happy Feast. Wadha would no doubt also come to wish me the same. If my feet didn't take me to Wadha's, I'd go back. I tried to think of something to occupy my mind but I couldn't. Perhaps because I was trying. The realization shocked me; I felt my head totally empty except for the wind whistling through it, as if they had taken away everything under the skull. I kept repeating in a soft voice, "I appealed to the soothsayers of Yamama . . ." and I heard the woman's voice coming faintly from afar, mixed with sobbing.

"Why are you standing there? What are you looking at?" the policeman standing outside the gate asked me. I was disconcerted. I was actually standing there looking at the small house with a garden that had palm and lemon trees. Outside the gate stood a young policeman carrying a rifle and on a small balcony on the ground floor sat Dr. Sayyid al-Gharib with his long scruffy beard, looking at me with great concentration. We had both been looking at each other for several moments.

"Sorry. I don't mean anything."

I answered the policeman and walked away. I found myself hurrying home. I didn't buy bread or cigarettes on my way back. I had enough anyway.

✧

In my room I found the television on. I had turned it on and when I found out that transmission had not started, I left it on making that white noise and went out. There it was, showing a *Telematch* program. The announcer sounded bizarre covering the German matches in formal classical Arabic. That was new to me. I had to eat some of yesterday's leftovers. I hadn't had my breakfast yet. Why had I gone out today? Just to see the house where Sayyid al-Gharib was under arrest, to bump into him on my way and to see him looking at me as though he were looking at somebody else, as if he were speaking and remembering at the same time? Why were they doing that to him, really? Why wouldn't they put him on trial and get it over with? Court procedures couldn't take that much time. The judge here was a religious scholar who only went by witnesses. There were no prosecutors, no lawyers, no pleading, and no indictments. Gharib's story was most probably forgotten. If someone, anyone, had brought it to the attention of the emir's office, it would have been resolved somehow. But nobody had done that so far. Should I do it?

I got busy preparing the food. I ate and slept then got up when I heard knocks on the door. I was going to open the door and find a woman asking for a drink of water and then fainting. I would carry her to my room; she wouldn't come to until the night. She wouldn't leave in the night. By the morning she would have become accustomed to staying with me.

A wind rattled the steel gate outside. I began rubbing my eyes and the knocks on the door became more distinct. I got up and left the room, taking my time. I smiled and walked slowly. No woman could be knocking on the door. I stopped for a moment in front of the door. What if it really were a woman? I wouldn't let her in. I opened the door and I saw an old man in tattered clothes, an old *ghutra* and a faded black *uqal*, holding out his hand to me. A beggar? In the Kingdom of Saudi Arabia? Persistently knocking on the door! I said to him, "May God provide for you." He didn't move; he was also barefoot. He didn't say anything I could hear but muttered something or other. Actually it was just his beard moving up and down. His hand remained held out. I hurried back to the room and brought back ten riyals; he took the money and left. I stopped in the roofless courtyard. A vast darkness surrounded me but the moon, which was nearing fullness, cast a little luster on the world. I hadn't realized it was evening already. The television was broadcasting the call to the sunset prayers. I hadn't had my lunch but I wasn't hungry. One meal was enough today. I began to listen to the heartfelt invocations after the call to the prayers.

The Prophet, God's Peace and Blessing be upon him, has said, "He who dies on this road, going or coming, will be received by God Almighty on the Day of Judgment without being held to account and will be admitted into Paradise." He also said, "He who goes on pilgrimage or on the minor pilgrimage of umra to this house and does not commit acts of lewdness or abomination, will be as sinless as he was on the day he was born." And he said, "He who goes on pilgrimage with an outstanding debt, God will settle his debt." Said ibn Musayyib has said, "I was sitting between the tomb and the minbar of the Prophet when I heard a voice saying, 'O God, I ask of you a righteous job, a profitable livelihood, and a contented life. O God, suffer nothing to separate us from You. O God, if my sustenance be in heaven, cause it to descend to earth; if in the earth, make it accessible; if it be little, cause it to grow; if slight, cause it to increase. O God, save me from subjugation and humiliation. O God, make me the poorest of Your creatures to You and the richest with Your bounty. O God, provide me with abundant subsistence and cause me to be content with it."

✧

The invocation tonight was different. Not because I was alone or because I hadn't gone on pilgrimage. It reminded me of my father, who recited many invocations after prayer. He had been dead for seven years now. Had it not been for a small plot of land that he had kept, I wouldn't have finished my last two years of college. He left behind just enough to last until the day I took over his mission. It was as if he had planned everything for me. Why hadn't I kept a single photograph of my father and why had I forgotten what he looked like? I got up suddenly and picked up a notebook that I used for writing letters, and wrote:

"The Principal of Taher Bek Preparatory School in Wardian in Alexandria:

"Greetings. I, Ismail Khidr Musa, teacher of English in your prestigious school, have traveled to Saudi Arabia using a passport issued on the basis of a forged identity card in which I did not record my occupation as a teacher so that the Ministry would not prevent me from leaving. Please consider the days of my absence as unpaid vacation until I return after a year."

I tore up the paper and wrote:

"The Principal of Taher Bek Preparatory School:

"Please keep my job for me. I am coming back as soon as possible."

I tore up the page and wrote:

"Principal of the School:

"I am not coming back and I am not staying here. I am going to explode."

I tore up that page also and jumped off the bed into the middle of the room. One, two, three, four, one, arms to the shoulders, two, arms to the sides, three, up, down, one, two, three. Those accursed flies had spent the night here in the room with me in spite of the cold and have stuck to the electric wires. Should I chase them? They'd just go everywhere but out. And this calendar on the wall must be torn up. November.

After two months, a new year would begin, and it would end after twelve more months. I won't place a calendar in the room in the new year. This was hung by Faruq. He had furnished the room fully for me. Where was Faruq now? He hadn't come back and he hadn't sent a letter. I turned off the television and turned on the radio: "This is the voice of Arab Egypt greeting you from Baghdad. In a few days it will be the ill-fated anniversary of the treasonous visit by the Egyptian president Anwar al-Sadat to Jerusalem. Today the Gulf Soccer Tournament began with a minute of silence in mourning for the imminent anniversary of that treasonous act. Oh, how happy the Egyptian president must be with the Arab news!" One. Two. Three. I jumped up in the air and opened the door of the room. A rectangle of light coming from the room poured out into the roofless courtyard and extended along the floor. I saw the almost full moon in the sky. I had seen it when the beggar knocked on the door. It hadn't moved much. Time was not passing. From now on it wasn't going to pass quickly. I wouldn't make it alive to the fourth day of the Feast. Hello, full moon! You're a king. Here I am standing in the cold, saluting you, alone in this empty house in this silent neighborhood in this sleepy town in the middle of the desert. Won't you come down and sit with me a while, great king? No woman to speak with and tell her that her face is like the full moon, or that I saw you in her face. Do you know who said you were a king? It was Ibn al-Mutazz, the caliph poet who used bad similes and metaphors. I still remember. Perhaps his adversaries killed him after they had castrated him. But no, suddenly it dawned on me: it belonged to Urwa ibn Hizam, author of the lines that the weeping woman was singing the morning before, the same Urwa who died a martyr of his love for his cousin Afra and whom Ibn al-Khattab, had he had a chance, would have helped marry his beloved. O full moon king, where will you sleep in the morning and when? I also wanted to sleep. I went into the room and closed the door to stay warm. One. Two. Three. What was that sound coming from the kitchen? A repeated scratching sound, then nothing for a short while. It was a mouse. A mouse having fun. A mouse that realized that Said, the expert at catching its kind, was in Mecca now, exactly as the huge white dog I'd seen the day before realized that the town was deserted and went there. What a smart mouse! And what an ingenious trap Said had made! He didn't use a regular trap; he invented a brutal, disgusting method. Mice always went to the kitchen. So, he placed a wooden board under the kitchen sink, which formed an acute angle with the wall. Said would chase a mouse until it was forced into the angle whereupon he would press the wooden board with his foot and the mouse would be crushed between the board and the wall. Then Said would carry it in a piece of paper and throw it out into the street over the top of the door. He killed a mouse every day until two weeks ago, when he stopped since the mice had disappeared. He said they could feel winter coming and didn't leave their holes. This mouse had probably been loitering somewhere else, and didn't go back to its hole. I would let it go off on its own, and would turn off the radio and turn the television on. Someone was knocking lightly on the steel door of the house. I could hear it clearly. It couldn't be another beggar. The call to the last prayer had been sounded. The announcer was now reciting a hadith of the Prophet. Who could it be at such a time? Who knew me here who hadn't gone on pilgrimage?

"Mansur!" I shouted when I opened the door. He was smiling. I couldn't take my eyes off the monkey's blue testicles on his shoulder.

10

The Pakistanis had tans and were more energetic and merrier after they came back from the pilgrimage. I asked Arshad, who had come into my office and stood there, silently, "Was it that hot?"

"It was cold, Mr. Ismail. We slept outdoors and traveled in an open semi truck." Once again he was silent. It was about seven thirty. Then he said irritably, "What's the story with Mr. Abed, Mr. Ismail?"

"Has something new happened?"

"Last night, after our return, we talked about the camp budget for this week. He's come back from the pilgrimage even more stingy than he used to be."

"Pardon me, Arshad. You know I can't get involved in that."

"I know, Mr. Ismail, but somebody's got to help us. Shall I talk to Mr. Abdallah?"

"No."

He looked long at me, then left without comment. I suddenly realized that Abed only did things that pleased Amm Abdallah. Then, after Arshad left, I thought, "Did he really come here to tell me that?" He must have wanted to speak to me about something else. So Arshad was once again reluctant to talk with me.

When Nabil came in carrying the coffee, he was smiling broadly. He placed the cup in front of me and said, "I didn't see you during the Feast."

"How could you see me when you were on pilgrimage?"

"I wasn't on pilgrimage."

My eyes grew wide with surprise. I smiled, thinking he was joking. He said, "I came back after going half way, well, two thirds of the way actually. One of the things that bothered me during the Feast was that I didn't know where you lived. If I'd known, I would have visited you and spent some time with you. I was very depressed here alone. I went into town several times and walked around in the hope of bumping into you but I wasn't lucky. I only found a stray dog."

"You really didn't make the pilgrimage?"

He laughed and swore that indeed he hadn't. Then he tried to suppress his laughter and said, "I'll tell you what happened. We arrived at Biar Ali, Abed and I. Biar Ali is near Mecca and it is there that *ihram,* the first step in the pilgrimage, begins. It's not a city or even a village. It's just a spot on the road where there's water and a small mosque. There we met a group of Egyptians who were riding a big bus. We all had to spend the night there. Among them was a young man who may have been sane or insane, I don't know. At any rate, he was quite a pain. He was the imam who led them in prayer, preached to them, and talked to them about the rites of the pilgrimage. Of course Abed and I joined them to listen to him talking about the requirements after *ihram*: no cutting down of trees or plants, no shaving, no trimming your fingernails, and, of course, no obscenity or licentiousness, and no killing of any animal, even a louse. Even if a lion came near you, you shouldn't kill it unless it attacked you. That's what he said and of course he's right: if a lion came near me I wouldn't kill it because it would kill me." We laughed enthusiastically and Nabil continued. "At night I saw a wolf, a real wolf standing near us. The women were sleeping in the bus and the men were sleeping on the ground. I was the only one awake. I wished I were asleep. I was afraid and waited for the wolf to leave, but it didn't."

"And of course you attacked the wolf?" I interrupted him sarcastically, laughing. He was silent for a short while then he said, "You won't believe it but Abed can confirm what I'm saying. The whole of Tabuk knows the story. How come it didn't reach you?"

I fell silent. Nobody had told me anything about it. Said and Wagih talked about all sorts of interesting things and difficulties they encountered during the trip, but not this story about the wolf. Nabil continued, "I picked up a stone and threw it at the wolf. I have a very strong arm. In Egypt I could throw a stone from Kitkat and it would go all the way across the Nile to Zamalek. Anyway, the stone hit the wolf on the head and it howled and ran away. If it hadn't howled, nobody would have found out anything. The men woke up, and some of the women, and that guy, the imam. He asked me if I had heard the wolf. Stupidly I told him the whole story. He went over to look at the stone, which I had pointed out to him, and found traces of blood on it. He told me my *ihram* was no longer good and that I had to do it all over again. How? You undo your *ihram*, then you declare your intention and you do your *ihram* again. He told me it was easy. Everyone told me it was easy. But it didn't make sense to me. Early next morning they went on their way to Mecca and I found a truck carrying cars coming from Jedda, heading for Tabuk and I hitched a ride. Would you believe that as I was putting my foot onto the truck I felt I was making a mistake and I almost went back and did what I was told. But I told myself that this truck had come at the time God had willed me to leave. Maybe God wanted to spare me something dangerous that would have happened during the pilgrimage. Who knows?"

I looked long at his eyes. He hadn't stopped smiling while he was talking. He said, "I know that you will never believe me, exactly as that guy didn't believe me when I told him that the wolf was about to attack me. He said I had to wait until it did. Maybe before, it was just roaming, unaware of my existence. As if I could have fought off the wolf if I waited for it to attack me!"

"So you didn't do the pilgrimage on behalf of your mother," I said.

He got up and said, "That woman doesn't deserve it."

He went out. I was laughing so hard I only stopped when Amm Abdallah's car came into the forecourt, blowing up a storm of dust.

✧

Abed came into my office, agitated, and said, "Take Aaron Bounkerd's file to Amm Abdallah."

He sat behind the desk next to the safe. I got up, picked up Aaron's file from the cabinet and asked Abed, "What's the story?"

"Amm Abdallah will tell you."

I went into Amm Abdallah's office. I found him lying back in the big chair, with his *ghutra* and *uqal* off, and fighting off sleep. He probably hadn't slept the night before. I saw his bald head for the first time. The only hair he had was above his ears. Without changing his position he said, "Prepare Aaron's 'termination'"—he said the word in English. "Tomorrow morning he should be in Thailand."

I was taken aback. Why this sudden firing?

"Why don't you get a move on? Finish the procedure then bring me the file."

I had nothing to say and he continued, "I know that Aaron has borrowed three months' salary from the company and I know that you approved the loan. Go." This was the first time that he had spoken angrily to me. In fact, I didn't approve the loan for Aaron. The only thing I did was intercede with Abed on his behalf. So, Abed had lied. The ugly game had begun. But what could I tell Amm Abdallah? He was a serious director who had no time to waste on facts. Whatever he heard first was always the truth.

I went into my office. Abed looked at me with an expressionless smile. He seemed ready to respond to whatever I had to say, so I didn't say anything. He went back to his office and I sat down finishing the paperwork on Aaron's termination. There was a form I had to fill out that Aaron had to sign. I had to contact the passport department so they would send the follow-up officer, who would take the passport and enter the "exit without return" stamp and book the ticket for the flight. I sat down to work and suddenly saw Mansur coming into the forecourt in his big Caprice, with Aaron next to him.

✧

"Did you finish the termination?" Mansur asked me as he entered the room followed by Aaron. I almost laughed when I heard him use the English word 'termination.' Amm Abdallah knew English well from his former job at Dammam, but where did Mansur learn it? Perhaps he had heard it many times, I said to myself. I was surprised that Mansur didn't have the monkey with him.

"I'm finishing it now," I said.

He had sat down behind the desk next to the safe. Aaron sat down on one of the leather chairs. Mansur yelled at him in Arabic, "Don't sit." Aaron understood, perhaps because Mansur had used a hand gesture. Aaron frowned, then stood up, smiling at me awkwardly. Mansur asked me, "What's taking you so long?"

I stared at him for a few moments without answering.

"Come on. Finish it," he said. Then he got up and left the office, giving me no opportunity to give him a piece of my mind. I motioned Aaron to sit down and asked him, "What happened?"

"They found some liquor."

This was the second time he had talked about alcohol.

"Did you really make liquor?"

"Yes, Mr. Ismail. Mr. Abdallah knows. I used to give him some."

I was taken aback for a moment. He continued, "Everything was going fine. During the Feast vacation I was almost all by myself in the camp so I made a lot of it. Mr. Abdallah was in Amman. He only came back yesterday. The day before that the Pakistanis came back. They all knew. One of them told me not to do it again. He said after the pilgrimage he wasn't going to tolerate the presence of liquor in the camp. I paid no attention to him. The idiot called the police."

"I'm afraid you won't be able to return to Saudi Arabia, Aaron."

"I know, Mr. Ismail. I'll go to Iran. I used to work there years ago."

"But there are big demonstrations in Iran now, and explosions, and the Shah is using airplanes against the people."

He smiled and said, "I know, Mr. Ismail."

I realized that talking wouldn't do any good. Aaron was going to be deported and we'd both forget each other. I gave him the termination form to sign and said, "I'll send you the passport and the ticket at the camp. I'll book you a flight in two days time so you can take care of things."

"Thank you, Mr. Ismail. Is there a problem about the loan?"

"No."

"Thank you, Mr. Ismail. I'll never forget you. You're a good Egyptian."

I smiled and said, "It's important that you buy a house in Bangkok!"

He stood up and said, "I will. Definitely."

I got up to shake his hand. He took my hand in both his hands, then went out hurriedly, looking like a small boulder, rolling.

✧

When Aaron had left, Mansur came into my office.

"I'll go back with you today," he said without any preliminaries.

"I saw you coming in, in your Caprice. What happened?"

"It broke down."

I looked at him sharply as he sat down at the desk next to the safe, and said, "Listen, Mansur. You asked for something and I promised to do it when the right time comes. Don't bug me."

He was silent for a while then said, "I'm afraid that you'll let me down. It's such a simple thing, it doesn't need that much time."

When Mansur came to my house the second day of the Feast, I was surprised to hear him say that he wanted to know when Said was going to marry his fiancée, Widad. It surprised me that he knew them. I was looking at him as he sat, polite and shy, in the room. I noticed that he had *kohl* around his eyes. I found out later that most men here used *kohl* during Feasts in emulation of the Prophet's tradition. He looked very strange. It was the first time I had seen a man wearing *kohl*. I couldn't take my eyes off his eyes. He said, "Let me explain, brother Ismail, so there's no confusion. I've known Widad for three years. She's a teacher in the middle school where my sister is a student. She used to come to the store with her mother to buy fabric. We have a big store on the main street. I thought of marrying her myself, and so my father, mother, and I went to her house, as you do in Egypt, and asked for her hand. But her mother said no, she was already engaged. But she was not engaged, brother Ismail. Her mother adamantly refused, and turned down the hundred-thousand-riyal dowry. She turned me down, brother Ismail, even though I know that Saudis go to Egypt all the time and marry there. Widad became engaged to Said later on and that hurt me a lot."

As he spoke he looked genuinely upset. I didn't know what to do to ease his pain. I made him tea three times and he drank it every time and it seemed he was never going to leave. And all the time the monkey was sitting on his shoulder, looking at me. I said, "Maybe they knew each other from before."

"No."

"How do you know?"

"I know."

"So . . ."

He didn't let me finish.

"She preferred the Egyptian to me. Saudis, brother Ismail, marry Egyptian women every day, easily," he said.

This time he bothered me. How could I explain to him that those marriages were not real marriages, it was no more than a Saudi infatuation with Egyptian flesh—or that the Egyptians were so poor they didn't ask for exorbitant dowries as they did in Saudi Arabia?

"What does that have to do with me?" I said.

"You are living with Said. I would like to find out from you when they are planning to get married."

I remembered his angry look at me when he saw us in the bank and his rudeness toward me most of the time. What good would it really do him to know when they were getting married? I was somewhat apprehensive. Mansur appeared to be an extremely complex character.

"I do live with Said, but we don't talk about private matters," I said.

"Then talk and find out," he said bluntly and got up to leave.

That night I wasn't able to sleep until the morning. Actually that helped me to sleep all day long the third day of the Feast, to skip one of the days of silence. When Said came back on the fourth day I couldn't help staring at his face from time to time. I was afraid that Said might catch me looking at him and ask me about this sudden, new condition. But Said remained unaware and I managed, after two days, to stop staring at him. Now Mansur has come expecting a quick response to his question. I had to lie, so I said, "If I told you when the marriage will take place, would you tell me what good that would do you?"

"It won't do me any good. I just want to know. That's all there is to it."

"In two years, Mansur."

I saw him look at me with sudden happiness.

"Are you being truthful with me, brother Ismail?"

"Very truthful."

"God bless you. May God give you long life."

He got up to shake my hand, laughing, happy like a child who has found his lost toy and said, "The Caprice is not broken down. I am not going back with you."

✧

"How did your car break down?" I asked Munzir, who caught up with me just as I was leaving the forecourt in my car.

"It's a goddamn piece of junk, a 1971. It fell into a big pothole. The tow truck took it to Arshad," he said as he climbed into the car. He sat down and said, "All day long they keep saying, 'Come, Munzir; go, Munzir; electricity, Munzir; mechanical work, Munzir; the water's cut off from the army, Munzir; we're running out of cement, Munzir.' At least they should give me a good solid car. Tomorrow I'll get one. Without Munzir, no work. Without car, Munzir no work."

I laughed and watched the road, enjoying the cool air coming from the open window of the car. Suddenly I remembered that I hadn't seen the old Yemeni man today. Did I really not see him or was it just that I hadn't looked in his direction? Most probably I hadn't looked. Mansur had so distracted me.

"What do you think of Mansur, Munzir?" I asked without thinking.

"Mansur! I told you before he's a nutcase; he's crazy."

"I know, but what do you mean exactly?"

He laughed long. "You want to know the whole story?"

"Yes."

"Listen. Mansur comes from a big family that has a huge business on the main street. He left his father's business and came to work as a driver for Abdallah. Isn't that nuts?"

"But Abdallah doesn't give him much work."

"Abdallah knows his family."

"Is that all?"

"Mansur is madly in love with an Egyptian school teacher who he wants to marry. He's crazy about Egyptian women. This isn't the first Egyptian woman to turn him down."

"That's really weird."

He laughed again and said, "You know everything, brother Ismail. You just want to make sure."

To change the subject, I said, "How far have you gone with your beautiful neighbor?"

"I beg you, please, don't remind me. She's now my wife's friend. My wife is young and foolish."

I laughed and he continued, "When I see her, Ustaz, it's like being in the war."

"She must be really beautiful."

"I tell you it's war, Ustaz, an ambush for Munzir."

Suddenly he bared his chest.

"Look, my right breast was blown off by a shell, look at this depression in my leg, and this arm has ten stitches."

He kept uncovering parts of his body where he was injured. I couldn't keep up; my eyes were on the road.

"I come from a family of freedom fighters, brother Ismail."

I didn't know what to say. We were silent for a short while then he said, "Please forgive me if I've bothered you. I don't know exactly what I'm doing. Last time I wasn't nice to you. But I swear I really love Egyptians. I only hate Sadat. Do you blame me?"

His voice was breaking as if he was about to cry. I found myself saying, "And I hate him too, Munzir."

"God bless you, Ustaz."

He lit a cigarette for himself and one for me then said in a soft voice, "Don't tell anybody about what you saw of my body. If they found out I was a freedom fighter, they would deport me, Ustaz."

"Really?"

"Oh yes."

"Send you back to Jordan?"

"What do you think? To Palestine?"

11

Forgive me, Wadha. I feel I've just escaped from hell.

✧

On my way to Wadha's house I thought I would spend a long time with her. But I saw it: the beautiful house with the garden, and the palm, and lemon trees. A vicious-looking policeman stood guard outside the door. On the balcony Sayyid al-Gharib sat, wrapped in a blanket. He saw my car and stood up, but I didn't stop. I felt claustrophobic even though everything was wide open in front of me. I couldn't understand how nobody could tell the emir that the "judge" had forgotten to put the Egyptian doctor on trial, neither imprisoning him nor setting him free, just hanging him out to dry in the fullness of time. I told Wagih, "The court couldn't forget a case like this one. I think it's intentional." He said, "That's quite possible. I thought of going to the Emirate and asking to see the emir and then I suddenly realized Gharib had been under house arrest for a whole year and nobody had thought anything of it. It made me so frustrated, I didn't go."

I saw the house today and decided to forget about the lesson, maybe also to forget about the new lesson for our landlord's son, Salih Sanyur al-Thaqifi. When Wagih introduced him to me I couldn't believe he was a student. Wagih told me teaching Salih might open the door for me to teach others and so make as much money as I could in the shortest possible time. I accepted and today we were supposed to begin, only after I was done with Wadha's lesson. More than once I caught myself fretting impatiently for the appointed time.

Today I was supposed to explain to her a lesson on Helen Keller and the human will. I was more afraid than I have ever been, thinking how, ever since I saw her on the police car, I had had a feeling that I would meet her, that I would be the end of her story. I was afraid for her because of myself and for myself because of her. I had declared the shores of the lake off limits a long time ago, so how come I was traveling all those miles to throw rocks into it? One of us was going to be killed. I didn't want to die nor to commit a sin in every country. Should I tell Wadha that? Would she understand? Would it do any good? Let our story then run its predestined course. But when I saw the beautiful house and Dr. Gharib, I felt great anguish, and I thought of going back.

✧

Wadha welcomed me. She opened the outside gate for me and led the way in. I entered the big room, my head bowed and my heart rolling before my feet. I imagined that I was visiting her at night, that there was nobody else in the whole world but the two of us. I kept my head down so I wouldn't see her uncovered face or her hair that invited me to bury my head in it. Wadha, small like a bird as she was, had a presence that filled the whole room. I had to raise my head and look at her.

"Where's the homework?" I asked abruptly. She handed me the notebook with a trembling hand. I probably frowned and I chose not to look at her face, which most likely had disappointment written all over it. She didn't know that I had lowered my eyes so as not to succumb to the invitation of her trembling lips.

"Ustaz, is it necessary to write the name before the address?"

"I don't think the mailman would return a letter just because the address was written before the name. But these are the conventions of writing letters in a foreign language."

"I don't know why, but I wish letters could be received without the writing of names."

"They can, of course, if you write a post office number."

I only understood too late what she was driving at, and sensed her face cloud over. Another disappointment. I realized how stupid I was and how determined she was.

I looked at the open door and saw an elderly man in a wheelchair.

"Grandpa."

She called out and rose quickly to go to him. Who was it that had pushed him to the door and left him there without a word? What would have happened if I hadn't looked and seen him?

She wheeled him into the room. I was struck by how small he was, no bigger than a child. His complexion was very dark and furrowed. I saw his hand lying limply on the blanket that covered his legs. The diaphanous skin on his hands revealed white bones and swollen, dark blue veins.

"This is my Egyptian grandfather. Khalid told him about you and he wanted to meet you."

She left him at a distance, next to the wall. I was struggling to see the color of the eyes that were looking at me. Were they white or green, or had their color faded? I couldn't tell. They were small and sunken, that was certain.

"This is the Egyptian teacher," Wadha told her grandfather loudly. I saw him smile. It was the first time that I had seen such an old man smiling in delight like a baby. She whispered to me, "Speak, my grandfather is blind."

I didn't speak. I got up and went over to him, then held his hand and shook it. When I let go of it, it fell on his lap. How could I go back to the lesson? It had started with stupidity preceded by malaise on account of one who was imprisoned by cowardice and forgetfulness, and was brought to an end by the presence of this old man. Who really wheeled him to the door? Why didn't I see anyone in this house except Khalid and Wadha?

"Did I bother you today?"

"No."

"Then why do you want to leave?"

"I'll make it up to you next time."

I saw her almost crying but kept up the strict facade. She didn't know that I wished I could go around the desk and take her in my arms.

"Your fiancée is not well?"

For the second time she mentions my fiancée. Do we really need all this stupidity today?

"As you can see, I am neither engaged nor married."

I turned my hands up and down, then left quickly. I knew she was silently crying behind me, but what could I do? I felt like someone escaping from hell. I also had to find another route that didn't go past the house surrounded by palms, lemon trees, and forgetfulness.

✧

"Hello, Ustaz."

Salih welcomed me warmly into his house, which was not different from Wadha's, a two-story building with a yard without any trees. He led me into a long room with green carpeting and cushions lying scattered on the floor. There was no desk and no chairs. A big television set dominated the room. Under the glass TV stand was a VCR, and next to it a small table on which were videocassettes. On the opposite side of the room sat four young men, who, like Salih, were about twenty. They stood up as soon as I entered and shook my hand, smiling, then sat down again, looking at each other and laughing noiselessly.

"My friends. You don't need to know them," Salih said, smiling while I was still standing. I smiled at them and they laughed and clapped their hands in unison like children.

"Don't be surprised, Ustaz. They come here to eat and drink and watch movies."

I realized that the situation did not lend itself to teaching so I sat in silence.

I was surprised when he asked me, "You want to see a film, Ustaz?"

"All right."

They cheered again. I didn't know why I agreed just like that but I also wished I could drink some liquor as well.

One of them got up and brought a number of films. Salih went out to make tea for us himself, or so he said.

"Explain to us the titles of the movies, Ustaz," the one carrying the videocassettes said as he handed them to me. Another one said, "The Ustaz will translate for us."

They laughed and cheered in delight. I placed the films on

the floor in front of me. They gathered around me and I picked up the films one by one.

"This is *Midnight Cowboy.*"

"We know it."

"This is *Straw Dogs.*"

"Great film but we've seen it lots of times."

"This is *Death in Venice.*"

"Ha, the one with the little boy!"

"This is *The Servant.*"

"That's the one where the man pisses," they laughed.

I was silent for a few moments. They had seen most of the films, so why did they want me to translate for them? I had seen these films too, in Alexandria cinemas. I had seen *The Servant* about ten years ago but I didn't remember whether someone in it urinated or not. I loved Dirk Bogarde. I always saw in his face a touch of profound sadness. I had also read about Harold Pinter as an avant-garde dramatist in England and I saw his name on the poster as the writer of the film. My God, that was back when I used to read. A long time had passed since then. Another young man got up and brought the rest of the films and placed them in front of me on the floor.

"This one is *Moby Dick.*"

"It's about the whale. We don't want that."

They killed my excitement over the one film I had not seen and would have loved to watch. I had never read *Moby Dick,* though I had read about Herman Melville's melancholy. I had always wanted to read it but never came across it. Be that as it may. Why did I want to bring up to the surface the profound sorrow that lay so deep down? What was the worth of reading, which I had let slip by in the midst of the responsibilities my father had laid out so well for me? What would have been the value of writing if I had written?

Anything that one forgot was meaningless. One only lost those things that one did not want in the first place.

"This is *Love Story*."

"That's a bad one."

"Okay. This is *Going Home*."

One of them grabbed it from my hand and, opening his eyes as wide as he could, said, "We want this one. This one has a paralyzed man who uses his tongue."

They laughed. One of them chided him, "What do you mean we want this one? Wait until the Ustaz explains to us the rest of the movies."

I was surprised to see the first young man shrink back and fall silent. He folded his arms around his chest and sat down cross-legged as if he were a little pupil in a Quranic school. I noticed that his *gallabiya* was dirty, and his feet were big and had little pimples with white heads. I saw him staring at me with big wide eyes that looked even wider because his face was pale and small. I thought the whole situation was silly. If only Salih would come back and save me. At last he did come in, carrying two films.

"This is *The Message*," he said. "Do you want to see it, Ustaz? It's banned in Arab countries." I was just about to say yes, but a gloom descended on everyone else's faces, and Salih said, "Forgive me, Ustaz. We'll see *The Message* later. Ghalib here wants to see this one and I can't refuse Ghalib anything."

He was pointing to the young man with the pimples on his feet. They all cheered and laughed. Ghalib jumped up and grabbed the film from Salih and placed it in the VCR, then adjusted the television and sat down, using the remote control to start the film.

Salih went out again and didn't give me a chance to leave, nor did I ask for one. He brought the tea in halfway through the film. He placed the big silver tray with the teapot and the little glass cups in front of us on the floor. No one drank or even thought to fill the little cups.

The film began with soft music. Then green, red, yellow, and blue dots began to form lines that zoomed and faded and intersected in lyrical rhythms, suggesting tormented bodies meeting after long suffering. Then the music grew softer gradually and the colors faded out. The legs of a man close together began to enter the frame from the left. I understood everything. I forgot the disrespect and rudeness. The man's huge, unshakable erection appeared. The woman came in, naked, her contours defined more clearly the closer she got. She stood in front of the man's organ and looked out at us, laughing loudly, then bent over to place her mouth around it.

Should I lie and say that I didn't need to see that, at least not today? I didn't feel I was doing anything morally wrong. After all I was going to leave this country and couldn't care less about what Salih might say about the teacher who hadn't asked to set up the place properly for a lesson but rather sat down and watched pornographic movies. What got to me throughout was Ghalib, whose mouth was open wide with surprise the whole time and who freeze-framed the film using the remote control—which he adamantly refused to relinquish—every time a woman's organ was shown. I would not be lying to say that he disgusted me. But I waited until the very end. For three whole hours none of us said a word. I didn't translate for them and they didn't ask for translations.

✧

I don't know at which point in the film I became so totally detached I saw the Nile Valley from the cataract in the south to the Mediterranean: roosters crowing, the sun causing the white flowers of fava beans to open all along the Nile; the sun shining on the mountains and the men who had slept next to their rifles waking up and standing to attention as if they were banners; the sun shining on the ancient temples and the face of Ramses laughing in the deepest south and rams running around bleating and butting each other after being too long fettered. I saw the sun shining over the Delta and the cows lowing and the children getting up and, barefoot, leading the cows to the fields. I saw the men who got up washing contentedly then praying and walking, carrying their hoes on their shoulders or riding their donkeys. I saw the sun shining in Cairo and grown men and students with red fezzes on their heads shouting in the streets and bringing the city to a standstill and the police firing on them and on a high balcony I saw the British High Commissioner standing, watching, and the pipe never leaving his lips. I saw the sun shining gently in Alexandria as a breeze came from the sea, laden with the smell of iodine and a fine spray that looked for lungs to take it in, finding only the lungs of the foreigners who had occupied the north and left the narrow, stifling south to the city's own people and to strangers who had come from the countryside, lured by its mirage. Then I saw the valley of the Nile shrink and its south get close to its north and its right get close to its left and become a room or the small hall of a house filled with old furniture and tired men, women, and a few children. I saw one of the men, in his thirties, getting up at dawn wearing an old *gallabiya,* taking a cloth bag containing a little bread and salt, slipping his feet into a worn out pair of shoes and sneaking out quietly as a thick fog enveloped everything and dew moistened the land. I saw him walking, seeing no one and unseen by anyone, parting the thick fog; alone, obviously knowing where he was going. I saw him ride a train and get off, cross a canal and stand in total awe of the vastness of the desert and wonder, "Will you walk on all this sand?" and answer, "Yes, I'll walk." I saw him walk through Sinai, sleeping at night and walking during the day, and if he was close to dying of thirst, water sprang from the ground for him and if he was close to dying of hunger, God sent him down a feast from heaven, until he entered Palestine and saw the Palestinians hanging on the gallows, the English beating them from the front and the Jews beating them from behind. He still had to answer the mysterious call to the Hijaz. He crossed the river and walked through the Jordan valley until he reached the desert of Tabuk, full of faith in God, with neither water nor food. He saw empty Diba and ruined Tima and accursed Tabuk and went on to see the enigma of Qaliba. Then he went on until he arrived at Medina where he sat at the door of the Prophet's mosque selling grain to those going in, then his business prospects improved. He became a peddler and traveled the country until he was in Tabuk again, where he sold some goods to a woman and followed her to her family's tent. They gave him food and he said, "Your food is delicious and your life salubrious; how could I bear to be apart from you, a stranger everywhere I travel the land? Give me sanctuary." They did, and the woman became his wife and begat a daughter, who begat Wadha bint Sulayman ibn Sabil. He was her grandfather and she his granddaughter.

For all the countries, states, cities, towns, and villages, it is still such a tiny world!

12

Mansur came into my office in the morning with the monkey on his shoulder and said, "Get ready to go to Medina."

I smiled. Whenever Mansur spoke with me I tried to fake a smile. I said, "Nothing bad I hope?"

He said, "You're to go to the Social Security organization and bring back the forms to insure the workers. It's a new system. I think you have something like that in Egypt."

I was surprised at how much he was meddling in my job, though I forgot that Amm Abdallah often gave him the opportunity to do just that. I said, smiling, "Are you our new director, Mansur?"

He sat at the desk close to the safe and said, "I want to give you this monkey."

I burst out laughing. I no longer feared him, as he had appeared to calm down following my lie to him about Said's marriage to Widad.

"But I don't like monkeys."

"Not for you. I want you to take it to my cousin in Medina. He wants one from Amman but I'm not going to Amman anytime soon."

I looked at the monkey and it stared at me. How could I carry the monkey, really? Are monkeys allowed on airplanes?

"Did you believe me, brother Ismail? I was just kidding."

I heaved a sigh of relief.

"But I swear I was ready," I said.

"God bless you, brother Ismail."

He fixed his eyes silently on the desk. I don't know what came over me. I felt like crying. I was so touched by this weak man's naiveté and goodness. If only I knew exactly what he wanted!

✧

We arrived an hour and a half later. It was a small plane that kept being rocked by air turbulence. We landed at a small airport not unlike the one at Tabuk. Since this was a domestic flight, there were no problems on arrival. There was a large group of men sitting on the floor in the glass-enclosed arrival lounge, with policemen standing around them. A mix of Egyptians and Asians, they were sitting so close to each other you couldn't count them. Their faces and clothes were dusty; some were barefoot. I left the building. Outside was a vast open space, high open sky, and a broad asphalt parking lot where cars and taxis waited. Half an hour from the airport to Medina, I was told. I expected a driver to appear but none did. People like me coming out of the airport were heading for the cars in silence. A man sitting in the passenger seat was beckoning in my direction. I looked around but there was nobody else. He must have meant me. What did he want?

"Get in quickly before the driver comes," he said. I didn't understand but I got in the car in the back seat. The driver appeared and opened his door saying, "Your brother has come?"

"Yes."

The man turned to me and smiled. The driver, who did not turn, said, "Hello."

He started the car. I was extremely perplexed.

"Your brother works in Saudi Arabia?"

"My brother and also my cousin. We left our families back in Egypt."

The young driver laughed.

"You did the best thing."

He kept laughing as the car sped forward. "Goddamn women," the driver said and turned to me. "Beg your pardon, brother," he said and I saw an old man's face. He was not young as I had thought. I thought the best thing to do was to keep my mouth shut. The man who asked me to get in was Egyptian. He wouldn't do me wrong.

The road was long and narrow, crossing dark, red mountains, their peaks at different heights, rocky and shining. At the foot of these mountains were dry gullies created a long time previously by the rains. On the flat land between the mountains were several old volcanic fields that emitted an almost transparent smoke, as if they were the mouths of volcanoes long extinct. There were no sands and no dunes. For some unknown reason I remembered the huge white dog that looked like a stray donkey, which I had seen on the road in Tabuk. I smiled. Here they probably killed dogs in the city and the desert. The man turned to me and said, "These are volcanic mountains like the mountains of our own Eastern Desert."

I didn't say anything. I needed to know his name so I could address him. But I'd had a good look at his face. He looked like an ordinary man about whom one could predict nothing one way or the other. He didn't appear to be well off;

his shirt collar was dirty, the top button was missing and the pullover he had on was old. He had a fair face, slightly red, his hair was all gray, and his eyes were small and tired. He continued talking, now to the driver.

"The mountains of Mecca and Jedda used to be connected to the mountains in the Eastern Desert in Egypt and they were part of the same range."

"I beg your pardon, Ustaz. I've never seen Egypt. I've only seen Turkey."

The driver seemed genuinely ashamed as he said that. The man turned to me and said, smiling, "The whole western part of Saudi Arabia was connected with the Egyptian Eastern Desert. In the remote past Egypt and Arabia were separated by the Great African Fault, as you know."

He was talking to me as an educated man, wanting to reassure me. I began to feel comfortable. Medina began to appear in the distance. There were a lot of tall high-rises among the low houses. I saw the minarets of the Prophet's mosque and the green dome gleaming in the sunlight. The man said, "Medina is beautiful. Its air is pleasant and its people are good. They are the ones who gave refuge and support to the Prophet."

"God bless you, Ustaz."

The streets did not look much different from those in Tabuk. Perhaps the streets here were cleaner and wider. There were more Asians. Medina was a bigger city.

The driver stopped in front of the Prophet's mosque. Huge crowds were going in and out quickly and silently. Crowds gathered around the elderly vendors sitting on the ground in front of the mosque selling wheat to feed the pigeons, flocks of which filled the sky over the mosque, exulting in their special status. We got off. The man paid the driver twenty riyals and after the car was gone told me, "You can give me ten riyals. I gave the driver his fare."

"I can give you the twenty."

"No, no, just the ten. You might need every penny here." So that was why he invited me to ride with him. I was not in the mood to chat, so I gave him the ten riyals. He asked me, "Do you know anyone here?"

"No."

"Then come with me. I know the cheap hotels."

Above us the sun was sending down strong hot rays. We were in the south, away from Tabuk. The daytime here was more like autumn, and autumn here was like summer in Egypt. I was puzzled by the women in front of the door of the mosque. We had moved in front of another door. There were women going in with uncovered faces; there were green eyes, and blue eyes, and dark eyes, and just as you could tell the nationality of the men from their complexions and their dress, in the case of the women you could tell it from their eyes, even if their faces looked similar. At least that was what suddenly occurred to me as I looked at those ripe faces, like roses floating on a sea of light. True, the *abaya*s were black, but underneath them were shining bright green, red, and white dresses. True, the *abaya*s were black, but contrasted against the white light of the day they gave the lovely faces an opportunity to reveal their charm. And right here in front of the noble Prophet's mosque I couldn't raise my eyes to heaven or lower them to earth; my eyes were in the same line of sight as the women's faces, the women's eyes, the women's lips, and their rosy cheeks. Umar ibn Abi Rabia, the famous love poet, was not mad when he went on pilgrimage to flirt with women and compose love poems for them and about them. What would happen if I went to Mecca?

I asked God Almighty to forgive me. What would I do about those captivating eyes and the comfort the soul found in those faces? I was in a dream world.

"Women here uncover their faces. Don't be surprised; it's a topsy-turvy world," the man said, bringing me back to reality. He walked and I followed him like a child following his father.

He took me to a narrow alley, and even though it was very crowded, things flowed smoothly and quietly; no sound of a hum, or voice, or a radio, or a cassette recorder. The whole place was permeated with the fragrance of incense and perfumes. There was silence and a sense of awe, as if the alley and all the houses were inside a big mosque.

"You're lucky there's no *umra* at the moment; if there was, you wouldn't have found room even for your foot. During the *umra* people sleep in the streets."

I said nothing. I let him guide me. We went into a small hotel named Hiraa. In a narrow, dark hall we met a smiling young Egyptian who accompanied us to a room upstairs. It couldn't have been more than three meters by three. It had two small, separate beds and a metal cabinet that was less than a meter in width and less than two meters high. There was a sink attached to the wall with a glass shelf above it, with a single cup. Above the shelf was a small mirror with rusted edges and dimmed glass. There was a ceiling fan, but I felt I was about to suffocate, as if the heat and humidity had been locked up in the room and were now attacking us. There was no window to the street, but a small window to a narrow skylight. I asked the young Egyptian to open the window. He smiled and opened it. Nothing changed. I told him to turn the fan on. He did and left. I sat on the edge of one of the two beds. My companion sat on the other bed and opened a small suitcase, then quickly took off his clothes and put on a *gallabiya* from the case. I did the same, except that I put on pajamas. I haven't liked *gallabiya*s since I was young; they always rode up and I felt the cold air on my thighs and my back. Whenever someone suggested that I wear a *gallabiya*, I immediately felt the cold air. I was very surprised how widespread the wearing of *gallabiya*s had become in Egypt. People were now wearing them on the street and sometimes at work. It was a new habit introduced by Egyptians coming back from the oil countries. I don't know how come people didn't feel cold air on their thighs.

"We'll rest here for an hour then have lunch at some other place," said my companion.

"I'm not hungry."

"Well then, we'll have lunch after the midafternoon prayer. We missed the noon prayer. We'll do them both in the Prophet's mosque."

I suddenly felt that he talked too much, but I ignored it and tried to sleep, but neither of us could. I saw him moving about restlessly on the bed then get up and take a book out of the suitcase and go back to lie down and read.

"My name is Ismail Khidr Musa," I said.

He smiled and said, "I should have introduced myself. I'm Kamil al-Beltagi. Please forgive me. It must all have been so confusing for you."

"Don't worry about it. I figured out what was happening."

"I think I can tell about people."

He fell silent for a while then asked me, "Do you like reading?"

"I used to read."

He got up lightly and took out another book and offered it to me. "This is a wonderful novel—and short, as you see."

I took it and said, smiling:

"*Le quai aux fleurs ne répond plus.* I know it, but it'll be fine to read it again. I read it a long time ago."

I didn't really need to read what he gave me. I wanted to know what he was reading, and I caught a glimpse of Chaim Herzog's book on the 1973 war, a black book with Golda Meir's face on the cover. I had heard about it but had never read it. Instead I began to read Malek Haddad's novel. I finished it in two hours. The little novel captivated me as it had the first time I read it. I saw him get up and take off his *gallabiya*, saying, "You probably need to take a walk."

It was as if he had called me away from an enchanted world. I rubbed my eyes and went to the sink to wash my face. I felt I was a new person who had shed his skin and acquired a new, brighter one. I sat once again on the edge of the bed looking at him in silence. Then I said, "When I first read this novel I felt I was the one jumping under the wheels of the train. Now I don't feel that. My heart just beat a little faster."

He looked at me for a while and said, "I read it often. Perhaps because of that. I'll wait for you in the lobby."

He went out quickly. Why did he suddenly look so ill at ease?

✧

We went to the Prophet's mosque to perform both the noon and midafternoon prayers at the same time. The first thing I thought as we were leaving the hotel was that I shouldn't look at women's faces. Entering the Prophet's mosque was not a routine thing. During the Feast of the Sacrifice I didn't quite grasp the idea that you could take a car, go on pilgrimage and come back in a few days. Now I didn't quite believe that you could go out of the hotel and enter the Prophet's mosque in a few minutes. I expected to shake and cry. Perhaps that was why nothing of the sort happened. I entered the mosque and looked at the pigeons filling the space over the open part. I was struck by how vast the mosque was and how crowded. It was divided into two sections, the right section for men and the left for women. I could no longer see the women's faces. All our faces were now turned to the *qibla*. If all the women turned their faces to me, I'd be dead in an instant. All one needed to go to hell was to see this vast number of women's faces all at once. A hellish devil was encircling me! Beltagi said, "We won't be able to reach the Prophet's tomb before the end of the prayers."

We sat in the open section of the mosque, then the call to prayer was made and we prayed. A sense of total awe enveloped the whole world as the kindly voice of the shaykh who led the prayers filled the place. I would be lying if I said that I was swayed into belief, since I wasn't an atheist in the first place. I would also be lying if I said that I didn't feel anything.

We were done. Beltagi said to me, "Wait a little for the crowd to let up."

I was thinking, "How can time pass so easily in the presence of the Prophet?" Ever since we were little we had heard the adults dreaming of making this visit. We never tired of hearing, at home and in school, the story of Muhammad's flight from Mecca, how the Prophet and his companion, Abu Bakr, hid in the cave and how doves laid eggs at the entrance and a spider wove its web. Abu Bakr was scared when he heard the hooves of the infidels' horses, but the Prophet reassured him, "Fear not, for God is with us." My father said that a lot when he saw me crying with the people when Israel invaded the country and Gamal Abd al-Nasser announced that he was stepping down: "Don't grieve, God is with us."

I got up to go to the Prophet's tomb.

"'Between my pulpit and my tomb is one of the gardens of Paradise' is a hadith of the Prophet. And this is the noble garden, Ismail," said Beltagi as I made my way with difficulty through rows of Asians reading intensely from small Qurans and swaying as they read aloud, almost oblivious to the people trying to go through.

"The tombs of the Prophet and Abu Bakr were in Aisha's house. Umar requested in his will that he be buried with them. And from the time Umar was buried in her house, Aisha became very meticulous about the way she dressed around the house, out of embarrassment. That's what she said. Later the house became part of the mosque."

Beltagi was speaking but I didn't bother to respond to him. I decided to recite the opening chapter of the Quran and ask for God's mercy for my father, health for my mother, and success for my brother and sisters. I stood in front of the tomb of the Prophet and his two companions and was on the point of turning back. How come I wasn't crying? Who was going to save me from this state of spiritual void that had taken hold of me for so long? Ever since my father held the hands of my brother and sisters and handed them over to me, ever since she said as she cried, "You left me on the fifth of June. Does that date remind you of anything? It's not a date that comes and goes every year as the other days do. It will always be with us. Even if we went to war and we won and everyone else forgot about it, I would never forget it because you left me on that day. Why, Ismail? Why don't you know how to choose? The wound you inflicted on me will remain forever and victory over Israel one day can never heal my wound. My hurt and my sorrow will never end."

We went outside. He asked me right away, "Do you really pray?"

"No." I answered without looking at him. I wished I could lie and tell him yes.

"Nor me. I don't pray but I was afraid of you. Come on, let's see Medina."

✧

Mount Uhud. Broad, stretched out, dark red, calm, serene, and mysterious. The light bathed it and stayed inside, without being reflected back, as if here its journey ended in rest. The air around it was cool and refreshing. The mountain that bounded Medina from the north stood steadfast and silent like a sentinel guarding against the vicissitudes of time, a mountain inspiring sadness and awe at the same time. There were a few people around selling dried dates, henna, small bottles of perfume and *siwak*s, and the two of us. It was as if we were the only strangers in Medina today. None of the vendors shouted or even spoke.

"Dried dates, henna, perfume, and *siwak*s as well as *kohl* are all part of the Prophet's tradition."

Beltagi was the only one who spoke there that afternoon. He added, "The prophet was clean and full of love for life. He loved everything and accepted no limits, except on possessions and food. Look, this is where Khalid ibn al-Walid came from."

He pointed to the site of the famous battle.

"And the Muslims stood here."

He pointed to two rectangles of small bricks on the ground.

"The bricks mark the graves of Hamza and Musaab ibn Umayr, the most illustrious martyrs of that battle. Do you know about them?"

"I know about Hamza, the one whose liver Muawiya's mother ate," I said. Suddenly, Beltagi's voice shook as if he were fighting off tears.

"Musaab was the flower of the youth of Quraysh, the most handsome and the richest. When he embraced Islam, he left everything behind. He suffered hunger and nakedness as he was besieged with the Muslims in the ravine of Abu Talib and he never surrendered. He was the standard bearer that day and he never let go of it until his body was torn and he died."

He fell silent. From the top of the mountain a cool, gentle breeze blew. It was approaching sunset when the night took its time to spread. The sun, now to our left, was sadly retreating from the world. I saw the Muslims leaving their posts on top of the mountain and descending so as not to miss out on the spoils, now that the battle was about to end in victory. Then Khalid ibn al-Walid appeared with his troops like a mountain on the mountain and attacked the Muslims from the rear. The Prophet stood his ground, his tooth was broken, and the Muslims were defeated. At school we always had to answer the question: What was the lesson of the defeat? The answer: Obey the chief. Why was the question repeated so frequently?

Beltagi started to move, so I followed suit.

✧

In the dimly lit room I felt claustrophobic, so I requested another, bigger lamp. I was surprised that Beltagi hadn't noticed how dim the light was, since he looked rather near-sighted to me. I lay down on my bed, thinking what I was missing that night. The television? I could always go to the lobby of the hotel, where I had caught a glimpse of a television set as we came back after our meal in a small restaurant behind the hotel. But what kind of guests would I sit with? Pakistanis, Afghans, Turks. All Muslims, and from all countries. Only Muslims could enter Medina. How could I be sure the Asians would sit quietly? They might talk in their rapid-fire way and ruin my evening. I decided to stay in the room. Beltagi asked me, "How long have you been in Saudi Arabia?"

"Almost three months."

"Do you have a regular job?"

"I don't understand what you mean."

He was busy making two glasses of tea on a small electric water heater that he had taken out of his suitcase. He explained only when he was done and we were drinking the tea.

"I mean, do you have an official contract or are you like me?"

"I had a contract before I came. How can you work here without a contract?"

He smiled and said, "You should have figured that out for yourself. Don't you see that I have my own tea-making equipment?"

He pointed to the suitcase lying next to the wall and said, "It has everything I need. It's small as you can see, but there's a lot in it."

He got up and opened it and took out an air mattress, a sleeping bag, and all sort of other things. He said, "I came for *umra* a year ago and I haven't gone back to Egypt. They issued a warning to everyone who was working here without an official contract to rectify his situation before last Rajab."

"So, why didn't you get a contract before the deadline?"

"Because I might leave at any time."

I was silent. He must have realized how confused I was. He said, "It would have been easy to get a contract before the last decree. Employers liked my kind of work arrangement, because it didn't entail any rights for the workers. But after the new decree it became dangerous for both parties to work or employ without a contract. But I chose not to get a contract, because I can still find employers who will take risks hiring me. I can do all sorts of things, least of which is typing. Anyway, that's what happened. It's not the safest situation and I sometimes find myself on the run. When you arrived at the airport I was one of those people who were arrested to be deported because they were working without contracts. But I managed to escape. Every time I get arrested, I escape."

I looked at him in total amazement and said, "All those men surrounded by the police were under arrest?"

"More than that are deported every day."

We were silent for a while then he said, "Most probably you will ask me how I escaped."

"What surprises me," I said sadly, "is how an educated and cultured person like you can accept such a difficult situation."

✧

It was as if that night had been preordained for me. When I set foot on the plane on my way to Medina I had felt that my great fear that things between Wadha and me were moving too fast was going to be allayed. She had let me hold her hand during the lesson the day after I'd seen her grandfather. She suddenly said, "Why are you being so cruel to me?"

I had been yelling for no reason as if I wanted to scare her away. I patted her on the back of her hand. She did not withdraw it so I took it between my palms feeling as if a little sparrow lay between my hands, wanting to but unable to move, a warm sparrow with blood coursing fast in its veins. Luckily I let go of her hand a moment before Khalid came in. He hadn't met me when I arrived at their house because he had just returned from a short trip to Riyadh. He had never before come into the room during the lesson. That day he did, and he came in to greet me. I trembled as if he had actually seen me. I needed time to get my breath back after he left. She must have known how I felt; she was writing and smiling at my fear and confusion.

Why was it so difficult to stay away from Wadha bint Sulayman ibn Sabil and at the same time so painful to be near her? She was too young for all that trouble. She had gone back to her old ways. Now she had been caught in flagrante delicto with the Egyptian, Ismail Khidr Musa. She would be stoned and he would be stoned. He would not be deported but thrown out of a plane into the desert of the Empty Quarter. An accursed Egyptian, like his president who the Muslims curse and wish dead day and night because he set his unclean foot on the soil of Jerusalem and sat with the Jews, who God has ordained us to kill wherever we encounter them.

O Lord of Mercy! O Salih Sanyur al-Thaqifi, help me! Show me another film. I had gone to Salih. Ghalib was the only one there and he was crying and Salih was cursing him. I said, "Salih, he is a wretched, poor, skinny boy with tattered clothes."

"Please, Ustaz, stay out of this," said Salih. "He's neither wretched nor poor. He has syphilis, Ustaz. Look at his feet. It's all over his body and not a word from him, the dog. I've torn up all the video tapes and here they are, piled up in front of you. I've also removed the VCR and the television from the room. These scum, they want to kill me. Get out, you brother of a whore!" Ghalib was crying his heart out and Salih was pushing him with a little stick so as not to touch him or his clothes. Then, turning to me, he said, "His father kicked him out of the house when he found out. He smashed the seven television sets in their house and the VCRs. His father is crazy. He bought a television set and a VCR for each of his sons so they wouldn't argue and fight among themselves. The problem, Ustaz, is that this dog doesn't content himself with pornographic movies, and syphilis is a very serious disease, Ustaz. Don't you know that?"

"I know, Salih. Let's begin the lesson."

"No lesson today, Ustaz. Don't worry about your fees; you'll get the money."

"Who said I could accept money without working for it, Salih?"

"Who said I needed any lessons, Ustaz? I can easily pass. The teachers come to our store before the exams and they take blankets, and silk, and wool dresses, and I pass. Don't look at how old I am. I flunk deliberately. I choose not to sit for the examinations. I give the teachers what they want and I get what I want and I don't take the tests. My father is a jackass who brings me a teacher every month and I kick him out. You I liked, and I'll ask my father to give you a higher salary on condition that you don't teach me. Let's sit down and talk about anything but school stuff."

I walked. It was darker than usual. I got into my car unaware of the route I chose. I saw the house where Sayyid al-Gharib was under arrest, dark inside and out, the doors and windows all closed, with no sound except for the monotonous rustling of the palm tree tops. I moved on and found myself in a narrow but well lit street with small lamps above the doors of the houses. I saw Ghalib stretching out in a corner, leaning his back to the wall of an old house, his legs stretched in front of him on the ground, with cats around him and on his legs, jumping and running about. I was disgusted by everything.

At home I wouldn't go along with Said and Wagih, who thought I should keep up the charade. I told Wagih he shouldn't have picked me to teach such a boy. I said to myself

I'd forget it all in Medina, but in fact I met Beltagi, who told me, "Here, Ismail, my friend, the airports bring dreams and wishes rolling in front of the feet of those who come here, very close to their hands, if only they stoop. You can find everything from anywhere in the world here: toys from Hong Kong next to eggs from communist Romania, grubby clothes from Taiwan next to chicken from communist Bulgaria, perfumes from Paris next to fake watches from Korea and good ones from Japan. Here you can buy and sell any currency as easily as you breathe. Here they have a police force for the small crimes. The big crimes, they usually get swallowed up in the dark. Here is a strong flowing river obstructed by neither cataract nor rapid, a river of profit. All you have to do is abbreviate some years of your life and forget about having friends or loving anyone, to be like me, to be content with whatever you have and not even think about what you eat. It can be cheddar cheese from Australia or feta cheese from Cyprus, lamb from Jordan or the local, tasteless lamb. I am a man who got stuck on a certain idea and the whole world stopped before me. That was a very long time ago, before the July revolution, the army movement. I still hadn't finished my study of law at the university. I was in jail when the revolution broke out. They released me from jail with all the nationalists. But they arrested me again in 1954; I had finished my degree and gotten married. They said I belonged to the Muslim Brotherhood. But they soon released me when they looked at the file they had on me, the file the young republic inherited from the days of the monarchy. They came back and arrested me again in 1956, for a few months, saying I was a communist. They let me out a few days before the tripartite aggression, when Britain, France, and Israel attacked Egypt. I went to fight in the Suez Canal zone and came back after the war and returned my weapon. Did you know that only a few volunteers returned their weapons? Most of them either sold them or hid them. They came back for me in 1957, and didn't release me until 1964. I saw my son, who was then nine years old, and my daughter, who was seven. They arrested me again in 1966 and let me out a few months after the setback of 1967. Then they arrested me in 1970; Gamal Abd al-Nasser's turn with me was over. Sadat took over and discharged us, leaving me out on the streets for four years, then he arrested me in 1975 on the first day of the year and let me out three months later, only to arrest me in 1977 but let me out again soon after. Finally I let myself out of Egypt. Did I really need all that time to come to hate my country? Or did I leave because my wife had turned our apartment into a kindergarten to compensate for losing me and our son, who lives in Sweden now, and our daughter, who married a teacher seconded to Algeria? I don't know why out of all the countries in the world I chose to come here. I used to go to jail and come out stronger, whatever you've heard about the horrors of jail. It was my wife who broke. She deteriorated and aged fast. A woman, like the land, dries up without water. Don't ask me why I didn't go to Europe, as many have done, or why I didn't go to other Arab countries to be given a forum in the newspapers and radio to attack the government."

He started crying and continued, "I'm a stupid masochist who derives pleasure from torture. I refused to have a contract so I could constantly face the threat of deportation. I'm a sick man; my disease is at such an advanced stage, it's incurable. Or do you think I really wish that someone would send me back home, that somebody would force me to love my country? I was never a communist, and of course I wasn't a Muslim

Brother. They forced me into becoming addicted to prisons, because I started my life loving my country."

He was now sobbing. I got up from my bed not knowing what to do. I sat down next to him on his bed.

"It's okay, Ustaz Kamil."

"Do you know how many swords would be at my throat if they knew anything about me? If an ant were to stray from its appointed path here, it would find a thousand feet on top of it. If a rooster were to crow before dawn here, it would not live to see another dawn. Here you can see the sign over Dante's inferno. Sadat did it and we were all lost. One man causes a whole nation to be lost? What a herd!"

✧

I didn't hear Beltagi again until it was almost dawn. I had felt a strange kind of weariness coming over me, and we had fallen asleep. The call to the dawn prayer that woke me up was mixed with a muffled sobbing coming from an unknown source. It took me a few moments to figure out where it came from. I couldn't get up to talk with him again for fear of embarrassing him. I stayed as I was, lying down and breathing regularly.

I remembered what I had thought before I slept. The story must have some secret aspects that he did not tell me about. Besides, what was it really that made him feel as if he were the one jumping under the wheels of the train every time he read Malek Haddad? I wished he had talked to me about the novel again. I wished I had told him that I myself was also at one time a potential writer of stories, but I forgot. My father's mission in life kept me suspended between heaven and earth and all the books and paper and pens were sucked up by space. He took me unawares by his story, the poor helpless man! The greatest gift that God had given me was the ability to forget. Had it not been for this ability I would have turned out like him. Each of us has a prison where he has lost something valuable, though my imprisonment was not long.

I slept again and I saw it: the huge rooster whose head was high up there and whose crest was in the seventh heaven while its body extended down to earth and its wings filled the air with bright colors. Then it began to beat the air with its wings, and winds and hurricanes blew and it got cold; then it ceased moving and it got hot. Once again it began to beat its wings and cold air almost froze me as I looked up in great fear; then it ceased moving again and I almost drowned and died in a sea of sweat.

I felt that someone was holding my head and pushing it down in a barrel full of water and I almost drowned and started beating the air with my arms, and just as I was about to die, my head would be brought back up and I would breathe in big gulps of air. Then the rooster crowed, "Cock-a-doodle-doo, Praise the Lord Most Holy, cock-a-doodle-doo." Then all of a sudden the rooster's head fell on its chest and blood gushed out, filling the air with red and drenching the earth in red. Then I heard a noise outside and I woke up in a great fright, to find neither Beltagi nor his suitcase. He had left me *Le quai aux fleurs ne répond plus*, and the sound of train wheels.

13

Here a person could forget everything. I knew that very well. Busy time and idle time could cause you to drown. The morning after I arrived back in Tabuk, I had to begin filling out the Social Security forms I had brought back from the main office in Medina. I had only stayed in Medina the following day; in the morning I went to the Social Security office and got the forms, and in the evening I took the plane back to Tabuk.

I kept thinking that I was going to run into Beltagi again on the street or perhaps at the airport. But that wasn't to be. It was as if it were all a dream. Now as I sat in my office filling out the forms, his face wouldn't leave me. I stopped working, stood up and moved away from the desk, pacing the room trying to remember where I had seen Beltagi's face before—in a newspaper, an Egyptian newspaper. That was one, maybe two, three years ago. I couldn't remember exactly. And I saw the face more than once, but on which page and why it was there I had no idea. I sat down at my desk again, unable to get back to work. So it was destined that I would forget the man twice. "Tabuk makes you forget your mother and your father" is a real proverb here. A person needed to forget only for one day and he would forget forever. I didn't need more than a few minutes with Mansur to forget everything but Mansur, a few moments with Nabil to forget everything but Nabil, or Arshad, or Munzir. Seeing the old Yemeni, who always came on time, moving the *siwak* in his mouth, or something stupid that Abed did, both had the same effect. But Tabuk was more generous. The door of the room was lit by a bright face, silky blond hair and brilliant blue eyes. A woman with an uncovered face stood at the door, looking at me with a self-confident smile, a real woman wearing a pair of tight jeans, a blouse with a red collar and a blue pullover, on her shoulders and back a white scarf.

"Good morning," she said as she entered and sat in front of me and asked me if I spoke English, all at the same time. She didn't stop looking at me with that brilliant fullness of her eyes.

She seemed about to laugh at my confusion. She said I could sit down. I discovered that I was still standing, so I sat down. She asked me to order a coffee for her from Mr. Nabil. So, she knew Nabil. She asked me, "Where's Mr. Abed?"

"In his office."

"He's not there."

"He must have gone out on some short errand. Can I do anything for you?"

Nabil appeared at the door, smiling and saying in affected surprise and in a loud, theatrical tone, "Oh, Mrs. Rose!"

She laughed and I smiled. He came in to shake her hand. She gave it to him without moving. He kept it in his hand for a while as he said to me, "Rosemary, Mr. Larry's wife, the most beautiful foreigner in the country."

He let go of her hand, she winked at me, shrugged her shoulders, and asked me what he had said. I translated it for her and she laughed and said, "I'm the only foreign woman here."

I smiled and felt at ease. Here was an uncomplicated woman who gave you a sense of familiarity. I asked Nabil to make two coffees for us. As soon as he left the room I began to wonder how she really knew Nabil. I had been there three months and I'd never seen her. Did she usually come after working hours?

"Are you new here, Mr. . . . ?"

"Ismail. I've been here for three months."

"I am sorry I didn't see you before. I was in America the last few months."

"Do you work here?"

"Larry, my husband, does. Officially I can't work but I do, privately and illegally, in Mr. Abdallah's day-care center."

"I didn't know Mr. Abdallah had a day-care center."

"It's well-known. His wife runs it, in town. How come you didn't know?"

She laughed and I told her, "Perhaps because I'm a bachelor."

She laughed and said that Mr. Abdallah's wife was huge — he was tiny—and that she ate almonds all day long, which was very dangerous for the health. Nabil brought the coffee and before leaving asked her, "America is good, Rose?"

"Good, Nabil. Very good."

The three of us laughed and then Nabil, blushing visibly, left the room. We talked for a long time. Every time she tried to leave I encouraged her to wait for Abed and she would stay while I hoped that Abed wouldn't come back and that nobody would come into my office. It was now one o'clock and I hadn't even noticed the smile of the Yemeni man. I saw him now, suddenly, and remembered that we hadn't exchanged smiles yet, which we immediately did. Then Abed was at the door.

"Hello, Rose," he said as he came in to shake her hand. She shook his hand, still sitting down. He looked upset and said, "Won't you come to my office?"

She got up and said, “I have to go to the camp. I don’t have time now. I just wanted to see you.”

She shook my hand and dashed out. She waved to him and Abed abruptly said, “Has anyone asked about me?”

“Rose.”

I don’t know why I said that. He looked askance at me and went to his office. I felt really sorry for answering him without thinking like that.

✧

On the desk were the stupid forms I was filling out. Really I wanted to toss them in the garbage. Rosemary, what a beautiful name! Her perfume was still in the room, evoking a presence that was as light as a feather, a swallow, crazy and frank. She expressed surprise at all the answers I gave her: a philosophy major ending up as an English language teacher in Egypt in charge of personnel here, what a mess! But that was exactly my situation, not a unique one among the Egyptians here. There were men with advanced degrees working as plasterers and ceramic tile layers. It was a regrettable situation but it was reality. I didn’t want to go on about how this was the era of the new janissaries, when third and fourth class occupations drove out the intellects with whips or irony. The scales of justice were not quite balanced in our country. Perhaps it was the same in your country, otherwise why have you come here? At least we’ve got an excuse, which you haven’t got. Petroleum, high master of these times, has stopped short of our eastern and western borders as if saying that the land of Egypt was forbidden land, a geographical conspiracy. Would anybody believe that? I would. Our country has always been fraught with conspiracies; if they weren’t engineered by the enemy, we would engineer them ourselves. We've got the time, tons of it. We've got newspapers and magazines and broadcasts that could turn black into white and white into black, or into something odorless, colorless, tasteless. I didn't tell her any of that. I just remembered Kamil al-Beltagi, but I told her, "You're a sociologist yet you work here secretly in a day-care center. We're not that different from each other then." She said her husband was a big expert. She laughed and challenged me as if she had known me for some time. She said it was he who pushed her to work at the day-care center because she couldn't have a job, legally. She wasn't a doctor, or a teacher, or a nurse. Then she softened and said she understood and didn't blame me. She said her life's dream was to do research on the contemporary Bedouins, on the changes taking place in their lives. But the authorities wouldn't give her a permit because she was not affiliated with any academic institution. That was why she went back to America and got a letter from the University of Chicago to the authorities to facilitate her task. She hadn't anticipated any further problems. But the authorities requested that she have a chaperone to accompany her while doing the research because it was not proper for a woman to travel alone among the Bedouins. Larry wouldn't leave his job to do that. The only one who could help her was her brother George, who would not leave America to live in a country where people were whipped if they drank alcohol. Thus she had lost her chance forever. She asked me if I'd seen the Bedouins here and I said no. I did see a beggar who came to town on the day of the Feast, but I didn't tell her that. She invited me to visit her and her husband in the camp. Why, when she hardly knew me?

✧

I saw the Yemeni man sitting with the *siwak* in his mouth. His smile today was more beautiful than usual. The sun was white, enveloping the earth in a lovely warmth. It was getting colder during the nights. Now the sun would get up with us, tired, ascending the sky slowly, seeming to rule the space only at noon. The cold during the day was not so bad. I left my office, still imbued with the delight that Rose had left behind in the room. I went into the kitchen, and Nabil stood up in alarm, "Abed has gone into town. How can you sit here?"

"What could happen? A stupid telephone call about something even more stupid? Do you have another chair?"

When I went in he was sitting on the only chair there, reading the magazine *al-Watan al-arabi*, 'The Arab Nation,' bringing his nearsighted eyes very close to the page. He said, "You sit here on the chair. I'll sit on the floor."

He spoke and crouched there immediately, the magazine still in his hand. I sat down.

"Please excuse the modest kitchen," he said.

The kitchen was very small and dirty. It reminded you of the kitchens of government offices in Egypt. There was a small, rusty metal cabinet, without doors, hanging on the wall. On its three shelves were boxes and jars of tea, coffee, and sugar. Below the cabinet was a gas stove on a wooden table that looked as if Nabil had made it himself from uneven scraps of old wood. On the table were glasses and two cups. In the other corner of the kitchen was a big Westinghouse refrigerator.

"It's very strange! They're calling Sadat horrible names. All the magazines here are doing it."

"Do you like politics?"

"No. Abed buys the magazines and doesn't read them, so I read them."

We laughed, then he said, "They say he's responsible for the war in Lebanon and the loss of Palestine, and that he's an agent of the Americans. I know that he's an agent of the Americans. Everything in Egypt is American now; refrigerators, and washers, and clothes. I'm not going to buy anything here because now they have everything in Egypt."

He fell silent for a moment then hit his forehead with his hand. "They don't mean it like that, they mean agent as in spy."

He threw the magazine on the floor and left it there, and stood up.

"Tea?"

"Coffee," I answered, laughing. I picked up the magazine and started leafing through it as he made the coffee and gave it to me, saying, "And the thing about it is that when you see Sadat on television you pity him. Sometimes he reminds me of the comedian Fuad al-Muhandis. Yes, sir. But . . . Palestine was lost a long time ago and the war in Lebanon has been going on for a long time. Does it make any sense that Sadat is responsible? This politics stuff is all bullshit."

He picked up the magazine I had put on the floor, tore it up, and tossed it in the garbage can. I laughed until tears came to my eyes. We were both silent for a long time until he said, "My daddy, God have mercy on his soul, dabbled in politics."

"Your father?"

"I think it's quite obvious, Ismail."

We both laughed. I hadn't meant anything by the question. His wit and manner of speaking today surprised me.

"A long time ago my father was one of the Muslim Brothers who took part in the Palestine War. He came back missing an arm and a leg, the right leg and the left arm. Unbelievable but true."

Suddenly Nabil looked serious. "He caused the family great misery. No job, no ability, and no one cared. The Revolution came and the Muslim Brothers became worthless: that's what my father used to say and what my mother told me later on. I was born on July 23, 1952, the very day of the Revolution. Don't ask me how my father managed that. I look exactly like him, more so than my brothers. We still have his picture hung in our house. I had a crazy maternal uncle who helped us and took me to the broadcasting station every anniversary of the Revolution, as soon as I was able to walk and talk. Lots of other kids who were born on the day of the Revolution went the same day. They would announce our names and give every child some chocolate and a fifty piaster note. My mother said it was a pound. My uncle would take the money and give me the chocolate. Anyway. Please don't laugh. These are facts, not stories. Believe me. One day my father was stretched out sunning himself in the courtyard, as usual. He did it every day. In the morning my older brother would go out to work, my mother would go to the market and my father would crawl to the courtyard, and I would play nearby. Our house was a very old house, going back to the time of the Mamluks. The rooms were very big and each family lived in one room. The house had a huge gate with two jambs made of tree trunks and encased in steel. The gate was always open because it was so stuck in the dirt nobody could move it. Over the gate the opening chapter of the Quran was inscribed in a faded blue, and underneath the inscription was a sign that said 'Khan al-Sanjakdar' without the name. There was only the name of the builders of the house: Master Muhammad Ibrahim and his two sons, Ishaq and Yahya. That was written on the gate.

"We left that house later on and moved to an apartment of our own in the same neighborhood, the slaughterhouse quarter in Imbaba. We grew up and became men and women, three brothers and four sisters. One of my brothers is now in jail. He worked for the post office and embezzled from savings accounts. Yes, sir. Please don't laugh. Now we go back to my father.

"On that very strange day, a crazy camel went into the courtyard. It was a huge camel, as big as a train. He trampled my father who could neither move nor scream. Perhaps he did scream but his screams never came out. I was at the edge of the courtyard, shouting and screaming as the camel trampled my father over and over again then backed off and attacked him again, raising its front legs, and I could see its broad black hooves coming down on my father, who was raising one arm that couldn't reach the neck of the camel and a leg that didn't reach its belly. The women and children all came out of the rooms screaming. There was not a single man there. All the men had gone out to work at the slaughterhouse. Suddenly there jumped into the courtyard five men, dusty, with disheveled hair, frightening like the devil. They had ropes and cleavers and knives, but they stood in shock. They were the owners of the camel. The camel was foaming profusely at the muzzle, and moved away from my father, who had stopped moving altogether. The exhausted camel stood there breathing then calmly knelt down on the ground as the foam flowed from its muzzle onto the dust, then stretched its neck as if to sleep and turned on its side. The men who looked like devils approached it cautiously then slit its throat and ran back. The camel did not get agitated or even get up. It only kicked twice then stopped moving, like my father."

Nabil fell silent for a long time and looked at the floor trying to hide the tears that were trying to flow. Then he raised his face, wiping it with his hands, and looked at me, smiling.

"I took your advice," he said. "I didn't send my fiancée any money this month. I haven't received any letters from her yet. Also I didn't send anything to my mother. I haven't heard from her, either."

✧

I went back to my office feeling a heavy burden on my shoulders. It seemed as if the old Yemeni man sitting in the sun was waiting for me to smile, but I did not.

I almost went over to him to yell at him, "Why do you hover around with your idiotic smile every day? Who gave you the right to sit there without working? What do you know about me to smile at me like that?"

But I went into the room, and heard a car come quickly into the forecourt.

Whoever it was, I had a ready answer to their stupid question. Nobody has called asking about anything in your absence, Abed or Amm Abdallah.

It was Abed who came into the office accompanied by a well-dressed, handsome, bespectacled young Egyptian man, whose black hair was neatly combed. He carried a shiny Samsonite briefcase. Abed didn't ask me about anything. He sat behind the desk next to the safe. The handsome man sat in front of him.

I sat at my desk.

"Ustaz Ismail, our colleague," Abed told the young man, who got up to shake my hand politely then sat down. Abed said, addressing me, "Ustaz Abd al-Hamid, representative of the Delta Bank, has come here to promote bank bonds. Would you like to buy some?"

"Not now."

"I thought not."

Then, addressing the young man, he said, "I'll buy twenty thousand dollars worth." He said that and looked at me. The representative opened his briefcase to take out his papers. I got up and left the place.

Abed had been in town and could have finished the transaction there but he brought the representative along in response to what he deemed to be an insult from Rosemary, who came to ask about him and ended up sitting with me, extended an invitation to me to her house in front of him, and didn't go with him to his office.

✧

My feet took me to the garage. Arshad saw, as we were drinking tea, that I was staring at the English-language edition of the newspaper *Asharq al-Awsat* on the little table between us.

"Don't worry about that, Mr. Ismail. These are our problems in Pakistan," he said, and did not take the paper or apologize for its being there in the workplace. He no longer feared me. There was a long article in the paper with the headline, "Public Opinion Pressure to Save Bhutto." I knew from the papers and the radio that Bhutto was awaiting another trial after his appeal against the death sentence. Arshad said, "Zia-ul Haq is applying Islamic *sharia* laws. He is begging from Saudi Arabia, Mr. Ismail."

"You think he will really execute Bhutto?" I asked him.

"Yes, he will. And if he could do it twice he would, Mr. Ismail."

Nabil came into the garage agitatedly and said to me, "Come quickly. Amm Abdallah is asking about you."

He ran ahead of me and I followed quickly. I caught the panic that I saw in his eyes. But I was thinking, "Did Arshad think I really cared that much about politics?" I was also thinking that the whole day had been ruined.

14

It was getting colder. It was the twenty-second of December. In the morning we found the water frozen in the faucet. That only happened in Arabian-style houses with their roofless courts exposed all night. Walking the short distance from the room to the bathroom was like swimming in a sea of ice. Television now was different; it no longer reminded me that there was a big, wide world out there. Now it gave me warmth. We watched it in Faruq's empty room.

"We don't need a fourth roommate," Wagih said and Said added, "We can turn his room into a living room."

We had no news of Faruq at all. He sent us no letters nor was his name mentioned in the letters I received from my family. His three-month exit and re-entry visa had expired. He was not coming back. We moved a table and some chairs to the room and used it as a dining room, and left Faruq's bed as it was. I left the volume on the television high, which surprised Said and Wagih. I told them the sound waves chased the cold waves out of the room. They said I was going crazy. We laughed. At six-thirty in the morning I left the house to find my car, parked in front, washed with dew. Every day a thick fog filled the air and didn't lift until nine o'clock. After getting into my car, shivering, I closed the door and started the car and blew the steam out of my mouth, and remembered my contests with the other children on our way to school to see who would steam the longest. I did that now and laughed. But today it was different. I felt sick so I went to the bathroom and stayed there for some time trying to throw up but nothing happened. I went back to my room, unable to stand. I stretched out on the bed and drew the cover over my face, thinking of not going to work, but I did. I debated whether to go or not for half an hour, so I arrived late.

✧

"Where am I?"

I saw gray things and white things and was unable to make out Aida's face near me.

"Don't touch the wound. It's out of danger now."

I heard her voice. I remembered that when I woke up again. Dr. Wagih was sitting on a chair next to my bed moistening my lips with a piece of water-soaked cotton as I lay stretched out on the bed. There were three other beds in the room with three men whose faces I couldn't see, sleeping in them. So I was in the hospital and it was night, for the lights of the room were on.

"What happened, Doctor?"

"Nothing. Your appendix acted up so we removed it."

"Really?"

"That happens to people every day."

"Did you perform the surgery?"

"Did you want somebody else to do it?"

"No, thank you very much."

I felt sorry. I hadn't meant anything by my question. He said, "Don't speak too much. It's best if you sleep, it's midnight now. In the morning try to walk a little."

Then he got up and said, "There's a doctor on call and a nurse. If you need anything, just press this button. Do you need anything before I go?"

"Where's Aida?"

"She works days. You still remember her?" he said, and left right away. He didn't forget to turn off the lights.

✧

I stayed awake in the dark. Now I remembered everything. I had arrived late and Abed told me that Amm Abdallah was angry, that he had had to open my desk drawer to take out the sign-in books for the employees. When I asked him how he opened the drawer, he said I shouldn't forget that the desk and the whole room were his before.

I was ill at ease and I felt a sudden stomach ache and I wanted to throw up again. I was so sick I almost lost my balance. I hurried to the bathroom and stood at the sink emptying my stomach. I hadn't had breakfast yet and I thought my stomach would jump out of my mouth. I was sweating profusely all over. I felt a fever in my face. My feet were no longer capable of supporting me so I held on to the faucet of the sink with both hands.

Then I felt nothing until I woke up in the hospital that night. I must have fallen to the floor. That damned appendix took me by complete surprise. Could death be different from the time I spent under anesthesia, feeling nothing? I didn't think so. Death must be easy, then. I didn't know why I thought about that at that time. Perhaps because it was the hospital where Philip had died a few days earlier. I had hurried after Nabil when he called out to me at Arshad's garage. At the gate he stopped and said, "Philip is dead. Amm Abdallah is very upset."

He didn't say anything else. He went into the kitchen and let me continue slowly to Amm Abdallah's room, in great shock. I saw muffled anxiety on his face. He said, "Prepare severance pay for Philip, a month and a half for every year and tell me how it adds up."

I knew that Philip and other employees were only entitled to one month's pay per year of service as severance pay and because I knew that Philip had been working for five years I said, "Thirty-seven thousand and five hundred riyals."

"Are you sure?"

"Yes, his file was on my desk in the morning. I was filling out the Social Security form for him."

"Make it fifty thousand. Say it was authorized by the director." Then he said to Abed, who was standing next to me, "And you, in the morning take the money to his wife. Now go and arrange for the box for shipping to Sri Lanka. Pay the bill and the price of the tickets for his wife and children and book the earliest flight for them."

"Isn't he going to be buried here?"

Abed asked, and Amm Abdallah shouted at him, "What do you mean, buried here? Because he converted to Islam? Let him be buried in his own country among his people."

He fell silent and we left. I felt sorry for Abed who appeared to be more royalist than the king. I went to my office and was sitting in silence when Mansur, who disappeared frequently, reappeared with the monkey on his shoulder and after sitting down, said, "Ha! He wanted to get a Saudi citizenship. He wanted to stay in the Kingdom and he got himself killed. Today he went to the Shaykh in the courthouse to proclaim his conversion to Islam. It was all taken care of and he was referred to the hospital to be circumcised and he died."

"Circumcised?"

"Of course. Don't you have circumcision in Egypt?"

I looked at him unable to get over my surprise. He continued, "Circumcising a man like Philip is not easy. It requires surgery."

I wasn't satisfied with what I heard but no one knew anything more. At home I asked Wagih and he didn't tell me anything more. I still couldn't believe it. Wagih didn't explain to me how Philip had died. He was hiding something from me. Wagih was the chief surgeon at the hospital. How could I be sure he didn't make a mistake and cause Philip's death? But could a surgeon like him make a mistake in circumcision? I didn't think that the spirit of superior arrogance could find an outlet for self expression in the operating room. The operating room was like a temple of worship where the surgeon worked faithfully on the patient who had surrendered himself to him. Could Wagih be so bad?

When I looked at Wagih he would avert his eyes. Perhaps he guessed what I was thinking; perhaps that was what made him ask me if I would have liked someone else to have performed the surgery on me. It was hard to accept Philip's death. At work I didn't want to talk. In the evening I went to Wadha and she said, "Why do you look out of sorts so much these days, Ustaz? Does our country bother you so much?"

I fell silent. I looked at her eyes. She lowered her eyelids. But she had to raise them again. Whenever I went to her, my soul was always totally drawn there, my heart full of joy, exuberant—but there was always something to cause me dejection. I told her the story of the Egyptian doctor under house arrest whose house I saw on my way once and she turned pale. I told her the story of Philip, and she smiled shyly, and said that such things happened all over the world, that I would forget it. Then she said angrily that she did not understand why these people converted to Islam. She did not believe that they stayed Muslim when they got back to their countries. Her intuition told her the whole thing was a lie, exactly as Mansur had seen it, but in Philip's case I detected some truthfulness, though I couldn't defend him. A man over fifty with ten children didn't lie. Maybe he was a weak man, afraid of going home without achieving what he wanted for his children, so he chose the more difficult path: to uproot himself.

I told her I would try to go to her with a carefree mind. She smiled and her face lit up beautifully. Once again I started looking at her thick hair and a hidden energy woke up in me. I smelled her mysterious perfume, and drew back, assailed by fears. She said she loved Egypt very much and wished she could visit it, that her grandfather said that he had a big family in Egypt and that if one of his progeny went there the family would take good care of them. She said the problem was that her grandfather did not remember where his family lived nor where he himself used to live. Then she smiled and said the poor man was now senile. She asked me if I knew Egypt well. I told her I knew Alexandria but it wouldn't be difficult if she came to Egypt to get to know Cairo, or Aswan, or any place in Egypt. We looked long at each other, then she said she loved Egyptian movies, that most of the time she did not believe them, but she was surprised at how beautiful the women were. We kept looking at each other and suddenly I said, "You are more beautiful." She lowered her eyes shyly and said, "The heat has taken its toll on us, Ustaz." I said with deliberateness, "In my eyes you are more beautiful." I read her face and found her lost in thought and I saw shades of sorrow and anguish on her face. She said, "Do you know why you are giving me the lessons, Ustaz? Do you know why we didn't approach any of the teachers?" She had taken me by surprise. I looked at her face and told her, "I know, Wadha, I saw you on the car under the sun." I saw her eyes fixed and the tears flowed as if they had been waiting behind a door that suddenly opened. She gasped and said, "They killed me, Ustaz." She lowered her eyes to the desk. I reached out my hand and started to stroke her soft, thick hair, then my hand descended to her smooth cheek, which felt ice cold and I raised the face by the chin. No torment in the world could equal the torment that I saw on her little face. I took some tissues out of my jacket and began to wipe her tears and the *kohl* that smudged her cheek. I didn't speak and nor did she. It was impossible to continue the lesson that day. We stood up. I went closer to her. She opened her eyes in total surprise. Her lips quivered. I bent down and she raised herself; she must have stood on tiptoe. But I noticed that the door was open, as usual. I went to the door to close it, but then quickly I went out.

Yesterday I went back to Wadha but she was not there. Khalid said that she had gone to Riyadh and would be back in a week. He laughed and said she had a maternal aunt in Riyadh who frequently missed her and Wadha couldn't say no. He asked me to sit down but I took my leave. I walked, thinking, "Was Khalid telling the truth or did Wadha decide to stay away?" And there I was in the hospital, most probably also for a week. Sleep was overcoming me as I heard the call to the dawn prayer far away in the sleeping town.

15

I woke up at about nine. I could still hear the chirping of the birds outside the window. As I opened my eyes, I saw the three other patients in the room: Koreans, talking, their eyes gleaming with delight, with a strange sound in their voices. I saw their mouths move at an astounding speed as they spoke. I smiled at them and they all said, merrily, "Good Morning! Good day *inshaallah*!" I smiled again. I saw Aida come into the room with a magnificent smile on her beautifully brown face, her wide dark eyes gleaming and her white uniform shining bright.

She stood by the bed and said, "You have to get up now and walk as much as you can in the room."

I didn't respond but kept looking at her face and said, "Aida?"

She came closer and said, "Come on, get up. I'll help you."

She held my arm to help me get up. I said, "I'll walk by myself."

"Okay, then. Hurry up."

She left me and went out of the room.

✧

I got up and walked a little, holding on to the walls for support, then I went back to bed, tired. I saw the Koreans standing in white *gallabiya*s packing very small bags. Aida came in with a syringe. I rolled up my sleeve.

"*Al-salaamu alaykum*," the Koreans intoned as they were leaving. Aida paid no attention to them. I waved to them. I saw them walk, keeping their legs slightly apart. Aida must have guessed what I was thinking and she saw the surprise in my eyes when she said, "Koreans. They announced their conversion to Islam yesterday."

I smiled. On her way out she said, "Don't try to drink anything today. And of course, don't eat."

She didn't come back until noon. She came into the room followed by Numan, wheeling in a patient, assisted by a huge Egyptian woman who Aida called Um Zaynab as she asked her to place the patient gently on one of the beds. Numan and Um Zaynab went out, pushing the empty gurney. Aida said, "Another appendix. A young Saudi on his way from Mecca to Turkey by car. He told us that before the operation. He felt sharp pain in the abdomen, so he came to the hospital."

Dr. Wagih came in, wearing a white coat. He looked very tall, as if I were seeing him for the first time. He said, "Hey, how's it going? Did you walk today?"

I nodded and smiled.

"I'm very busy. Maybe I'll see you this evening. Come on, Nurse, let's go to the next operation."

He went out followed quickly by Aida. In spite of the antipathy between them that I had noticed the first time I saw her, Wagih relied on Aida a great deal, as I learned later.

Said came to see me at three. He brought with him a *gallabiya* and helped me take off the dirty hospital gown. I smiled and told him how I felt when I saw a *gallabiya*. He laughed and said I could put up with the cold air on my thighs for a week. He also brought me a huge jar of powdered orange juice, three plates, a glass, a spoon, a fork and a knife, some underwear, and a blanket to place between me and the hospital's old blankets. After Said, Nabil poked his face through the doorway, laughing. He brought me a box of candy and said he almost died when he saw me lying on the floor in the company bathroom. He said he heard a big thud when he was in the kitchen. He went out to investigate but couldn't see anything out of the ordinary. He didn't know what inspired him to go to the bathroom, where he found me stretched out on the floor. He laughed and said, "You're very heavy." It was he who carried me, after shouting for help. Abed came running and they took me to the hospital. He said that Arshad was very upset on my account and that Munzir shouted and said that the water of the well was cursed. Nabil laughed and said that Rosemary had called to ask about me. He was at the office that day so he answered the telephone and she said, "Is that Ismail?" and he said, "Ismail hospital." She was surprised and said, "Hospital?" and he said, "Yes, operation." He asked me if he had made any mistakes in his English. When I laughed the area of the wound hurt because I shook so much. I got hold of myself and told him to stop it, as I wouldn't be able to laugh anymore. He laughed and said, "Let me depress you, then, and talk about Mansur." I tried to restrain my laughter. He added, "He and the monkey are going to visit you." He kissed me on the forehead and left.

I couldn't fight my thirst anymore. My throat and lips were very dry. Numan came into the room, and I asked him to moisten a piece of cotton, which I kept touching my lips with. I saw him stand, confused, above the head of the Saudi patient. Then he turned to me and asked, "Did he wake up from the anesthesia?"

"Yes, he did. He talked a lot but I didn't understand what he was saying."

He laughed and said, "Everyone here talks. I came to wake him up."

He left after removing the pillow from under the young man's head and placing it at his feet, saying, "Um Zaynab is a donkey." The young man opened his eyes and looked at me, then fall asleep again.

✧

The morning of the following day everything around me seemed brighter. I became more aware of how pale and thin I had become. I felt as if my body had become ether-like, as if it were something floating between the sky and the earth. I felt as if I were resting after a difficult journey or as if I had climbed a high mountain and sat on its shining peak, opening the pores of my body to the pure air. I thought how beautifully the day before had gone. Abed also visited for a few minutes, then Arshad came and sat in silence, looking at me in disbelief. The night-shift nurse told me that someone called Munzir had come to inquire after me, and, finding that I was asleep, didn't stay but left a package for me. I opened it and found a new *gallabiya*, a new big towel, and a bottle of Old Spice. I was overwhelmed; all those people came so quickly to see me and wish me well. Things must be different from the way they seemed to me.

Aida appeared at the door with a smile even brighter than that of the day before. Or was it that I felt better and was more receptive to what I saw?

"Today you may have something to drink."

She stood next to the bed preparing a glass of orange juice, which she offered to me saying, "Not all of it."

I drank as she looked on, smiling all the time. I placed the glass on the nightstand and asked her with a smile, "How come I didn't see you at the end of the day yesterday?"

"We had so many operations and I was so tired I went straight home."

"You seem to be smiling about something that you want to say."

"Not at all."

Then she smiled again and asked me, "Who's this Wadha whose name you kept repeating when you were under? Is she Egyptian? That's a Saudi name."

So, I had spilled the beans. I ignored her question and asked her, "Did I say any other names?"

She smiled and said, "Al-Beltagi, Kamil, . . . Aaron. It's the first time I've heard that word, is it a name?"

I nodded, smiling, as she continued, "And Philip, you repeated the name Philip a lot, more than all the other names, more than Wadha. Also, Sayyid al-Gharib, do you know him?"

I motioned her to sit on the chair next to the nightstand. She looked like an obedient student. I sighed and said, "I want to ask you about Philip."

"I don't know him."

"Philip Sousay Biliya, a tall black man with a strong face, a Sri Lankan who converted to Islam, came here for circumcision and died a few days ago."

She closed her eyes. Her face clouded over slightly then she smiled and said, "That happens a lot."

"I want the truth."

"It wasn't Dr. Wagih, anyway. It didn't happen during our shift. A novice Saudi surgeon. But it wasn't the surgeon's fault, anyway. It was the lab's fault. They mixed up another patient's blood sample with Philip's; the tests turned up okay, but Philip had very severe hypertension. The blood gushed out, there was no way to stop it . . . so he died."

So that was what happened, a minor mistake. But why did Wagih keep it a secret from me? Was it perhaps because the surgeon was Saudi? Aida mentioned that the lab technician was also Saudi. She asked me, "Why are you so interested in him?"

"He was my friend."

Suddenly the young man in the room with me started sobbing hard. Aida got up and went over to him.

"Why are you crying, Yasir? Does the wound hurt?"

Yasir, whose name I was hearing for the first time, said, "The wound is nothing, Miss Aida."

She sat on a chair next to his bed and said, smiling, "Do you want to go back to Mecca?"

"I want to see my mother."

She looked at me in surprise. True, Yasir seemed young, about twenty, but nobody would think that someone his age would cry to see his mother. She said, "You'll see her in a few days."

"My mother is here in Tabuk."

Once again she looked at me in surprise.

Yasir said, "I'm from Mecca but my mother is from Tabuk. I haven't seen her since I was born. My father divorced her and went to live in Mecca and took me and my sister with him. He never allowed us to see her or inquire after her and she never came to see us. I know she is from Tabuk, that her name is Salha, from the Khatham tribe. I want to see her."

He said that and started sobbing again. Aida seemed lost in thought for a few moments, then she said, "I will bring you your mother on condition that you stop crying."

He looked at her with wide, imploring eyes and said, "I will. Please bring her, for God's sake."

Then he stopped crying and immediately fell soundly asleep. Aida got up and came closer to me, saying, "Here a man marries more than one wife and the wives live without rancor. I've never heard of a man depriving his wife of her children. Sometimes a wife even rejoices when her husband marries a new wife, because he'll have to give her as much gold as he gives the new one."

"Are you really going to find his mother?"

"I will. We have a Saudi maid here named Wakhaba who knows everything and everyone in Tabuk. She'll find her."

She left and I watched the young man, who was sleeping as innocently as a little child.

✧

Footsteps hurrying in the corridor outside the room and women's laughter from a distance. I got up slowly, left the bed and pushed the door, to look at the crowd that had gathered at the far end of the corridor. I saw some male patients and a number of nurses. I saw Aida standing at the office door, motioning me to go back to my room. I went toward her.

"What's happened?

"Something stupid."

She went into her office angrily, I didn't know why. I was so curious I kept going in the corridor until I reached the crowd. Suddenly Dr. Wagih appeared and angrily yelled at the crowd to leave. No one remained standing except a female Pakistani doctor and I. Wagih saw me but didn't talk to me. He addressed the Pakistani in English, "What are you doing, Doctor?"

"There's no other way."

"That's not done. Not in a hospital!"

"The two of them requested it. Besides, it's my job."

He looked at her, extremely vexed, then left without looking at me. Then he suddenly stopped and turned around to the Pakistani doctor.

"This is a hospital, Doctor, not a police station," he said.

She didn't seem to care. The crowd of patients and nurses returned. The Pakistani doctor kept looking at them in a strangely idiotic manner.

I heard a noise inside the closed room: indistinct voices, meowing, howling, snorting, shrieking, insults, and hard breathing, then hurrying footsteps, things falling, then a long silence and tired breathing. Then the door was opened and a middle-aged Saudi man with torn clothes and angry eyes emerged. Behind him I could see a woman sitting on the bed covering herself with a white sheet, her hair disheveled, with tears in her eyes.

"This woman is crazy," the man shouted and went through the crowd as a knife would through butter. His *ghutra*, which had slipped to his shoulder, fell to the floor. He didn't bother to pick it up. The Pakistani doctor went into the room and closed the door. We heard the sound of prolonged, uninterrupted weeping. The crowd dispersed.

The story spread quickly in the hospital. Everybody learned that Dr. Sardar, the Pakistani doctor, had allowed a man to have intercourse with his wife in a room in the hospital. He had come to complain about his wife and how she didn't like him to be intimate with her. His wife was with him and she said it was he who couldn't, that she had come with him to help him see a doctor but he had deceived her and taken her to a gynecologist. Sardar calmed them down and sat a long time with them, speaking in halting Arabic about the psychological calm that was necessary before coitus. Suddenly the man swore that he was going to take his wife in that very room so the doctor would know he was all right. His wife challenged him to do it; Sardar closed the door.

✧

"How can that happen?" I asked Aida, who had come in to give me an ampicillin tablet. Without looking at me she said, "It's a crazy world."

A dark black, short, fat woman appeared at the door. Aida said, "Hey, Wakhaba, did you find her?"

"She's here with me."

She stepped inside and another woman, also short and fat, entered. She had a lot of gold on her wrists, her fingers, and her chest. Her face was covered with layers of black silk. Aida asked her, "Are you Salha?"

"Yes."

"This is your son, Yasir."

The woman didn't say anything. She went forward; Wakhaba had backed away from the door. I looked at Aida, whose eyes were welling up with tears. I expected a stormy, tearful, scene.

The woman sat on a chair next to the head of her son's bed. Aida went over to wake him up. Yasir opened his eyes and looked at the seated woman. Aida said in a choked voice, "This is your mother, Yasir."

Yasir quickly sat up and leaned back in the bed and said in a soft voice, "Mother."

The woman said loudly, "How are you, Yasir, and how's your sister, Hissa?"

She didn't lift the multi-layered veil. Yasir whispered, "Fine."

"How's the old man?"

"Fine."

"You live in Mecca?"

"We still do."

"God be with you."

She got up and left. Aida looked at me and I looked at her then looked at Yasir.

He shrugged his shoulders and said, "My mother's gone crazy."

Then he fell silent and didn't look at anybody.

✧

It wasn't difficult to kill time. A car came the following day and took Yasir to Mecca. There were always one or two other patients with me in the room, but no contact or conversation. Wagih had turned my room into an observation room where a patient would spend a little time before he was discharged or moved to another hospital room. He turned the original observation room into a long reception area. He did this out of concern for my comfort, he said. I made it my full time pursuit to snoop around and find out what was happening. The day after Dr. Sardar's incident, the police came to investigate a claim by a Bedouin that he had brought his little sick daughter to Pediatrics and that the Egyptian nurse had kidnapped her. I saw the nurse standing in the hall surrounded by three policemen, one of whom was an officer. She looked very frightened. Aida and a few nurses were smiling and laughing. The accused nurse said that the man's daughter was there, that she was the one holding her hand. The man denied that this was his daughter. She was a three-year-old girl of dark complexion, with rich hair and wide, hazel eyes, wearing a pink dress with a hem bordered with ruffled green lace. On each side of her head were bows of red silk. She was really a beautiful doll, an effect enhanced by the fact that she was totally silent. The nurse said that she had merely seen a beautiful girl in dirty clothes and taken her to the nurse's residence, where she had given her a bath, cut her fingernails, combed and perfumed her hair, and given her this nice dress to wear. The man was still swearing that the girl was not his daughter, that he would never give up on her, and would insist that the Egyptian nurse go to jail. Suddenly the nurse's eyes seemed to lose focus and it appeared that she was no longer aware of her surroundings. Then she began to let out long shrieking sounds. The officer and two policemen appeared terrified. The nurse backed off, still making the same shrieking noise. Aida and the other nurses hurried to prevent the nurse from falling to the floor and were able to get her inside the nurses' room nearby and close the door. We heard a noise and continued crying and suddenly, in an extremely bitter and sarcastic tone, she was singing, "I loved you, I love you, and I will love you forever." The officer looked very confused. He ordered the man to take his daughter and go. "Who says this is my daughter?" "I do," the officer yelled at him. "I am going to the king." "Go to the devil." The man carried his daughter and left hurriedly and angrily. The officer and two policemen left even faster.

✧

I lay down on my bed unable to restrain my laughter. I laughed alone in the room, audibly. Aida looked in on me laughing, then said, "Of course you must find this all very strange."

I kept laughing, then realized it was no longer appropriate, so I stopped and looked at the delightful face. She must have felt that a sense of repose had come over my body and soul as I felt my eyes gleaming and my face at ease, for she lowered her long lashes and spoke.

"The nurse who was screaming is called Warda. She only started here six months ago. She was at the Diba clinic before that, where they didn't have housing for single nurses. Only married nurses usually went there. But that's where Warda's appointment was. The doctors and nurses left the clinic every day at two o'clock and went home. All the doctors and nurses were married. All, that is, except Warda, who had to stay in the clinic itself. She slept in a room on the roof. It was a big clinic with more than ten rooms on the first floor. She had to spend the time between two in the afternoon until the following morning by herself, every day. You can imagine the ideas that can rob one of one's reason in a faraway, empty place. Warda suffered a severe nervous breakdown and was transferred here."

Aida laughed, saying that Warda was now living in the nurses' residence, and that she often laughed uncontrollably. She remembered how she used to kill time by singing on the roof. She sang to the sky and to the air and ran and jumped, then suddenly slapped her own cheeks. At night she cowered in the farthest corner of her room and sobbed. "At present, after midday, Warda's mind wanders away then comes back and she starts to sing the way you heard her; we call it the 'Diba syndrome.'" "I thought she was afraid of the officers," I said and couldn't help laughing. Aida also laughed loudly. Whenever our eyes met we laughed, but it wasn't possible to laugh all the time.

✧

I was awakened by frantic screaming. Normally I woke up every morning to the chirping of birds I couldn't see, and Aida's delightful face. Now I left my bed in panic. I went out of the room looking for the source of the screaming, which was coming from the corridor that was at a right angle to my room and which led to the women's ward.

Two policemen were grabbing at a little woman who was trying to get away from them as they pulled her harshly and angrily. She was a blonde, with very long hair that covered her face, her chest, and her shoulders, reaching half way down her back. They brought her closer and I could see her green eyes and red face, bearing the marks of earlier slapping. She would fall to the floor and they would lift her as she tried to cling to their legs. Women patients stood crying at the doors of their rooms, and nurses from various departments sobbed.

Warda came quickly, carrying a little black baby who she took to the nurses' room, where I soon realized Aida was standing next to me. There was a young Egyptian doctor standing behind the woman and the two policemen, removing his glasses and wiping his eyes. He took a step every time the two policemen took a step with the woman. They were able to drag the little woman forcefully and she no longer fell to the floor. She let herself be dragged along. And as each held her by one arm, the brown robe opened, revealing a green dress with white and orange flowers, and a dazzling neck and neckline. They descended the stairs with her, followed by the physician.

Aida went into her room. I found myself going in after her. I saw Warda sitting, holding the baby to her bosom, patting him on the back and crying. Aida, who sat behind the desk, with her head in her hands, was also crying. Before I said anything the woman who had been dragged by the policemen came into the room in a frenzy. She snatched the baby from

Warda, who didn't try to stop her. Then the woman sat on the floor, quickly pulled the collar of her dress and uncovered her breast, and placed the nipple in the black baby's mouth. She kept looking at me with terrified glistening eyes.

Then the two policemen appeared like demons. The young Egyptian doctor caught up with them and shouted, "Leave her alone."

They were just about to pounce on the woman but they stopped and looked askance at him.

"Go downstairs," he said. "I will bring her to you. It's my responsibility."

They looked at him sharply then started to move, stamping the floor. The doctor looked at me then collapsed into a nearby chair for a moment then raised his head to look at the woman, who was holding the baby close to her bosom as if she wanted to hide him there and cover him with the robe so we wouldn't see him.

She lifted her face to look at us. Her tears poured down as she looked at the young doctor.

"Give her something to drink, Warda," the doctor said. Warda opened a small refrigerator, from which she took a pitcher of orange juice and offered a glass to the woman, who took it and gulped it down. It seemed she was not the only one drinking. She quickly set the glass down beside her on the floor and bent over the baby to feed him. When the baby was full she covered her little breast again and fell back to lean against the wall, as if resting forever.

"I've told you, sister, it's no use. I've let you come back to see your son five times already."

The beautiful little woman leaned her head back, lifting her eyes to us, and said tearfully, "My chest is killing me, Doctor. Look at the gown."

I also looked and saw the traces of milk on her chest. Warda's sobbing got louder as she stood in a corner, her face to the wall. Aida kept wiping her eyes with a small handkerchief. The beautiful little woman spoke again in a heartrending voice, "My chest, Doctor. Whenever I went away, it ached with yearning and milk flowed."

She fell silent, letting her tears speak. The young doctor took off his glasses and dried his tears with a tissue. Then he looked at his watch and seemed to be getting a grip on himself. He told her, "I have taken your address and Nurse Warda and Nurse Aida also have it, and I promise you I will send you the name of the family that will take him. Be assured that one day you'll be able to come back to the Kingdom and see your son again. We would never let a family take him without knowing their address."

He got up calmly and extended his hand to her. She got up with the baby close to her bosom then, as if in a daze, gave him to Warda who held out her arms and took him. The woman kept looking at Warda—at Warda, not the baby. Did she want to make sure that the one who took him from her was a human being?

✧

I didn't want to know the story. When they brought down the lifeless body of Abdallah ibn al-Zubayr and placed him on the lap of his mother Asmaa, who was close to a hundred years old, she bent over to kiss him. It was said that she started to menstruate and milk flowed from her breast.

I didn't leave my room nor did I eat until the evening, when Aida came in followed by the Egyptian maid, Um Zaynab, carrying the food.

"I forgot to bring it to you at lunch time. You can't spend the whole day without food."

"I've never seen a mother in such anguish."

"You've never seen a mother being separated from her son to the end of time."

"Isn't she coming back?"

"Impossible. Women in her situation are placed on the blacklist."

"But the baby is not a newborn?"

"She spent a year in jail feeding him. In such cases the woman doesn't leave her baby until it is one year old. Poor Dr. Ahmad! He arrived here only a week ago and they gave him the assignment of accompanying her to the airport. It's a merciful measure, they let a doctor keep the woman company so she doesn't harm herself, or die, or commit suicide. Death would be more merciful. Can you imagine that for a whole year she's refused to tell the police who the baby's father is?"

The picture was now clear, a girl seduced by a local man. Why didn't she reveal his name? Did she hope to take her son? They left her in jail for a year to nurse him. The state had to take custody of a healthy baby.The mother couldn't prevent the year from passing. How many fantastical hopes the poor woman must have hung on to! Perhaps she thought that God might end this world all of a sudden and she would make it to the other world with her baby in her bosom.

Aida said that the woman was Lebanese, that her family lived in Tabuk but that they had disowned her. They didn't want to go back to Lebanon. Where would they go when the war was everywhere?

"She's left us her address. But . . ."

We were silent for a long time. The food sat there between the two of us, untouched by me. I said, "It's a beautiful baby!"

"Abdallah?"

I said, "I don't know his name."

She said they gave him that name. All illegitimate babies were placed in pediatrics wards in hospitals until a family or an emir adopted them or until they were transferred to an orphanage in Riyadh, but she and her fellow nurses liked to take the babies to their residence. The worst day was when the baby was adopted by someone. It usually didn't happen until they had all gotten used to the baby and it had gotten used to them. It would have more than one mother crying over the separation and it would cry for all those mothers.

16

It was as if I had entered through a door leading to a hell with no exit. I couldn't stay any longer even though I had caught myself anticipating Aida's joyous entry into my room in the morning. I had forgotten the world outside. Nobody had come to visit me again. I no longer remembered whether I knew anyone here.

I no longer knew anything except hurrying footsteps carrying plasma bags to save an injured person, nurses crying over those who died and who could have been saved if only this or that had been done, doctors shouting at the patients not to leave their beds, or to leave them and walk so the blood in the their legs would not clot. I knew only of the ululating sounds of joy coming from Obstetrics where a young woman had given birth to her first baby after three days of labor, pain, and waiting on the part of her family. I could see the joy in the eyes of the lonely, young foreign man as the nurses got busy, getting, at their own expense, clothes for his baby boy and gifts and hot food for the young mother. I only knew a screaming that sounded as if it were coming from a long-forgotten bygone era, from a man confined in a basement room awaiting transfer to the mental asylum in Taif in a few days. I could always hear the gurneys scurrying in the corridor, with

Numan the orderly yelling at poor tired Um Zaynab. Here was a Saudi servant who had his own servant from a distant land. My room was close to the burns unit, where the nights turned spooky with the screams of the patients tied down and swathed in cotton and gauze, dying for a drop of water. I only knew that cars were accidents waiting to happen: boulders from mountaintops suddenly falling on them or the cars themselves falling off the mountain or pushed by fate to Qaliba where cars overturned. Qaliba was an old village with an old name: how did camels overturn? From which country did I come and which town? Leaden ants were crawling over my memory, though I had spent only a few days here. Aida's delightful, joyous face was no longer enough in the midst of this hell of screams and laughter and death holding on to life. How come the doctors didn't die and the nurses didn't commit suicide? What devilish power did God give humans, that ultimately they seemed stronger than rocks?

Khalid visited me and looked as though I had known him earlier in a dark well. I could barely recognize his face or even remember his name. "Wadha says hello," he said and I thought of asking who Wadha was. He was very nice. He said he had found out from Said that I was sick and told Wadha in Riyadh. She was very alarmed and sent her greetings. "What greetings?" I was about to say. He said, "Wadha is coming back in two days." I didn't tell him that I was getting discharged from the hospital in two days. That was what Wagih had decided, even though I begged him to let me out earlier. A long silence fell upon our meeting. I suddenly became aware of his delicate face. Had it not been for his moustache, the black *uqal* and the *ghutra*, he would have looked exactly like Wadha. So, I still remembered the face of someone I knew! He left, wishing me a speedy recovery. I didn't speak. I was waiting for the last night in the hospital, though I still caught myself anticipating Aida's joyous entry. That day Aida started working nights.

✧

By midnight I had a desperate need to talk. Everything was quiet and I could only hear faint sounds of breathing. Lights were dim. I was alone in the room, unable to sleep even though I was leaving the hospital in the morning. I left the room and stood in the dimly lit corridor in front of the door of Aida's room. I hesitated to knock. I had a desperate need to talk with her. That was the only reason I left my room, though I didn't know what I was going to talk with her about. I heard the voice of Nagaat al-Ṣaghira singing softly and the sound of someone sobbing. At the very moment I thought of going back the door opened and she stood there looking at me in total surprise.

"I am sorry, very sorry."

"No need to be. I heard your footsteps and was startled. Please come in."

I went in, embarrassed. She sat behind the desk.

"I didn't mean anything."

"I know. Please sit down."

I sat down. I was about to tell her that I had heard her sobbing quietly and could still see the traces of tears in her eyes, but she stood up and said, "I am going to make you a cup of tea. It's cold, and I want some too."

She went to a small cupboard and took out an electric hot plate on which she placed the teapot. As she moved she appeared very small. I said what I didn't want to say:

"Is it all right if I ask you why you were crying?"

"You just did."

She answered with a smile. We both fell silent. She went about making the tea then gave me a glass and took one herself, and once again sat behind the desk.

"Sometimes one feels like crying."

I thought perhaps it was Nagaat's song coming over the small radio on the desk that made her cry. That easily happened to the homesick.

"I hope I haven't imposed on your feelings."

"On the contrary."

"Aren't you happy here?"

"I'm extremely happy, otherwise I wouldn't have stayed. I've gotten used to the job and in the nurses' residence we have lots of fun. We live like one happy family. Of course we've got problems like everybody else: there's a woman whose fiancé swindled her out of her money, a woman whose family refuses any suitor so that she can continue to lay golden eggs for them, a woman who married and left her husband behind to come to work here and when she returned on vacation she found that he had married another woman in the very apartment that she herself had furnished. And there are women who have decided against marriage altogether."

"Really? To that extent?"

"There are smart women who have bought apartment buildings and land, and some who have found happiness in marriage. Anyway, together we have a good life, an easy life, at the residence."

We fell silent for a while. Nagaat had finished her song and Abd al-Wahab's beautiful voice filled the night with a sweet taste.

"Do you like Abd al-Wahab?" she asked me with a smile.

I said, "Is there anybody who doesn't?"

We fell silent.

We didn't embrace when love enticed us
Our hearts and souls embraced many times.

"It's a beautiful poem. Aziz Abaza wrote it for his wife."

She smiled and said, "I'm afraid to tell you that I like the songs of Abd al-Halim Hafiz too, in case you make fun of me."

"Why? I like Abd al-Halim as well."

We were silent again, until I found myself asking, "Which one of the women you told me about are you, Aida?"

It was the first time I had addressed her by name. The question was a surprise to me. My unconscious was always ahead of me, revealing that which I wanted concealed.

"Me?"

She didn't say anything else. I looked at her eyes until she blinked, then she said, "Let's drop the subject."

But she didn't.

"Medicine is a horrible profession. It turns you into a cold instrument. If it didn't, you'd break and be no good. I've seen people here turn into poor animals that scream like beasts from the even more beastly pain. I've seen people who are worthless, idiotic corpses. I endured all that for the sake of my brothers, who are happy now. All my happy brothers objected to my going to nursing school, all except Hashim, my immediate elder brother. He was a law student and a source of constant joy at home. He was always an optimist, always smiling. He believed that everything changed with time, even ancient ideas. But he was also a source of constant worry for the family. He took part in demonstrations at the university, and the secret police came many times at night to arrest him. He always came out of jail more joyful and optimistic. His body was so small that nobody could figure out where he got the strength to endure jail. Hashim graduated from the university in 1973, and in 1974 during Nixon's visit to Egypt, when they paid people to stand along the railroad tracks to greet Nixon and Sadat on their way to Alexandria, he couldn't stay in Damanhur, our hometown, so he went to Alexandria to stay with some friends there from his school days. He was hit by a car and they brought him to the government hospital where I worked after I graduated. That day I was working in Emergency and I looked after him."

A tear fell from her eye, then the tears flowed. She got some tissues from one of the drawers and dried her eyes.

"I am very sorry."

"Can you imagine, he's the only one who writes to me."

"So he's alive."

"Yes, but he can't move. He lives with my elderly parents and a maid."

"So that's why you're here," I said to myself. What unbearable pain! Had Aida been a man it would have been different. A remarkably beautiful woman. I found myself patting her on the hand and saying, "Did I upset you?"

"No, you haven't upset me."

Abd al-Wahab's song was over and I heard the announcer say, "The One O'Clock News Summary, from Cairo." He said things about Begin and Carter and Sadat that I didn't understand or care about. I changed stations and the voice of Abd al-Halim Hafiz flowed beautifully and warmly:

O gold flowing between two banks, beautiful and brown,
Without your brown color in the eye it wouldn't be bright.

O sweet brown one,
O sweet brown one,
O sweet brown one.

I smiled and I saw her smile and her eyes brighten up with dazzling brilliance.

17

I was discharged from the hospital on the last day of December. I left Wagih in the hospital and didn't find Said at home. There was nothing I needed more than sleep. I had left Aida's room just before dawn. I described my situation to her and told her that I had recently discovered that I was the victim of a plot hatched by my father, a plot in which I acquiesced—out of unparalleled moral stupidity. It had erected a dam between women and me. I told her that I was seriously contemplating marriage. We bowed our heads in silence for a long time and then I saw her glance at her wristwatch and that brought me back to reality. She is a female and I am a male, in a country where the very air reports tender feelings to the police. I got up with the feeling that she hadn't told me everything. Even angels had things to hide. We both had things to hide, things we couldn't say, but whenever I looked at her face I felt close to her and wished I could rest my head on her bosom. I didn't tell her that it was I who bungled the love stories. And even though I had made it to the land that the original Sindbad had ignored but that was now the destination of thousands of Sindbads every morning, the land from which one returned to find all windows, doors, and paths wide open, I still felt the ice of my heart on fire. All

I had done with Wadha, everything I felt when I visited her was a lie. I lied when I said that I wanted to get married now. My old wound had still not healed. I still wished I could get out of my very self and punish it, kill it. She had asked me, "Why do you keep reading Naguib Mahfouz's *Khan al-Khalili* over and over again?" I said I loved Ahmad Akif. She said, laughing, "I don't know anybody by that name." I said, "Here, take it." She came back, laughing and saying, "Which one is Ahmad Akif in the novel?" We laughed and fell silent. I said I wanted to go to the Antoniadis Gardens. It was spring and they had a festival of flowers. She said, "I didn't know you liked flowers. You are in love with love and you want to go because it was there that we first declared our love, on our first day." Her white face lit up and her hazel eyes engulfed me, and we started on our way. The plants around us in the college were greener than any other day; the air was clearer and the sky higher than any other day; the orange roof tiles of the college were brighter than any other day. She said as we passed through the gate, "I've often wondered, why is it that you understand logic better than any of us?" I told her I just studied more. She said I was lying and I was.

We were now in front of Chatby Maternity Hospital with its vast exterior and extensive grounds and the whiteness of everything about it, which blended with the white, wide open space. She saw my eyes lingering on the hospital so she nudged my arm saying, "Do you know anyone giving birth today?" I said it was the best possible location for a maternity hospital because of the vast sea in front of it. She said, "You say the strangest things." I hailed a cab and we got out at the zoo, in silence. We walked slowly, moving closer to each other then farther apart. I don't remember what we talked about. We came upon the gate to the Antoniadis Gardens, which had a sign on top saying 'Public Not Permitted.' Why? The policeman said, "The Army has taken it over. It's a military post." Before that, they had taken the beautiful promontory of Silsila and left the statue of the Alexandria Mermaid all by itself, without lovers to keep it company. The policeman smiled without understanding. She said, "The zoo is bigger." I asked her, "Why didn't you read the novel carefully?" We were silent again then she asked me why I hadn't given her the stories I wrote to read. I said I didn't think I would continue writing. "Why? Why are you giving up all the beautiful things in your life? Why this closing of the windows?" I stopped trying to explain, but we wrote letters to each other and kept seeing each other. It was evening, that last minute we had together at the college with the beautiful garden. We walked on the lawn up to the garden of the College of Commerce. The mute devil told me that candor was better than deception, so I was candid with her and told her that for me love meant marriage and I wasn't going to get married now or ever. We walked in silence and at Raml Station we saw Saad Zaghlul with his back turned to the city, pointing to the sea, to someone drowning. She jumped up and kissed me on the cheek, and everybody in the square saw us, and she hurried away. I didn't go that Sunday nor any Sunday after. I was never in love with her; I was in love with love, as she said. The woman who didn't read stories had seen me for the fool I was, completing the mission of a man who made it past the age of sixty-five but didn't finish the job.

"Life is a tragedy and the world is a boring stage. The play is tragic but, curiously enough, the actors are clowns. The message, strangely, is sad not because it is sad in itself but because, meant to be taken seriously to the extreme, it produces a totally farcical effect. And, because for the most part we cannot laugh at the thwarting of our hopes, we cry and the tears blind us to the truth: we think the play is a tragedy when in fact it is a farce."

So said Hamlet, and Naguib Mahfouz, and poor Ahmad Akif, who read all the classics of Arabic belles lettres but didn't become a writer or find a beloved. How did it come to end in madness and death? The letters kept coming, in red ink, green ink, blue ink, and black ink. Why didn't I pay any attention? It was the fifth of June, a day that no Egyptian would forget. "People might forget it if we have a victory but I, alone among a whole people, will remember it." I found out about her death only a few days before I came to this place. I went to the college to get a copy of my diploma and I met Samya, our friend who knew everything about us. She had come like me to get a copy of her diploma to go to the Emirates. Samya told me and I hurriedly left the country. She had never shown any sign of losing her mind, let alone her life. Who would release me from my death now? Who would burn my secrets? Wadha or Aida? Or am I the death of everyone? How I longed for sleep.

✧

"I knew you were here," Said said as he came in carrying a cardboard box, which he took into the living room and placed on the table. He stood, panting, and said, "We will celebrate your homecoming and the new year."

It was three o'clock in the afternoon. I had slept soundly. He opened the box and brought out the things and put them on the table as he spoke.

"Feta cheese, Egyptian olives from Siwa. Ha ha ha. These presidents are very peculiar: one of them called them 'liberty olives' and the next called them 'the crossing olives.' Fava beans from Qaha, Bulgarian eggs. Look at the size of these eggs, each as big as an Egyptian chicken. In Bulgaria when they want to call someone a coward they say he's as cowardly as an egg. Ha ha ha."

He kept emptying the contents of the box, speaking and laughing the whole time. He looked very strange to me. I realized for the first time that he was shorter than I thought he was. He moved like a rubber ball.

"And we have Romano cheese from Italy, the genuine article; cheddar cheese from Australia. Look at the box, it's pressed down like the aborigines, who must be as extinct as the American Indians. They're all gone. Nothing endures but God. And here is the most important item: twenty bottles of alcohol-free beer, Moussey, made in Europe. The Europeans are con artists who bamboozle the Arabs. Our celebration of your homecoming and the new year is going to be splendid beyond your dreams."

I looked at his eyes for a long time and said, "Something happen to your head today?"

"You want the truth?"

"Yes."

"I met Widad."

"Is that the first time?"

"Of course not. But today I met her and I kissed her. I kissed her, here in the kingdom that lies to the west of Asia, overlooks the Red Sea, the Indian Ocean, and the Arabian Gulf, the kingdom that houses the *qibla* that Muslims from all over the world face when they perform their prayers and from which all the jinn and the demons have fled on account of the heat and the cold."

He began to laugh and clap and jump up in the room. I couldn't help laughing. Suddenly he stopped and said, very seriously, "Man, I didn't know deprivation could be so terrible."

✧

After lunch I stayed alone in my room. I was surprised to hear Said snoring for the first time. I smiled as I recalled his behavior before lunch. Said must have been pulling my leg; there was nothing easier than kissing a woman here. Widad was his fiancée and lived with her mother. He visited them and the mother must have given them the opportunity for that and more. Yes, and more. One kiss could not produce all this madness. I thought of going to Wadha. She must have returned from Riyadh.

At six o'clock Said was still sleeping. I also had slept again and woken up. Wagih must have come back while we were asleep and ate and slept. All this sleeping took place in our house during the day.

I drove my car, which did not let me down despite being idle for a whole week. I drove it through the alleys around the main street, avoiding the potholes that might affect the wound; the stitches had been removed only that morning. I found the policeman standing in the middle of the street, preventing me from continuing. My God, I had forgotten, and here I was, once again, in front of the house where Sayyid al-Gharib was under house arrest. The policeman ordered me to turn around. So, they had closed the street to traffic. I saw al-Gharib sitting on the balcony wearing a black *abaya*, with a dimly lit lamp above his head. But I saw his face clearly; I didn't know whether he saw mine or not. I had stopped in the dark.

I turned away from the house and kept going, suddenly hoping not to find Wadha at home, not to finish the lesson with her today either. But it was she who let me in. Her eyes grew wide with joy and she didn't speak. She took my hand in her hands and pulled me to enter, oblivious to my wound and to my inability to move suddenly. But I walked, and I felt strength coming to my body. When I entered the room she wasn't with me.

I waited a long time. Every moment I expected someone to enter the room, Khalid or her disabled grandfather, or her mother or father, or any of her brothers who I hadn't seen. My heart didn't stop pounding until I saw her. She had changed her clothes and came back wearing a long, dark blue dress with white flowers, and on her shoulders was a white shawl, her hair cascading down her shoulders and back. On her wrists were two bracelets of gold inlaid with rubies and on her chest was a golden rose pendant with rubies on the rose petals too. All this was preceded by her perfume. I found myself standing up and holding out my hand. She extended both her hands and I took them, then she came close to me, then turned to her chair. I let go of her hands and she sat down and I sat across from her, looking at her face and eyes. She had gotten a little pale in Riyadh.

"I was afraid you wouldn't come."

"Having your appendix out is not that serious."

"You shouldn't drink the city water."

"I was told about that but I don't like mineral water."

"I'll send you large quantities of it."

"I really don't like it. Besides, a person can have only one appendix."

She smiled and said, "I couldn't come to visit you."

"Shall we start the lesson?" I asked stupidly and without meaning to, with my usual foolishness. She bowed her head in silence then raised it, saying, calmly and in pain, "Why do you think so little of me?"

She burst into tears.

"Wadha," I whispered.

"I sent you a letter from Riyadh. Haven't you read it?"

"I haven't been back to work yet."

Tears kept flowing down her cheeks. I brought my chair closer to her. I placed my left arm around her shoulders and with my right hand lifted her head toward me. She rested her head on my chest and wept. I could hear her breathing and her heart and I could smell her mysterious perfume, drowning my face in her soft rich hair.

"Wadha," I whispered, and she raised her face to me. Her eyes grew wide with a light I had seen once before, her lips quivered with a desire that I had seen once before. I looked involuntarily toward the door and she whispered, "Don't be afraid." It was she who said that and nobody else, Wadha, in my arms now. I reached my right hand to her left armpit and felt her breast small in my hand. She was as light as a dove as I brought her to her feet and stood up. Had she grown taller or did I perhaps stoop? She was in my arms, my mouth on her mouth, pressing as hard as I could, eating her lips with my lips, my teeth hitting her teeth. The moment our faces drew apart to catch my breath I saw joy almost jumping out of her eyes. Once again I held her close to my chest as my lips kept squeezing her moist lips. I felt her lips moving with my lips and between them and around them. She was not just yielding herself to me; she was kissing me. I forgot about the open door and about death hanging over our heads. At the moment it seemed she had melted and dissolved, I saw on her face the likeness of another face, Aida's. I moved my head back and looked at her, her eyes now closed. I kissed her again bringing her feet down to the floor. I felt pain in the wound and thought about my boldness and the consequences of what I was doing in a country where the very air reported things. I stood up with difficulty. The wound was really painful, even though I was helping her to stand up. She opened her eyes and seemed to emerge from a distant dream.

"Don't go. Don't make me feel guilty."

"Sit down, Wadha."

"You sit down first."

We both sat down on our chairs. We bowed our heads in silence. I didn't know what she was thinking about, but I knew what I was thinking about.

Aida had stopped me cold by saying as we were talking that she would not think of marriage before Hashim recovered and could walk, even if that cost her twenty years of work here. There she was, her face looking in on me.

"Will you take me with you to Egypt?"

"I will take you, Wadha, and no one else."

She got up and took my head in her chest and kissed it, then, like a proud princess, said, "You may go. I don't need a lesson today."

✧

My body is alive and is not just something I inhabit. Alive. Alive. Alive. I opened the car window despite the cold. I longed for gardens of roses. My senses were all awakened and they wanted to be satisfied. It wasn't fair to shut down the senses, but I couldn't dance into the house naked. I had to hide everything from Said and Wagih and come back as I had left, a weary soul in a sick body waiting for recovery. Said had lied to me. He hadn't kissed Widad, he hadn't gotten anywhere with her.

How wonderful to keep your love secret, savoring the pleasure and reliving the joy, rising higher and higher while people around you are naive idiots!

I went back home and found Said and Wagih standing in the living room with Salih, the landlord's son. "Hello, Ustaz. Why have you stopped visiting us?" He talked to me but it wasn't easy to bring me back down to earth. They had removed the table from the room to the hall and placed cushions around the now big room. Next to the television they had put a VCR with videocassettes on it.

"We've borrowed the VCR from Salih for tonight only."

"No problem, Doctor. Keep it until you're tired of it." He took his leave.

"Sit down," Said said to me.

"Let me change," I said and went to my room, where I changed my clothes and returned lighter than I had been. They had placed the Moussey beer all over the room and Wagih was sitting with a small white bottle in one hand and a dropper in the other.

"Alcohol from the hospital. I'll put a drop in each bottle and let's see who can handle it," Wagih said.

Said went out to the kitchen and came back carrying a tray with three roast chickens and large pieces of kebab.

"When did you cook that?"

"Wagih bought it. We agreed to buy everything tonight. Tonight we splurge." He laughed. I had never celebrated new year's eve before. I just stayed home and watched television. Said and Wagih were behaving like two country bumpkins visiting the city for the first time.

"Choose us a film to start with."

I picked up the four films: *Doctor Zhivago, Frankenstein,* Bruce Lee's *Fist of Fury,* and *Some Like It Hot.* What a strange mix! Anyway, none of the films was pornographic. We started with Marilyn Monroe. We sat down drinking and eating as the VCR ran without any of us looking at it. That drop of alcohol did a real job on us. Wagih said, "Eat a lot and you won't get drunk." Said said, "Damn you," and recited:

Cry not for Layla and delight not in Hind.
Drink wine that's red like a rose.

We laughed and Wagih said, "But this is yellow." And we laughed even more. Said recited again:

O Friends from Bani Makhzoum,
Cure with me the daughter of the vine.

We laughed and Wagih said, "But this is the daughter of barley." Said said, "Daughter of a dog," and our laughter grew more boisterous. I told them to listen to me. Their eyes grew wide with anticipation.

I do not know why they call wine spirits.
Is it because it is light and aromatic?
Or because it lifts its drinker's spirits?

The house must have shaken to its foundations from our shrieks of laughter. Said asked me how I knew the verses and I told him that I knew many things. He asked why I had been hiding it from them and invited me to a contest, but I just stared at him. Suddenly he cried out and pointed at the food saying we had to keep the donkey away. "What donkey? I don't see anybody but you in front of me," Wagih said and I laughed, but Said continued to cry. He got up in fright and moved away toward the wall saying the donkey had put its head in the food and that we must take it away. He kept repeating that. Then we heard quick, hard knocks that almost broke down the outside door. I got up and in the courtyard I laughed and opened my mouth to drink in the cold air. As soon as I opened the outside door they pushed me aside and rushed into the room: three policemen like devils with shining brass buttons. Their huge boots hit the floor like blocks of basalt falling one after the other. A cold blast came in with them to the courtyard and to my soul. A young officer came in after them and said, "Carry everything as it is." I saw their guns clearly. One of them pulled the bedsheet and put everything in it and when his foot hit the alcohol bottle and spilled its contents, I saw Wagih heave a sigh of relief.

They took us in our house clothes in the Jeep, which sped off in the silence of the cold night. Then they took us to a room without furniture in the police station: around us the cold walls and under our feet the icy floor, with nothing except Said's crying for a long time in fear of the donkey's head that kept appearing to him.

In the morning they took us to the officer in charge, a high ranking officer who smiled to Wagih and said, "Hello, Doctor. How was your night?"

Wagih smiled and said, "Ask your student who put us in jail, Abu Hakim."

"I owe you one, Doctor."

Then he motioned the young officer who arrested us to leave and he ordered coffee for us and kept leafing through papers in front of him. An elderly man came in with a coffeepot and a cup and started serving us. Wagih and Said drank twice but I didn't. I couldn't stand the bitter Arabian coffee. Suddenly Abu Hakim shouted, "What's that? Salih ibn Sanyur al-Thaqifi? He's nuts."

We looked at each other. We gathered that Salih had informed the police that we were drinking and making too much noise and disturbing the neighbors. Abu Hakim continued, "He's nuts through and through. Aren't you living in their house, Doctor?"

"We are."

"Why the hostility then?"

"I don't know, Abu Hakim."

Abu Hakim laughed and held the little dropper. "What's that for, Doctor? You drop alcohol into the beer?"

"This is for my eyes, Abu Hakim."

"You put booze in your eyes?"

He laughed. We didn't. He began to change the subject.

"You know me and you know how I choose my friends, Abu Hakim."

"I know you are the pride of the Egyptians. I am going to let you go. The problem, however, is that that lieutenant boy notified the director of this one's school," he said, pointing at Said. "And the director telephoned us demanding that he be deported."

He fell silent for a while then said to Said, "I am very sorry, Ustaz, but that's what happened."

18

I missed my work and there I was driving my car fast and opening the car's windows to the cold morning air to clear the fogged up windows. I cut short my leave and went. It was no longer possible to stay at home for a long time. We had gone back home in silence. Wagih left us and went to the hospital before the news spread. He said his going there first would make a difference. Said entered the house resignedly. He changed his clothes and when I asked him where he was going he said, "To the school. Do you think they'd deport me while I'm here at home?" I took a hot shower after that cold night and saw the wound. It was red and the scar looked like the footprints of a scorpion on my skin. I put a new bandage on it and went to sleep. Said woke me up at three in the afternoon. It was as if I were seeing him for the first time. Said was being deported and I would forget him forever.

As we sat eating lunch slowly Said said, "I knew some calamity was waiting for me."

"But you were happy yesterday."

"I was lying. I didn't kiss Widad. I only met her. We've been having problems for a few months."

I said nothing.

"She has a cousin who worked as an accountant in Egypt who's been after her for a long time. He went to Kuwait and managed to get a better job contract. She wants to go."

"But she was going back with you this year and you were going to get married. You told me that yourself."

"Yes, I did, and we'd agreed, but what do you expect should happen to somebody whose family ate up half his wealth and crooks the other half?"

He got up, carrying the dishes, not realizing I hadn't finished eating. I got up and helped him with them. As soon as I went into my room I changed my clothes and then went out and drove my car fast, paying no attention to my wound or the potholes in the alleys. What vicious motive made Salih complain about us? How did he convince the police to raid our house? I arrived at his house and knocked several times on the door.

"Who's there?" replied the feeble voice of an old woman from behind the door.

"This is Ismail. Where is Salih?"

"Salih who?"

"Al-Thaqifi."

"Nobody here by that name."

"Salih, the student in the middle school whose family has a business on the main street . . ."

"Nobody here by that name. Go away."

I heard the feeble footsteps moving away. I looked around to the right, and to the left, and behind. This was the house. This was not an enchanted city where everything you saw disappeared. I drove my car again to the main street.

"What can I do for you, Ustaz?" he said very calmly, as I went into his store. He was standing there selling blankets and fabrics. I stood there eyeing him angrily. He didn't wait for my reply.

"You want a tiger-skin blanket. We have tiger skins that the Egyptians like very much. You are Egyptian, Ustaz, aren't you? It seems you're new in Tabuk."

As he talked he kept looking at two boys who I had seen at his house before. They were smiling and seemed to be enjoying themselves. "You don't want anything? Well then please make room for someone else. Would you like something cold to drink?"

I realized the foolishness of what I was doing. This boy, who wasn't quite twenty yet, had mocked me twice and there was no possible revenge. I returned home slowly. I went into the room and looked at the wall calendar. It was the first of January, 1979. If only this day and night would end so I could go to my work in the morning. I saw Said bringing out his suitcases to get ready for his journey. He said that the school had sent to the Ministry of Education for an opinion and he knew that the opinion would be deportation in a few days. Then suddenly he said I shouldn't have refused to teach Salih. I said I hadn't; I just refused to be paid for watching pornographic movies. He said I didn't know the country. "Salih uses bribery with all teachers from all nationalities. No one turns down his bribes or his gifts. You refused to give him the upper hand."

"That never occurred to me, Said. Salih is too young to think as you say he does."

"Salih is a merchant, Ismail. Most students here are merchants: young in years but with big egos."

Said's words left me baffled. I told him, "These are sick egos," and he said, "Perhaps they are innocent, like children. The least thing hurts them and they don't know how to defend themselves. Here if someone gives you something, take it without hesitation. If someone asks something of you, do it or give him hope that you will do it until he forgets. You never know how the wind will blow."

I was silent for a long time then I told him that I had gone to Salih a short while earlier. He smiled ironically and said, "You made him happy for free."

✧

In my office I kept looking at the glass cabinet and the chairs and the clock on the wall and the carpeting and the loud air conditioner and the safe and the desk next to it. This was a room that I loved without knowing it. At least time passed in it; how else could one explain the passage of those four months. Today everybody joyfully welcomed my return: the Asians, Nabil and Munzir, even Abed smiled, and Amm Abdallah liked the fact that I had cut my leave short and came to work. At nine, the telephone rang and I heard Rosemary's voice. Good Lord! I had forgotten. She said she did that every day, and that she was waiting for me to accept her invitation to lunch. I said I accepted it if it was for today. She laughed and it sounded as if she were overcome with joy. What she didn't know was that I just didn't want to go home. She said she would come at three in her car and that I could follow her in mine. As soon as I finished the conversation Abed came from his office to ask if I had accepted Rose's invitation. He had been listening in on our conversation as our telephones were on one line. Why did he come to ask me then? I told him, "As you heard." His face remained impassive and he said, "There's a letter for you."

I picked up the letter and examined it. How come I had forgotten so much? It was unmistakably Wadha's handwriting, so this was the letter she told me about; Wadha, whose secret had burst forth only the day before yesterday and which I had forgotten about as if it had taken place in the distant past.

"Do you know anyone in Riyadh?"

She did not write her name on the envelope but he read the postmarks.

"I have a relative there," I answered without looking at him.

✧

At twelve o'clock, after I saw the old Yemeni man sitting on the floor with the *siwak* in his mouth and after he smiled at me more broadly than ever before and I laughed because I had forgotten all about him, Nabil came in carrying a coffee that I had not ordered. He sat down and said, "I got two letters today, one from my mother and one from my fiancée. What do you think?"

"About what?" I asked, smiling. Nabil's way of speaking, which I had forgotten, brought me back some joy.

"About the two letters."

"I don't know what's in them."

He took them out of the upper part of his *gallabiya* and placed them on the desk, saying, "My mother says my fiancée threatened her that if I didn't send her a large sum of money as a down payment on an apartment, she would leave me. My fiancée says that she is waiting for me as a swallow awaits the break of day to sing."

I started laughing, feeling blood coursing through my veins.

"Don't make fun of me. Here's my fiancée's letter, read it for yourself."

"I missed you, Nabil."

He looked at me, smiling, and said, "I want your opinion."

"I told you before to go back to Egypt."

"And I said I couldn't. I have another solution. I should send power of attorney to my older brother so he can get me married to my fiancée by proxy, then I can send her an entry visa. Then she can come in her wedding dress to live with me here."

"Very good idea."

He was silent for a few moments then said, "The problem is, my older brother is a little crazy and the other brother is in jail, as I told you. I really don't know how to get out of this mess."

He got up and left me, surprised but feeling better and healthier.

✧

At quarter past three Rose came. Munzir was the last worker to leave. He came close to me and whispered in my ear, "I've got stories, Ustaz." Then in a loud voice, "Either you wreck your car or I wreck mine so we can ride home together every day."

As usual he left in a great hurry.

I saw her stop the car outside the forecourt, her face and hair shining in the light of a day taken over by the sun after a foggy morning. She got out of the car to shake my hand. I knew that Abed was standing in the door of his office looking at us because she waved to him. She drove her car and I followed with mine. We drove for quite a distance on the asphalt road, then turned onto a side street paved with little white compacted stones. I thought I saw something at a distance in the sand: a huge white dog, walking slowly.

It was a long road and the desert was vast around us. Suddenly some gray clouds appeared, blocking the sun, and several low, wooden houses painted green with sloping roofs came into view. This was the compound where the Americans worked. Rosemary indicated to the guard that I was with her, and we went through the gate. I saw three rows of houses forming three sides of a quadrangle; each house separated from the other by a small circular garden surrounded by a hedge. Between the walls of the houses and the hedges were winter flowers of different colors.

"This is our house," she said after she stopped and left her car. I left my car and climbed three white steps. She turned the key in the door and told me to come in. Why didn't she ring the bell? What was going to happen to me now? Was there going to be another mistake? She went ahead of me and I followed awkwardly, but I heard a husky voice speaking in English and asking her if I had come. This was undoubtedly Mr. Larry. I heaved a sigh of relief and found him in front of me in the short corridor, and smiled. I don't know why, but I thought I saw that the soil in the garden was black. Mr. Larry was tall with a strong build. He was wearing the green khaki overalls that he wore when he visited our offices. His appearance gave the impression that he was a man who had a lot to do and that visits should not take too long. Be that as it may. But where did they get the black soil from?

"Hello, Mr. Ismail. How are you?"

"Hello, Mr. Larry."

He pulled me by the hand to go inside. Rose smiled at us then went ahead of us and disappeared. We sat in a large living room. In one corner there was a bookcase that had books, records, cassettes, and a television, a VCR, and a stereo. In another corner was a handsome, broad and short curio cabinet with little knickknacks in it. In a third corner, opposite the seating area where we sat, was a simple, shiny black table around which were four chairs: a simple living room set of hardwood with separate cushions. I noticed that the table was set already: it had a white tablecloth with green flowers, three big plates and three small plates, empty, arranged in front of three seats, and next to each place setting was a knife, a fork, and a spoon. To the side was a pitcher of water, three cans of 7UP, and three glasses.

"Beer, Mr. Ismail, or juice? We have local beer"—and he winked—"and some other beer."

"Juice," I said quickly, so that he wouldn't mention beer again. I didn't want anyone reminding me of the night before last. He got up and went to a small refrigerator that I hadn't noticed and took out a lemonade bottle. He filled a glass and gave it to me and started talking loudly in a strange American accent that didn't pronounce the ends of the words. I heard Rose answering him from some place I didn't know, but I couldn't see her or understand what they were saying.

In a few moments Rose came back, smiling, wearing a short green dress that stopped above her knees, its collar open, revealing a great neck sitting confidently on full shoulders and a rich bosom. She wore a necklace of shiny white pearls and a mysterious perfume that took my very breath away. This was not the same beautiful Rose that I had seen before. She may have realized what my glances meant for she smiled.

"What's up, Mr. Ismail? I see that your thoughts are somewhere else," she said after sitting in front of me next to her husband. What did she mean by that question? I replied, "Nothing."

"Are you afraid of our food?"

Larry laughed so loudly he almost shook the walls of the house. I looked at him with surprise mixed with displeasure. He seemed embarrassed as he said, "Don't be afraid, Mr. Ismail. We are all foreigners and all foreigners eat the same food."

Rose asked me, "Aren't you happy at work with Mr. Abdallah?"

"Mr. Abdallah is an excellent man. You both must know him better than I do. Mr. Larry works for the company and you in his day-care center."

We were silent. It seemed I had put my foot in it. After a short while Rose said, "Yes, Mr. Abdallah is an excellent person." We were silent again. Was the gathering going to be a drag? Had words run out so fast? But Larry asked me, "Are you from Cairo, Mr. Ismail?"

"I am from Alexandria."

"Beautiful city."

"Did you visit it, Mr. Larry?"

"No, I read Durrell's *Quartet.* You must have read it yourself. Rose says you are very well read."

I was surprised by his flattery and said, "Alexandria is different now. No more foreigners and no more Jews, especially."

"But the Jews are going back now, Mr. Ismail."

"I don't think so, Mr. Larry," I said, looking at Rose's back as she went to prepare the food. A beautifully proportioned back. I wanted to get up and put my arms around it, as her legs glowed wonderfully. But noticing that Larry was looking, I bowed my head.

He got up and put on a cassette tape of light, pleasant music and came back to sit in silence. I couldn't help steal glances at Rose as she brought things to the table or went back to the kitchen. Once again he asked me, "Do you really think the Jews don't go to Egypt nowadays?"

"They go but nobody pays any attention to them."

"But Sadat keeps talking about peace every day."

"Sadat is not the Egyptian people, Mr. Larry. There's a lot of bad blood between us and Israel." He fell silent and I fell silent too. I felt as if I was ruining everything. But Rose stood up, extended her arms, and said in a delightful voice, "Everything is ready."

We went over to the table. The lunch was not different. It was exactly what Mr. Larry called it, foreigners' food: slices of cold cuts, slices of hot meat, some rice, a little bread, sautéed vegetables, a big bowl of salad, and a bottle of Portuguese red wine with a three musketeers logo.

Larry said, "We must apologize for offering you wine that has traveled by plane."

I didn't understand, so he added, "Wine loses a lot of its flavor when it's transported. The best wine you drink in its place of origin."

"These are very complex matters, Mr. Larry. Besides, I don't drink."

Rose changed the music and played some waltzes by Strauss. Larry asked me if I liked music. I talked about Stravinsky and *The Rite of Spring* and Tchaikovsky's *Marche Slave*. Larry seemed impressed with my knowledge of music, which I knew was quite limited. When he said he liked Haydn's music very much I said that that reactionary church composer couldn't last a minute vis-à-vis somebody like Wagner, for instance. Tension seemed to fill the room but Rose smiled and said with enviable tact, "Why don't we eat in silence and listen to Strauss's butterflies hovering all around us?"

✧

After lunch Rose said the camp cinema was showing *Last Tango in Paris* that day. Larry said, "I think such films are banned in Egypt." I knew he was trying to get at me any way he could and, to tell the truth, I don't know why I started being hostile to him.

"Yes," I said. "They are banned in Egypt."

He smiled as if he had scored a point against an adversary. It didn't bother me that he had found a chance to get at me, for he had fallen into the trap. He told me I could go and take a nap in their room if I was tired. He thought that, as an oriental, I would decline and leave. I declined but I didn't leave. I said I would stay and watch the film.

Larry was really weak and fragile. Suddenly he started talking about America, telling me it wasn't like what we saw in the movies, that there was poverty and hunger in America, that he himself had worked so hard to try to come to Saudi Arabia. He seemed like someone talking with a Saudi official who had power over him. Rose, who sat next to me after lunch, seemed to have more self-confidence.

When we went out to go to the cinema it was much colder outside, perhaps because here we were in the middle of a vast desert. I saw several couples coming out of the houses, walking slowly, laughing and talking loudly, heading for the cinema, which was small and elegant with comfortable leather seats and air conditioning.

We sat down. The film that was banned in Egypt was shown. I left truly fascinated by Marlon Brando's performance. I saw Amm Abdallah look at me in surprise; he was at the cinema too, in the company of a short, fat American. He seemed displeased at seeing me, but he ignored me and left with the American man. I felt a little uneasy, then found myself thinking about the beautiful last dance in the film as Marlon Brando dropped his pants and the little old ladies fled in horror. Then I remembered Marlon Brando asking the young woman to put her finger up his ass and how he took pleasure in the pain as she complied.

19

We were now living in total silence. Said did everything quietly; he sat down and stood up as if he were a mere apparition. When he ate, his teeth operated independently of the rest of him and very slowly. He didn't speak and didn't turn on the television. He prayed a lot and read the Quran silently. I learned that Aida had left Tabuk, so I joined in his silence.

On my way back after Rosemary's invitation I felt pain in my wound. It was night and very cold; the vast desert seemed to shrink in the darkness around me. I had a pressing need to empty my bladder, so I stopped the car and got out and stood next to it. I saw that blood had leaked through the bandage on the wound. It seemed that movement had caused a tear in the suture. I could have gone on home and Wagih could have taken care of it. Instead I headed for the hospital, where I was seen by Warda instead of by Aida, who I really wanted to see. Warda took me to a Pakistani doctor who had a thin neck and a very small head. When he heard the ambulance siren, he told her to take care of the wound herself and dashed off.

"Where's Aida? I thought she was still working the night shift," I asked Warda.

She was surprised by my question. She blushed and reluctantly said, "In Diba."

"Diba?"

"Yes."

"Why?"

"They needed a nurse and we were all terrified, so she requested to work there."

"But I was here only two days ago, she didn't tell me anything."

"It all happened yesterday, and today she left."

"That fast?" I asked in a whispering voice as Warda looked at me. She applied a new bandage, then rushed out to tend the accident victims. How come Wagih didn't tell me? Why did she make such a decision?

I fell deeper and deeper into silence so Wagih, whenever we were together, also became silent since there was no one to talk to him. We lived on in total silence.

The following day I was supposed to go to Wadha. I knew I wouldn't see her either. Khalid welcomed me amiably as usual and took me to the big room. I didn't see the desk and I decided not to worry.

"Please sit down, Ustaz." He pointed to the floor. I didn't sit down and I said nothing.

"Wadha is very sick, Ustaz. The doctor has forbidden her to see anyone for two weeks to a month. God alone knows what might happen after that."

We shook hands. So, Salih Sanyur al-Thaqifi had spread the news of our drunkenness throughout Tabuk. At the outside door, Khalid said, "I know your house, Ustaz. When Wadha is well again, I'll come to you."

I said nothing. The tribe of Thaqif had chased the Prophet with stones when he went to them. From Thaqif came al-Hajjaj ibn Yusuf who entered Kufa, took off his turban, and issued the first decree threatening to cut off the heads of the Iraqis. But I didn't think Salih was from Thaqif; he was just a rash, vindictive youth. Who would leave the lush south for the dusty, dry north these days? The silence became even more profound. On my way back I did my best not to make the mistake of passing by the house of Sayyid al-Gharib, the forgotten prisoner of fear and defeat. I couldn't be stricken with silence forever.

Said left and I didn't go to work that day. I went to the airport and saw the happy faces of the Egyptians all around, lots of baggage and constant movement. The sun shone more brightly than usual and the Egyptians laughed loudly. They were at the gates of a wide open world. Said, however, remained silent, and I descended even deeper into silence myself.

I went back home and read the papers that Wagih had bought but never read. Begin declares that talks with Egypt will resume in a week or two in the United States. Conflicting reports about the Shah's departure. Shahpour Bakhtiar, the new prime minister of Iran, announces that Iran might stop exporting oil to Israel. Dozens of flying saucers are seen in the Australian sky; shiny blue objects fly at random over the eastern coast of Australia and then their color changes to red and they send mysterious signals; scientists say these sightings are the planet Venus, which appears at its brightest now and can be seen twelve hours a day in such a way as to give anyone the illusion that it is a moving body.

Wagih came back at three and was surprised I hadn't had lunch yet. He said that as of today we would always lunch together. I was surprised that his voice had become loud all of a sudden, but before I could figure out quite what he meant, he said, "I'll be working nights for one or two months."

"So I'll be spending the night alone," I said to myself as he added, "I don't think we need anybody else to live with us, unless it's too much for your budget to handle half the rent?"

I said decisively, "We don't need a third roommate. We don't even need this house."

"How so?"

"Do you really want to go on living in a house owned by Salih Sanyur al-Thaqifi?"

✧

I almost fell asleep after lunch even though I had declared war on sleep, which had declared war on me. In two consecutive days, Aida and Wadha were gone; nobody was left but Rosemary, who I knew would be no more than a parenthetical clause. Now Said too was gone and sleep's arsenal became more potent. For five days I had been using all the weapons available so as not to fall asleep. I took more than one bath a day. I had light lunches even though I had lost weight after the operation. I didn't sit on the bed. I exercised in the room and thought out loud. But sleep, like a sneaky whisperer, always managed to seize a moment when my eyelids relaxed, and laid down a heavy cover of darkness, and pulled me by the foot to the bottomless abyss, and stood over my head sending down its nightmares and visions. Sleep had me terrified now and I saw it sitting everywhere in the room, smiling slyly, comfortable in the knowledge that it was master of the universe. I am ready to surrender, Master, if only you would change these visions. Why are you terrifying me so when I haven't wronged anybody? Wadha's book was now closed forever and my intuition was proved wrong. She vanished as simply as the slightest hand movement. I didn't believe the story would have any other ending, for everything I felt had been nothing but a thirst. Do you think that I desired Rosemary, whose invitation still baffled me? You could see, Master of Eyes and Bodies, Lifegiver and Soulsnatcher, how I behaved so testily with her husband, placing boulders in the path of the sweet flowing waters. Perhaps you were blaming me for Aida's sake. Was it wrong to believe that a relationship with a woman could only be for the purpose of marriage? What wrong have I done when I was so close to avowing my desire? It was she who closed the door and opened a wound that could not heal. She was going to stay here for twenty years, until Hashim, who was hit by a car the day Nixon visited the country, was cured. Politics besieged me. Please don't forget that I was the one besieged. Let me sleep once like a child. I did no wrong when I told Amal that the only way I understood love was for marriage. How could I know her mind was so fragile and her soul so transparent? I was the victim of duty and outworn family values. I have committed no crime or sin even though Amal was dead and every one was lost. In this time of ours, nobody died of love, these were old stories. So, was it my fault that somebody did die of love? Are you still watching me even now I am sitting on a chair, resisting your crawling army of ants and the temptation to nod off for a moment on the bed? I am going to take a bath and will give you no opportunity today. Today at least. Even if my eyes were blinded and my nerves shattered.

I left the chair tired and stretched out on the bed fighting a desire to cry. I really had desire for three women. Now only one remained, and a hopeless one at that. What frustration after frustration! Some of those frustrations were of my own making; others were thrown in my way. I pulled the cover over me and the three faces came in with me under it. I saw them, those fierce-looking guards with black faces, yellow teeth, and constant smiles, their glances fixed on the faraway high horizon, paving the ground and sprinkling it with water. They were putting up a high wall and waving their hands at the sky, from which little boys and big boys, old men and young men, women and girls came hurtling down. Stones rose from the ground. The eunuchs grabbed me and threw me upward; I found myself sitting on top of a mountain surrounded by water and I couldn't get down. I saw Wadha collapsed in a heap on the ground next to the wall, her head between her knees and her arms. She woke up and saw those who had come down from the sky grabbing the stones that had risen from the ground. She was terrified and ran to the right and still saw them, and to the left and still saw them. They had blocked the way in front and there was no way she could climb the wall. I couldn't get down; she could hear my screams as she raised her arms to me in terror and as one stone after another hit her and blood spurted from her head. Rose stood on top of a mountain that burst suddenly from the ground opposite me. She was laughing and taking off her clothes and throwing them in the air. Then the ground was level again and everybody went back to the sky. The water around my mountain receded and I was able to get down slowly and make my way toward Wadha, who had collapsed in a heap again, sobbing like a child who had just stopped screaming after receiving a painful spanking, who, at an early age, understood the meaning of humiliation. The wall broke into pieces of ice that formed a very cold pond. A hand held me up by the arm as I sat with my head between my knees and my arms around my head, sobbing, and raised my head until I saw Aida with tears in her eyes. I walked with her and she fell down a hole in the road. I walked alone crying and wiping the tears with my hands. The road kept getting longer. I changed my clothes and went down the main street screaming. My God, why this hell? Two hells a few moments apart. I had come to the market only to get tired so that if I slept I would sleep a thousand skies above sleep's sky, so it would forget me. But all the cars on the street came back one way, screeching and honking their horns loudly, almost jumping on each other. I moved quickly in the street, seeing the southern horizon blackened with thick smoke rising over the flames that filled the sky with a frenzied red. Successive explosions followed, pieces of wood and big objects and small objects that I couldn't make out flew high into the air. Men and women ran in terror, carrying children or dragging them mercilessly, as red charred debris kept falling on nearby houses and screams rose in many languages. I moved forward, paying no heed to the choking sensation I felt, and ran with the foreigners, dragged the men, women, and children who had fallen on the street, moving them quickly to the northern part of the street, away from the fire and the smoke. The sounds of the sirens came from behind but the ambulances themselves could not move because of all the cars left behind by their drivers who had run away. It was up to us who didn't know one another to carry the dead and the dying to where the ambulances were stuck, as the fire trucks blasted their sirens and skirted around the jam to go through the side streets to the fire, which had devoured the whole southern half of the main street. The huge hoses appeared from the small alleys, but they suddenly slipped from the hands of the firefighters and writhed on the street like scared giant snakes. As fiery debris fell on them, the hoses writhed more frantically; the firefighters fled as the water drowned the street rather than be directed at the fire. A big cloud passed above darkening the street. There were cries of "God is great!" in all accents, and arms rose in supplication praying for rain to fall. But there was no rain. The cloud passed, paying no heed to us. We could hear the roar of huge yellow helicopters on the sides of which I could read 'US Air Force' written in big letters. The helicopters were close to the ground, dumping clouds of white smoke and torrents of water on the street.

A very long time passed before I found myself alone in a scene of total destruction. I was wet from head to toe, but I wasn't tired. What supernatural force had possessed me, when I had been discharged from the hospital only eight days earlier? I felt no pain in my wound; I could only smell a pervasive smell of roasting: was it charcoal, wood, stone, or human flesh? I didn't know, but I saw the shocked eyes of men and women searching among the burn victims, where screaming filled the sky. I also saw people who had ceased all movement and sound and turned into charred corpses. All the women's faces were uncovered and all the headdresses had fallen off the heads of the men. The call to prayer rose from the big mosque and all the mosques. I approached the area of Omdurman, which had been spared. Did the mosque protect it or were its inhabitants not from this era? I stood trying hard to remember who I was looking for among the dead and the injured. Said was the one who always went to market with me. But Said had left; I had seen him off myself at the airport.

20

I now had to try hard to forget. Nothing here made you forget anything. Tabuk didn't make you forget your mother or your father. The long and short of it was that it was the foreigners who came here to forget.

Our moving to a new house helped distract me for some time. Wagih had left the whole matter to me. With difficulty, I was able to rent a small two-room Arabian-style house in the same neighborhood, Faysaliya, west of town. The house, at the edge where the neighborhood met the desert, was brand new, still smelling of mortar and paint. I got rid of the excess furniture by selling it to a dealer in second-hand goods.

As I entered the new house for the first time, I felt as if I had just come from Egypt and hadn't known anyone here. I said to myself that perhaps sleep would restore me and indeed I slept deeply and wasn't disturbed by the mouse that apparently had been waiting for me, making a nest in the kitchen. I didn't think of killing it or chasing it out. I sat down and wrote a letter to Aida. Wadha's book, which my foolishness had opened, was now closed forever. Rosemary's book was an illusion from beginning to end. Wadha was a girl who had pledged herself to death and I should never have taken one step on her path, stirring up a sorrow I had buried deep in the ground. Now I had to pray to God in praise and gratitude for I came here neither to kill nor to die. Maybe the days I spent with her would be preserved as a memory of a sweet adventure that taught me something about the vitality of the body, the expansiveness of the world, and the lie of morality. Rosemary represented the longing of a villager who spends one day in the city then goes back to his family and friends to tell them about conquests inspired by their own warnings to him. Now there was no escaping Aida, who alone soothed the wounds of my imagination and filled the emptiness that was my world.

I only wrote, "Why did you do that?" Her reply, if any, would provide the ending of the story. On the envelope I wrote, "Aida Abd al-Salam, Diba Hospital," and I felt great relief. Sleep now proved to be a good friend. More than once I almost got up to look for the mouse, to smile at its frightened face and encourage it to stay. I lost all fear, of anybody, or for anybody. I realized that a month had passed since I I had last seen Rosemary and that I hadn't made any effort to see her or she to see me. I was prepared to forget, and my letter to Aida was the last drop of balm for my soul, which had inexplicably become sick. The beginning of the effort to revive the memory of the beautiful woman was the realization that no female of this world was able to undertake the duty she had prepared herself to perform. So what could really prevent me from being a gallant knight in this country? Every gallant knight in history had come to the rescue of the woman he loved and who loved him. Today, three days after my letter to her, I was driving my car to work in an ethereal mood despite the barren clouds that hid the sky, separating the sun from us and trapping the bitter cold down here. With the car windows closed I lit cigarette after cigarette.

I saw the Pakistanis standing in front of the camp, moving incessantly as their suitcases were piled on the ground. When they saw my car as I turned off the main road to get to the company forecourt, they waved to me from a distance. Ten of them were leaving for Pakistan for their annual vacation. Of the nine who had spent five uninterrupted years working for the company, five had finished their contracts and were not coming back. Arshad, who went on vacation every year, was the tenth. He would begin his fifth year of work after coming back from vacation.

They had said good-bye to me the day before as I gave them their tickets and passports. They asked me if I wanted anything from Pakistan. All of them, including those not coming back, made gestures of generosity. Arshad, however, seemed ill at ease. I didn't want to see him. I told myself perhaps it was all due to the anxiety preceding a long trip. Today the Pakistanis, in their white, loose-fitting pants and blue and green jackets and their incessant movement in front of the camp, seemed like children on a feast day. I went into the forecourt elated with delight.

I sat by myself after the workers had come and signed in. I started to translate some reports, then I thought to myself, "Why didn't Wagih bring one of his two wives to live with him?" He was over forty-five years old and was at that stage in his life when he should be enjoying a happy bed and a comfortable home, good glances from a good wife, happiness as he saw the children reliving their father's experience in learning, love, and hopes.

A strange bird this Wagih, working hard to bring happiness to two faraway wives who he married only to stay away from.

"Did you see the Pakistanis?" said Nabil as he came into the room smiling, bringing me my coffee.

“They are monkeys, I swear. All night long: ‘Come, Nabil, help us find some rope; come, Nabil, help us find an empty box. What would you like from Pakistan?’ ‘I don’t want anything. Please let me sleep.’ ‘Stay up with us Nabil, we won’t see you again.’ They spent the whole night singing.”

“And Arshad?”

“Arshad’s very strange. He didn’t say a word. Why? Do you know?”

I had no answer; I really didn’t know. We were silent for a few moments then Nabil said, “What’s the story with those flying saucers these days?”

“What flying saucers?”

“Don’t you read the newspapers? Don’t you listen to the news? Before, they were far away in Australia, New Zealand, Japan, America, but now they’re talking about them in India, northern Iraq, and Turkey. This is too close.”

“Why should that concern us?”

“Are you kidding? Don’t you know? Flying saucers mean that the people who live far away from us, on Mars or Saturn, are preparing to invade Earth.”

I began laughing loudly as he looked at me in surprised embarrassment, and with a faint smile interrupted only by the sound of a car entering the forecourt and Amm Abdallah’s voice speaking English to somebody as he came in.

“Oh God!” Nabil jumped up and ran to the kitchen. A few moments later Abed stood at the door of my office telling me that Amm Abdallah wanted to see me.

✧

“Do you have problems in Egypt?” Amm Abdallah asked me after Larry, who was with him in the room, shook my hand.

"What kind of problems?"

"With work or the army. I know lots of you run away from the army and forge your papers."

"I don't have any problems with anyone," I said, looking long at his face.

"Well then. You'll go to Cairo in two days. Larry will explain everything."

He got busy pushing telephone buttons. Larry got up, saying, "We can talk in your office."

I went ahead and he followed. We sat on two opposite chairs. He must have noticed my distraction before he spoke.

Egypt. Now. When Amm Abdallah said it, my heart pounded with joy. Now. Perhaps that meant recovery from everything. Egypt. How could I immediately contact Aida to get her family's address and meet Hashim, the optimist who she loved better than all her brothers and who had erected a solid wall of waiting around her without knowing it? In what way was I related to her that I could send her a telegram, which anybody could read? There was no telephone service between Tabuk and Diba. No telephone? Damn the oil, the riyal, the dinar, and the dollars that kept the distances so long!

"How are you, Mr. Ismail?"

"I'm fine, Mr. Larry."

"The trip to Egypt should be nice, anyway. I nominated you in particular for this task, as soon as Rose saw you. She said you spoke English, and we need that."

"Tell me what needs to be done, Mr. Larry."

"In this envelope is a bill of lading for equipment worth three hundred thousand dollars, ten boxes of important equipment that I had shipped four months ago from San Francisco, California, but that have not arrived yet. On the lading bill, as you can see, are the flight numbers, and dates, and the company, Lufthansa. You'll find also the itinerary: San Francisco, New York, Munich, Cairo, Jedda, Tabuk."

"So why do I go to Cairo, Mr. Larry?"

"Because the only likelihood now is that the equipment has been lost in one of the airports, and Cairo airport is a strong candidate for that. You know Egypt better than I do, Mr. Ismail," he said and smiled, but I didn't smile. My feeling of defiance toward him returned, and I felt even more strongly that feeling that had inexplicably erupted between us.

"Couldn't we reach these airports by telex from here?"

"We did, but so far, no response. It's bizarre, Mr. Ismail. But don't worry too much. We'll find the equipment in the end."

He took out of his inner jacket pocket a small roll of riyals, a piece of paper and a pen.

"Here's five thousand riyals to cover your expenses in Cairo. I know that money moves everything in Cairo. Please sign this receipt."

I didn't find a way to return the insult. He was undoubtedly right. I felt thwarted because I didn't know how to triumph over him. I signed the receipt quickly. He got up smiling and said, "Now you have to call Saudi Airlines to book a flight the day after tomorrow. Don't forget to request an exit and return visa for a month or a month and a half so you'll have plenty of time."

✧

Larry left and at the same time Arshad came in. He was pale but there was a lot of anger in his eyes. He threw himself on the nearest chair.

"Arshad? Impossible!" I looked at the clock on the wall. It was ten. The plane was supposed to take off at nine.

"Was the flight delayed, Arshad?"

He raised his eyes to me and shook his head. He was still very angry.

"Why have you come back, then?"

"Bhutto, Mr. Ismail. Bhutto and Zia-ul Haq."

"Did they kill him?"

"The Supreme Court upheld the death sentence and turned down the appeal that he had filed. Bhutto didn't ask for a pardon. The court does what Zia-ul Haq wants."

"Arshad, you are my friend. At least I think so. These big issues should not stop us. Bhutto can kill Zia-ul Haq or Zia-ul Haq can kill Bhutto. To hell with them."

"I agree, Mr. Ismail. But . . ." He began to sob. "We made all the preparations to travel. We sent cables to our families and they made preparations to wait for us. We are all crying now, Mr. Ismail. We all love our children, and wives, and parents, and brothers and sisters. Wahhaj is crying. Ghulam is crying and so are Sarwar, Khurshid, Jounah, and Muhammad. We are very unhappy."

Nothing had made any sense yet. I was at a loss. Nabil, who had heard news of my trip to Cairo, came in, saying loudly, "Congratulations!"

When he saw Arshad he stopped talking to me and said, "What's wrong, Arshad my friend? Why are you crying? Problems with cumin?"

I needed great strength to stop myself from laughing. Arshad didn't raise his head to him. I said to Nabil, "They sentenced Bhutto to death again."

"Bhutto? Who's Bhutto? Oh, Prime Minister Bhutto. Is he your relative, Arshad?"

Once again I kept myself from laughing and winked to Nabil to stop talking. I asked Arshad, "I still don't understand why you've come back from the airport."

"The demonstrations, Mr. Ismail, they are all over Pakistan. The government closed down the airports. They told us that, here. They also said it would be best to postpone the flight rather than wait in Jedda or Bombay in India."

The three of us fell silent. Nabil was still standing. I said, "I don't think a country would close down its airports for more than a day or two. So, tomorrow or the day after is not so far off, Arshad."

He said nothing. We fell silent again. Then he asked, "What do we do now, Mr. Ismail? Do we go back to work?"

"No. Stay in the camp. I'll count your waiting period as working days. Don't worry, Arshad."

He stood up and said, "Thank you very much, Mr. Ismail. Please forgive my crying."

He shook my hand and kept it in his for a few moments. I said, "I like you, Arshad. I like all Pakistanis."

He pressed my hand humbly and left.

✧

No one gave me a chance to sit by myself. Abed sat with me for a long time explaining his address in Matariya, gave me a thousand dollars to give to his father, then left. Nabil hadn't told me yet what he wanted and hadn't left the office yet. He spoke to me about Imbaba, which he missed, about sitting in the café with the butchers and renderers, who, no matter how clean their clothes, still had traces of blood on them. He didn't ask anything of me, but at one point he fell silent for a long time and then told me that he was having dreams about standing on the Kitkat side of the river and throwing stones to the other side in Zamalek. It was a dream that recurred a lot but that he didn't understand. He used to do that as a boy and his friends envied him and expressed amazement at the extraordinary strength of his arm and at the same time his inability to swim in the Nile with them, due to his great fear of the water. Once again he was silent for a long time and then said that he was very frightened by the flying saucers that the papers and broadcasts were talking about. What would happen if one of those flying saucers were to fall on their home in Imbaba? The houses there were old and hardly stayed standing; they could all burn down. He refused to believe that it was all nonsense, that to date no one had produced a flying saucer or a creature that came with one and shown its picture or displayed it on television. "Why are they talking about it if it's nonsense?" I told him I didn't know why they were talking about it either but I remembered that in Egypt after the 1967 defeat they said that the Virgin Mary was appearing every night in a church near Cairo. He said, "Yes, in Matariya, and it did happen." He had gone with his mother and the women from their street and saw her. I told him it turned out afterwards that it was all staged by the Egyptian secret police so that people would forget the defeat. He hit his forehead with his hand and cried, "My God!" Then he said he didn't believe me. I didn't wish to continue. He said the newspapers were talking about flying saucers in lots of countries; that these were signs of the Day of Judgment. He left and I saw that it was twelve o'clock so I looked at the forecourt to look for the old Yemeni man and found him standing in the door of the room. I stood back in amazement. He was going to speak to me. He came up to me and shook my hand smiling that broad smile of his.

"You're going to Egypt?" he said.

"Yes, would you like me to bring you something back?"

He frowned and left me to go sit in his place chewing on his *siwak*. What did he want from me and why did he ask me?

I didn't understand. Abed came into the office and said that he had thought about it and decided not to send anything to his family after all, because he had sent a large sum a week earlier. I was surprised but gave him the thousand dollars. Mansur, who had disappeared for a long time, came into the forecourt in his car, stirring up a dust storm.

✧

"I heard you were asking about me," he said as he came in with the monkey on his shoulder. I had not asked about him. I thought of him once. I wanted to tell him about the breaking off of Said and Widad's engagement, not because I liked him but because I disliked Widad, who I hadn't seen but who had driven Said to the celebration that resulted in his termination here. I didn't know what Mansur had in store for them but it couldn't be anything good. Should I do it now and tell him?

After he sat down behind the desk next to the safe and looked at me expecting an answer, I said to him, "I didn't ask about you but I did want to see you."

"I know the whole story."

"What story?"

"The New Year story. Your friend is gone." I fell silent. How did he find out about Said's departure? Did Salih know something about Mansur too? I ignored Mansur and began to translate the reports that I hadn't begun working on yet. Mansur didn't budge. Then the monkey jumped on the desk and then onto the floor, where it stood looking at me as if it knew me or was trying to remember me.

"Come here," Mansur yelled at it. I had stood up in fear of the little monkey's glances and its red eyes; it looked like it was about to do something or other. Mansur came out from behind the desk and held out his arms to the monkey, which didn't respond.

"Come here, dog."

The monkey didn't move, just looked right and left. Mansur took off the tightly woven *uqal* and snapped it in the air, making a sound like a lion-tamer's whip. The monkey ducked its head and the whip missed it. It recoiled in fear then flipped over in the air; now it was facing the door so it ran jumping to the light of the big forecourt, "Stop, don't move, dog," Mansur yelled and ran behind it brandishing his *uqal*, with the result that his *ghutra* fell off from his head to his shoulder to the floor. He was now in the forecourt whipping the air with the *uqal* behind the monkey, which was shrieking in a thin, intermittent voice. I stood at the door and saw Nabil standing at the door of the kitchen and the old Yemeni man sitting still in his place, not caring and not moving; he only stopped moving the *siwak* and his eyes grew wider and brighter. Mansur stood near him and snapped the *uqal* so hard in the air that I thought that if it caught the monkey it would cut him into two halves. The monkey jumped on top of the white Cadillac that belonged to Amm Abdallah, who had left that day in his yellow Mercedes. Mansur ran around the car as the monkey was moving on it, unable to escape, or so it appeared to me. Mansur started waving the *uqal* calmly in the air and holding out his left arm so that the monkey would jump onto it. It was as if the monkey knew what Mansur intended to do. The moment that Mansur swung the *uqal* hard, it jumped upward and let out a long, thin, convulsive shriek and stood once again on top of the car, looking viciously at Mansur.

"Leave it alone, it'll come down on its own," shouted Nabil, who was standing at a distance in front of the kitchen, but Mansur was in no mood to listen to anyone; he jumped up to get onto the car from the front. The monkey made a big jump over Mansur's head as he was climbing onto the car so his foot slipped and he fell face down on the windshield of the car. I gasped in fear but the glass didn't shatter and I saw the monkey run toward the gate of the forecourt, but it didn't get out. It ran along the wall, frightening the old Yemeni man, who had not left his place and who now got up for the first time, but soon stumbled and fell. The crazed monkey leapt past him and reached the kitchen. Nabil ran into the kitchen and closed the door. The monkey ran around the walls and almost crashed into me, but I backed up and it passed in front of me. Mansur had by now collected his wits and was standing at the gate of the forecourt, blocking it by waving the shiny *uqal*. The monkey stood, motionless, not far from him. They eyed each other in tense readiness. I saw Mansur's hair, black and long but now disheveled. His eyes bulged and reddened with anger. He relaxed his arm and let the *uqal* fall to the ground, then advanced slowly, holding out his arm for the monkey: "Come on. Don't be afraid. Come." But the monkey ran again and with amazing speed toward the door of the kitchen, where Nabil appeared at the door again then made a giant leap upward, going beyond the kitchen and the company wall in one fell swoop. Mansur ran out of the gate, but I knew he wouldn't catch up with it. He came back alone and without uttering a word he got into his car and sped off. I stood there wondering where the monkey had gone. It most probably joined the stray white dog that roamed the endless sands.

21

Cairo. We were now flying over it, but I could see nothing. A dust storm was delaying the landing. The captain announced that we might be forced to land at Luxor airport. I wanted very much to see the Nile and the Pyramids but the only thing I could see was a yellow horizon through the glass of the small window next to which I had taken pains to sit. On my way over I had not paid any attention to where I sat as I was too busy being afraid of flying for the first time in my life.

On my way back the storm frustrated my wishes. Of all of Egypt I could only see the jaws of the Red Sea, wide open and silent. The plane was circling over Cairo; I could feel the circling but I could see nothing. I suddenly thought of not going back to Saudi Arabia; nobody would ask about me and no harm would come to anyone. I had left behind in Tabuk more money than the five thousand riyals, in unpaid salary, bonuses, and compensation for unused vacation days. "We ask all passengers to remain in their seats and put on their seat belts in preparation for landing." I tried to keep busy by sitting in an upright position, listening to Quranic verses being muttered around me and observing the tense silence hanging in the air. The captain was going to land despite the storm.

"Please extinguish your cigarettes." Silence continued as the firm tires of the plane hit the runway hard. There were no cries of panic, only the sound of the engines shrieking as the plane moved on the ground. "We rejoice with you on our safe landing. It is now three in the afternoon, Cairo time, the temperature outside is five degrees Celsius." I heard the sirens of ambulances and fire trucks, but the Egyptian stewardesses were standing there smiling at us, so these must have been just precautions. A long time passed before the doors were opened. We ran to the little buses, which took us in no time to the almost empty arrival lounge. By the time we had finished entry procedures, our baggage had arrived and everything was over very quickly, Mr. Larry. And please, Mr. Larry, don't tell me the dust storm had caused the cancellation of many flights. As I left the airport I couldn't see the wide open space in front of it, just people running about hiding their faces in their chests, their clothes flying every which way, the dust getting into their throats and noses, causing eyelids to drop over eyes. I got into the first cab and motioned the driver to put my suitcases in the trunk.

"Thank the Lord for your safe arrival."

"Thank you."

"Where to?"

"Alexandria."

"In weather like this it will be thirty pounds."

"Fine."

"Well then, have a cigarette."

The driver turned around to give me a cigarette, his thin, brown face covered with a scarf that also covered the head and neck. He sped off, turning on the cassette player; Um Kulthum's voice filled the car.

"Have no fear. We'll make it safely, God willing. Two tapes and we'll be there. The first one is *Why have you renewed your love?* and the second one is *Memories,* Ustaz." He laughed and added, "Or would you rather listen to *Who shall I go to?*"

He laughed once more; I smiled. He turned on the heater; I felt warm and confident. The trip seemed to take only a few minutes. I was immediately in the center of the welcoming clamor of joy, laughter, and my mother's tears. From the television news we learned that Tehran had fallen to Khomeini's supporters; mystery surrounded the fate of Bakhtiar; King Hasan declared that the Shah would stay in Morocco as an ordinary citizen; the Shah thanked Sadat for the days he spent in Egypt after leaving Iran; Zia-ul Haq refused to heed international appeals to pardon Bhutto, saying there was nothing he could do about the court's verdict. Arshad had told me yesterday morning that Bhutto's execution was inevitable now that Zia-ul Haq had lied when he stated that he didn't interfere in the judgment of the courts. Arshad smiled as he told me that airports in Pakistan had been opened and that he was taking the evening flight that day. "It's a long flight, Mr. Ismail. But it's beautiful: Tabuk, Jedda, Bombay, Lahore, Peshawar, then my wife Amina, and Zaynab, my daughter, then my friends, Mr. Ismail." My mother looked apprehensive when she saw that my face was pale and learned that I had my appendix out. I told her that that was two months ago, and that I didn't think I was as pale as she said I was. She laughed and I laughed and my sister Sanaa laughed and said I was in the best of health. My brother Bahaa said I looked great. "Here is a Rado watch, a bottle of Chanel perfume, three French Montagu blouses, pure silk fabric for a dress, and a piece of English Held wool for a suit for you, Sanaa." My sister, beside herself with joy, kissed me on the cheek.

"An Orient watch, wool fabric for a suit, and a Sheaffer pen set for you." Bahaa, smiling, thanked but didn't kiss me.

"A silk scarf, velour fabric, a chic black coat, and a Moroccan *abaya* for you, Mother." She thanked me and cried.

"This suitcase with everything in it is for Rawhiya and her two sons and Aliya and her two daughters. Nobody touch it." We laughed. "The third suitcase has pistachios, almonds, apples, Lipton tea, orange juice powder, bars of Lux soap, black pepper, cardamom, and lots of other stuff that you can divide equally among everybody, Mother. Don't laugh, this is what all the Egyptians do. I've learned from them."

"What did you get for yourself?"

"Lots, Mother, but I left them there."

There? Did that mean I was going back? Not because I had bought things and left them but because I longed to return. My longing increased as the days went by and as I walked the streets of Alexandria as if it were some city I didn't know; the crowds were unbearable, transportation slow, the streets muddy, the paint on the walls faded. Television was showing strange programs that lacked the intimate quality that had developed between me and *Television Magazine*, *A Drop from Every Sea*, *ABCD*, *Telematch*, *The Incredible Hulk*, or the programs of Shaykh Tantawi. The call to prayer here lacked that wounded note of sadness coming from a faraway mountain, nor were they accompanied by those plaintive, prayerful chants that moved the soul to seas of serenity. One couldn't find the dry air of Mount Uhud here or the dark red color of the tranquil mountain. I really wanted to go back; I was expecting a letter from Aida, who was spending her nights alone on the roof of a frightening building in a town inhabited by silence and ghosts, where the voice of Abd al-Halim Hafiz was never enough.

"What's wrong, Ismail?" my mother asked every day and always found me smiling; but she didn't know I was responding to the Yemeni's strange smile; laughing, but she didn't know I was listening to Nabil; looking perplexed, but she didn't know that Mansur was sitting there frowning, with the monkey on his shoulder; upset, but she didn't see Abed giving me a letter from Wadha that he knew was sent from Riyadh. Wadha's letter? Where was that letter that I hadn't even opened? Did I take it home or leave it at the office? How could I not open it for such a long time? I tried very hard to remember where I had hidden it. I was worried that Abed might find it in the office and open it. I tried to reassure myself by saying that I must have taken it home with me, that it must be with my papers there. Then I would say to myself that even if Abed did find it and read it, what more could happen? Wadha and her story were gone forever.

"Why are you so silent, my son, and how come you don't ask your sister or brother how they are doing in school?" What a mother, my mother! She didn't want me to forget my father's conspiracy against me.

A week passed and I said that was enough staying there, that I had work to do in Cairo. Everybody fell silent. My mother took me to my room, which they said they had kept clean in my absence, and told me that Alaa, son of Abbas the pastry maker, had proposed to Sanaa and had been waiting for my return. Without giving me a chance to recover from the surprise, she added, "Alaa graduated from the Faculty of Law last year, as you know."

I remembered him, a quiet, mild-mannered boy whose father gave a big banquet for the poor when he passed his exams.

"Alaa is ambitious; he's thinking of opening a practice."

My mother didn't leave me any choice. Another week passed during which Alaa and his father came to our house. The father complained to me about inflation in the prices of sugar, flour, butter, oil, syrups, artificial colors, dairy products, sesame, chocolate, and everything related to pastry making. He told me the only people who made real money were fava bean and felafel vendors, contractors, thieves, and big businessmen. My mother and my two sisters let loose ululations of joy. The house was filled with guests, and we had a simple engagement party. I felt proud to see beautiful Sanaa next to Alaa. Overcome by a parental feeling, a tear dropped from my eye. I took them to the Mustafa Darwish restaurant for dinner. I was dazzled by the white lights, white tables, white tablecloths, and the white uniforms of the waiters. Alaa told me about his plan to buy an apartment and an office. He said he was prepared to a certain extent. To a certain extent!? Sanaa said that Alaa liked me very much; that he said he wouldn't talk to anyone about the engagement except me, even if I didn't come back for ten years. It wasn't possible to stay for ten years, Sanaa. I said nothing. I saw the vast darkness of the sea and felt the severe cold, which was different from other years in Alexandria, famous for its warm weather. At home, my mother said Sanaa shouldn't wait more than a year, as marriage offered a girl protection. "What do you think?" What do I think? You've already arranged everything. I didn't say anything and headed for my room to sleep. She followed me. "Haven't you thought of marriage, yourself?" I smiled and said nothing. I was in search of sleep, which had forsaken me. I got under the covers. Now I had to go back, finish my first year, and give whatever I made that year to Sanaa and Alaa. In what dark corner was this Alaa lurking for me? Be that as it may. Every conspiracy must come to an end.

Anyway, I didn't think that Aida would fall for the gallant knight in less than a year.

I fell asleep then got up very early. I asked my mother about Faruq, who I suddenly remembered. She fell silent for a moment then said that she no longer kept up with his news since he had approached her to ask for Sanaa's hand in marriage and she had turned him down. How could she agree to his marrying Sanaa when he had a son from his previous marriage? I was surprised to hear this. She went on to tell me that he had told her that he was working in a land development company on the north coast and that he was making more money than he was in Saudi Arabia. Sanaa, however, had read in the papers that his company had just grabbed state land, subdivided it, and sold it to people for millions of pounds; that people were unable to use the land and that there were many lawsuits filed against the company. I told my mother that I had to go to Cairo. She cried, but I had to go. Sanaa cried and Bahaa shook my hand and I left in tears. There's no such thing as a good farewell; so why did I want to leave so soon?

I arrived in Cairo at eleven in the morning. I got off the bus in front of the Hilton hotel and I saw the frightening Tahrir Square. I climbed the pedestrian bridge and took it to the top of Suliman Street as Abed had directed me before I left. Suddenly I had a sense of relief; the street was cool, the height and breadth of the buildings on both sides gave me the feeling that I was walking in a cellar where, if I wanted to, I could sleep.

It didn't take me long to find the Lufthansa office to my right. I pushed the heavy glass door and talked to one of three pretty young women. She accompanied me upstairs, where I stood in front of a smiling, neatly dressed, middle-aged man. "Please have a seat." I sat down and began to speak. "Where is the bill of lading?" he said. He examined it and smiled. "It's a forgery."

"What?"

"Yes, a forgery. Here, have a look at this." He gave me one that was in front of him. "Do you see a difference?"

"No."

"We can tell the difference. Unfortunately there are lots of international rings that work this scam, especially in America. Why are you shaking?"

"I don't understand anything, sir."

"Are you the owner of the company?"

"I only work there."

"Then go back and tell them what I've told you; I can give you a letter to this effect. Why are you trembling?" I didn't tell him that nobody would believe me. It was me and Larry. Larry would win.

"Tell me what I can do to help."

"Thank you, sir. I would like to send telexes to all those airports and take the responses with me."

"That's easy. And, to reassure you even more, go to Lufthansa's freight terminal at the airport. There you'll see Engineer Magdi. He'll help you look for the equipment and send all the telexes you want."

I couldn't get up. He started to explain to me what I already suspected.

"Imagine that you want to buy a million pounds worth of merchandise for a company and one of the members of the ring met you and tempted you by offering a forged bill of lading in return for ten percent of the merchandise that you hadn't bought. You agree and take the bill. You've just made nine hundred thousand pounds and he's made a hundred thousand, and neither of you did anything for it. Many of the agents sent by the Gulf countries to buy merchandise from America do it. It doesn't matter what happens afterwards. The agent just absconds with the money. The country or company that sent him would get entangled in legal battles with shipping and insurance companies—which they lose. No one so far has been able to win the war against these American rings. Here is a pass to the airport and Lufthansa's freight terminal."

I got up in disbelief. Five thousand riyals to finish the job in Cairo, Mr. Larry, and three hundred thousand dollars for you. Every country really got what it deserved. You made a good choice when you chose me, Larry, you and Rose had a good plan. An intelligent, poor Egyptian who knew that Amm Abdallah would never listen to him. Anyway to hell with all people, all countries, and all oil money. Suliman Street was coming to an end and I couldn't cross the street ahead. I stood. It was cold. The huge red buses were racing down the wide street, spewing black smoke and rumbling. Around it ran microbuses, taxicabs, and cars. People crowded on the sidewalk and crossed the street hurriedly from every point to every point, and at the intersection a number of traffic officers and policemen stood helplessly in the midst of the frightening chaos. Should I go back to Suliman Street, where cars moved slowly but there were no buses and people walked in dense crowds, but at least on the sidewalk? I had noticed several movie theaters along the street; should I go back and go into one of them until the crowds thinned out. I didn't think that would happen until nightfall. Seeing a sign on a big building that said Grand Hotel, I jumped over the iron railing along the sidewalk and ran across the street. "I want a room, quick." I told the receptionist, panting from crossing the street. I stood trying to get my breath back. The receptionist examined me closely.

"Sorry. Do you have a room for one person?" I looked around me involuntarily, still confused, and said, "I'm very sorry. I'm rather afraid of your city. I come from Alexandria and I'm not used to this chaos and crowds. I'm also very hungry. Is there any food in the hotel?"

"We have everything."

I finally saw the smile that hotel workers normally affect. I gave him my passport and a fifty-pound deposit. An old Nubian man led me to my room, and I lay down on the bed forgetting my hunger and my terror. I'd only been in Cairo three times in my life. The last time was when I flew to Saudi Arabia and I didn't even enter the city; the second time was to get my papers approved, so I stayed close to Tahrir Square and only went to the Saudi Consulate in Garden City. The first time was a long time ago.

It was 1968. We had come on a routine school trip for secondary school seniors to visit Aswan and Cairo. We spent two days in Cairo, at a very shabby hotel in Clot Bey Street. My classmates and the teachers visited al-Azhar and al-Husayn mosques, the citadel, the Islamic museum, the military museum, and the pyramids. I escaped from them at al-Azhar and al-Husayn. I walked a lot in Gamaliya and sat at a cheap café in Bayn al-Qasrayn Street, a café that was almost underground. I didn't see a single face that reminded me of Ahmad Abd al-Gawwad, or Fahmi, or little Kamal, or reckless Yasin, or Aisha, persecuted by fate, or Amina, or Khadiga, or the grandchildren. Instead I saw women with huge bottoms, and women with not much on, and I heard obscenities used by men and women. I wondered how and where Naguib Mahfouz's books fitted into all that. I realized for the first time that writing was nothing like what happened to me—a beautiful feeling, and pride in what I wrote. It was a great hardship. I wondered afterwards, would time give me the ability to experience that beautiful hardship? And when I saw Midaq Alley, that very short, narrow, cool, black alley, I wondered how all the characters I had lived, laughed and cried with, lived in it. I was surprised only by the arcades on both sides of Clot Bey Street, the many shoe and handbag stores, and the small, narrow cafés where old women hardly capable of moving, with faces heavy with hilarious make-up, sat and smoked the narghile. At that time Cairo seemed to me to be older than Alexandria, older than time itself. Brick barricades had been erected in front of house entrances, streetlights were turned off in the evening, the smell of defeat was still in the air.

Now Cairo was a publicly grumpy city, unaware of anyone and indifferent to its visitors; its vehicles crushed the toughest bones. I wasn't going to stay long. Day after long, dreary, boring day passed. The Nubian servant told me I could get better food at the neighboring restaurants in Tawfiqiya and drink tea in its cafés. The first restaurant I came to was al-Sham; I went in, and it was big and elegant, but I ate there alone every day. On the other side there was the little Casablanca cafeteria, where I drank my tea with one or two other customers sitting in silence. From the newsstand in front of the hotel I bought all the newspapers and magazines, then went into my room and read, and tossed and turned on the bed. I went to the airport only twice, taking a cab from in front of the hotel. The first time I told Engineer Magdi about my story. The second time he gave me the replies to the telexes. No equipment had left San Francisco and none had arrived at New York, Munich or Cairo.

"Did you have to come to Cairo to do that?"

I smiled, and by the way, Mr. Larry, he refused to take a single penny as a bribe. I was now spending the day in the hotel waiting for the five days to pass, reading the newspapers and magazines, which were talking about the imminent departure of the Egyptian delegation to America, headed by Mustafa Khalil, to prepare for the final signing of the Camp David agreement. I was also reading about harrowing cases of rape, furnished apartments run as brothels, Sadat's picture laughing on every page, with his famous pipe in his mouth. I went out only at night now, and crossed the street confidently. I went to Cinema Metro to watch *Earthquake* because I liked Ava Gardner. The following day I went to Cinema Miami to watch *Ragab on a Hot Tin Roof* and didn't think Adel Imam was very funny. The third night I went to Cinema Cairo Palace to watch the new actress Marie-France Pisier because she was playing opposite Raf Vallone, who had a very expressive face. I wasn't surprised by the frequent intervention of the censor in this beautiful film, which they dubbed as *Destructive Desire* when its real title was *The Other Side of Midnight*. Time didn't pass, so after nine o'clock I walked to al-Husayn. Why did I do that? I wanted to get tired. To be tired at night meant to be able to sleep during the day and meant the passing of the five days despite Cairo's cold nights. Every night I saw the trees of Azbakiya garden like black giants enveloped in darkness. The green and red lights from the cafeterias there looked ugly. I crossed the garden in silence. Looking around I saw people sleeping, covered with sackcloth. Al-Azhar Street was empty, the stores were closed already, and only I and a few cars speeding past me were about. I kept thinking what Azbakiya garden looked like when the French tested their hot air balloon before the frightened and dazzled eyes of the Egyptians. I didn't sit at any cafés or eat in any restaurant in the neighborhood of al-Husayn, as the large numbers of policemen who were out and about determined my route for me. I turned around and caught foul smells coming from the little alleys. I tried to remember what I had decided to do in Cairo that night, my last night there. I remembered. The next morning I was going to visit Said. He had left me his address before leaving. How wonderful it would be to surprise him by visiting him early, I said to myself on my way back to the hotel. It was past one o'clock, and I was walking alone along 26th of July Street. I was very close to the hotel, when a hand grabbed my shoulder and violently pulled me into a dark side alley then pushed me to the wall. There were two of them, with fiery eyes. One carried a sword and the other a long thick iron chain.

"Take out everything in your pocket, you son of a bitch."

I heard the man with the chain and I saw my death in his eyes. The man with the sword backed up and raised his sword in the air. I stalled. Out of total fear I stalled. Death looked me in the eye. The man with the chain backed up and delivered a crushing blow to my arm, which lit a fire in my head; then another one to the side of my left foot. I fell to the ground and crawled in terror; they kicked me repeatedly in the back, then the huge one with the chain lifted me and leaned me against the wall as the one with the sword shouted in a muffled voice, "Leave him to me; I'll kill him."

"I beg you," I implored in a voice that was hardly audible.

"You beg me, you son of . . ."

"Take whatever you want."

He let me fall to the ground. They emptied my pockets.

"He has riyals and dollars. Where are you from, boy?"

"Alexandria."

"So you're one of those harbor thieves."

They both kicked me in the ribs and suddenly disappeared.

The ground felt cold. I was unable to get up. I was so overcome with fatigue I almost slept there. Then I remembered that the rest of my money and my passport were in the hotel. I felt some strength coming back. Supporting myself on my arms, I crawled to the street, then stood up leaning against the walls and walking, almost falling down every step of the way. They really could have killed me. Around me I saw nothing but lampposts that shone into a dark void without even a cold breeze.

22

No Aida, no Wadha, no Rosemary, Arshad, Munzir, or Nabil; no Abed, Mansur, Wagih, or Salih Sanyur al-Thaqafi. No one and nothing enticed me to return or to stay, just a mysterious feeling propelling me forward, and another, equally mysterious, pulling me back. I was leaving Egypt to go to Tabuk. Twenty days earlier I had left Tabuk to come to Egypt. So where was I from? And in what other place was I born, and where did I grow up? The plane took off at five o'clock local time; we arrived at half past seven local time. The flight took one and a half hours, but they were one hour ahead of us. I arrived home at half past eight and found the house dark. Clearly I was going to have to spend the night alone. Wagih was still on night duty.

I went in, changed and looked for food. There was none. I made a cup of tea and stretched out on the bed under the covers. I began eating some cookies I had left in the room and always had on hand for breakfast. I was surprised at how small the room was. This was my room and this was our house, which I opened with my key. I jumped out of bed and turned on the television. When I heard the sound of the mouse in the kitchen, I smiled but decided to start a campaign against mice the following day.

✧

"Didn't you bring me a letter from my mother?" Nabil asked me as he came in with the morning coffee. The morning here was still bitterly cold even though February was over. When I got up, Wagih had not yet returned from the hospital. I wrote him a note, which I left in the kitchen. I told him I was back and asked him to prepare lunch.

Abed was the first to meet me. He didn't ask me about my mission and I chose not to tell him anything. He gave me two letters, saying one was from Riyadh and the other from Diba. He asked me if I knew someone in Diba too.

I said nothing. I looked in my desk for Wadha's earlier letter but couldn't find it. I couldn't ask him about it. I would look more carefully for it.

"You didn't ask me, Nabil, and you didn't give me the address."

I looked at his beard, which he had let grow, and saw a sad smile that I hadn't noticed before. Before I could ask him what had happened to him in my absence, he said, "Yes, perhaps I didn't ask you. You should have gone all the same."

He left, leaving behind gloom in the room. Had I not noticed the two letters in my hand, I would have forgotten about them too. I put them in my jacket pocket and got ready to receive the workers who had begun to arrive for signing-in. They all smiled at me, but Munzir stood talking to me after embracing me and patting me on the back and kissing my cheeks affectionately.

"I left the house, Ustaz," he said.

"Which house, Munzir?"

"The house where I lived. I told you I had stories, but you didn't give me a chance."

"You still remember, Munzir?"

"By God, I want to forget but that whore won't let me. I've rented an Arabian house. Guess who objected? My wife. She's such an idiot."

"If you had told her the story she wouldn't have objected."

"Come on, Ustaz, Egyptian! Me tell my wife? Do you think I'm crazy? Women aren't very smart. She would never believe me. She'd say me and the woman were having something on the side and my life would become a living hell. The stupidest men are those who tell their wives the truth. A woman, Ustaz, can only see what's in her own head."

He left me as I laughed. I began to take out the reports that Abed couldn't translate in my absence, but Amm Abdallah arrived and I heard him asking Abed about me, so I realized he was going to send for me.

"What have you done, Ismail?" he asked when I went into his office. Larry, who was with him, shook my hand warmly. Amm Abdallah shook it indifferently. I didn't answer his question, but gave him the reply telexes.

"What's that?"

I made a point of not looking at Larry and said, "They're replies to telexes. No equipment has left San Francisco and none has arrived at any of the airports."

Amm Abdallah was visibly annoyed and looked at Larry, who was smiling impassively. "What do we do, Larry?"

"Well, someone better go to San Francisco."

Amm Abdallah looked even more annoyed and said, "Well, get ready to go then."

He got up to leave, then suddenly smiled and said, "Don't forget to take Rose with you. Don't leave her alone in the camp."

Amm Abdallah laughed and so did Larry and followed him out.

✧

Hardly half an hour had passed since Amm Abdallah and Larry left when the telephone rang. It was Larry asking me to accept another invitation to lunch.

"I don't think I can come today, Mr. Larry."

"This is Rose's wish, Mr. Ismail. You have to come."

"No, really, I'm busy today, Mr. Larry."

"Then we'll expect you for dinner, Mr. Ismail."

Before I could say anything he said, "Don't even try to say no, Mr. Ismail."

He didn't give me a chance. I wasn't surprised by his lying. When did Rose find out that I had returned? I knew the ending of the story and I was going to go to let him know that I knew.

I felt my jacket to make sure the letters were still there. I couldn't read them in the office, not out of fear of anyone, but out of fear of losing them. I resolved to set aside a place at home for letters—which I knew would continue to come.

"Who? Mansur?" I said when I saw him at the door with a little monkey on his shoulder. It looked exactly like the other one except that the hair around its neck was gray.

"How are you, Ismail? How was Egypt?" he said as he came in and sat behind the other desk as usual.

"Fine, Mansur."

"You saw the family and found everyone all right?"

"Everything in Egypt is fine, Mansur."

"I know, brother Ismail. I was there too."

"In Egypt?"

"Of course. I went there first and spent a week there, then I went to Sudan. Didn't you see Said there?"

"I wanted to visit him but I ran out of time." I didn't want to tell him what happened to me that last night and how I almost missed my plane because I couldn't get up before noon.

"I visited him, brother Ismail. Poor Said now has a beard and holds prayer beads and speaks to no one."

Mansur didn't give me a chance to think. He said, "I got his address from Widad. You know her?"

I didn't answer nor was I able to. He added, "Widad is getting ready to quit her job here. She's leaving soon for Kuwait."

"She's getting married to a relative of hers."

"No, she's not marrying anybody. What do you think of this monkey?"

I smiled. Mansur struck me as a ludicrous clown.

"I went from Egypt to Sudan and I bought ten monkeys and had them shipped to Tabuk. You want a monkey?"

"No, Mansur. I don't want anything. I have work to do."

"Don't worry, brother Ismail. I'll leave you in peace."

He went out leaving me almost suffocated. I no longer wanted to work or to talk to anyone. I didn't think the day would pass in peace. I spent the time thinking of the riddles I was confronted with. I couldn't make much of anything. At twelve o'clock I looked at the forecourt. The old Yemeni wasn't there.

✧

What would happen if I went to Rose and Larry at lunch time? That would throw a monkey wrench in their plans. I would tell them what I'd found out and then it would all be over. I'd go home, having said good-bye to Rose forever and I'd read Wadha's and Aida's letters slowly. Wadha's letter would be no more than a nice good-bye. How else could the story end?

Then Aida's letter could take up the whole night. I wondered what she thought of my being so late responding to her letter because of the time I spent in Egypt. Again Egypt was causing one to lose everything. I was sure that Aida would not close the door forever. Oh, what a wretched job it was that sent a crazy person my way every moment! I really wanted to read Aida's letter but I couldn't. Nabil came in silently with coffee.

"I didn't order coffee."

"You never ordered it before. Shall I take it back?"

I looked at his sad face and long beard.

"Sit down."

He sat, looking at the floor.

"What happened to you while I was away? Did anybody bother you?"

"Not at all."

"Then why do you look so pale and why haven't you been shaving?"

He didn't answer but looked at me with a defeated look. Then he said, "Don't you read the papers or listen to the news?"

I didn't answer. What was in the papers that could upset Nabil so much? Iran had fallen to Khomeini, Shahpour Bakhtiar had disappeared; Carter was getting ready to invite Begin and Sadat to sign the peace treaty. Yesterday they inaugurated the 6th of October bridge in Cairo. The British queen was visiting Saudi Arabia, where they organized a camel race for her. I didn't think any of that would bother Nabil.

"You don't want to believe me when I tell you that flying saucers are for real."

"You still remember, Nabil? The newspapers aren't talking about that anymore."

"They'll be back and the papers will talk about them. I'm scared."

I smiled encouragingly and said, "What are you afraid of, Nabil?"

"If one of them fell here, we'd all burn. Wouldn't we?"

I said nothing. I never believed that what he said was the reason behind his sadness, or his beard. He would never tell me anything. There was no point in continuing the conversation. There were a lot of reports that I hadn't begun to work on, so I decided to start. It was not likely that anyone would distract me in the little time I had left.

✧

"Mr. Ismail? What a surprise!"

Rose opened the door incredulously. She gave me a beaming, broad smile and invited me in.

"Larry's not here now but that's okay. He'll be here soon. He must have been held up for some reason or other with Mr. Abdallah. He told me you were coming for dinner. Please make yourself at home. Give me a few minutes to change."

She spoke very fast and in obvious confusion. Then she left and I sat down on the chair I hadn't used the previous time. She disappeared and I heard her whispering with somebody whose voice I couldn't make out. I smiled. It couldn't be anybody else but Larry. She was a smart woman and she handled the situation ably. Then suddenly I realized the foolishness of what I had done. Just because I knew their secret, why had I come? To tell them that was not enough reason. What was the use of that now? There was no connection between me and these people except for a hostility that I developed as a boy and a young man. I never believed what Sadat repeated over and over about the "American friend." I never hated seeing anybody as much as I hated seeing them the day they landed in Alexandria after Nixon's visit and walked in the streets in their Marine uniforms and crew cuts, big and tall, looking at people and stores, waving a greeting to whoever they came across. That day I remembered the films about American sailors when Gene Kelly or Tony Curtis would disembark and go into town and have a fight in one of the bars. There were lots of them after Nixon's visit, walking down the corniche, cheerfully riding horse-drawn carriages and singing. Now there were so few of them you hardly saw them anymore.

I realized that my visit didn't make any sense and thought of leaving. But I saw Rose coming toward me looking radiant, preceded by a perfume that did a number on my senses. She wore a low-cut blue dress that revealed her cleavage and plump arms.

When Rose turned her face to the refrigerator I saw a large area of her back and her thick blond hair tied with a thin blue ribbon. She brought two glasses of wine, put them on the little table between us, and sat down. She said, "I couldn't leave without seeing you."

"Thank you."

"You must be hungry, Mr. Ismail. Shall we eat now or wait for Larry?"

"I'm not really hungry—and as you know, I don't drink."

"Then let me show you something pretty."

She took me by the hand. I got up and found myself standing in the bedroom.

"Don't think badly of me, Mr. Ismail. That's not the way to seduce you." I smiled. This was Rose who dazzled me the first time I saw her, the same Rose who shared my bed in my dreams and mocked me in my nightmares. I found her appealing once, I lusted for her once, I confess, but now I saw her like a piece of bad meat.

"What's the pretty thing you want to show me?"

She pointed to the bed. I sat on its edge and she sat next to me.

"You're very intelligent, Rose."

"I don't approve of what Larry did. But after all I am his wife and I have to protect him."

"I wish you had chosen someone else. Why did you pick me?"

She came closer and whispered, "You won't believe me, Ismail. I was going to do it to somebody else. But I liked you and I wanted to find a way to reach you."

"There's nothing I can do, Rose. I'm an Egyptian. People here wouldn't believe me and not you. You didn't need to go through all that. Do you know what really bothers me? Do you remember our first meeting here in your house? I was very rude but Larry was even ruder. He wanted to appear superior to me. He didn't have to do that. Did he have the right to do that when he's . . . ?"

I didn't complete the sentence. We fell silent for a long time.

"Please let me kiss you," she said.

I let her take my face between her hands and kiss my lips, my cheeks, my nose then go back to pressing my lips. She didn't try to bring her body closer to me nor did I try. I was busy looking at her eyes, which were closed. When she opened them, they were ecstatic. I got up.

"Good-bye, Rose."

"Good-bye, Ismail."

I saw pain in her eyes so I hurried out. She didn't come after me. As I made it to the door of the house I heard her yelling, "You are the stupidest man in the world, Larry, and I'm not going to let you get away with everything."

23

"Ismail, why did you let them do that to me? I love you. Don't forget me. Wadha."

I wish I hadn't started with your letter. I drove from Rose's house at full speed to be by myself and open the letters. Did you know that I started with your letter out of carelessness and with the knowledge that the story had ended, that what happened was no more than a whim or a fit of madness? Wadha bint Sulayman ibn Sabil, delicate like a little sparrow, what do you expect from me, who came from the lands of the Nile trailing thousands of years? Was that the reason you cleaved to me? Why did you pick *me*? The police paraded you the day I arrived and your body quivered in front of my eyes; my friend recommended me to your brother then I met you face to face and I couldn't run away. I advanced without fear, or have you forgotten? But there are those among your people who are hell-bent against me. Salih Sanyur al-Thaqifi is stronger than all of us, armed with foolishness and frustrated innocence. I haven't left you, Wadha. Now, would you let me read the other letter? It's not your first letter. I don't know how or where I lost it. That was not a good omen.

✧

I realized suddenly when I came home that Wagih was not there. He didn't usually go to the hospital before six o'clock. I found no lunch prepared, despite my note to him in the morning. I hadn't seen him yet. I hadn't had my lunch either. I opened the refrigerator, but there was nothing but cans of juice. I went into his room and found a can of tuna on a small table. I ate it quickly and stretched out on the bed, reading.

"Dear Ismail, there was nothing I could do but accept. Fate has always been on my side. I didn't seek to go to Diba. They asked for one of us and everyone was terrified. I volunteered to go right away, but I came to realize later on that it was somebody else who volunteered, not me, someone else who spoke and agreed, not me. But I don't regret it. Diba is not hell. On the contrary, it's a beautiful small town near the sea, the Red Sea. People here are kind. The fishermen come by to the hospital every day and offer me the best fish they have for free. I have enough fish here to feed the whole of Tabuk. Do you think I can eat all that fish? Nobody would take any fish from me, because all the townspeople have even more fish than I do. It is very strange that I am telling you all of this. Please forgive me. I only wanted to let you know I am doing fine. I know you need to know that. I saw you the first time when you came to the hospital to spend the evening with Dr. Wagih, and I know that I'll see you again. But . . . everyone here likes me. The women know how lonely I am so they come after hours to sit with me, and so time passes easily. Some of them even send their daughters to spend the night here with me; a rare display of courage for Saudi women. Well, maybe not so rare. After all, the Arabians are known for their generosity, as we learned in our schoolbooks. How else could women be so generous to fellow women? Please forgive me for my inelegant style. I often think of my fellow nurses and I laugh. What comes over them in this quiet, beautiful place? True, if you thought of the vast expanse around and of the old town of Diba, which was deserted by its inhabitants when they moved to the new town, you might go crazy. Old Diba isn't far from here. I can see its old, ruined houses at night from the roof, like cemeteries filled with ghosts. But I try not to look in that direction. During the day I see it the way you see an archaeological site that deserves to be visited, but I don't visit it. In short I can escape feeling lonely by doing things. I rearrange the room, rearrange the medications in the pharmacy. I always do everything after hours. The hospital is very big, but I lock it up from inside. After hours, the patients go to the doctors in their houses, then come to me and I give them their prescription drugs through a hole in the door. I am only bothered by patients who come in the middle of the night, but all the rooms here are well lit; I leave the lights on all night. During the day the light of the sun is stronger than any other light. I am never frightened when somebody comes at night. I am only bothered by the cold when I leave my room and go down to help somebody. Is it still very cold in Tabuk? My brother Hashim always said, "Say to anyone who worries that no worry lasts forever. Just as joy fades away, so do worries." He always said that to me and got me out of my daydreams. Sometimes he sang it to me. Why did I have so many daydreams when I was a young schoolgirl? Everyone wondered about that, my parents, my brothers, my classmates, and the teachers. You know I do not love anyone in this world as much as I love Hashim. I always believed him. I still do."

I reread the letter and almost screamed. What kind of pernicious madness was creeping into Aida's head without her knowing it? Every word in the letter spoke of it. I read the letter again to respond to every word in it, to rearrange it and show her that she was on the road to ruin, that she was riding a most obstinate horse. But she wouldn't listen to me. She wouldn't listen to anyone. Noble, chivalrous gestures were neither useful nor needed.

I placed the two letters in front of me on the bed and stared at them. My mind stopped working; my imagination was blank. Then I heard the key turn in the outside door, so I hurriedly hid them under the pillow. Wagih came in with the young doctor I had seen at the hospital the day the young Lebanese woman was deported. I remembered him well despite his pale, sad face—or perhaps that was why I remembered him.

Wagih shook my hand and embraced and kissed me. He said how surprised he was at my sudden return. The young doctor appeared totally oblivious to us and began biting his fingernails. He was so exhausted he started leaning against the wall.

"Please have a seat, Dr. Ahmad," said Wagih and pointed to a seat in my room. Ahmad sat down and kept biting his nails, oblivious to us. Wagih asked me, "When did you come back?"

"Yesterday."

"I didn't come back from the hospital in the morning."

I realized only then that he, too, looked very tired. He stretched out on my bed and said, "If you go into my room you'll find a small box of eggs and canned stuff under the bed. I bought it a couple of days ago but didn't have time to put it in the kitchen. We need a proper supper."

He kept looking at the ceiling, his hands joined under his head. I went to his room wondering how he couldn't find the time to put the stuff in the kitchen when he could have come in from outside directly into the kitchen. Anyway, I prepared a supper of boiled eggs, sliced cheese, cold cuts, and olives. I went into the room carrying it on a big tray. Ahmad suddenly got up.

"You must eat something," said Wagih, but Ahmad continued to bite his nails.

"You want to sleep?"

Ahmad nodded. Wagih got up and took him to his room, then came back. Before he sat down, he said, "An unforgettable day. Let's eat."

I placed the tray on the floor and we sat down around it. Wagih picked up an egg, placed it, whole, in his mouth and said, "Do you remember Dr. Rafat?"

"The urologist who went back to Egypt a few months ago?"

"Yes."

He had another egg and added, "He went to America and bought all the equipment for the clinic, and died before the clinic opened."

I fell silent. I kept eating slowly as he picked up one egg after another and placed them each, whole, in his mouth.

"Strange, isn't it?" he said.

I said nothing. Said, who had decided to go back to Egypt for good at the end of the year, had to go earlier than he planned. Rafat, who was happy because he was able to decide when to go back, went back and died. Why hadn't I met Wagih yesterday? If I had we would have talked about something else. I wanted to read Aida's letter once again. I wanted to write to her. Why is everybody reiterating the lesson of this country? This is a land that insists on holding on to whatever and whoever falls onto it, never letting go. If he rebels, it kills him; by a stroke of fate or misfortune, or a naive mistake, it kills him. It kills in any case. Killing is the end. Aida knows and she is digging her own grave. Salih Sanyur al-Thaqifi is a good son of this land. Small and fragile he might be, but he insists on having the upper hand, even in charity. The nomad has come into wealth but he doesn't realize it's not his handiwork. Woe unto all city-dwellers.

How could I write a letter to Aida now with Wagih sleeping in my narrow bed, snoring and leaving me such a small part of the bed? I could hardly move. He said he had taken the whole day off because it was impossible for him to work two nights in a row without sleep. During the day he was busy with Ahmad, who, said Wagih, should never have left Egypt. He also said he knew Ahmad's family and was an old friend of his folks. He was very happy when Ahmad came to the Kingdom, but Ahmad was as delicate as lace and couldn't take it. Less than a week after he arrived the director of the hospital assigned him to accompany the young Lebanese woman to the airport. Today, the director assigned him to go to the military base to attend the execution of a soldier who had shot his officer. It was not a beheading but death by firing squad in the military tradition. Ahmad had to go place a mark in white paint around the heart of the soldier for the firing squad to aim at, then he had to examine the body and confirm the death. Ahmad had initially refused to go but the director insisted, so the poor man went, and placed the mark around the heart. Bullets were fired; they hit every part of his body except the heart. They took the soldier and Ahmad in the same ambulance to the hospital; the soldier to the morgue and Ahmad to the doctors' lounge. Ahmad was leaving for Cairo in a few days. He had requested that his contract be terminated as soon as he recovered from his breakdown. Wagih had spent the whole day with him and failed to persuade him to stay, so he brought him home out of fear for him.

24

No letters from anyone.

"Please forgive me for being so late in writing to you. I have been in Egypt, where I spent twenty days on urgent business that I couldn't beg off. Did I, perhaps, need to go without knowing it? Once I was there, I felt I needed to come back. Now I want to travel again, but not to Egypt. If there's one reason for my coming back here, it is you . . . I can't say any more. I would love to come and visit you, but I am afraid. What sense would there be if you were to receive me warmly and then I had to return? I fear staying too long and ruining the whole thing.

"Our days here are like your days there and so are the nights and the sky. The dust storms beat down on all of us with equal force. But I don't have your strength. You were born to give; I was born to learn too late. I'd like, for once, to be certain, in time. Many times, awake and in my sleep, I have seen you take me by the hand and lead me away from death. I would like to take you by the hand and lead you away from your impossible choice. Would you accept me as your husband, Aida?"

No letters. Every day I look at Abed's eyes. It is he who goes into town more than once during the day and passes by the post office. Abed has nothing for me except orders to wait until he returns.

We made a dent into the month of March. Spring began to dispel the cold of the morning with its early light. It didn't prevent the dust storms.

✧

"Where's Arshad?" I asked the Pakistanis, who had come back from their vacations and gleefully came into my office that beautiful morning.

"Sarwar knows, he lives near him in Peshawar."

Sarwar came in a few minutes later; a short man who bounced rather than walked, with gleaming eyes, always smiling.

"Poor Arshad, Mr. Ismail. He's in jail."

"Jail?"

"Yes, Mr. Ismail. He was arrested as soon as we arrived. He's not coming back, Mr. Ismail."

I said nothing.

"Arshad works with the opposition, Mr. Ismail. The opposition sends its members to many countries in the Gulf to raise funds. That's what the press says, Mr. Ismail."

Again I said nothing.

"I am sorry, Mr. Ismail. I know he was a good friend."

Sarwar left. So, Arshad will never be coming back. My God, what are they doing to him now?

"The military are stupid, Mr. Ismail," he had told me. Did the military hear him?

I saw Abed at the door, smiling. He asked me, "Have you seen Munzir?"

"He hasn't come yet."

"He's not coming."

Nothing.

"He was arrested yesterday and charged with attempted rape. He's still with the police."

"I'm not working today."

I hurried to my car and sped off, paying no heed to Abed's repeated pleas to return nor to the look of mortified surprise on his face.

✧

The light opened up the world in front of me; vast expanses of majestically brilliant sands. Above me were scattered wisps of clouds and above all an unbelievably blue and clear sky. Why was it that since my arrival in this town I hadn't seen a single bird in the sky? I did not even see the sparrows that I heard chirping outside the window in the hospital, not a single one of them came in and stood for a moment on the ledge to look at us then fly away. A country without birds, how could that be? Or was it that I no longer looked upward?

I struggled not to look at the spot where I had seen the dog once. Why was I overcome with the desire to look today? I looked and I saw it. The white dog, as big as a stray donkey, hadn't changed. I kept driving my car at a tremendous speed until I came to the end of the road and then slowed down to turn onto the main street. It was at that moment only that I realized I was going to the police station to see Munzir. It was also at that moment that I wondered whether that was possible. I didn't wait for an answer, nor did the Caprice that swerved toward me forcing me to go off the road, cross the small median and end up in the other lane. There, my car hit another car head on, my chest hit the steering wheel and my head the windshield. I felt nothing until people started to pull me away from the front of the car and the windshield, which had totally shattered. I had a terrible pain in my head and face and a stifling sensation in the chest.

"Nothing serious, nothing serious," said the pleasant, smiling face of a young Egyptian who I didn't know. There was a large crowd around me as I sat stretched out on the sidewalk, trying to stop myself from fainting and feeling hot blood on my face. I saw a young Saudi police officer yelling over and over again, "You!"

Then Wagih's face appeared from out of the crowd.

"Come on, let's go to the hospital. Put him in my car."

"Nothing serious, God willing," the young Egyptian with the pleasant face said as he held my arm helping me to walk to Wagih's car.

"He's not going to the hospital. The police station first," the officer yelled at Wagih, who yelled back, "I am Dr. Wagih, chief surgeon at the hospital. This young man will bleed to death here or in the police station. Are you willing to take responsibility for that?"

"So are you responsible for delivering him to us?"

"I am."

Wagih took me by my other arm and we got into his car, I and the young Egyptian with the pleasant face who kept saying, "Nothing serious, God willing. Don't worry."

He didn't stop smiling in my face so I smiled and saw that his smile was very sweet. I asked, "What happened?"

"A little accident," the young man said.

But Wagih told me, "Not so little. You hit a police car, Ustaz. Thank God I was coming back from the hospital now and saw you."

The young man asked, "Do you know him, Doctor?"

"Of course. He's my roommate."

"Thank God. Well, can you drop me off here? I don't think you need anything from me. Do you?"

"No. Thank you very much," Wagih said, and I smiled and with difficulty I held out my hand to shake his. He patted it and left.

✧

Wagih didn't take me to the hospital but to the main clinic on the main street. There I stretched on the examination table as he and a dark-complexioned Egyptian nurse began to pick the little pieces of glass from my head wounds. He had to cut the hair off my whole head, and he started to laugh when he saw my shaved head. He found only two pieces of glass in my forehead. He was relieved when he found my ribs intact. Then he said, "I'm going to have to write a big report to strengthen your position vis-à-vis the police."

"Does it need all that?"

"Of course. You swerved off the road, ended up in the wrong lane and hit a police car. In ordinary cases you can pay damages to the wronged party, but with the police, I don't know what might happen. Couldn't you find any other car to hit?"

"I didn't hit anybody. I saw a Caprice heading straight for me so I swerved. I don't know how I went over the median."

He laughed. "You can look at yourself in the mirror and laugh, anyway. I'll bandage your head with gauze, even though you don't need it, so the police will take pity on you."

He bandaged my head, looked at his watch, and said to me, "Nobody's come. You can go home now."

"But I want to go to the police station."

"What?"

"I had left work to go to the police station."

"Why?"

I didn't answer. The officer who was yelling at the time of the accident came in. He asked me to go with him. Before Wagih could say anything, I said, "I can go with you."

I saw Wagih looking at me in troubled surprise. "I will come with you too," he said.

✧

Wagih's plan was to telephone Abu Hakim before we went there. He had tried twice but couldn't find him. He was afraid the case would be turned over to the court in the absence of Abu Hakim, in which case it would be a month in jail at least. That was why he wanted to stall the officer, not knowing that I wanted to go as soon as I could to see Munzir before he was deported or sent to jail. But why did I really want to see Munzir?

When we arrived, Abu Hakim welcomed us and I saw Wagih breathe a sigh of relief.

"Sorry for bothering you, Egyptian brother. We will pay you the indemnity, Ustaz Ismail, if you waive charges against that crazy dog," said Abu Hakim suddenly after we sat down. An elderly man came with a teapot. Wagih looked at me in surprise and tapped my foot with his foot. I assumed he wanted me to say nothing.

"We caught the Caprice driver," continued Abu Hakim. "People led us to him. What's between you and this boy, Doctor? I'm going to get this lout; he will not get away. But it should be over something worthwhile. What does he want from you, brother Ismail?"

"I don't know what you're talking about."

"Salih al-Thaqifi. I think you left his house."

"We left him in peace," answered Wagih after warning me with his eyes not to say anything. "We have good relations with him. I don't think Salih meant anything."

I was still thinking about what Abu Hakim was saying. Was Salih al-Thaqifi really the driver of that Caprice? What did he want from me? Did he want to kill me or set me up in a big crash? I didn't know. Who could guarantee that the thin line between setting me up and killing me would remain intact? I said resignedly, "I don't believe he meant anything either."

Abu Hakim laughed and said, "You, Doctor, have come to know us well. But your friend doesn't know us yet. Let him speak freely." Then he said, "Don't fear anything, brother Ismail. Here we have laws and a police force that can protect you."

"Thank you—but that's the truth."

"And the indemnity, will you waive it?"

"I'll waive it."

"You Egyptians are something else!"

The elderly man came by again, carrying a coffee pot. I drank a small cup for the first time; it had that bitter taste I couldn't stand. I drank another cup and said, "I have a little problem here, Abu Hakim."

✧

Munzir came in, looking crestfallen and very pale. He saw me and I saw his red eyes as he smiled ironically

"I left the apartment building, Ustaz, for an Arabian house, a beautiful old house with lemon and palm trees. My wife is pregnant, so I said to myself the garden is for the boy, Jihad. I'm going to name him Jihad. And what happened, Ustaz? Munzir doesn't forget. Munzir never gets tired.

Without Munzir everything comes to a standstill. Then came that damned husband of hers, the old man who walks and talks and does everything with great difficulty, if at all. He asked me to go with him to fix the air conditioning in the apartment building. I went from apartment to apartment until I got to his. I went in; he came with me then went out without me realizing it, and the police came as I stood on the ladder fixing the cables. It's almost like a movie, Ustaz, and you'll see. There will be no trial and I will not go to jail. I'll be deported."

"Deporting you would be difficult, Munzir. Palestinians are tried, jailed, and punished, but not deported."

"The Palestinians, Ustaz! Now I am Jordanian and I am not so unhappy about it. Deporting me means I have a homeland to go back to. They found me a homeland, Ustaz, and nobody turns down a homeland!"

"Get going, boy," said Abu Hakim, motioning a policeman to take Munzir away. The only thing I could do was to hug and kiss him. "Forgive me, Ustaz. I love you. I love Egyptians very much, The only one I hate is Sadat, Ustaz. One of my ancestors is an Egyptian, one who refused to take part in digging the Suez Canal and fled to the Levant." The policeman pulled him and he went along.

"Don't be so sad, Egyptian. That's the way the world goes, as you say in Egypt. Don't believe this boy's story."

How had Abu Hakim heard him when he was speaking so softly?

"God's greetings."

"God's peace."

Wagih held out his hand and shook Abu Hakim's. I didn't hold out my hand nor did Abu Hakim hold out his to me. I didn't believe that Munzir's new house had a garden with lemon and palm trees. The only house I knew like that was the one where Sayyid al-Gharib was waiting.

✧

I returned home exhausted. Wagih went into his room to sleep. I lay down on my bed. "It's a trap set for me, Ustaz. I know." Munzir had walked into the trap, of his own free will and with his eyes wide open. I picked up one of the magazines lying on the floor next to the bed and looked at its cover. Why did I open it at the last few pages to look at the readers' letters?

"We have received a letter from our friend Wadha bint Sulayman ibn Sabil from Riyadh, in which she says that she loves Egypt very much, and that she wishes the Egyptian president hadn't gone to Israel, causing this rift between Egypt and Saudi Arabia. She asks whether Egyptian universities are accepting Saudi students now and whether the Saudi government approves of young Saudis enrolling in Egyptian universities. To our friend Wadha we say that, like you, we wish he hadn't gone there, but one does not attain all one wishes for, as our great poet al-Mutanabbi said. As for enrolling in Egyptian universities, we now have universities of the highest caliber here, so there is no reason for our youth to go to Egypt for education."

So Wadha was sending me messages in these indirect letters. Who told her I read the local magazines? She must know that time does not pass though lifetimes are stolen.

25

The world is beautiful and life is truly worth living for we live only once. Here and now, my head is opening up little by little and the vitality and rush of youth are being poured into it. I can remember every book I've read. Who said that, Ismail? Ostrovsky, as he ran through the White Army with his sword and bullets, behind a vanguard of optimism. But I am an old connoisseur of writers' lies and shouldn't deceive myself now, otherwise it would be quite laughable. I do not need any new pain. The world appears to me like a woman taking off a layer of clothes every day, revealing more charms. As March progresses I shed some of my own clothing. The guard of the wind has imprisoned the dust storm in his cave and killed its dusty rooster on realizing that even with its wings clipped, it was still able to blow the dust through its beak. I haven't yet received any reply from Aida. Every day I decide to go visit her and every day I wait.

I devised a system to kill the mice. I placed a wooden board under the kitchen sink in such a way that it formed an acute angle with the wall. I began to chase them until they got between the board and the wall then I pressed the board with my foot, crushing them. So far I've killed three. Today I thought of starting a body count. I had gotten up feeling refreshed, jubilantly had two eggs for breakfast and ran to the courtyard to look at the clear sky. I breathed in the pure air then suddenly stopped and decided to take a body count of my victims.

I stood in my room holding the letter pad to record the number of my dead victims, whose names I didn't know. Today is the 26th of March, 1979. Suddenly the room felt bigger and I felt as if cool, refreshing water was being poured into my chest. Why don't I keep a diary, starting today? Keeping a dairy would make of me a third person who can see without burdening the heart with sorrows. Which wicked author wrote that? I don't remember and I don't care. I should go to work right away.

✧

I never started a diary. It wasn't easy to become a third person. I chose the wrong time to feign strength. Amm Abdallah always came in a great hurry and the dust was always there; whatever got blown away during the day was returned by the devils during the night.

Abed came into my room with terrified eyes.

"Did you do anything wrong?"

"No."

"Amm Abdallah is very angry. He has sent for you. Go, and don't talk back to him no matter what he says."

I got up and left my office in surprise. I was also thinking, "Why was Abed so gentle all of a sudden?"

"What did you do in Egypt? What did you do about the equipment?"

"Nothing. I couldn't find it anywhere. I told you that."

Amm Abdallah threw a small piece of paper, which didn't reach me or end up on his desk. I bent down and picked it up from the floor. He yelled at me, "Read."

"Sorry, Mr. Abdallah. I am not coming back to the Kingdom. Bye. Larry."

"Do you know what that means?"

"Mr. Larry is not coming back."

"Larry is a thief who stole three hundred thousand dollars. You are a sly Egyptian pharaoh; you went to his house, where you ate and drank liquor and slept with his wife. Did you or did you not sleep with Rose?"

"No."

We fell silent and everything around us was silent. I said "no" in an almost inaudible voice and was about to say, "It is you who sleeps with Rose in Abed and Nabil's room; it is you who breaks the laws of the Kingdom by giving her a job in a day-care center and makes it possible for her husband to rob the company blind. After all, it's not your company; you're only the director, you only care about your own affairs, and Abed spends more time dealing with them than he does with the company." But I just stood there, silently wondering where the explosion would come from, after all this silence.

"Go. Get out of my sight," he said in obvious discomfort. I left, not displeased with myself. What bothered me was that I really hadn't slept with Rose.

✧

The Yemeni did not show up today either. I looked at the clock; it was twelve. I looked at the forecourt; he wasn't there. I had forgotten that he hadn't shown up for a few days. I also forgot to find out why. Nabil came into the room bringing the coffee. His beard was getting longer. He wanted to speak with me. He stood hesitantly, then sat down and asked, "What's going to happen now?"

"About what?"

"The American satellite."

"The one that stopped working in space?"

"Yes."

"It will come down somewhere. That's what the radio says."

"And are you happy about that?"

Nabil's question took me by surprise. I said, smiling and puzzled, "What can I do about it?"

He fell silent for a moment then said, "Nobody said where it was coming down exactly."

"They said Australia was the most likely spot."

"But it hasn't come down yet. Three people in Australia committed suicide out of fear, but it hasn't come down."

We fell silent. I couldn't laugh. I began to think seriously about finding a way to help him cope with these ideas of his but couldn't. I didn't understand the reason for the new direction his reasoning was going. I said, "The flying saucer phenomenon is over and nothing happened. The satellite thing will also pass peacefully."

"I don't think so. This is a real satellite with real owners."

"Nabil, maybe it's better that you tell me about yourself. How are you these days? Do you get any letters from Egypt?"

"I got one from my mother telling me that my fiancée has married the cab driver."

We fell silent again. Tears were welling up in Nabil's eyes.

"Take care of yourself, Nabil. With time you can forget everything; you can start over again."

"I don't think my mother is telling the truth," he said, and left.

✧

I went home and had lunch with Wagih. We didn't say much. I wanted to finish quickly so I could be by myself in the room. Abed had brought me two letters. He gave them to me as he was leaving the office, but one or two steps later he turned and smiled at me. Aida's name was written on the back of one envelope and my brother's name on the other. Abed's gesture diminished my joy at receiving the letters. I expected him to come back to the office to see me reading them. I don't know why I was reminded of Uriah Heep in *David Copperfield*, which I had started to translate at one time but never finished. I could hardly believe the day was over and I could go home and be by myself reading my private correspondence.

"I received your letter as I was getting ready to travel. It seems you didn't have a good time in Egypt. You didn't tell me what happened exactly but everyone who goes back to Egypt comes back and says the same thing. Why is that so? And when they are there they also complain about here.

"Of course you could have visited me. There's no problem with that provided you come early in the day. It wouldn't have been difficult to introduce you to my colleagues, men and women, as a dear friend. Now, however, you can't visit me because I am leaving in the morning. It would have been wonderful if you had come. Now there's nothing I can do. The minister of health visited our hospital and heard that I was doing an outstanding job. He laughed a lot when he found out I spent the nights all alone in the big hospital. He wondered how I wasn't afraid or going crazy. He said I must be rewarded and ordered that I be transferred to Abha, in the south. Abha is a really beautiful city. They say it has a European climate. The minister's visit came at a crucial time; I had begun to lose some of my strength, and fear was beginning to find its way to my heart. The hospital is horrible at night. The sky above is beautiful but I couldn't spend the whole night looking up. We don't have television here yet. The radio is my friend but the radio only brings pain. The sound of the wind on the roof terrifies me now and every time someone knocks on the door for medicine, I think it's the security forces come to arrest Hashim. They always came at night. Do you know what intrigued me the last few days? A bizarre situation: Diba is made up of two towns, Old Diba and New Diba nearby. People moved out of Old Diba en masse but New Diba is exactly the same as the old one. How do you explain that? I will send you my new address. Until then, peace."

No answer to my question. I heard a mouse moving around in the kitchen. I got up and chased it from behind the cabinet into the space between the wooden board and the wall and crushed it.

✧

Wagih did not go to work today.

"There's something I've been keeping from you, Ismail. I'm transferring to al-Malik Hospital in Medina. I can recommend an Egyptian to be your roommate."

"Are you moving for good?"

"Pretty much. And I'm leaving tomorrow."

"I don't need any roommates."

"You're going to live alone in the house?"

I said nothing. As if he didn't know that I had been living alone ever since I came here. He also didn't know that my brother's letter contained the news that my mother was sick and that they needed two hundred pounds. My brother did not tell me what my mother had. His letter made me forget Aida's letter for a few minutes and Wagih's news made me forget both letters. The announcer speaking at that moment made me forget everything. He said the station was going live to cover the ceremony of the signing of the Camp David Agreement in the American White House. "We are not providing this live coverage of the event to support it or bless it but so that the people can see the treason with their own eyes."

Carter is standing, smiling, at the center of a long, white table, with Sadat standing to his right and Begin to his left. Flowers almost cover the whole table; on both sides of the big lawn, politicians and the press, watching and taking pictures. Carter is speaking about the painstaking efforts exerted by the three leaders to reach this agreement, and the great hopes of ending the conflict in the Middle East. He speaks of peace in the Old Testament and the Quran: "And if they incline to peace, incline thou also to it," saying it in Arabic. Carter's voice fades off as the voice of the local announcer is heard saying: "The Quran also says, 'And make ready for them all the force you can muster and all the horses of battle to strike fear into the hearts of the enemies of God and your enemies.' God Almighty speaks the truth."

✧

At dawn I got up and sat on my bed and turned on the light and said I was not going to sleep in this town after today. I went into a big theater that had no seats, just a square stage. I was the only spectator sitting on the only seat at the door. On the stage, nineteen men, women and children stood at the sides. At the far end of center stage was a woman tied by the hands to the back of a bed, bending her legs at the knees, a white sheet covering her lower body. She was screaming and raising her upper body, sweat covering her face, her eyes bulging in horrendous pain. The eyes of the men, women, and children bulged with terror. Above the woman Satan sat in a suspended chair. He had two blue horns and his face was covered with red, blue, and yellow.

Spotlight zooms in on him.

Satan: *(screaming and laughing boisterously)* I can allay your fear.

Men: *(in supplication)* How, master of fire and the dark?

Satan: *(hissing)* You choose one to die.

(The men and women exchange glances in pain. The women hold the children's hands in fear.)

Men: What a difficult choice! *(They kneel on the floor and raise their arms in supplication)* Why are you doing this to us who have chosen you as our teacher and guide?

Satan: *(laughing)* Because of your deeds, you have been placed in my power.

Women: *(boldly to the men)* Don't listen to him. He is a deceitful liar who deceived our parents and caused us all this misery.

Satan: *(laughing, with his voice amplified)* Well then, wait until she gives birth. Labor is getting harder.

Blue and red spotlights are trained on the woman tied to the bed. Her screams blend with the strobe lights. Nobody knows whether they are hearing or seeing. A young man, about thirty, jumps onto the stage suddenly. I see him and realize that it is me.

How did I get up from my seat and jump up without being aware of it?

I: *(shouting at the men)* None of you will die. This is not Satan. What would make Satan torture you so much? This is your conscience coming back to life after hundreds of years. This is the first drop of the rain. The woman will give birth and none of you will die. Did you live in the time of Muhammad?

Men and Women: No.

I: Has any of you seen him?

Men and Women: No.

I: Have you heard that God punishes the children for their parents' sins?

Men and Women: No.

I: If he were to come to you now, would you deny him water?

Men and Women: No.

I: *(to the men)* Then get up and leave until the woman gives birth. The woman is having a hard time of it because it is unheard of for a woman to give birth in the midst of men. *(The men get up but do not move.)*

Men: Our feet are stuck to the floor.

Satan: *(laughing viciously and talking to me)* Do you know the truth of this town?

I: *(advancing toward him, looking up as the blue light blinds me)* I know it.

Satan: Have you come to save it from the curse?

I: Yes.

Satan: You should have sacrificed yourself for their sake. *(Addressing them)* Ask him if he is ready to do that.

They all look at me. The children come to me and cling to my legs, crying. No one talks. The sound of crying of a newborn baby is heard.

Satan: *(laughing)* The woman has given birth. One of you will now die unless you voluntarily offer one.

The men fall to the ground writhing in pain. The women rush to the children, each hugging her child. I back up bit by bit. Before I fall off the stage, the men stand up and quickly jump on me and raise me up then throw me to Satan, sitting above. He carries me by the arms and throws me into an abyss between two high mountains filled with white, blue, and red smoke, which engulfs me. The hot smoke gets into my chest almost suffocating me as I tumble down. The two arms, between which I can make out my mother's frightened face, cannot reach me. I do not reach the bottom of the abyss.

26

The mice kept coming and I kept killing them. I have been by myself since Wagih left for Medina two weeks ago. We had a five-day heat wave that scorched the town then subsided, giving way to dust storms that blew all the time. No letter from Aida telling me her new address. No explanations for the many letters from W. S. S. appearing in the local and Arabian magazines I began to buy regularly.

"Sister W. S. S. from Taif has sent us a letter asking: 'Can a *fatwa* be issued by the Kingdom banning marriage if the difference in age between the man and the woman is more than twenty years?' Of course no such *fatwa* or legislation can be issued, sister W. S. S."

"Sister W. S. S. from Dammam has sent us a letter asking why it is all right for women to be unveiled in the holy places but not in all other parts of the country. The reason, Sister, is obvious: people in the holy places devote all their attention to God Almighty and avert their gaze as our good religion enjoins us to do. In the rest of the country, people have various interests, and commerce and work, and interdependent relationships, and should use all means to put out the fires of lust."

"Sister Wadha bint Sulayman ibn Sabil from Riyadh has

sent us a letter asking us to name the poet who wrote the following line of poetry and to provide the line that comes after it:

The abodes of the valley are as delightful in place
As spring is delightful in time.

This line was written by Abu al-Tayyib al-Mutanabbi, the greatest poet of the Arabic language. He composed it when he visited the Valley of Bauwan in Fars. The line that follows it is:

But the Arab lad in their midst
Is a stranger in face, hand, and tongue.

Sister Wadha always sends us wonderful letters containing many fine verses. We have received another letter from her, which we have been tardy in responding to, asking us the meaning of the following line of poetry:

Sorrow before death is weakness.
After separation, it is pointless.

This line also was written by al-Mutanabbi, famous for his extraordinary sagacity. Here he is not calling for patience in the face of the death of the beloved as naive commentators might think, but points to man's helplessness in the face of the certainty of death hanging over all beings. How wretched and miserable man is, who can face the certainty of death only with silence."

Wadha is killing me with all this poetry she's asking about even though she knows it well; Wadha, whose very name spells clarity. So who is that W. S. S. who writes to all the magazines from these different cities? Yesterday was Friday and Shaykh Ali Tantawi said, "We received a letter written in a beautiful hand and on beautiful paper signed by Tormented W. S. S. This "tormented," by the way, shows the influence of Egyptian magazines. In any case, these Egyptians with their sweet talk enter all our homes. The Tormented W. S. S. asks, "Does Islam permit a seventy-year-old man to marry an eighteen-year-old girl?" I say to Tormented that this is the worst kind of torture, but that Islam permits it for a reason. When God created man he gave him reason and distinguished him from the beasts. No man with reason will do that, but money has corrupted many a head. The family of the girl should reject such a marriage without feeling any guilt. Some might use the argument that some of the Prophet's Companions and Followers did just that. That, however, was a different era with a different caliber of moral character. Men then were real men. I ask God's forgiveness."

How many Wadha bint Sulayman ibn Sabils were sending letters to the editors of all these magazines, letters in code to me who can do nothing? And not a single letter from Aida to console me or from my brother to reassure me about my mother and explain her illness.

✧

I laughed so hard I almost fell off the chair as I read a letter from Wagih, brought to me by Abed who announced, "This is a letter from Dr. Wagih, your former roommate."

So, he had read the sender's name as usual. I didn't care. I can read this letter at work. Wagih had married in Medina a Lebanese woman, who he said was stunningly beautiful. "Her family is very wealthy and they have a flourishing business in Medina. This is number three, Ismail. Only one more to go.

But I don't think I'll do it. This one is worth hundreds of women in beauty and wealth."

Nabil came into my office, surprised at my laughter, which he could hear in the kitchen. He smiled and said, "Aren't you afraid of Amm Abdallah hearing you?"

"Oh, so you are finally smiling, Nabil. Amm Abdallah's not here. Sit down for a while."

He sat as his smile faded away and said, "Two days ago I performed some additional prayers to ask God that the satellite fall down away from my head. God has answered my prayers; it fell down in the ocean near Australia."

"Then you must shave off your beard."

"I won't shave it off until I am in Egypt."

"You're really going?"

"At the end of next month, May. I don't believe my fiancée has gotten married. She's either sick or my mother has ruined everything. The problem is, this is not the time for my annual vacation. I'll send word to my brother to send me a telegram informing me of my mother's death. What do you think?"

"No need to do that. I can persuade Amm Abdallah to give you leave. I'll explain your circumstances and he'll agree."

"That dog Abed refused to do that."

✧

Mansur came into the office, smiling.

"Greetings, brother Ismail."

"Greetings, Mansur. Where have you been?"

"In Kuwait. I got back yesterday."

"Really?"

"Of course you're surprised. Are you saying I'm crazy?"

"No."

"Then do you know why I went there?"

"No."

"To Widad. She has broken off her engagement with Said."

"That happened a long time ago."

"No. There was still a wrinkle left. She was still wearing the engagement ring."

"Oh."

"And we agreed to get married."

"I thought she went over there to join a relative?"

"No. That's a story we made up for your friend. It was me that got her a visa to work in Kuwait, and I invented this story of her relative, the accountant."

"I see."

"What do you think of this solution? Detective work, eh? Like Egyptian movies."

He got up and walked toward the door and said, "Get ready for next Friday. I'm going to fix a big *kabsa* here. Do you know what *kabsa* is?"

"I know what it is, but I've never tasted it."

"In all this time?"

"No."

"I'm going to slaughter lots of animals and all the workers are coming. You will taste it here in the forecourt."

He hurried away, with the monkey looking at me over his shoulder.

✧

I have killed more than fifty mice. I was now killing them at night, too. As the call to the dawn prayer filled the town where heat had driven the air away, rendering any sound as loud as a drum beat, I would get up and spend the two remaining hours chasing mice. I was killing day and night, throwing the dead out of the door and hearing the fighting of the cats, which I knew were as big as tigers. I had gone to the hospital to see Warda. She didn't laugh or smile. Her face grew pale and sorrowful.

"You've come to ask about Aïda?"

"Yes. I want her address in Abha."

"Aida's moved to the east; to Dammam."

We fell silent. I swore I would kill the first person to speak to me on the street.

I didn't kill anyone nor did anyone speak to me. I just kept killing mice. I was only catching little mice, inexperienced idiots that wandered into the killing field that I had prepared for them. The wooden board was no longer just lying there; it was now hinged to the wall in such a way that whenever I pushed it with my foot it was pressed against the wall without any possibility that the board would slip and let the mouse escape. These were tiny mice, some white with red bellies that had not grown hair yet, and which sounded like cockroaches. Where are the big mice that gave birth to them? And why do they let them come here? How come they didn't realize that their children were being killed every day? This night I was confronted by the big mice. "Are you Ismail Khidr Musa?" "Yes." "Why do you kill our children and little brothers and sisters every day, for no reason?" "I do not kill at random; I am a stranger in a foreign land. I like my guests to ask permission before they come in. Your brothers and sisters and children disturb my sleep night and day." "You're a liar. You hate sleep." "But sleep doesn't hate me and beats me in every encounter and then your mice disturb me. Do you want me to eat them? I have sealed the cracks through which they could come in, but they still do come in." "You don't just kill mice; you use a horrible method." "For that horrible method I pay the price of loathing." "You are a traitor to bird and animal. We mice are not of your world but there's affection and love between us and birds and animals." "Animals and birds hate you. Cats, for instance, eat you, and so do kites." "It's not cats and kites; it is hunger that ruins character. Look at the doves; they don't eat us. Doves are meek. And we have many such friends ever since our father saved the ringdove from the hunter's net." "That is a fable from a book." "This is the truth. You just don't know. You must know also that lions love us, ferocious lions that are so dignified and proud." "That's only what you think; what kind of dignified and proud being lives on what his wife captures?" "You have to remember that our ancestor, the mouse, one day saved the lion from the hunter's net. We mice might be insignificant but, like everything else that is small in the universe, we are useful. You are an ignorant being. Don't you know that God has created a balanced universe that no one should tip this way or that?" "Nonsense. Germs are creatures too but we chase them and kill them before they kill us. You are cowards; you carry lice and you spread the plague that killed Abu Ubayda al-Jarrah in Syria and destroyed Napoleon's army in Palestine and took the lives of half the Egyptian population in Mamluk times. And now you are destroying the crops in Egypt and killing children in the countryside. You are spreading disease in the cities around the Suez Canal, where you prospered before our victory; it's as if you don't want our victory to be complete. You are my enemy and I am your enemy until the Day of Judgment." "Well then, dialogue with you is no good."

The black mice jumped at me, covering my body. I got up in a fright and ran to the kitchen, where I found one of them between the wooden board and the wall. I crushed it brutally.

27

It suddenly occurred to me that my mother's illness couldn't be anything ordinary. There would be no need to mention that in a letter. When I received a letter from my brother asking me to send a thousand pounds right away, I was certain. But he didn't mention what she had nor the steps taken for treatment. I had been in Cairo two months earlier and my mother was in the best of health. True, she was over fifty but that is not an age when illness suddenly strikes. My mother was too young for the diseases of old age. She was younger than my father; maybe that was why they had all those fights during the Feasts. I wrote to my brother asking him for details and sent him two thousand pounds.

Then I became aware of the talk of the town, which had made it to the company offices and which everybody was laughing about: the Pakistanis, Abed, and Nabil, who could not believe what had happened.

"Is that possible?" he asked.

"It's not so strange, anyway."

"You mean if I hit you or you hit me on the head, one of us would lose consciousness and the other would do to him whatever he wanted?"

"In the old days, before anesthesia, they used to hit the patient with a wooden hammer before the surgeon performed the operation."

Nabil felt his head and laughed.

"But she hit him with a pressure cooker?"

"A pressure cooker is heavier than a hammer."

"And she castrated him!"

"That's what they say."

"Can a woman do that?"

"Jealousy can be deadly."

Nabil laughed.

"The poor guy went to the hospital and they found one of his testicles stuck to his pants."

We fell silent. Nabil got up suddenly, saying, "Mansur left for Kuwait yesterday, just to get out of the *kabsa* party he promised. He's a miser; I know him well."

✧

So there was nobody at work I could talk to except Nabil. Wahhaj, who was now responsible for food in the camp, would come and Abed would agree to all his requests without hassle. I remembered Arshad always asking, "Why's Abed doing this to me?" I wished Abed would give Wahhaj a hard time or deny him something or another. But Abed seemed to read my mind. I remembered Arshad's bewilderment and sense of helplessness. I wished, more than once, to see Arshad coming in suddenly. Arshad had a three-month visa, which meant that he had only a few days. Would Arshad do it and come back? I didn't think so. Sarwar had spread the news that Arshad was arrested for political reasons. I didn't think he could ever come back. After his imprisonment, Arshad could go to any country except Saudi Arabia, and while in jail he could dream of going anywhere but Saudi Arabia. He must have forgotten the time that he spent here. Said is probably doing the same thing, and Munzir, and the young Lebanese woman, and Dr. Ahmad. Even poor Rafat, and Philip, who no longer needed to remember or to forget.

A strange rift develops between those who go back to their countries and this country. It's a rift that's built in; everybody comes here to go back. Does the old Yemeni man know that? Is that why he smiles at me? Does he see the whole world around him as a big farce? And how come he no longer appears? I asked Abed about him yesterday. He smiled and asked me, "Do you care about him?"

"I'm just asking."

He shrugged his shoulders indifferently.

✧

"Is there no way to get in touch with her in Dammam? Don't you have her number at work or the address?" I asked Warda at the hospital after I got off from work.

"It's difficult to get in touch with her in Dammam. We don't know exactly which hospital she's at. Didn't you write to her?"

"I did."

"She didn't write back?"

I said nothing. I got up, shook her hand, and left.

✧

I hated going home. I hated killing mice. I washed the wooden board every day with soap and disinfectant. There was no foul odor in the kitchen but I could smell it in the air. I thought seriously of looking for a small apartment in an apartment building. The chances for mice would be fewer. Arabian-style houses are no more than blocks of stones, which the mice easily climb or crawl under. I got to the main street in my car. I felt the need to see the police car parading someone in disgrace. Anyone at all.

I saw myself riding a donkey, my face toward its tail. As it walked forward, men and women laughed at me and kids threw stones at me. If I hadn't heard the car horns, I would have hit the cars in front of me.

I heard that orders had been issued prohibiting the public disgracing of people in the market place. Who had done that, when I needed to watch? I left my car and walked. I was going to Sayyid al-Gharib's house. I had to talk with somebody.

"Go away," the policeman yelled at me. "Go away."

Sayyid al-Gharib waved to me from the balcony where he sat.

"Why are you standing here?" said the policeman.

"Does that bother you?"

"Yes it does. I told you to go away."

"Where shall I go?" I asked the policeman suddenly, in surprise and confusion.

"If you don't go away I'll put you in the house with him and then you won't be able to leave."

I walked away and went back to the main street. I bought the newspapers and magazines. I passed Salih on the street; we ignored each other. Then, when he was behind me he stopped and called out to me. I stopped and he came up to me. "I want to give you a gift, Ustaz."

I said nothing.

"Please forgive me for not coming to apologize to you after you withdrew your complaint to the police."

I said nothing.

"You want a tiger-skin blanket? I can get it delivered to your new house. Do you find the new house comfortable, Ustaz?"

"God be praised."

"Have a good day, Ustaz."

He left me. Once again the sun shone so intensely it almost burned my face. The main street was filled with goods. The school and office supply store owned by Khalid, Wadha's brother, was closed. Khalid looked like Wadha despite the small moustache, and the white *ghutra,* and the *uqal.* There was now no trace of the fire in the street.

I drove my car and saw things running backward; everything was moving away from me. There was nothing more to be done except wait for one letter from my brother telling me my mother was all right. I saw her sitting next to me in the car patting my shoulder. "Don't cry, Ismail."

She wiped my tears with her cold hand and picked me up and took me through the glass of the car and placed me on the little white bed and covered me with the white cover. She sat next to my head, placing on my forehead handkerchiefs soaked in cold water. I heard the call to the dawn prayer. "Praise the Lord, Abu Ismail. The fever is gone."

"Praise the Lord." My father bent down and kissed me. "*Say: He is God, the One God, the Eternal, the Absolute; He begets not, nor is begotten; And no one is comparable to him. God! There is no god but Him, the Alive, the Eternal. No slumber or sleep can come over Him. To Him belongs whatever is in the heavens and the earth. Who is he that can intercede with Him except by His leave? He knows that which is in front of them and that which is behind them. They encompass nothing of His knowledge except what He will. His throne extends over the heavens and the earth and*

He is never weary of preserving them. He is the Sublime, the Supreme.

"Please, O God, take from me for his health and vigor; give me his subsistence and give me life that I may see his offspring. O God, I complain to You about my worry at night and my toil during the day, so please listen to my complaint and bring me closer to You and help me with my son, You who know everything about me, the Forgiver, Most Merciful. O God, I have pledged to slaughter a ram at the door to the mausoleum of Sidi Ibrahim al-Desuqi and a ram at the door of my house. Please heal my son, Ismail. Please God, heal our sick and have mercy on our dead and save us from the company of the unrighteous."

"And the two girls, Um Ismail? Are they all right? Did you look in on them?"

"Yes I did. They are fine and sleeping."

"Look in on them, Um Ismail."

"I told you I did."

"Okay, okay, I'm sorry."

Car horns from all directions.

"Why are you stopping and blocking the traffic?"

"Sorry."

"Go quickly."

I went quickly. All I had taken from the two older sisters I had to give to Sanaa and Bahaa, my younger sister and brother. To me went the chicken breast and the red meat and the egg with the double yolk and the whole bottle of Coca-Cola and the butter pies and the thighs of rabbits and the livers of fowl and the strings of undeveloped eggs and the hot water in winter and the fancy soap and the fine clothes and school trips and the visits to the parks. Why did I always like my father to take me to the railroad station so I could watch the trains as they came and went and the people and the music bands in the square in front of the station? I saw Salih Sanyur al-Thaqifi standing in front of the house with the landlord.

"Peace."

"Greetings," Salih replied with a booming voice, a broad smile, and a strong light in his eyes as the landlord muttered something I couldn't hear.

"Well?"

"All's well, God willing. Please open the door so we can come in, Ustaz," Salih replied in a strangely confident tone. How did he make it here before me even though I'd just seen him on the main street and he'd talked to me without mentioning anything. I opened the door. We went to my room. I didn't want to ask them to sit down but Salih sat on the edge of the bed and pulled the landlord to sit next to him. I remained standing.

"Don't make tea or coffee, Ustaz. We're leaving soon. Of course you have rented this house from this old man here. Now I want the house."

"Which one?"

"This one."

"But I am living here."

"I know, Ustaz. But I've bought it from this old man here and I've bought the one next to it. I'm going to get married here and tear down the other one and turn it into a garden. I'll plant Egyptian trees. I'll give you one month's notice to look for another house, Ustaz. Is that enough?"

"It's enough."

I didn't look at them after that. There was no sense in asking the first landlord whether what Salih said was true. Salih did not bring him over to conspire or lie. He had indeed bought the house and I had to move out, whether he got married in it and tore down the one next to it or married in the one next to it and tore this one down or tore them both down and didn't get married.

✧

I ate with an appetite that I didn't think I'd had since I came here. I grilled a huge amount of lamb and liver and started wolfing it down right there in the kitchen, without any bread. Today I could eat a whole lamb, a camel if I wanted to. I may even go outside in a fury and slaughter everyone I meet and grill and eat them.

I needed a long sleep. I stretched out on the bed. My hand reached to a magazine I had dropped on the floor close to my head.

"A crime shakes the Kingdom. Second such incident in one month. A seventeen-year-old woman hits her husband on the head with a heavy pressure cooker, then castrates him. The husband dies of shock when he comes to and realizes what has happened. The husband is A. S. S., seventy years old. The young murderer is W. S. S. from Riyadh. She is a student in middle school."

I turned the pages frantically to the readers' letters.

"We have received more than one urgent telephone message asking if W. S. S., the author of many letters to us is the murderer. The answer is, no. We would like to reassure our dear readers that our friend W. S. S. has talked to us by telephone since the incident, asking whether Khomeini's government in Tehran is going to close down schools and universities and go back to the practice of teaching in the mosques. The truth is we have no clear answer to that as yet. Like our friend, we hear many rumors about the new government in Tehran. It is certainly busy getting a grip on the reins of power and authority and getting rid of the opposition and the Shah's aides scattered all over the country. It is also certain that the veil has begun to reappear on women's faces all over Iran. This is a blessed step on the part of the new government, which we hope will be followed by other steps on the right path to the true religion."

I had seen Khalid's store in the market closed a few hours earlier. I jumped out of bed and into my clothes and drove, speeding on the northern road. It was Wadha. Wadha and no one else. I kept driving very fast, indifferent to the great void surrounding me or the dark that was enveloping everything. And there, very, very far away, as I came close to Hallet Ammar, gateway to Jordan, I realized that along the road I hadn't come across a sea to jump into.

28

It is not permitted for the sun to overtake the moon or for the night to outstrip the day. Each floats in an orbit.

I was inevitably going back where I had started; everything I drew close to had drawn away. How had I forgotten to be a smooth shiny mirror that raindrops fell off?

The night and the day and one man between them, and that one man is me. The Arabs called the night and the day 'the two fillers' because they filled the world with light and with darkness. How can one see in dazzling light or in pitch darkness? The Arabs called the night and the day 'the two new ones' because they were forever new with darkness and light. They stopped for no one. The day has never stopped to chat with me nor has the night. The day brings forth light from early dawn and runs from east to west until, spent, it is overtaken by the dark; a battle they wage against each other without any concern for anyone standing under or between them. As the day makes its appearance I rush to work not believing that I have slept and awakened and that the night is gone. I keep repeating to myself the Quranic verse, "I seek refuge in the Lord of Daybreak . . . from the evil of the darkness where it is intense," out of fear of the dark of the night as it sweeps in with no crescent, full moon, or stars.

I no longer know what day of the month it is. I saw my father going out before sunset looking for me in the street to go back to the house before dark, quoting the Prophet, saying, "Shelter your children from the pitch black of the early night." The Arabs called the night 'the unbeliever' because it hides people, and unbelieving is hiding and an unbeliever hides God's blessings and denies them. The word for hamlets far-flung from cities is also related to the word for unbelieving, because hamlet dwellers are so far away that they are hidden from large communities. The Prophet has said, "Dwell not in hamlets for hamlet dwellers are like tomb dwellers." Tabuk is far away from cities. In Egypt there are thousands of hamlets.

I see the night now as "darkness on a vast abysmal sea, covered by a wave on top of a wave above which is a cloud. Darkness upon darkness." I hold out my hand but can hardly see it. Every night I wait for the day and I wait for something that can carry me hence, something I do not grasp though I know it is not a letter from anyone.

✧

Mansur came back from Kuwait but I haven't seen him. Nabil told me that the *kabsa* banquet that Mansur had promised us earlier but didn't have, would now be on Friday. "It's going to be a big banquet," Nabil said, adding that we'd be seeing Mansur for the last time since he was going to Kuwait for a third time and was going to stay there to marry the Egyptian woman he had been pursuing for so long. Poor Mansur! He was born to fall in love with Egyptian women. Nabil laughed and asked me why I was surprised. I was wondering why Mansur had been going to Kuwait so frequently and for such short periods. Could it be that his marriage to

Widad was not a done deal as he had tried to convince me last time? And why didn't he come to work during the day so I could see him? Why did he send me news of the *kabsa* via Nabil?

I thought of not going to the banquet but came to the conclusion that that would be senseless; I was now totally cut off from everyone and everything. Aida was lost in the faraway sands. Wadha was a murderer and would undoubtedly be beheaded. The fact that W. S. S. was still sending her questions to the newspapers from different cities was no concern of mine, since I hadn't bought any newspapers the last few days. I had no memories associated with the house that Salih was going to take and demolish, or populate with women and children. All those I had known were now consigned to a remote part of my memory even though it hadn't been that long. The magical god of Tabuk was once again shooting arrows of forgetfulness at me. The dust storms were blowing all the time, a loud reminder that I was a stranger in a strange land. My brother Bahaa sent a letter saying my mother was fine. He didn't ask for more money and didn't give me any details about her illness. She recovered, just like that. So I will attend the Friday banquet.

✧

I had always turned down invitations from Wagih and Said to go with them to such banquets. Now for the first time I was longing to go to one and looking forward to it happily. My soul was calmer now that I was certain that all ties had been severed. Perhaps. But maybe because it was Mansur's banquet.

I have a strange and sudden sensation that I am standing at the door of the plane, the cool air on my back, my face and chest facing the sun as I make the first step, which nobody has made me take. Am I going to become, once again, a smooth and shiny mirror? I have come to know well everything I see, to inspect it like a judicious buyer. I have to begin keeping a diary that will makes things happen with me, not to me. A diary means consciousness, and consciousness means the defeat of emotion so that no grief will come to me afterwards. If only I could remember which wicked author said that! All authors are wicked and all readers are fools who believe them and live someone else's life; premeditated robbery of time and life and no one complains. It is said that when Goethe published *The Sorrows of Werther,* hundreds of young people committed suicide in romantic Germany, which Napoleon later overran brutally. Goethe killed his young compatriots with a small book during the writing of which he cried once or twice. Napoleon needed armies to kill them. Lorca's poems did not save the lives of the Republican soldiers who carried them in pockets close to their hearts. During my last visit to Cairo, Salah Mansur, with eyes so penetrating, died; he got up from his bed and stood next to it to deliver Hamlet's famous soliloquy. As soon as he said, "To be, or not to be," he went back to bed to sleep forever. I wonder how many people Shakespeare's handsome prince has killed over the last four centuries. And why should we go far? Take me, Ismail Khidr Musa, who always grasps things too late: Ahmad Akif and Naguib Mahfouz led me astray. I believed them and killed Amal. Yes, it was premeditated murder. I came to know what Ahmad Akif didn't, early on. I wasn't going to accomplish anything, so why overburden my heart and break the hearts of others? I succeeded in the first task but failed in the second, killing that which I wanted to live. To prepare for a career in writing I read hundreds of books, but not those few that Mahfouz's Ahmad Akif spent so much time on; then let writing itself slip through my heart to my foot to the road, to be trampled by oblivion and rust. Did I know that I was going to end up this way or did I come all this way to figure out the reasons? Here, hundreds of miles away from everything that touched my heart, causing it to stir or freeze, here and now I realize that I can go back to writing but I don't want my heart to bleed. I am my author and my reader, so undoubtedly I am my own killer when the wicked deception is played to the end, even though I am the wicked, deceitful author. I should prevail over feeling and stop the blood from coursing from the heart to the rest of the body.

✧

I didn't keep a diary and apparently never would. The night, once again, was harder to take. In times of grief the night usually grows longer. So why was it longer now that all ties between me and everything here had been severed? My nights were heavy and odious, but I made it to Friday morning. I stayed home until the prayers were over. I had lunch and stretched out on the bed watching television. I was beset by sudden anxiety; I really wanted to attend the banquet. Television was generous to me; it showed an exciting film about the sinking of the ship Poseidon. I didn't know anything about the ship and whether the story was true or not, but who isn't attracted to the kind of film that depicts people in a crisis situation and shows the human will at its strongest, and portrays conflicts at moments of strength and weakness? In all such films the viewer knows the ending, which never fails him: rescue always arrives at the end. I know that too, but in front of movies I turn into a captivated, innocent child.

Sleep was also generous to me; as soon as the film was over, my head grew heavy and left my body. Once again I saw Gene Hackman, the faithful priest who preached to the passengers not to despair of God's mercy and who remained strong despite their ridicule. When it looked like there was no way they could be rescued after they and he had exerted tremendous efforts, he shouted in anger and disappointment, "We don't want your mercy, just leave us alone. Let us face what's happening without intervening for us or against us." I laughed at his despair and his predicament. When I woke up I found the television showing *This Week's Magazine*. It was dark already. I hurried out to my car and drove to the company scared to death that I might have missed the banquet.

✧

I drew near and found a large number of cars parked in front of the gate outside: Caprices, Mercedes, Cadillacs, and Peugeots. Amm Abdallah's white Cadillac stood out from the others. Next to it was a black Mercedes with curtains behind the windows. In the middle of the roof, just like Amm Abdallah's car, was a two-way antenna. I left my old pickup truck outside and went in slowly, wondering who Mansur had invited to the banquet.

The place was ablaze with lights in the midst of a huge darkness; additional lights were placed around the wall. It all looked like a wedding in the middle of the desert. As I went into the forecourt I was met by the sight of people from the town sitting in two rows facing each other. Sitting in the middle was Amm Abdallah, who raised his face to me then ignored me as usual. Next to him sat a black man wearing on top of his *gallabiya* a black *abaya* embroidered with gold brocade.

On his head was a green *ghutra* with intersecting red lines. He too raised his head then ignored me. I was reluctant to go close to them. They were talking and laughing. Nabil appeared from the direction of the kitchen carrying a pitcher and a glass and silently walked toward them.

I saw Abed speaking on the telephone in his office. I started over to him with awkward steps. As soon as I went in, he put the receiver down and smiled, saying, "Surprise, no?"

"Who are all these people."

"These are the town notables and high-ranking officials of the Emirate. In the middle is Amm Abdallah and the emir."

"This is the emir of Tabuk?"

"You've never seen him before?

"No."

"He is a very courteous person. Come say hello to him."

Before I could say anything he took me by the hand. I didn't resist; I had a strange fear so I let myself be led by him. When we left the office I freed my hand from his; it wasn't seemly to appear that he was pushing me to greet them. Of course Abed didn't introduce me to anyone. As we came close to the emir, he left me and started small-talking with one of the notables. To get out of the whole situation I went over to shake Amm Abdallah's hand. He said hello tersely. The emir shook my hand while remaining seated. Amm Abdallah said, "This is Ismail. He knows English well. You can use him in the Emirate."

"Really?" the emir asked me without appearing to speak or move his lips. When I answered in the affirmative he nodded twice, closing his eyes. It seemed that he had dismissed me from his mind. I found myself hurrying toward the kitchen without shaking hands with the rest of the gathering. I sat, shaking on the only chair. I was overcome by a fear whose source I didn't know. How was it that my brother had sent me a letter saying my mother had recovered from an illness that he did not name or tell me anything about but that necessitated all the money I had sent? I noticed that the red carpet extending between the two rows of notables extended also beyond them to the side opposite the emir. I realized that the Pakistani workers were also coming to the party. Perhaps Mansur had also invited the Americans. Where would my place be? There was nothing to do except wait for the rest of the guests and sit with them. I couldn't sit with the notables. There was nothing I could say to any of them nor did I know a single one of them. I hadn't come to eat in silence. Somebody must talk to me. Abed would find it a great opportunity to talk with all the notables in front of me and exchange laughter and words that I didn't understand. He wouldn't say a word to me now and Nabil would be busy serving tea and Arabian coffee until Mansur and his food arrived.

Nabil came into the kitchen, his face noticeably red.

"I pray to God everything goes all right," he whispered.

"Where's Mansur?" I saked him.

"He'll be coming shortly with a truck load of food. He's having it cooked in town, at home. That's what he said. Why don't you go and sit with them? It's an opportunity to get to know them."

I smiled. He took another teapot and left. Me, get to know all these notables with their fancy *ghutras* and their elaborate *abayas* and their prosperous faces and short, shiny beards? I remained in my place but moved the chair in such a way as to see them from behind the open door without being seen myself. I saw Abed going around the whole time, stopping to chat with someone for a moment, laughing with another, bending to kiss a third's head or his shoulder, and everybody speaking words I didn't understand. A lot of them were laughing; I saw the emir from behind, not moving at all, and apparently not speaking.

Wagih and Said had often spoken about *kabsa* in front of me. They said one ate with one's hands, using only the right hand to tear into the meat of the roasted lamb, placed whole on a big tray of rice, sometimes a full meter in diameter; the rice, piled high, is drenched in butter and cooked almonds, raisins, pine nuts, and pistachios. You take the hot rice in your hand and press it in your palm before tossing it into your mouth. The more your hand oozes butter the more generous the host is deemed to be. If spoons are present at all, they should never be used; they are only provided if salad is served with the meal, in which case one should serve the salad with the spoon and with one's hand take the rice and salad, press the mixture into a ball and eat it. The rule of etiquette for *kabsa* is that no one starts before the head of the gathering. Today the head of the gathering is the emir with his little eyes buried under high eyelids. I have to observe all these rules.

I heard a loud noise outside the forecourt, then the Pakistani workers ran in laughing. Suddenly they stopped, stunned to see the notables. Some of them stood back; others went out quickly to warn those rushing in after them. They stood there awkwardly, not knowing what to do. Abed went over to them and pointed to the empty area around the red carpet. They proceeded to sit in silence, their faces turning red. Nabil came back to the kitchen, red-faced also.

"Mansur is very late."

I said nothing; I was watching the silence that had descended on everyone, including the notables and Abed, who went out and stood anxiously at the entrance of the well-lit forecourt. A cool, refreshing breeze blew and everything seemed nice and mellow. But I suddenly got worried.

"You think he might not show up?" I asked Nabil.

"I don't think so; he's invited the emir and all these notables. His father is here too. Don't you know him?"

I shook my head and he said, "He's the man in the brown *abaya.*"

I looked at the opposite row and saw him, a very elderly man with closed eyes and a closed mouth, so sleepy his nodding head almost fell on his chest.

"But what are you doing here?" Nabil asked me suddenly, then added, "You should be with them. People will be aware of your absence and that's not done. So long as you are here, you should sit with them."

✧

There was no place for me to sit except at the center of the row, facing the emir and Amm Abdallah; to the side and the front were the two rows of Pakistani workers next to two rows of notables. Abed would be able to sit next to me, and there was also room for Mansur, who should sit in the center. In this way I would end up to his right and Abed to his left. As for Nabil who hadn't sat down yet, he wouldn't sit down; he would have to make tea and coffee to serve them quickly after the meal to all those present. Maybe Nabil would eat some of the leftovers. There is usually a lot of food left, which is thrown out to the cats that are as big as tigers—to the envy of the outcast dogs, which are banned from entering towns. Tonight, however, the cats would envy the dogs since the leftovers would be thrown away in the desert. Abed came quickly from the entrance and sat next to me, saying, "The food is here."

He was shaking for no obvious reason, and smiling. I kept looking at the emir who looked fat, and shorter than the others.

"There's a pickup truck outside carrying the trays of food, but Mansur hasn't come," Abed said, looking rather scared. I smelled the pervasive aroma of the butter, and then two Yemenis came into the forecourt, each carrying a tray covered with white cheesecloth, and stood at a loss what to do. Nabil went over to them and directed then to where the emir was sitting. They placed the first tray in front of him and the second one a short distance away, and hurried back outside. Nabil motioned to three Pakistanis, who immediately got up and went with the Yemenis carrying the trays covered with white cheesecloth. The smell of the food filled the air; tips of tongues came out, licking at the lips and everybody began to salivate. The notables began to talk about Mansur not showing up and laughed raucously; then their laughter subsided. They pointed at his father, who opened his eyes and spoke inaudibly then again looked like he was fighting off sleep. The emir fidgeted but I gathered from his conversation with Amm Abdallah and from their subdued laughter that they weren't going to wait for Mansur to show up.

I counted twenty trays. The two Yemenis again stood at a loss after the three Pakistanis returned to their places. Nabil motioned the Yemenis to stand at the kitchen, and they did. Silence descended as everyone waited for the emir to begin. I expected a stone to fall on my head from the sky, and I recoiled within myself and genuinely wished to see Mansur.

The emir lifted the cheesecloth and the hands began to lift the cheesecloth from the trays in front of them. The air suddenly filled with angry voices. "Lizards! Lizards! What did that idiot fix? Lizards, Abu Muhammad, Lizards, Mansur, Lizards, Abdallah?"

There were no lambs on the trays but strange, short animals like small crocodiles with a tail of many vertebrae.

"It's a lizard," Abed whispered to me. I didn't need to be told. I saw anger in the emir's face and eyes, and surprise in the faces of the Pakistanis—one of whom got up screaming in horror and dashed out of the forecourt. Silence descended again. Amm Abdallah looked ill at ease. Mansur's father was still fighting off sleep. No one had noticed what I had realized: not every tray had a lizard; on three or four of them there was another type of animal, with four long legs and without a head. Their large, protruding buttocks made it clear what they were. Abed lifted the cheesecloth covering the tray in front of us and I saw the same type of animal. I felt my stomach almost jump out, as if a frog had jumped out of my belly to my mouth. That's how I felt exactly. I held my abdomen with my hands and got up to run to the bathroom, but couldn't help throwing up before I got there. Nabil quickly caught up with me and took me by my arms backward to the kitchen as I almost fell, fainting to the ground. I heard a commotion and screaming. Nabil stood at the door to find out what was happening. "My God, what is going on?" I got up with difficulty and stood next to him and saw a man I hadn't seen before chasing the two Yemenis and raining blows on them, until they managed to escape from the forecourt. He stood there retrieving his *ghutra,* which had fallen to the ground, and then moved toward the emir, who got up quickly and left in anger, without stopping. The man kept trying to catch up with him, succeeding only at the entrance to the forecourt, where he kept kissing the emir's head, his nose, and his shoulders. The notables talked, shouted, and laughed uproariously. Amm Abdallah yelled at the Pakistanis to throw the food out. I saw Mansur's father, stooping as he walked, shaking his head incessantly.

29

I was surprised to see the old Yemeni man again. Today he came early, at about nine o'clock. He just appeared, sitting in his place, the *siwak* in his mouth, looking at me and smiling the whole time. Ever since he reappeared his smile has been broader. He must have heard the whole story about Mansur. Poor Mansur. At the very last moment his older brother found out about the banquet. It was said that his mother was the one who told him, as he came back home from the store, that Mansur had slaughtered the monkeys he had purchased in the Sudan and that he had hired two Yemeni men to cook them. The Yemenis had loaded everything onto the truck and left. The older brother caught up with Mansur as he was getting into his Caprice, prevented him from going and and started beating him up. Mansur fought back, but the older brother managed in the end to tie him to a large palm tree in the courtyard of the house, and rushed to the company. It was him I had seen beating the two Yemenis and trying to pacify the emir.

At first I didn't believe the story, but I realized it was true when the news of Mansur being institutionalized in the mental asylum in Taif was confirmed. It was Abed who told us, then the Pakistanis who had heard the story from their friends in other companies began to talk about it. The whole of Tabuk knew the story and how it ended. Mansur had gone to Kuwait for the second time and found out that Widad had married her relative. He didn't help her with anything; everything he told me was something he had invented and believed himself. Mansur came back from Kuwait cursing the oil and the day it began to flow. Before, people used to eat the local animals. Lizards were a delicacy in the desert. Mansur, who didn't attend the banquet himself, must have prepared the monkeys for us foreigners. He probably wouldn't have agreed to the haphazard way the trays were placed.

✧

"How come you don't laugh anymore these days?" Nabil asked me. He was getting ready to go back to Cairo the day after next. I chose not to ask him why the old Yemeni man had reappeared, and why he had come early today. I also chose not to tell him that I felt somewhat responsible for what happened to Mansur. Besides, what good would it do to tell him how lonely I was and how I constantly thought about not finding anybody to talk to. Two weeks of the month's notice that Salih had given me to leave the house had passed. I hadn't looked for another place. I kept forgetting, and when I remembered I did nothing about it. I said to Nabil, "Sit with me a while."

His face brightened up for the first time in a long while. He sat down, looked at me for some time then closed his eyes and said, "I don't know why I keep remembering these days what my mother used to tell me all the time, that I have been touched and blessed by God. She always told me that and reminded me of my uncle who used to take my money from the radio station and give me only the chocolate, and how he drowned in the Nile even though he was one of the most famous swimmers in Imbaba. She used to remind me of the teacher who made me hate school by beating me up in primary school, and how an earthen water jar fell on his head and killed him instantly; and the officer who took me from the coffee house with some other boys and made me spend two years in the reformatory, how a balcony in the Giza Security Headquarters collapsed and killed him, even though it was only on the first floor. Then there's my fiancée, who left me for a taxi driver; my mother tells me her husband is divorcing her because he believes she's brought him bad luck since a big army truck wrote off his taxi, leveling it to the ground even though he had parked it under the window of his own house. Why am I thinking about all that these days?"

I had no answer for him. I needed his pleasant conversation to distract me from my own worries and he surprised me with his riddles. I asked him, "Are you finally convinced that your fiancée has married the taxi driver?"

"I don't think my mother lies all the time."

"So why are you returning?"

"I don't know."

Then he fell silent for a while and said, "Do you really think I've been touched and blessed by God? Am I so good without knowing it? Does God love me that much?"

I looked at him sympathetically and said, "I don't think God hates you, Nabil."

He shook his head and smiled. "I wish my uncle had given me the money and hadn't died," he said. "I wish the teacher had left me alone so I could finish school, and hadn't died. I wish the officer hadn't shoved me into the reformatory and lived. I wish my fiancée hadn't left me."

He started sobbing, then got up and left the room.

✧

I sat alone the rest of the day. I got busy translating reports whose authors were American technicians I didn't know, about work sites I hadn't visited in all this time. From time to time I couldn't help looking at the old Yemeni; he sat there looking at me and smiling the whole time. Before, when I looked at him he would feel my gaze and look back and smile. Today and the last few days, ever since Mansur's banquet, he never took his eyes off of me. When Abed came back from town carrying a letter for me, I read Alaa's name on the back of the envelope and postponed reading it until I went home. I didn't want to upset myself over something that Alaa might be asking of me or over a problem between him and my sister that he might ask my opinion about. At home I could turn the television on, or leave the house and walk freely about town.

30

"I didn't want you to reproach me one day, when we meet. Everyone has chosen to keep the news from you so it wouldn't interfere with your work. But I realize how courageous and how capable of handling difficult situations you are. Therefore I have chosen to inform you despite the pain: your pain because she is your beloved mother, and my pain because of my breaking ranks with your family in this matter. Your mother passed away a few weeks ago; we have buried her and given her a proper funeral. Please accept my condolences and my family's condolences. Your mother was the mother of all of us. I pray to God to give you strength to be exactly what I believe you are, a strong man who accepts God's will, and to continue in your job, confident that we here, my family and I, are looking after your brother and sisters as we do our own."

I didn't sleep at all last night; I don't think I will sleep tonight either. I couldn't go back to work to tell anybody and I couldn't stay home except after going through all the streets of town as if I alone was going through ruins where no one else breathed. Morning found me still hitting my head: how could I have lost the image of my mother's face so completely that I wasn't able to recall it even once? Do images die too?

I was quite dumbfounded at the stupor that had come over me, almost turning me into stone. I roamed the town unaware of anything around me. My mind stopped working. The night dragged on and on for too long and still my mind didn't work. Had I anticipated this end for my mother without knowing it? And he wants me to be what he believes me to be, a strong man who accepts God's will and continues in his job; Alaa, whose hiding place I didn't know and who jumped up to rob me of the fruit of my labor, wanted me, as did my brother and sisters, to carry on with my father's loathsome game. They hid the news from me so I would continue with my work. They didn't want me to interrupt my endeavor to provide for myself what all the youth of this age are striving for: money to help us overcome the evil that Egypt has thrown in our way. I long for a mouse, a single mouse that mistakenly makes it to this house after such a long absence. I will not kill it. I just miss hearing its feet scratching as it jumps and prances about, trusting the innocent world around it.

Neither Abed nor Nabil believed the news. They saw me working calmly; but I showed the letter to Abed who became perturbed.

"Are you going back?" he said.

"Tomorrow."

"But . . ."

"Amm Abdallah won't mind, not in a situation like this one," I told him decisively. A little later Amm Abdallah came to the office and before I went to him, he came to me. Abed had told him. He shook my hand and offered his condolences asking me if there was anything I needed. I thanked him. He told Abed to go to the passport office to get me a one-month visa and on his way back to buy me a ticket to leave the following day with Nabil. He didn't say with Nabil; it was I who thought of it as he gave his orders quickly to Abed. I wasn't bothered when the old Yemeni man showed up early today, nor by his ever-present smile. On my way back I wanted so much to go to the hospital to see Aida and tell her that there was no longer anything that tied me to anyone in Egypt. But I realized I wouldn't find her there. I remembered the whole story. And now, in my room, in the house that I had to leave to move out of for good so Salih could take it, I wished I could take my car and rush to Wadha's house and cry in her bosom. Now I remembered that, as I roamed the town last night silently, unaware of my surroundings, I saw her brother Khalid's store still closed. I thought, out of the blue, that they were twins; I remembered how strong the resemblance between them was. Then I remembered that Khalid was much older. Like yesterday, I longed for the company of a mouse that might accidentally come into the house. And unlike yesterday, I turned on the television, but transmission had ended a long time ago. I began to see the morning struggling to free itself from the dark of this hot, stifling night. I had to struggle to fight off the sleep that assailed me. If I fell asleep now I wouldn't wake up before the evening. Abed's attempts to wake me up by knocking on the door, to take me to the airport, would never succeed.

✧

"You look better than yesterday," said Abed when he came at eight o'clock in the morning and found me waiting for him. I said nothing; I didn't think I was any better. I picked up my big suitcase and he hurried to take it from me and left me a small one to carry. He looked surprised; I thought he was about to ask me how I had managed to buy all this stuff in the suitcases despite my apparent grief. I chose not to tell him that there was nothing in the suitcases other than my own things that I had brought over with me from Cairo and a few items I had bought before. Nothing of mine was left in the house except the television, which had been left behind by Faruq, then Said, then Wagih, and now by me.

He drove slowly, not because the plane wasn't taking off until ten o'clock but because of the solemn occasion. At least that's what I thought. I actually needed to see the town one last time, attentively. It wasn't possible to ask him for something like that; the distance between my house and the road to the airport was short and anyway the road didn't go through town.

"I took Nabil a short while ago," he said and I didn't say anything. "Nabil will keep you company."

I said nothing.

"Please come back soon. Death awaits all the living."

I didn't say anything. I sensed that he was embarrassed; he fell silent. I felt the old antipathy coming back.

✧

The car got onto the airport road with its shiny black asphalt that reflected the rays of the sun in such a way as to remind me how uneven its surface was. The sun had ascended the sky quickly and taken possession of the world too early. Around the road was nothing but sand and dunes. This was a road that I knew, but today I was seeing it as if for the first time. I kept looking to both sides to see anything besides the dunes. I saw the huge white dog that looked like a stray donkey running at high speed with something black on its back. Opening my eyes as wide as I could, I saw that it was a monkey riding the poor dog, which ran incessantly at a dazzling speed. Abed didn't notice the spectacle. I almost shouted at him to look but I held back, feeling my mouth dry. I twisted my neck to look at the rear view mirror and saw the dog still running and the monkey still on its back. The road was turning and the car was getting faster. The scene began to disappear as the company offices took the place of the dog and the monkey. I looked ahead and said to myself, "It must be Mansur's monkey."

✧

"All that's on it will perish, Ismail. We will be on a plane for an hour and a half, between heaven and earth. It could very likely crash."

Nabil was talking to me; I wasn't looking at him. At the beginning, when we arrived at the airport and after Abed left me and I went into the terminal, I felt everything around me was radiant with delight. There were a lot of Saudis and an even larger number of Egyptians, all wearing bright clean clothes, moving and talking ceaselessly. Children were running around the colorful suitcases and laughing innocently. The air conditioning felt good. The faces of the young men behind the check-in desk and the passport office were fresh and calm. I felt very comfortable and content and seemed to have quite forgotten about my mother's death. I lit a cigarette, gave one to Nabil, and smiled. But then I saw something that Nabil didn't. A jeep stopped in front of the terminal door and a young officer got out and headed for the passport office with a green passport, which he gave the young, smiling official. From the back of the jeep two policemen got out, pulling a man who got down and stood between them. They pushed him behind the officer. It was Sayyid al-Gharib, with his untrimmed beard and the same pants I had seen him wearing earlier; he wore a shirt that he had had no time or inclination to wash or iron. He saw me as soon as he got out of the car; I looked at him and he looked at me as if he knew I was waiting for him. He remembered me as I remembered him; I didn't see him look at anybody else. They led him through a door into a room and we didn't see him afterwards. But all the passengers now knew what was happening. The Egyptians began to speak softly. It wasn't difficult for Nabil to grasp the situation. After he talked to me he looked where I was looking and said, "A man under arrest is being deported. God spare us!"

I saw his face turn pale; he moved away from me and we kept going around among the passengers for quite some time.

I figured that Sayyid al-Gharib would get on the plane before all of us, since he had no baggage to weigh and he was being processed for departure now. Most probably the two policemen would escort him to where he would sit on the plane and we would see none of that but would find him sitting in the plane when we boarded. It seemed from the whispered conversations of the Egyptians that they knew his story, but many faces showed signs of surprise. I also saw fear on the faces of many of the women whose faces were uncovered now that they were in the airport. I saw Nabil talking with the Egyptians and realized that he was trying to find out the story of Sayyid al-Gharib. But why didn't he ask me?

"They say that he's a doctor."

"I know the whole story," I interrupted him.

But he added, "They released him today. They say a new undersecretary of health visited Tabuk and heard his story, so he asked to see him. The undersecretary had been his classmate in the university in Egypt, and arranged for his deportation without a trial. He's very lucky."

I didn't try to decide whether Sayyid al-Gharib was really lucky or not. I thought how people in Tabuk knew everything and I knew nothing. The passengers began to form a long line to weigh their baggage.

✧

In the short distance between the door of the terminal and the door of the plane, I felt that I and the universe were one thing: hot and empty. I understood why Nabil went ahead of us all to ascend the gangway, escaping the rays of the sun that burned though it wasn't quite half past nine yet. Nabil had looked afraid as he got close to the check-in desk. He said he was afraid of this trip, even though when he rode on a plane the first time he wasn't afraid. I told him it was natural to be frightened when one flew. But I didn't see the worried look leave his face until we left the terminal and got onto the tarmac.

He went ahead of us all. I hung behind, looking to the right and seeing a small ochre helicopter with an American flag on the side, under which I saw the words 'US Air Force.' I looked to the left and saw another helicopter.

I sat silently next to silent Nabil. I saw Sayyid al-Gharib sitting in the first seat behind the cockpit, far away from us all in first class where nobody else was. They must have picked that seat for him so nobody would talk to him. I expected him to comment on this generosity in a deportation, but Nabil was not looking at me; he was staring at nothing in particular. He began reciting the opening chapter of the Quran, more than once, in a voice I was able to hear in spite of the noise of the engines.

We fastened our seat belts and refrained from smoking. A stewardess passed hard candy around. The plane moved very fast on the runway as Nabil accelerated his recitation. The plane took off and I saw him closing his eyes and saying "Thank God." The plane reached a cruising altitude; the passengers undid their seat belts. Nabil sighed and said, "Now I don't care what happens."

I patted him on the thigh to give him courage. He said, "I'm not going back."

I looked at him in surprise. He said, "This is my irrevocable decision. Every girl I get engaged to will leave me and get married. I must stay in Egypt to protect my property."

He fell silent for a moment then said, "You shouldn't go back either."

I looked at him and said, "I'm not going back, Nabil."

"You'll stay in Egypt?" he asked me, his eyes lighting up with a sudden joy. I said, "No."

I saw surprise all over his face. I don't know why I gave him that answer but I really had no other answer. That was what I felt with certainty. Then we heard the captain's voice:

"Ladies and gentlemen, the plane will return to the airport due to a minor technical problem. We apologize for the inconvenience; we hope you will help us by remaining calm in your seats, refraining from smoking, and fastening your seat belts."

"Well, it seems we're not traveling today after all," I said, but Nabil didn't seem to hear. He turned pale; his eyes had a blank look and he shook in his seat as if he wanted to hide. "Nabil, what happened?"

He was looking at me with a terror that I thought no human being could experience. We hadn't climbed very high. I felt the plane descending and I had no time to call a stewardess, as I was busy fastening my seat belt and then Nabil's. He was hardly aware of my existence. The wheels of the plane hit the runway so hard it frightened us. The passengers cried out and I felt my heart wrenched as I saw Nabil shrinking even more. I heard the loud roar of the engine and the screeching sound of the tires as Nabil said in a barely audible voice, "There's no technical problem, Ustaz Ismail." At the moment the plane came to a stop, I saw through the small window a number of policemen approaching quickly.

"There's no technical problem, Ustaz Ismail. I wish you would leave my side right now. I robbed the safe. I finally learned the combination and took fifty thousand riyals. I hid it in my baggage."

The door of the plane opened quickly and then there were three policemen in front of me. They grabbed Nabil, as I sat helpless, incapable of even speaking. The passengers watched what was happening in great fear; the Egyptian stewardesses stood in a frightened daze, shrinking as they drew closer to each other.

I didn't see Sayyid al-Gharib's face. He remained seated where he was, not moving, not caring to know what was happening on the plane.

✧

From the small window I saw Amm Abdallah and Abed standing next to the high-ranking officer Abu Hakim and a number of policemen. The three policemen kept pushing Nabil toward the little crowd, hitting him on the back of the head and the neck with their hands and kicking him in the back. I saw Abed move quickly toward Nabil and kick him viciously in the abdomen. Nabil bent over as the policemen kept beating him on the back and the head and the neck. Then Abed took one step back and hit Nabil as hard as he could with his hand and his foot until Nabil fell to the ground on his back. I saw blood covering his face as they bent down and grabbed his feet and dragged him on the airport ground and took him behind the plane. It was no longer possible for me to see him but those sitting on the other side who had rushed to our side to try to watch with us now rushed back to their side and crowded around the small windows. I didn't try to look again.

✧

"Ladies and gentlemen, we apologize for what happened a few moments ago, and would like to inform you that we will be taking off again immediately. Please remain seated calmly, fasten your seat belts, and refrain from smoking. We wish you a pleasant flight and a happy time on board Saudi Airlines. Thank you."

The stewardesses moved fast; one of them began to pass hard candy around. The captain repeated his announcement, this time in English.

GLOSSARY

Abaya: a loose-fitting outer garment worn by both men and women covering the whole body

Fatta: a dish of bread soaked in broth and covered with rice and meat, traditionally served at mid-morning on the first day of the Feast of the Sacrifice

Fatwa: judicial opinion by a recognized Islamic religious scholar, who may or may not be appointed by the state to render such opinions

Gallabiya: a loose-fitting gown worn by men and women in Egypt

Ghutra: a scarf-like head cover worn by men in Arabia and the Gulf region

Kohl: powdered antimony sulfide, used to darken the eyelids and the eyebrows, purportedly in emulation of the Prophet Muhammad

Qibla: the niche in a mosque marking the direction of Mecca

Sharia: Islam's canonical law

Siwak: a short stick from a specific fragrant plant used as a natural toothbrush, purportedly in emulation of the Prophet Muhammad

Uqal: a band, usually black, surrounding the top of the head, to hold the ghutra in place

MODERN ARABIC LITERATURE

from the American University in Cairo Press

Ibrahim Abdel Meguid *The Other Place*
No One Sleeps in Alexandria • *Birds of Amber*
Yahya Taher Abdullah *The Mountain of Green Tea*
Leila Abouzeid *The Last Chapter*
Ibrahim Aslan *Nile Sparrows* • *The Heron*
Alaa Al Aswany *The Yacoubian Building*
Hala El Badry *A Certain Woman*
Salwa Bakr *The Wiles of Men*
Hoda Barakat *The Tiller of Waters*
Mourid Barghouti *I Saw Ramallah*
Mohamed El-Bisatie *A Last Glass of Tea*
Houses Behind the Trees • *Clamor of the Lake*
Fathy Ghanem *The Man Who Lost His Shadow*
Randa Ghazy *Dreaming of Palestine*
Gamal al-Ghitani *Zayni Barakat*
Tawfiq al-Hakim *The Prison of Life*
Yahya Hakki *The Lamp of Umm Hashim*
Bensalem Himmich *The Polymath* • *The Theocrat*
Taha Hussein *A Man of Letters* • *The Sufferers* • *The Days*
Sonallah Ibrahim *Cairo: From Edge to Edge*
Zaat • *The Committee*
Yusuf Idris *City of Love and Ashes*
Denys Johnson-Davies *Under the Naked Sky: Short Stories from the Arab World*
Said al-Kafrawi *The Hill of Gypsies*
Sahar Khalifeh *The Inheritance*
Edwar al-Kharrat *Rama and the Dragon* • *Stones of Bobello*
Betool Khedairi • *Absent*
Ibrahim al-Koni *Anubis*
Naguib Mahfouz *Adrift on the Nile* • *Akhenaten, Dweller in Truth*
Arabian Nights and Days • *Autumn Quail* • *The Beggar*
The Beginning and the End • *The Cairo Trilogy: Palace Walk*

Palace of Desire • *Sugar Street* • *Children of the Alley*
The Day the Leader Was Killed • *The Dreams*
Echoes of an Autobiography • *The Harafish*
The Journey of Ibn Fattouma • *Khufu's Wisdom*
Midaq Alley • *Miramar* • *Naguib Mahfouz at Sidi Gaber*
Respected Sir • *Rhadopis of Nubia* • *The Search*
Thebes at War • *The Thief and the Dogs* • *The Time and the Place* • *Wedding Song* • *Voices from the Other World*
Selim Matar *The Woman of the Flask*
Ahlam Mosteghanemi *Memory in the Flesh*
Chaos of the Senses
Buthaina Al Nasiri *Final Night*
Haggag Hassan Oddoul *Nights of Musk*
Abd al-Hakim Qasim *Rites of Assent*
Somaya Ramadan *Leaves of Narcissus*
Lenin El-Ramly *In Plain Arabic*
Ghada Samman *The Night of the First Billion*
Rafik Schami *Damascus Nights*
Miral al-Tahawy *The Tent* • *Blue Aubergine*
Bahaa Taher *Love in Exile*
Fuad al-Takarli *The Long Way Back*
Latifa al-Zayyat *The Open Door*